Celebrate ~~...~~ *Romance!*

Enjoy four ~~...~~ ~~...~~ ~~...~~ hood and
celebrate that ~~...~~ ~~...~~ ~~bond between~~ mother and child
with four extra-special Harlequin® Romances this month!

Whether it's the pitter-patter of tiny feet for the first
time, or finding love the second time around, these
four Romances offer tears, laughter and emotion and are
guaranteed to celebrate those mothers in a million!

For the ultimate indulgent treat, don't miss:

A FATHER FOR HER TRIPLETS by Susan Meier

THE MATCHMAKER'S HAPPY ENDING by Shirley Jump

SECOND CHANCE WITH THE REBEL by Cara Colter

FIRST COMES BABY... by Michelle Douglas

SUSAN MEIER

A Father for Her Triplets
&
Her Pregnancy Surprise

H HARLEQUIN® ROMANCE

Recycling programs
for this product may
not exist in your area.

ISBN-13: 978-0-373-74240-0

A FATHER FOR HER TRIPLETS

First North American Publication 2013

Copyright © 2013 by Linda Susan Meier

HER PREGNANCY SURPRISE

Copyright © 2007 by Linda Susan Meier

Printed in U.S.A.

www.Harlequin.com

CONTENTS

Susan Meier spent most of her twenties thinking she was a job-hopper—until she began to write and realized everything that had come before was only research! One of eleven children, with twenty-four nieces and nephews and three kids of her own, Susan has had plenty of real-life experience watching romance blossom in unexpected ways. She lives in western Pennsylvania with her wonderful husband, Mike, three children, and two overfed, well-cuddled cats, Sophie and Fluffy. You can visit Susan's website at www.susanmeier.com.

Books by Susan Meier

THE BILLIONAIRE'S BABY SOS
NANNY FOR THE MILLIONAIRE'S TWINS*
THE TYCOON'S SECRET DAUGHTER*
THE BABY PROJECT**
SECOND CHANCE BABY**
BABY ON THE RANCH**
KISSES ON HER CHRISTMAS LIST

*First Time Dads! duet
**Babies in the Boardroom trilogy

Other titles by this author available in ebook format.

A Father for Her Triplets

For the real Owen, Helaina and Claire… Thanks for being so adorable I had to write about you.

CHAPTER ONE

THE BEST PART OF BEING rich was, of course, the toys. There wasn't anything Wyatt Mc-Kenzie wanted that he didn't have.

Gliding along the winding road that led to Newland, Maryland, on a warm April morning, he revved the engine of his big black motorcycle and grinned. He loved the toys.

The second best thing about being rich was the power. Not that he could start a war, or control the lives of the people who depended upon him for work and incomes. The power he loved was the power he had over his own schedule.

Take right now, for instance. His grandmother had died the month before, and it was time to clear out her house for sale. The family could have hired someone, but Grandma McKenzie had a habit of squirreling away cash and hiding jewelry. When none of her family heirloom jewelry was found in her Florida town house, Wyatt's mother believed it was still in her house in Maryland. And Wyatt had volunteered to make the thousand-mile trip back "home" to search her house.

His mother could have come. She'd actually know more about what she was looking for. But his divorce had become final the week before. After four years fighting over money, his now ex-wife had agreed to settle for thirty percent interest in his company.

His company. She'd cheated on him. Lied to him. Tried to undermine his authority. And she got thirty percent of everything *he'd* worked for? It wasn't right.

But it also hurt. They'd been married for four years before the trouble started. He'd thought she was happy.

He needed some time to get over his anger with her and the hurt, so he could get on with the rest of his life. Looking for jewelry a thousand miles away was as good an excuse as any to take a break, relax and forget about the past.

So he'd given himself an entire month vacation simply by telling his assistant he was leaving and wouldn't be back for four weeks. He didn't have to remind Arnie that his gram had died. He didn't have to say his divorce was final. He didn't have to make any excuse or give any reason at all. He just said, "I'm going. See you next month."

He revved the engine again as he swung the bike off the highway and onto the exit ramp for Newland, the town he'd grown up in. After buying the company that published his graphic novels, he'd moved his whole family to Florida to enjoy life in the sun. His parents had made trips home. Gram had spent entire summers here. But Wyatt hadn't even been home for a visit in fifteen long years. Now, he was back. A changed man. A *rich* man. Not the geeky kid everybody "liked" but sort of made fun of. Not the skinny nerd who never got picked for the team in gym class. But a six-foot-one, two-hundred-pound guy who not only worked out, he'd also turned his geekiness into a fortune.

He laughed. He could only imagine the reception he was about to get.

Two sweeping turns took him to Main Street, then one final turn took him to his grandmother's street. He saw the aging Cape Cod immediately. Gables and blue shutters accented the white siding. A row of overgrown hedges bordered the driveway, giving a measure of privacy from the almost identical Cape Cod next door. The setup was cute. Simple. But that was the way everybody in Newland lived. Simply. They had nice, quiet lives. Not like the hustle and bustle of work and entertainment—cocktail parties and picnics, Jet Skis and fund-raisers—he and his family lived with on the Gulf Coast.

He roared into the driveway and cut the engine. After tucking his helmet under his arm, he rummaged in his shirt pocket for his sunglasses. He slid them on, walked to the old-fashioned wooden garage door and yanked it open with a grunt. No lock or automatic garage door for his grandmother. Newland was safe as well as quiet. Another thing very different from where he currently lived. The safety of a small town. Knowing your neighbors. Liking your neighbors.

He missed that.

The stale scent of a closed-up garage wafted out to him, and he waved it away as he strode back to his bike.

"Hey, Mithter."

He stopped, glanced around. Not seeing anybody, he headed to his bike again.

"Hey, Mithter."

This time the voice was louder. When he

stopped, he followed the sound of the little-boy lisp and found himself looking into the big brown eyes of a kid who couldn't have been more than four years old. Standing in a small gap in the hedges, he grinned up at Wyatt.

"Hi."

"Hey, kid."

"Is that your bike?"

"Yeah." Wyatt took the two steps over to the little boy and pulled back the hedge so he could see him. His light brown hair was cut short and spiked out in a few directions. Smudges of dirt stained his T-shirt. His pants hung on skinny hips.

He craned his head back and blinked up at Wyatt. "Can I have a wide?"

"A wide?"

He pointed at the bike. "A wide."

"Oh, you mean *ride*." He looked at his motorcycle. "Um." He'd never taken a kid on his bike. Hell, he was barely ever around kids—except the children of his staff when they had company outings.

"O-wen…"

The lyrical voice floated over to Wyatt and his breath stalled.

Missy. Missy Johnson. Prettiest girl in his

high school. Granddaughter of his gram's next-door neighbor. The girl he'd coached through remedial algebra just for the chance to sit close to her.

"Owen! Honey? Where are you?"

Soft and melodious, her sweet voice went through Wyatt like the first breeze of spring.

He glanced down at the kid. "I take it you're Owen."

The little boy grinned up at him.

The hedge shuffled a bit and suddenly there she stood, her long yellow hair caught in a ponytail.

In the past fifteen years, he'd changed everything about himself, while she looked to have been frozen in time. Her blue-gray eyes sparkled beneath thick black lashes. Her full lips bowed upward as naturally as breathing. Her peaches and cream complexion glowed like a teenager's even though she was thirty-three. A blue T-shirt and jeans shorts accented her small waist and round hips. The legs below her shorts were as perfect as they'd been when she was cheering for the Newland High football team.

Memories made his blood rush hot through his veins. They'd gotten to know each other because their grandmothers were next-door neighbors. And though she was prom queen, homecoming queen, snowball queen and head cheerleader and he was the king of the geeks, he'd wanted to kiss her from the time he was twelve.

Man, he'd had a crush on her.

She gave him a dubious look. "Can I help you?"

She didn't know who he was?

He grinned. That was priceless. Perfect.

"You don't remember me?"

"Should I?"

"Well, I was the reason you passed remedial algebra."

Her eyes narrowed. She pondered for a second. Then she gasped. "Wyatt?"

He rocked back on his heels with a chuckle. "In the flesh."

Her gaze fell to his black leather jacket and jeans, as well as the black helmet he held under his arm.

She frowned, as if unable to reconcile the sexy rebel he now dressed like with the geek she knew in high school. "Wyatt?"

Taking off his sunglasses so she could get a better look at his face, he laughed. "I've sort of changed."

She gave him another quick once-over and

everything inside of Wyatt responded. As if he were still the teenager with the monster crush on her, his gut tightened. His rushing blood heated to boiling. His natural instinct to pounce flared.

Then he glanced down at the little boy.

And back at Missy. "Yours?"

She ruffled Owen's spiky hair. "Yep."

"Mom! Mom!" A little blond girl ran over. Tapping on Missy's knee, she whined, "Lainie hit me."

A dark-haired little girl raced up behind her. "Did not!"

Wyatt's eyebrows rose. *Three kids?*

Missy met his gaze. "These are my kids, Owen, Helaina and Claire." She tapped each child's head affectionately. "They're triplets."

Had he been chewing gum, he would have swallowed it. "Triplets?"

She ruffled Owen's hair fondly. "Yep."

Oh, man.

"You and your husband must be so…" *terrified, overworked, tired* "…proud."

Missy Johnson Brooks turned all three kids in the direction of the house. "Go inside. I'll be in in a second to make lunch." Then she faced the tall, gorgeous guy across the hedge.

Wyatt McKenzie was about the best looking man she'd ever seen in real life. With his supershort black hair cut so close it looked more like a shadow on his head than hair, plus his broad shoulders and watchful brown eyes, he literally rivaled the men in movies.

Her heart rattled in her chest as she tried to pull herself together. It wasn't just weird to see Wyatt McKenzie all grown up and sexy. He brought back some memories she would have preferred stay locked away.

Shielding her eyes from the noonday sun, she said, "My husband and I are divorced."

"Oh, I'm sorry."

She shrugged. "That's okay. How about you?"

His face twisted. "Divorced, too."

His formerly squeaky voice was low and deep, so sexy that her breathing stuttered and heat coiled through her middle.

She stifled the urge to gasp. Surely she wasn't going to let herself be attracted to him? She'd already gone that route with a man. Starry-eyed and trusting, she'd married a gorgeous guy who made her pulse race, and a few years later found herself deserted with three kids. Oh, yeah. She'd learned that lesson and didn't care to repeat it.

She cleared her throat. "I heard a rumor that you got superrich once you left here."

"I did. I write comic books."

"And you make that much money drawing?"

"Well, drawing, writing scripts…" His sexy smile grew. "And owning the company."

She gaped at him, but inside she couldn't stop a swoon. If he'd smiled at her like that in high school she probably would have fainted. Thank God she was older and wiser and knew how to resist a perfect smile. "You *own* a company?"

"And here I thought the gossip mill in Newland was incredibly efficient."

"It probably is. In the past few years I haven't had time to pay much attention."

He glanced at the kids. One by one they'd ambled back to the hedge and over to her, where they currently hung around her knees. "I can see that."

Slowly, carefully, she raised her gaze to meet his. He wasn't the only one who had changed since high school. She might not be rich but she had done some things. She wasn't just raising triplets; she also had some big-time money possibilities. "I own a company, too."

His grin returned. Her face heated. Her heart did something that felt like a somersault.

"Really?"

She looked away. She couldn't believe she was so attracted to him. Then she remembered that Wyatt was somebody special. Deep down inside he had been a nice guy, and maybe he still was underneath all that leather. But that only heightened her unease. If he wasn't, she didn't want her memories of the one honest, sweet guy in her life tainted by this sexy stranger. Worse, she didn't want him discovering too much about her past. Bragging about her company might cause him to ask questions that would bring up memories she didn't want to share.

She reined in her enthusiasm about her fledgling business. "It's a small company."

"Everybody starts small."

She nodded.

He smiled again, but looked at the triplets and motioned toward his motorcycle. "Well, I guess I better get my bike in the garage."

She took a step back, not surprised he wanted to leave. What sexy, gorgeous, bike-riding, company-owning guy wanted to be around a woman with kids? *Three* kids. Three superlovable kids who had a tendency to look needy.

Though she was grateful he was racing away, memories tripped over themselves in her brain. Him helping her with her algebra, and stumbling over asking her out. And her being unable to keep that date.

The urge to apologize for standing him up almost moved her tongue. But she couldn't say anything. Not without telling him things that would mortally embarrass her. "It was nice to see you."

He flashed that lethal grin. "It was nice to see you, too."

He let go of the hedge he'd been holding back. It sprang into place and he disappeared.

With the threat of the newcomer gone, the trips scrambled to the kitchen door and raced inside. She followed them, except she didn't stop in the kitchen. She strode through the house to the living room, where she fell to the sofa.

Realizing she was shaking, she picked up a pillow, put it on her knees and pressed her face to it. She should have known seeing someone she hadn't seen since graduation would take her back to the worst day in her life.

Her special day, graduation… Her dad had stopped at the bar on the way home from the ceremony. Drunk, he'd beaten her mom, ruined the graduation dress Missy had bought with her own money by tossing bleach on it, and slapped Althea, knocking her into a wall, breaking her arm.

Her baby sister, the little girl her mom had called a miracle baby and her dad had called a mistake, had been hit so hard that Missy had taken her to the hospital. Once they'd fixed up her arm, a social worker had peered into their emergency room cubicle.

"Where's your mom?"

"She's out for the night. I'm eighteen. I'm babysitting."

The social worker had given Missy a look of disbelief, so she'd produced her driver's license.

When the social worker was gone, Althea had glared at her. She wanted to tell the truth.

Missy had turned on her sister. "Do you want to end up in foster care? Or worse, have him beat Mom until she dies? Well, I don't."

And the secret had continued….

Her breath stuttered out. Her mom was dead now. Althea had left home. She'd enrolled in a university thousands of miles away, in California. She'd driven out of town and never looked back.

And their dad?

Well, he was "gone," too. Just not forgotten. He still ran the diner, but he spent every spare cent he had on alcohol and gambling. If he wasn't drunk, he was in Atlantic City. The only time Missy saw him was when he needed money.

A little hand fell to her shoulder. "What's wong, Mommy?"

Owen. With his little lisp and his big heart.

She pulled her face out of the pillow. "Nothing's wrong." She smiled, ruffled his short brown hair. "Mommy is fine."

She *was* fine, because after her divorce she'd figured out that she wasn't going to find a knight on a white horse who would rescue her. She had to save herself. Save her kids. Raise her kids in a home where they were never afraid or hungry.

After her ex drained their savings account and left her with three babies and no money, well, she'd learned that the men in her life didn't really care if kids were frightened and/or hungry. And the only person with the power to fix that was her.

So she had.

But she would never, ever trust a man again. Not even sweet Wyatt.

Wyatt walked through the back door of his gram's house, totally confused.

Somehow in his memory he'd kept Missy an eighteen-year-old beauty queen. She might still look like an eighteen-year-old beauty queen, but she'd grown up. Moved on. Become a wife and mom.

He couldn't figure out why that confused him so much. He'd moved on. Gotten married. Gotten divorced. Just as she had. Why did it feel so odd that she'd done the same things he had?

His cell phone rang. He grabbed it from the pocket of his jeans. Seeing the caller ID of his assistant, he said, "Yeah, Arnie, What's up?"

"Nothing except that the Wizard Awards were announced this morning and three of your stories are in!"

"Oh." He expected a thrill to shoot through him, but didn't get one. His mind was stuck on Missy. Something about her nagged at him.

"I thought you'd be happier."

Realizing he was standing there like a goof,

not even talking to the assistant who'd called him, he said, "I am happy with the nominations. They're great."

"Well, that's because your books are great."

He grinned. His work *was* great. Not that he was vain, but a person had to have some confidence—

He stopped himself. Now he knew what was bothering him about Missy. *She'd stood him up.* They'd had a date graduation night and she'd never showed. In fact, she hadn't even come to his grandmother's house that whole summer. He hadn't seen her on the street. He'd spent June, July and August wondering, then left for college never knowing why she'd agreed to meet him at a party, but never showed.

He said, "Arnie, thanks for calling," then hung up the phone.

She owed him an explanation. Fifteen years ago, even if he'd seen her that summer, he would have been too embarrassed to confront her, ask her why she'd blown him off.

At thirty-three, rich, talented and successful, he found nothing was too difficult for him to confront. He might have lost one-third of his company to his ex-wife, but in the end he'd come to realize that their divorce had been nothing but business.

This was personal.

And he wanted to know.

CHAPTER TWO

THE NEXT MORNING Wyatt woke with a hangover. After he'd hung up on Arnie, he'd gone to the 7-Eleven for milk, bread, cheese and a case of beer. Deciding he wanted something to celebrate his award nominations, he'd added a bottle of cheap champagne. Apparently cheap champagne and beer weren't a good mix because his head felt like a rock. This was what he got for breaking his own hard-and-fast rule of moderation in all things.

Shrugging into a clean T-shirt and his jeans from the day before, he made a pot of coffee, filled a cup and walked out to the back porch for some fresh air.

From his vantage point, he could see above the hedge. Missy stood in her backyard, hanging clothes on a line strung between two poles beside a swing set. The night before he'd decided he didn't need to ask her why she'd stood him up. It was pointless. Stupid. What did he care about something that happened fifteen years ago?

Still, he remained on his porch, watching her. She didn't notice him. Busy fluffing out little T-shirts and pinning them to the line, she hadn't even heard him come outside.

In the silence of a small town at ten o'clock on a Tuesday morning in late April, when kids were in school and adults at work, he studied her pretty legs. The way her bottom rounded when she bent. The swing of her ponytail. It was hard to believe she was thirty-three, let alone the mother of triplets.

"Hey, Mithter."

His gaze tumbled down to the sidewalk at the bottom of the five porch steps. There stood Owen.

"Hey, kid."

"Wanna watch TV?"

"I don't have TV. My mom canceled the cable." He laughed and ambled down the steps. "Besides, don't you think your mom will be worried if you're gone?"

He nodded.

"So you should go home."

He shook his head.

Wyatt chuckled and finished his coffee. The

kid certainly knew his mind. He glanced at the hedge, but from ground level he couldn't see Missy anymore. It seemed weird to yell for her to come get her son, but...

No buts about it. It *was* weird. And made it appear as if he was afraid to talk to her... or maybe becoming an introvert because one woman robbed him blind in a divorce settlement. He wasn't afraid of Missy. And he might not ever marry again, but he wasn't going to be an emotional cripple because of a divorce.

Reaching down, he took Owen's hand. "Come on." He walked him to the hedge, held it back so Owen could step through, then followed him into the next yard.

Little shirts and shorts billowed in the breeze, but the laundry basket and Missy were gone.

He could just leave the kid in the yard, explaining to Owen that he shouldn't come to his house anymore. But the little boy blinked up at him, with long black lashes over sad, puppy-dog eyes.

Wyatt's heart melted. "Okay. I'll take you inside."

Happy, Owen dropped his hand and raced

ahead. Climbing up the stairs, he yelled, "Hey, Mom! That man is here again."

Wyatt winced. Was it just him or did that make him sound like a stalker?

Missy opened the door. Owen scooted inside. Wyatt strolled over. He stopped at the bottom of the steps.

"Sorry about this." He looked up at her. His gaze cruised from her long legs, past her jeans shorts, to her short pink T-shirt and full breasts to her smiling face. Attraction rumbled through him. Though he would have liked to take a few minutes to enjoy the pure, unadulterated swell of desire, he squelched it. Not only was she a mom, but he was still in the confusing postdivorce stage. He didn't want a relationship, he wanted sex. He wasn't someone who should be trifling with a nice woman.

"Owen just sort of appeared at the bottom of my steps so I figured I'd better bring him home."

She frowned. "That's weird. He's never been a runner before."

"A runner?"

"A kid who just trots off. Usually he clings to my legs. But we've never had a man next door either." She smiled and nodded at his coffee cup. "Why don't you come up and I'll refill that."

The offer was sweet and polite. Plus, she wasn't looking at him as if he was intruding or crazy. Maybe it was smart to get back to having normal conversations with someone of the opposite sex. Even if it was just a friendly chat over a cup of coffee.

He walked up the steps. "Thanks. I could use a refill."

She led him into her kitchen. Her two little girls sat at the table coloring. The crowded countertop held bowls and spoons and ingredients he didn't recognize, as if Missy was cooking something. And Owen stood in the center of the kitchen, the lone male, looking totally out of place.

Missy motioned toward the table. "Have a seat."

Wyatt pulled a chair away from the table. The two little girls peeked up from their coloring books and grinned, but went back to their work without saying anything. Missy walked over with the coffeepot and filled his cup.

"So what are you cooking?"

"Gum paste."

That didn't sound very appetizing. "Gum paste?"

Taking the coffeepot back to the counter, she said, "To make flowers to decorate a cake."

"That's right. You used to bake cakes for the diner."

"That's how I could afford my clothes."

He sniffed. "Oh, come on. Your dad owns the diner. Everybody knew you guys were rolling in money."

She turned away. Her voice chilled as she said, "My dad still made me work for what I wanted." But when she faced him again, she was smiling.

Confused, but not about to get into something that might ruin their nice conversation, Wyatt motioned to the counter. "So who is this cake for?"

"It's a wedding cake. Bride's from Frederick. It's a big fancy, splashy wedding, so the cake has to be exactly what she wants. Simple. Elegant."

Suddenly the pieces fell into place. "And that's your business?"

"Brides are willing to pay a lot to get the exact cake that suits their wedding. Which means a job a month supports us." She glanced around. "Of course, I inherited this house and our expenses are small, so selling one cake a month is enough."

"What do you do in the winter?"

"The winter?"

"When fewer people get married?"

"Oh. Well, that's why I have to do more than one cake a month in wedding season. I have a cake the last two weeks of April, every weekend in May, June and July, and two in August, so I can put some money back for the months when I don't have orders."

"Makes sense." He drank his coffee. "I guess I better get going."

She smiled slightly. "You never said what brings you home."

Not sure if she was trying to keep him here with mindless conversation or genuinely curious, he shrugged. "The family jewels."

Missy laughed.

"Apparently my grandmother had some necklaces or brooches or something that *her* grandmother brought over from Scotland."

"Oh. I'll bet they're beautiful."

"Yeah, well. I've yet to find them."

"Didn't she have a jewelry box?"

"Yes, and last night I sent my mom pictures

of everything in it and none of the pieces are the Scotland things."

"So you're here until you find them?"

"I'm here till I find them. Or four weeks. I can get away when I want, but I can't stay away indefinitely."

"Maybe one of these nights I could grill chicken or something for supper and you could come over and we could catch up."

He remembered the afternoons sitting on the bench seat of her grandmother's picnic table, trying to get her to understand equations. He remembered spring breezes and autumn winds, but most of all he remembered how nice it was just to be with her. For a man working to get beyond a protracted divorce, it might not be a bad idea to spend some time with a woman who reminded him of good things. Happy times.

He smiled. "That would be nice."

He made his way back to his house and headed to his grandmother's bedroom again. Because she'd lived eight months of the year in Florida and four months in Maryland, her house was still furnished as it always had been. An outdated floral bedspread matched floral drapes. Lacy lamps sat on tables by the bed. And the whole place smelled of pot-pourri.

With a grimace, he walked to the mirrored dresser. He'd looked in the jewelry box the night before. He could check the drawers today, but he had a feeling these lockets and necklaces were something his grandmother had squirreled away. He toed the oval braided rug beneath her bed.

Could she have had a secret compartment under there? Floorboards that he could lift, and find a metal box?

Looking for that was better than flipping through his grandmother's underwear drawer.

He pushed the bed to the side, off the rug, then knelt and began rolling the carpet, hoping to find a sign of a loose floorboard. With the rug out of the way, he felt along the hardwood, looking for a catch or a spring or something that would indicate a secret compartment. He smoothed his hand along a scarred board, watching the movement of his fingers as he sought a catch, and suddenly his hand hit something solid and stopped.

His gaze shot over and there knelt Owen. "Hey."

He rocked back on his heels. "Hey. Does your mom know you're here?"

The little boy shook his head.

Wyatt sighed. "Okay. Look. I like you. And from what I saw of your house this morning, I get it. You're a bored guy in a houseful of women."

Owen's big brown eyes blinked.

"But you can't come over here."

"Yes I can. I can get through the bushes."

Wyatt stifled a laugh. Leave it to a kid to be literal. "Yes, you *can* walk over here. It is possible. But it isn't right for you to leave without telling your mom."

Owen held out a cell phone. "We can call her."

Wyatt groaned. "Owen, buddy, I hate to tell you this, but if you took your mom's phone, you might be in a world of trouble."

He shoved up off the floor and held out his hand to the little boy. "Sorry, kid. But I've got to take you and the phone home."

Wyatt pulled the hedge back and walked up the steps to Missy's kitchen, holding Owen's hand. Knocking on the screen door, he called, "Missy?"

Drying her hands on a dish towel, she appeared at the door, opened it and immediately saw Owen. "Oh, no. I'm sorry! I thought he was in the playroom with the girls."

She stooped down. "O-ee, honey. You have to stay here with Mommy."

Owen slid his little arm around Wyatt's knee and hugged.

And fifty percent of Wyatt's childhood came tumbling back. He hadn't been included in the neighbor kids' games, because he was a nerd. And Owen wasn't included in his sisters' games, because he wasn't a girl. But the feeling of being excluded was the same.

Wyatt's heart squeezed. "You know what? I didn't actually bring him home to stay home." He knew a cry for help when he heard it, and he couldn't ignore it. He held out her cell phone and she gasped. "I just want you to know where he is, and I wanted to give back your phone."

She looked up at him. "Are you saying you'll keep him at your house for a while?"

"Sure. I think we could have fun."

Owen's grip on his knee loosened.

She caught her son's gaze again. "If I let you go to Mr. McKenzie's house for a few hours, will you promise to stay here this afternoon?"

Owen nodded eagerly.

Her gaze climbed up to meet Wyatt's.

"What are you going to do with a kid for a couple of hours?"

"My grandmother kept everything. She should still have the video games I played as a boy. And if she doesn't, I saw a sandbox out there in your yard. Maybe we could play in that."

Owen tugged on his jeans. "I have twucks."

Missy gave Wyatt a hopeful look. "He loves to play in the sand with his trucks."

He shrugged. "So sand it is. I haven't showered yet this morning. I can crawl around in the dirt for a few hours."

Missy rose. "I really appreciate this."

"It's no problem."

Twenty minutes later, Missy stood by her huge mixer waiting for her gelatin mix to cool, watching Owen and Wyatt out her kitchen window. Her eyes filled with tears. Her little boy needed a man around, but his dad had run and wanted nothing to do with his triplets. Her dad was a drunk. Her pool of potential men for Owen's life was very small.

Owen pushed a yellow toy truck through the sand as Wyatt operated a pint-size front-end loader. He filled the back of the truck with sand and Owen "drove" it to the other side of the sandbox, where he dumped it in a growing pile.

Missy put her elbow on the windowsill and her chin on her open palm. *She* might not want to get involved with Wyatt, but it really would help Owen to have him around for the next month.

Still, he was a rich, good-looking guy, who, if he wanted to play with kids, would have had some by now. It was wrong to even consider asking him to spend time with Owen. Especially since the time he spent with Owen had to be on her schedule, not his.

She took a pitcher of tropical punch and some cookies outside. "I hate to say this," she said, handing Owen the first glass of punch, "but somebody needs a nap."

Wyatt yawned and stretched. "Hey, no need to worry about hurting my feelings. I know I need a nap."

Owen giggled.

Wyatt rose. "Wanna play for a few hours this afternoon?"

Owen nodded.

"Great. I'll be back then." He grabbed two cookies from the plate Missy held before he walked over to the hedge, pulled it back and strode through.

Watching him go, Missy frowned thoughtfully. He really wasn't a bad guy. Actually, he behaved a lot like the Wyatt she used to know. And he genuinely seemed to like Owen. Which was exactly what she wanted. Somebody to keep her little boy company.

She glanced at the plate, the empty spot where the two cookies he'd taken had been sitting. Maybe she did know a way to keep him around. Since he was in his grandma's house alone, and there was only one place in town to get food—the diner—it might be possible to keep him around just by feeding him.

That afternoon Missy watched Wyatt emerge through the hedge a little after three. Owen was outside, so he didn't even come inside. He just grabbed a ball and started a game of catch.

Missy flipped the chicken breasts she was marinating, and went back to vacuuming the living room and cleaning bathrooms. When she was done, Owen and Wyatt were sitting at the picnic table.

Marinated chicken in one hand and small bag of charcoal briquettes in the other, she raced out to the backyard. "You wouldn't want to help me light the briquettes for the grill, would you?"

Wyatt got up from the table. "Sure." Grabbing the bag from her arm, he chuckled. "I didn't know anybody still used these things."

"It's cheaper than a gas grill."

He poured some into the belly of the grill. "I suppose." He caught her gaze. "Got a match?"

She went inside and returned with igniting fluid and the long slender lighter she used for candles.

He turned the can of lighter fluid over in his hand. "I forgot about this. We'll have a fire for you in fifteen minutes."

"If it takes you any longer, you're a girl."

He laughed. "So we're back to high school taunts."

"If the shoe fits. By the way, I've marinated enough chicken for an army and I'm making grilled veggies, if you want to join us for dinner."

"I think if I get the fire going, you owe me dinner."

She smiled. She couldn't even begin to tell him how much she owed him for his help with Owen, so she only said, "Exactly."

She returned to the kitchen and watched out the window as Wyatt talked Owen through lighting the charcoal. She noticed with approval that he kept Owen a safe distance away from the grill. But also noticed that he kept talking, pointing, as if explaining the process.

And Owen soaked it all in. The little man of the house.

Tears filled her eyes again. She hoped one month with a guy would be enough to hold Owen until…

Until what she wasn't sure, but eventually she'd have to find a neighbor or teacher or maybe somebody from church who could spend a few hours a week with her son.

Because she wasn't getting romantically involved with a man again until she had her business up and running. Until she could be financially independent. Until she could live with a man and know that even if he left her she could support her kids. And with her business just starting, that might not be for a long, long time.

While the chicken cooked, Wyatt ran over to his grandmother's house for a shower. He liked that kid. Really liked him. Owen wasn't a whiny, crying toddler. He was a cool little boy who just wanted somebody to play with.

And Wyatt had had fun. He'd even enjoyed Missy's company. Not because she was flirty or attracted to him, but because she treated him like a friend. Just as he'd thought that morning, a platonic relationship with her could go a long way to helping him get back to normal after his divorce.

He put his head under the spray. Now all he had to do was keep his attraction to her in line. He almost laughed. In high school, he'd had four years of keeping his attraction to her under lock and key. While she'd been dating football stars, he'd been her long-suffering tutor.

This time he did laugh. He wasn't a long-suffering kind of guy anymore. He was a guy who got what he wanted. He liked her. He wanted her. And he was now free. It might be a little difficult telling his grown-up, spoiled self he couldn't have her....

But maybe he needed some practice with not getting his own way? His divorce had shown him, and several lawyers, that he wasn't fond of compromise. And he absolutely, positively didn't like not getting his own way.

He really did need a lesson in compromise. In stepping back. In being honorable.

Doing good things for Missy, and *not* act-ing on his attraction, might be the lesson in self-discipline and control he needed.

Especially since he had no intention of getting married again. The financial loss he'd suffered in his divorce was a setback. He would recover from that with his brains and talent. The hurt? That was a different story. The pain of losing the woman he'd believed loved him had followed him around like a lost puppy for two years. He had no intention of setting himself up for that kind of pain again. Which meant no permanent relationship. Particularly no marriage. And if he got involved with Missy, he would hurt her, because she was the kind of girl who needed to be married.

So problem solved. He would not flirt. He would not take. He would be kind to her and her kids. And expect nothing, want nothing, in return.

And hopefully, he'd get his inner nice guy back.

When he returned to Missy's backyard in a clean T-shirt, shorts and flip-flops, she had the veggies on the table and was pulling the chicken off the grill.

"Grab a paper plate and help yourself."

He glanced over. "The kids' plates aren't made yet."

"I can do it."

"I can help."

With a little instruction from her about how much food to put on each, Wyatt helped prepare three plates of food for the kids. Owen sat beside him on the bench seat and Missy sat across from them with the girls.

It honest to God felt like high school all over again. Girls on one side. Boys on the other.

Little brown-eyed, blond Claire said, "We have a boys' side and a girls' side."

Wyatt caught Missy's gaze. "Is that good or bad?"

"I don't know. We've never had another boy around."

"Really?"

She shrugged and pretended great interest in cutting Helaina's chicken.

Interesting. She hadn't had another man around in years? Maybe if Wyatt worked this right, their relationship didn't have to be platonic—

He stopped that thought. Shut it down. Getting involved with someone like Missy would be nothing but complicated. While having a platonic relationship would do them both good.

So the conversation centered around kid topics while they ate. Wyatt helped clean up. Then he announced that it was time to go back to his grandmother's house.

"To hunt for hidden treasure," he told Owen.

Owen's head almost snapped off as he faced Missy. "Can I go look for hidden tweasure, too?"

"No. It's bath time then story time then bedtime."

Owen groused. But Wyatt had an answer for this, if only because he understood negotiating. Give the opposing party something they wanted and everybody would be happy.

He caught Owen by the shoulders and stooped to his height. "You need to get some rest if we're going to build the high-rise sky-scraper tomorrow."

Owen's eyes lit up as he realized Wyatt intended to play with him again the next day. He threw his arms around Wyatt's neck, hugged him and raced off.

An odd tingling exploded in Wyatt's chest. It was the first time in his life he'd been close enough to a child to get a hug. And the sensation was amazing. It made him feel strong, protective…wanted. But in a way he'd never felt before. His decision to be around this little family strengthened. He could help Owen, and being around Owen and Missy and the girls could help him remember he didn't always need to get his own way.

It was win-win.

Missy sighed with contentment. "Thanks."

"You're welcome."

With the kids so far ahead of her, she motioned to her back door. "Sorry, but I've got to get in there before they flood the bathroom."

Wyatt laughed. "Got it."

He walked to the hedge, pulled it aside and headed for his gram's house. He went into her bedroom again and started pulling shoe boxes filled with God knew what out of her overstuffed closet. But after only fifteen minutes, he glanced out the big bedroom window and saw Missy had come out to her back porch. She wearily sat on one of the two outdoor chairs.

Wyatt stopped pulling shoe boxes out of his gram's closet.

She looked exhausted. Claire had said they'd never had another man around, which probably meant Missy didn't date. But looking at her right now, he had to wonder if she ever even took a break.

He sucked in a breath. If he really wanted to help her, he couldn't just do the things he knew would help him get back his rational, calm, predivorce self. He had to do the things *she* needed.

And right now it looked as if she needed a drink.

He dropped the box, pulled two bottles of beer from the refrigerator and headed for the hedge. It rustled as he pushed it aside.

She didn't notice him walking across the short expanse of yard to the back porch, so he called up the steps. "Hey, I saw you come out here. Mind if I join you?"

"No. Sure. That'd be great."

He heard the hesitation in her voice, but decided that was just her exhaustion speaking.

He held up the two bottles of beer. "I didn't come empty-handed." He climbed the steps, offered her a beer and fell to the chair beside hers. "Your son could wear out a world-class athlete."

She laughed. "He's a good kid and he likes you. I really appreciate you spending time with him." She took a swig of beer. "Wow. I haven't had a beer in ages."

Happiness rose in him. He *had* done something nice for her.

"A person has to have all her wits to care for three kids at once. One beer is fine. Two beers would probably put me to sleep."

"Okay, good to know. This way I'll limit you to one." He eased back on the chair. "So tell me more about the cake business."

She peeked at him and his heart turned over in his chest. In the dim light of her back porch, her gray-blue eyes sort of glowed. The long hair she kept in a ponytail while she worked currently fell to her back in a long, smooth wave. He didn't dare glance down at her legs, because his intention was to keep this relationship platonic, and those legs could be his undoing.

"I love my business." She said it slowly, carefully meeting his gaze. "But it's a lot of work."

He swallowed. Her eyes were just so damned pretty. "I'll bet it is."

"And what's funny is I learned how to do most of it online."

That made him laugh. "No kidding."

He turned on his chair to face her, and suddenly their legs were precariously close. Nerves tingled through him. He desperately wanted to flirt with her. To feel the rush of attraction turn to arousal. To feel the rush of heat right before a first kiss.

Their gazes met and clung. Her tongue peeked out and moistened her lips.

The tingle dancing along his skin became a slow burn. Maybe he wasn't the only one feeling this attraction?

She rose from her chair and walked to the edge of the porch, propping her butt on the railing, trying not to look as if she was running from him.

But she was.

She was attracted to him and he wasn't having any luck hiding his attraction to her. This attraction was mutual, so why run?

"There are tons and tons of online videos of people creating beautiful one-of-a-kind cakes. If you have the basic know-how about cake baking, the decorating stuff can be learned."

He rose from his seat, too. He absolutely, positively wanted to help her with Owen, but a platonic relationship wouldn't get him over his bad divorce as well as a new romance could. And from the looks of things, she could use a little romance in her life, too. Even one that ended. Good memories could be a powerful way to get a person from one difficult day to the next.

He ambled over beside her. Edged his hip onto the railing. "So you baked a lot of trial cakes?"

She laughed nervously. "I probably should have. But I worked with a woman whose sister was getting married, and when she heard I was learning to bake wedding cakes she asked if I'd bake one for the wedding." Missy caught his gaze, her blue-gray eyes filled with heat. Her breath stuttered out.

He smiled. In high school he'd have given anything to make her breath stutter like that. And now that he had, he couldn't just ignore it. Particularly since he definitely could get back to normal a lot quicker with a new romance.

"Because it was my first cake, I did it for free." Her soft voice whispered between them. "Luckily, it came out perfectly. And I got several referrals."

He slid a little closer. "That's good."

She slid away. "That was last year. My trial and error year. This year I have enough referrals and know enough that I was comfortable quitting my job, doing this full-time."

He nodded, slid closer. He wouldn't be such

an idiot that he'd seduce her tonight, but he did want a kiss.

But she scooted farther away from him. "You're not getting what I'm telling you."

He frowned. Her crisp, unyielding voice didn't match the heat bubbling in his stomach right now.

Had he fantasized his way into missing part of the conversation?

"What are you telling me?"

"I was abandoned by my husband with three kids. We've been as close to dead broke as four people can be for four long years. It was almost a happy accident that the first bride asked me to bake her cake. Over the past year I've been building to this point where I had a whole summer of cakes to bake. A real income."

She slid off the railing and walked away from him. "I like you. But I have three kids and a new business."

His chest constricted. He'd definitely fantasized his way into missing something. He hadn't heard anything even close to that in their conversation. But he heard it now. "And you don't want a man around, screwing that up?"

She winced. "No. I don't."

The happy tingle in his blood died. He wasn't mad at her. How could he be mad at her when what she said made so much sense?

But he wasn't happy, either.

He collected the empty beer bottles and left.

CHAPTER THREE

THE NEXT MORNING, Owen blew through the kitchen and out the back door like a little boy on a mission, and Missy's heart twisted. He was on his way to the sandbox, expecting to find Wyatt.

She squeezed her eyes shut in misery. The Wyatt she remembered from their high school days never would have hit on her the way he had the night before. Recalling the sweet, shy way he'd asked her to the graduation party, she shook her head. That Wyatt was gone. This Wyatt was a weird combination of the nice guy he had been, a guy who'd seen Owen's plight and rescued him, and a new guy. Somebody she didn't know at all.

Still, she knew men. She knew that when they didn't get their own way they bolted or pouted or got angry. Wyatt wasn't the kind to get angry the way her dad had gotten angry, but she'd bet her next cake referral that she'd ruined Owen's chances for a companion today. Hell, she might have wrecked his chances for a companion all month. All because she didn't want to be attracted to Wyatt McKenzie.

Well, that wasn't precisely true. Being attracted to him was like a force of nature. He was gorgeous. She was normal. Any sane woman would automatically be attracted to him. Which was why she couldn't let Wyatt kiss her. One really good kiss would have dissolved her into a puddle of need, and she didn't want that. She wanted the security of knowing she could support her kids. She wouldn't get that security if she lost focus. Or if she fell for a man before she was ready.

So she'd warned him off. And now Owen would suffer.

But when she lifted the kitchen curtain to peek outside, there in the sandbox was Wyatt McKenzie. His feet were bare. His flip-flops lay drunkenly in the grass. Worn jeans caressed his perfect butt and his T-shirt showed off wide shoulders.

She dropped the curtain with a groan. Why did he have to be so attractive?

Still, seeing him with her son revived her

faith in him. Maybe he was more like the nice Wyatt she remembered?

Unfortunately, until he proved that, she believed it was better to keep her distance.

After retrieving her gum paste from the refrigerator, she broke it into manageable sections. Once she rolled each section, she put it through a pasta machine to make it even thinner. Then she placed the pieces on plastic mats and put them into the freezer for use on Friday, when she would begin making the flowers.

She peeked out the window again, and to her surprise, Owen and Wyatt were still in the sandbox.

Okay. He might not be the old shy Wyatt who'd stumbled over his words to ask her out. But he was still a good guy. She wouldn't hold it against him that he'd made a pass at her. Actually, with that pass out of the way, maybe they could go back to being friends? And maybe she should take him a glass of fruit punch and make peace?

When Missy came out to the yard with a pitcher and glasses, Wyatt wasn't sure what to do. He hadn't worked out how he felt about her rebuffing him. Except that he couldn't take it out on Owen.

She offered him a glass. "Fruit punch?"

She smiled tentatively, as if she didn't know how to behave around him, either.

He took the glass. "Sure. Thanks."

"You're welcome." She turned away just as her two little girls came running outside. "Who wants juice?"

A chorus of "I do" billowed around him. He drank his fruit punch like a man in a desert and put his glass under the pitcher again when she filled the kids' glasses.

Their gazes caught.

"Thirsty?"

"Very."

"Well, I have lots of fruit punch. Drink your fill."

But don't kiss her.

As she poured punch into his glass, he took a long breath. He was happy. He liked Owen. He even found it amusing to hear the girls chatter about their dolls when they sat under the tree and played house. And he'd spent most of his life wanting a kiss from Missy Johnson and never getting one.

So, technically, this wasn't new. This was normal.

Maybe he was just being a pain in the butt by being upset about it?

And maybe that was part of what he needed to learn before he returned home? That pushing for things he wanted sometimes made him a jerk.

Sheesh. He didn't like the sound of that. But he had to admit that up until he'd lost Betsy, he'd gotten everything he wanted. His talent got him money. His money got him the company that made him the boss. Until Betsy cheated on him, then left him, then sued him, his life had been perfect. Maybe this time with Missy was life balancing the scales as it taught him to gracefully accept failure.

He didn't stay for lunch, though she invited him to. Instead, he ate a dried-up cheese sandwich made from cheese in Gram's freezer and bread he'd gotten at the 7-Eleven the day he'd bought the beer and champagne. When he was finished, he returned to his work of taking everything out of his grandmother's closet, piling things on the bed. When that was full he shifted to stacking them on the floor beside the bed. With the closet empty, he stared at the stack in awe. How did a person get that much stuff in one closet?

One by one, he began going through the shoe

boxes, which contained everything from old bath salts to old receipts. Around two o'clock, he heard the squeals of the kids' laughter and decided he'd had enough of being inside. Ten minutes later, he and Owen were a Wiffle ball team against Lainie and Claire.

Around four, Missy came outside with hot dogs to grill for supper. He started the charcoal for her, but didn't stay. If he wanted to get back his inner nice guy, to accept that she had a right to rebuff him, he would need some space to get accustomed to it.

Because that's what a reasonable guy did. He accepted his limits.

Once inside his gram's house, tired and sweaty, he headed for the bathroom to shower. Under the spray, he thought about how much fun Missy's kids were, then about how much work they were. Then he frowned, thinking about their dad.

What kind of man left a woman with three kids?

What kind of man didn't give a damn if his kids were fed?

What kind of man expected the woman he'd gotten pregnant to sacrifice everything because she had to be the sole support of his kids?

A real louse. Missy had married a real louse.

Was it any wonder she'd warned Wyatt off the night before? She had three kids. Three energetic, hungry, busy kids to raise alone because some dingbat couldn't handle having triplets.

If she was smart, she'd never again trust a man.

A funny feeling slithered through Wyatt.

They were actually very much alike. She'd never trust a man because one had left her with triplets, and he'd never trust a woman because Betsy's betrayal had hurt a lot more than he liked to admit.

Even in his own head he hadn't considered wooing Missy to marry her. He wanted a kiss. But not love. In some ways he was no better than her ex.

He needed to stay away from her, too.

He walked over to her yard the next morning and played with Owen in the sandbox. He and Missy didn't have much contact, but that was fine. Every day that he spent with her kids and saw the amount of work required to raise them alone, he got more and more angry with her ex and more and more determined to stay away from her, to let her get on with her life. She ran herself ragged working on the wedding cake every morning and housecleaning and caring for the kids in the afternoon.

So when she invited him to supper every day, he refused. Though he was sick of the canned soup he found in Gram's pantry, and dry toasted-cheese sandwiches, he didn't want to make any more work for Missy. He also respected her boundaries. He wouldn't push to get involved with her, no matter that he could see in her eyes that she was attracted to him. He would be a gentleman.

Even if it killed him.

But on Saturday afternoon, he watched her carry the tiers of a wedding cake into her rattletrap SUV. Wearing a simple blue sleeveless dress that stopped midthigh, and high, high white sandals, with her hair curled into some sort of twist thing on the back of her head, she looked both professional and sexy.

Primal male need slid along his nerve endings and he told himself to get away from the window. But as she and the babysitter lugged the last section of the cake, the huge bottom layer, into the SUV, their conversation drifted to him through the open bedroom window.

"So what do you do once you get there?"

"Ask the caterer to lend me a waiter so I

can carry all this into the reception area. Then I have to put it together and cut it and serve it."

By herself. She didn't have to say the words. They were implied. And if the caterer couldn't spare a waiter to help her carry the cake into the reception venue, she'd carry that alone, too.

Wyatt got so angry with her ex that his head nearly exploded. Though he was dressed to play with Owen, he pivoted from the window, slapped on a clean pair of jeans and a clean T-shirt and marched to her driveway.

As she opened the door to get into the driver's side of her SUV, he opened the door on the passenger's side.

"What are you doing?"

He slammed the door and reached for his seat belt. "Helping you."

She laughed lightly. "I'm fine."

"Right. You're fine. You're run ragged by three kids and a new business. Now you have to drive the cake to the wedding, set it up, and wait for the time when you can cut it and serve it." He flicked a glance at her. "All in an SUV that looks like it might not survive a trip to Frederick."

"It—"

He stopped her with a look. "I'm coming with you."

"Wyatt—"

"Start the SUV and drive, because I'm not getting out and you don't have another car to take."

Huffing out a sigh, she turned the key in the ignition. She waved out the open window. "Bye, kids! Mommy will be back soon. Be nice for Miss Nancy."

They all waved.

She backed out of the driveway and headed for the interstate.

Now that the moment of anger had passed, Wyatt shifted uncomfortably on his seat. Even though it had been for her own good, he'd been a bit high-handed. Exactly what he was trying to stop doing. "I'm not usually this bossy."

She laughed musically. "Right. You own a company. You have to be bossy."

"I suppose." Brooding, he stared out the window. She wanted nothing to do with him, and he wasn't really a good bet for getting involved with her. And they were about to spend hours together.

She probably thought he'd volunteered to

help in order to have another chance to make a pass at her.

He flicked a glance at her. "I know you think I'm nuts for pushing my way into this, but I overheard what you told the babysitter. This is a lot of work."

"I knew that when I started the company. But I like it. And it's the only way I have to earn enough money to support my kids."

Which took him back to the thing that made him so mad. "Your ex should be paying child support."

Irritation caused Missy's chest to expand. She might have been able to accept his help because he was still the nice guy he used to be. But he hadn't offered because he was a nice guy. He'd offered because he felt sorry for her, and she *hated* that.

"Don't feel sorry for me!"

He snorted in disgust. "I don't feel sorry for you. I'm angry with your ex."

Was that any better? "Right."

"Look, picking a bad spouse isn't a crime. If it was, they'd toss me in jail and throw away the key."

She almost laughed. She'd forgotten he had his own tale of woe.

"I'm serious. Betsy cheated on me, lied to me, tried to set my employees against me. All while she and her lawyers were negotiating for a piece of my company in a divorce settlement. She wanted half."

Wide-eyed, Missy glanced over at him. "She cheated on you and tried to get half your company?" Jeff emptying their tiny savings account was small potatoes compared to taking half a company.

"Yes. She only ended up with a *third*." Wyatt sighed. "Feel better?"

She smiled sheepishly. "Sort of."

"So there's nobody in this car who's better than anybody else. We both picked lousy spouses."

She relaxed a little. He really didn't feel sorry for her. They were kind of kindred spirits. Being left with triplets might seem totally different than having an ex take a third of your company, but the principle was the same. Both had been dumped and robbed. For the first time in four years she was with somebody who truly "got it." He wasn't helping her because he thought she was weak. He wasn't helping her because he was still the sort of sappy kid she'd known in high school.

He was helping her because he saw the injustice of her situation.

That pleased her enough that she could accept his assistance. But truth be told, she also knew she needed the help.

When they arrived at the country club, she pulled into a parking space near the service door to facilitate entry. She opened the back of her SUV and he gasped.

"Wow."

Pride shimmied through her. Though the cake was simple—white fondant with pink dots circling the top of each layer, and pink-and-lavender orchids as the cake top—it was beautiful. A work of art. Creating cakes didn't just satisfy her need for money; it gave expression to her soul.

"You like?"

"Those flowers aren't real?"

"Nope. Those are gum paste flowers."

"My God. They're so perfect. Like art."

She laughed. Hadn't she thought the same thing? "It will be melted art if we don't get it inside soon."

They took the layers into the event room and set up the cake on the table off to the right of the bride and groom's dinner seating.

Around them, the caterers put white cloths on the tables. The florist brought centerpieces. The event room transformed into a glorious pink-and-lavender heaven right before their eyes.

Around four, guests began straggling in. They signed the book and found assigned seats as the bar opened.

At five-thirty the bride and groom arrived. A murmur rippled through the room. Missy sighed dreamily. This was what happened when a bride and groom were evenly matched. Happiness. All decked out in white chiffon, the beautiful bride glowed. In his black tux, the suave and sophisticated groom could have broken hearts. Wyatt looked at his watch.

"We have about two hours before we get to the cake," Missy told him.

He groaned. "Wonder what Owen's doing right now?"

"You'd rather be in the sandbox?"

"All men would rather be playing in dirt than making nice with a bunch of people wearing monkey suits."

She laughed. That was certainly not the old nerdy Wyatt she knew in high school. That kid didn't play. He read. He studied. He did not prefer dirt to anything.

She peeked over at him with her peripheral vision. She supposed having money would change anybody. But these changes were different. Not just a shift from a nerdy kid to a sexy guy. But a personality change. Before, he'd seen injustice and suffered in silence. Now he saw injustice—such as Owen being alone—and he fixed it. Even his helping her was his attempt at making up for her ex abandoning her.

Interesting.

White-coated waiters stood at the ready to serve dinner. The best man gave the longest toast in recorded history. In the background, a string quartet played a waltz.

Wyatt looked at his watch again. Silence stretched between them. Missy knew he was bored. She was bored, too. But standing around, waiting to cut the cake, was part of her job.

Suddenly he caught her hand and led her outside, but a thought stopped her short. "Is the wedding bringing up bad marriage memories?"

He laughed and spun her in a circle and

into his arms. "Actually, I'm bored and I love to dance."

"To waltz?" If her voice came out a bit breathless, she totally understood why. The little spin and tug he'd used to get her into his arms for the dance had pressed her flush against him. His arm rested on her waist. Her hand sat on his strong shoulder. And for a woman who'd been so long deprived of male-female contact, it was almost too much for her nerves and hormones to handle. They jumped and popped.

She told herself to think of the old Wyatt. The nice kid. The geeky guy who'd taught her algebra. But she couldn't. This Wyatt was taller, broader, stronger.

Bolder.

He swung her around in time with the string quartet music, and sheer delight filled her. Her defenses automatically rose and the word *stop* sprang to her tongue, but she suddenly wondered why. Why stop? Her fear was of a relationship, and this was just a dance to relieve boredom. Mostly his. To keep it from becoming too intimate, too personal, she'd simply toss in a bit of conversation.

"Where'd you learn to dance like this?"

"Florida. I can dance to just about anything."

She pulled back, studied him. "Really?"

"I go to a lot of charity events. I don't want to look like a schlep."

"Oh, trust me. You're so far from a schlep it's not even funny."

He laughed. The deep, rich, sexy sound surrounded her and her heart stuttered. Now she knew how Cinderella felt dancing with the prince. Cautiously happy. No woman in her right mind really believed the prince would choose her permanently. But, oh, who could resist a five-minute dance when this sexy, bold guy was all hers?

His arms tightened around her, brought her close again, and she let herself go. She gave in to the rush of attraction. The scramble of her pulse. The heat that reminded her she was still very much a woman, not just a mom.

He whirled them around, along the stone path to a colorful garden. As they twirled, he caught her gaze and the whole world seemed to disappear. There was no one but him, with his big biceps, strong shoulders and serious brown eyes, and her with her trembling heart and melting knees. Their gazes locked and a million what-if's shivered through her.

What if he hadn't gone away after college?

What if she'd been able to keep their date?

What if she wasn't so afraid now to trust another man?

Could she fall in love with him?

The dance went on and on. They never broke eye contact. She thought of him being good first to Owen and then to all three of her kids. She thought of him angry when he'd jumped into her SUV. Righteously indignant on her behalf, since her ex was such an idiot. She thought of him wanting to kiss her the other night, and her already weak knees threatened to buckle. If it felt this good to dance with him, what would a kiss be like?

Explosive?

Passionate?

Soul searing?

"Excuse me? Are you the lady who did the cake?"

Brought back to reality, she jumped out of Wyatt's arms and faced the woman who'd interrupted them, only to find a bridesmaid.

Missy's senses instantly sharpened. "Yes. Is there something wrong? Do I need to come inside?"

"No! No! The cake is gorgeous. Perfect." The woman in the pink gown handed her a slip of paper. "That's my name and phone number. I'm getting married next year. The third week in June. I'd love for you to do my cake. Could you call me?"

Happiness raced through her. Her cheeks flushed. "I'd love to. But I have to check my book first and make sure I don't have another cake scheduled for that day."

The pretty bridesmaid said, "Well, I'm hoping you don't." Then she slipped back into the ballroom.

Slapping the little slip of paper against her hand, Missy joyfully faced Wyatt again.

He leaned against a stone retaining wall, watching her with hooded eyes.

"Look! I'm already starting to get work for next year."

He eased away from the wall. "Yeah. I see that."

She'd expected him to be happier for her. Instead he appeared annoyed. Her heart beat against her ribs. Surely he wasn't upset that they'd been interrupted?

She licked her lips and fanned the little slip of paper. "She hasn't tasted the cake yet. This might not pan out."

"Everybody who ate at the diner loved your cakes. You know they're good."

She grinned. "I do!"

"So you're a shoo-in."

"Yeah."

She took a breath. He glanced around awkwardly.

Then she remembered they'd been dancing. Her heart had been pounding. Their gazes had been locked. Something had been happening between them. But the moment had officially been broken.

And now that she was out of his arms, away from his enticing scent, away from the pull of their attraction, she was glad. Really. This wasn't a happily-ever-after kind of relationship. He'd be around only a short time, then he'd go back to Florida. And her divorce had left her unable to trust. Even if she could trust, she wouldn't get involved in something that might distract her from her wedding cake business. She'd never, ever find herself in a position of depending upon a man again.

She turned to go back into the country club ballroom. "It's about time for the bride and groom to cut the cake. Once they get pictures, our big job starts."

She didn't even look back, just expected him to follow her. Even Wyatt with his sexy brown eyes couldn't make her forget the night she'd sat staring at the babies' cribs, knowing she didn't have formula for the next day—or money to buy it.

She would build her business, then maybe work on her trust issues. But for now, the business came first.

CHAPTER FOUR

AFTER THE BRIDE AND GROOM cut the cake, Missy sliced the bottom layer, set the pieces on plates and the plates on trays. Waiters in white shirts scrambled over, grabbed the trays and served the cake.

Wyatt glanced around. "What can I do?"

"How about if I cut the cake and put it on dessert plates, and you put the plates on the trays?"

It wasn't rocket science, but it was better than standing around watching her slender fingers work the knife. Better than wrestling with the hunger gnawing at his belly. And not hunger for food. Hunger for a kiss.

A kiss she owed him. Had she not stood him up, their date would have ended in a kiss.

Hence, she owed him.

When the last of the cake was served, she packaged the top layer, the one with the intricate orchids, into a special box. They packaged the remainder of the uncut cake into another, not quite as fancy, one. The bride's mom took both boxes, complimented Missy on the cake, then strode away to secure the leftovers for the bride.

As the music and dancing went on, Missy and Wyatt gathered up her equipment and slid it into the back of her SUV.

Just as they were closing the door, a young woman in a blue dress scrambled over. "You made the cake, right?"

Missy smiled. "Yes."

"It was wonderful! Delicious and beautiful."

Her cheeks flushed again. Her eyes sparkled with happiness. "Thanks."

"I don't suppose you have a card?"

She winced. "No. Sorry. But if you write down your name and number, I can call you." She headed for the driver's side door. "I have a pen and paper."

The young woman eagerly took the pad and pen and scribbled her name and phone number.

"Don't forget to put your wedding date on there."

After another quick scribble, the bride-to-be handed the tablet to Missy, but another young woman standing beside her grabbed the pad and pen before she could take them.

"I'll give you my name and number and wedding date, too. That was the most delicious cake I've ever eaten."

"Thanks."

When the two brides-to-be were finished heaping praise on Missy, she and Wyatt climbed into the SUV and headed home.

He'd never been so proud of anyone in his life. He didn't think he'd even been this proud of himself when he'd bought the comic book company. Of course, the stakes weren't as high. As Missy had said, she had three kids to support and no job. He'd been publishing comic books for at least six years before he bought the company, and by then, given how much influence he had over what they published, it was almost a foregone conclusion that he'd someday take over.

But this—watching Missy start her company from nothing—it was energizing. Emotional.

"You need to get business cards."

She glanced over at him, her cheeks rosy, her eyes shining. "What?"

"Business cards. So that people can call you."

She laughed her musical laugh, the one that reminded him he liked her a lot more than he should.

"It's better for them to give me their numbers. This way they don't get lost, and I control the situation."

He sucked in a breath. She liked control, huh? Well, she certainly had control of him, and it confused him, didn't fit his plans. Probably didn't fit her plans. "That's good thinking."

"I'm just so excited. I'm already starting to get work for next year." She slapped the steering wheel. "This is so great!" But suddenly she deflated.

He peered over. "What?"

"What if all the weddings are on the same day? I can't even do two cakes a week. Forget about three. I'd have to turn everybody down."

"Sounds to me like you're borrowing trouble."

"No. I'm thinking ahead. I might look like an uneducated bumpkin to you, but I've really thought through my business. I know what I can do and what I can't, and I'd have to turn down any cake for a wedding on the same day as another booking."

He nodded, curious about why her fear had sent a rush of male longing through him. He wanted to fix everything that was wrong in her life. The depth of what he felt for her didn't make sense. He could blame it on his teenage crush. Tell himself that he felt all this intensity because he already knew her. That his feelings had more or less picked up where they'd left off—

Except that didn't wash. They were two different people. Two new people. Fifteen years had passed. Technically, they didn't "know" each other. The woman she'd become from the girl she had been was one smart, sexy, beautiful female. And how he felt right now wasn't anything close to what he'd felt when he was eighteen, because he was older, more experienced.

So this couldn't be anything but sexual attraction.

A very tempting sexual attraction.

But only sexual attraction.

She had goals. She had kids. She'd already warned him off. And he didn't want another relationship...

Unless she'd agree to something fast and furious, something that would end when he left?

He snorted to himself. Really? He thought she'd go for an affair?

Was he an idiot?

He lectured himself the whole way home. But when they had unloaded the SUV and stood face-to-face, her in her pretty blue dress, with her hair slipping from its pins and looking sexily disheveled, his lips tingled with the need to kiss her.

She smiled. Her full mouth bowed up slowly, easily. "Thanks for your help."

"Thanks for…" He stopped. Damn. Idiot. She hadn't done anything for him. He'd done a favor for her. He sniffed a laugh to cover his nervousness. "Thanks for letting me go with you?"

She laughed, too. "Seriously. I appreciated your help."

He nodded, unable to take his eyes off her. The way she glowed set off crackling sparks of desire inside him. Even though he knew he wasn't supposed to kiss her, his head began to lower of its own volition.

Her blue-gray eyes shimmered up at him. Her lips parted as she realized what he was about to do. He could all but feel the heat from her body radiating to his—

She stepped back. Smiled weakly. "Thanks again for your help."

Then she spun away and raced into the house.

He stood frozen.

It took a while before he realized he probably looked like an idiot, standing there staring at her back porch. So he walked into his grandmother's house and dropped onto the guest room bed without even showering. He was tired. Crazed. Crazy to be so attracted to someone he couldn't have, and it was driving him insane that this attraction kept getting away from him.

Two minutes before he fell asleep that night, he wondered if somehow her excitement for her business had gotten tangled up in his feelings for her and morphed into something it shouldn't be.

That would really explain things for him. Normally, when he decided someone was off-limits, he could keep her off-limits. So it had to be the excitement of the day that had destroyed his resolve. That was the only thing that made sense.

The next morning he strode over to her

house. Ostensibly, he'd come to get Owen to play. In reality, he had decided to test out this attraction. If it had been seeing her excitement about her business that had pushed it over the line the day before, then he'd be fine this morning.

Her door was open, so he knocked on the wood frame of the screen door. "Hey. Anybody home?"

"Come in, Wyatt."

Her voice was soft but steady. No overwhelming attraction made her breathless. In the light of day, they were normal. Or at least she was.

Now to test him.

He pulled open the screen door. "I came for Owen...."

Papers of all shapes, sizes and colors littered her kitchen table. But she had a pretty, fresh, early morning look that caused his heart to punch against his breastbone. So much for thinking it was her excitement about her wedding cake opportunities that had gotten to him the day before. It was her. Whatever he felt for her was escalating.

He carefully made his way to the table. "What's up?"

She peeked up, her blue eyes solemn, serious. "Doing some figuring."

He sat on the chair across from hers. "Oh?"

She rose, took a cup from her cupboard, filled it with coffee and placed it in front of him.

"What I need is an assistant."

"Do you think—" Because his voice squeaked, his cleared his throat. "Do you think your business is going to pick up that fast?"

She refilled her own coffee cup and sat again. "I plan for contingencies. I don't want to be known as the wedding cake lady who can't take your wedding."

He laughed. "There's something to be said for playing hard to get...." Maybe that's why she was suddenly so attractive to him? Didn't he always want what he couldn't have? Maybe he'd only been kidding himself into thinking he was trying to get his inner nice guy back? And her playing hard to get had just fed his inner selfish demon? "Everybody wants what they can't have. You could charge more money—"

"The more cakes I bake, the more referrals I get. I don't need to be exclusive. I want to start a business, a real business. Someday have a building with a big baking area and an office."

Their knees bumped when she shifted, and her gaze jumped to his as she jerked back. Her voice was shaky when she said, "I've been going over my figures, and if I didn't save money for the winter I could hire someone."

He tried to answer, but no words formed. Mesmerized by the gaze of those soft blue eyes, everything male in him just wanted to hold her.

He frowned. *Hold her. Protect her. Save her.*

Was he falling into the same pattern he'd formed with Betsy? Once they'd started dating, he got her a great apartment, a new car. All because he didn't want to see her do without.

And he knew how that had ended.

Owen came running into the room. "I made my bed!" He jumped from one foot to the other, so eager to play that energy poured from him.

Wyatt scraped his chair away from the table. "Then let's go."

Missy swallowed and she rose, too. "Yeah.

You guys go on outside. Mommy has some things to think about."

Wyatt's gut jumped again. He could solve all her problems with one call to his bank. He glanced at the papers on the table. Was it really an accident that she'd picked today, this morning, after he'd nearly kissed her the night before, to run some numbers?

He sucked in a breath. He had become a suspicious, suspicious man.

But after Betsy, was that so bad? Especially if it caused him to slow down and analyze things, so neither he nor Missy got hurt?

"Come on, O. Let's go haul some dirt."

He and Owen left the kitchen and Missy squeezed her eyes shut. Since that dance, she'd had trouble getting and keeping her breath when he was around. And she knew why. He was good-looking, but she was needy. Four years with no romance in her life, four years of not feeling like a woman, melted away when he looked at her. His dark, dark eyes seemed to see right through her, to her soul. And since that dance, every time he looked at her she knew he was as attracted to her as she was to him.

They could be talking about the price of

potato chips and she would know he was thinking about their attraction.

And everything inside her would swing in that direction, too.

Luckily, she had a brain that wouldn't let her do anything stupid.

They hardly knew each other. What they felt had to be purely sexual. She had kids who needed protecting. And the only way she could truly protect her kids was to make her business so successful she'd never have to depend on a man. Keeping her eye on the ball, creating the best wedding cake company in Maryland, that's what would keep her safe, independent. Eventually, she might want a relationship. She might even marry again, if she didn't have to be dependent on a man. But it would be pretty damned hard not to become dependent on Wyatt when she was broke and he had millions.

He had to be off-limits.

No matter how good-looking he was. And no matter how much she kept noticing.

Playing with Owen cleared Wyatt's mind enough that he made a startling realization as he was eating another dry sandwich for lunch, this one peanut butter from a jar he'd found in a cabinet.

His relationship with Betsy ultimately had become all about money. But so did a lot of his relationships. He hired friends who became employees, and the friendships became working relationships. He invested in the companies of friends and those friendships became business relationships.

Because money changed things. If he really wanted his feelings for Missy to cool, all he had to do was give her money for her business. Then his internal businessman would recategorize her.

Sadness washed through him. He didn't want to recategorize her. He wanted to like her. But he ignored those thoughts. He was recently divorced. With his limited time, all he and Missy would have would be a fling. She deserved better.

Walking to the back door of his grandmother's house, he sniffed a laugh. It looked as if he'd gotten what he wanted. His inner nice guy was back. He was putting Missy's needs ahead of his.

He strode through her empty backyard, knowing the kids were probably napping. He and Missy wouldn't just have time to talk privately; they could go over real numbers to determine exactly how much money she'd need.

His heart pinched again. He kept walking. This was the right thing to do.

On her porch, he knocked on the wood frame of the screen door.

She turned and saw him.

Time stopped. Her eyes widened with pleasure. When he opened the door and stepped inside, he watched them warm with desire. Her gaze did a quick ripple from his face to his toes, and his gut coiled.

"Hey."

"Hey."

"I didn't expect you back until the kids woke up."

He scrubbed his hand across the back of his neck. Offering her money suddenly seemed so wrong. She was pretty and she liked him and he'd always liked her. The house was quiet. He could slide his hand under that thick ponytail, nudge her to him and kiss her senseless within seconds.

The very presumptuousness of that thought got him back on track. She'd already rebuffed him twice. She knew what she wanted and was going after it. She wouldn't sleep with him on a whim. No matter how attracted they were.

He needed to behave himself, think rationally and get them both beyond this attraction.

"I've been considering what you said this morning about hiring someone."

"Oh?"

"Yeah. Can we sit?"

"Sure."

She sat on the chair she'd been in earlier that morning. He sat across from her again.

"You need to buy a new vehicle. Maybe a van."

She laughed. "No kidding."

"So the way I figure this, you need salary for an assistant, day care for the kids in the morning and a new van."

She nodded. "Okay. I get it. You just talked me out of spending my winter money on an assistant. It won't work to hire an assistant if the SUV breaks down."

"Actually, that's why I'm here." He took one last look at her face—turned up nose, full lips, sensual blue-gray eyes. His hormones protested at the easy way he gave up on a relationship, but he trudged on. "Rather than you using your winter money, which isn't enough anyway, I'd like to give you a hundred thousand dollars."

He expected a yelp of happiness. Maybe a scream. He got a confused stare.

"You want to *give* me a hundred thousand dollars?"

"There are hidden costs in having an employee. I'm guessing a good baker doesn't come for minimum wage. Add benefits and employer taxes and you're probably close to fifty thousand. A van will run you about thirty thousand and I'm not sure about day care."

She rose. "You're kidding me."

"No. Employer taxes and benefits will about double your expense for an assistant's salary."

"I'm not talking about the taxes. I'm talking about the money." She spun away, then pivoted to face him again. "For Pete's sake! I don't want your money! I want to be independent."

"Your business can't stand on its own."

"Maybe not now, but it will."

"Not if you don't get an influx of cash."

She gasped. "I thought you had some faith in me!"

"I do!"

"You don't!" She leaned toward him and the hot liquid he saw in her eyes had nothing to do with sexual heat. She was furious with him. "If you did, you'd give me a few months to work through the bugs and get this thing going! You wouldn't offer me money."

"You're taking this all wrong. I'm trying to help you."

"So this is charity?" She looked away, then quickly looked back again. "Get out."

"No. I…" Confused, he ran his hand along the back of his neck. What had just happened?

"Get out. Now. Or I won't even send Owen out to play with you."

Wyatt headed for the door, so baffled he turned to face her, but she'd already left the room.

She sent Owen out to play after his nap, but she didn't even peek out the window. Confusion made Wyatt sigh as he trudged up the steps at suppertime. He opened another can of the soup he'd found in the pantry. Seeing the sludgelike paste, he checked the expiration date and with a groan of disgust threw it out.

What the hell was going on? Not only was he eating junk, things that had been in cupboards for God knew how long, but he was attracted to a woman who seemed equally attracted but kept rebuffing him. So he'd offered her money, to give them a logical reason to keep their relationship platonic, and instead of making her happy, he'd made her mad. *Mad.* Most people would jump for joy when they'd been offered money.

She should have jumped for joy.

Maybe what he needed was to get out of this house? He hadn't really cared to see a lot of the people from his high school days, but he was changing his mind. A conversation about anything other than Missy Johnson and her wedding cakes and her cute kids might be just what he needed to remind him he wasn't an eighteen-year-old sap anymore, pining over a pretty girl who didn't want him. When it came to women, he could have his pick. He didn't need one Missy Johnson.

He straddled his motorcycle and headed for the diner. He ambled inside and found the place almost empty. Considering that it was a sunny Sunday afternoon, Wyatt suspected everybody was outside doing something physical. A waitress in a pink uniform strolled over. He ordered a hot roast beef sandwich and mashed potatoes smothered in brown gravy. For dessert he ate pie.

After a good meal, he felt a hundred percent better. He hadn't seen anybody he recognized or who recognized him, but it didn't matter. All he'd needed to get himself back to normal was some real food.

He paid the bill, but curiosity stopped him from heading for the door. Instead, he peeked into the kitchen. "Hey, Monty. It's me. Wyatt McKenzie."

Missy's dad set his spatula on the wood-topped island in the center of the diner kitchen. "Well, I'll be damned."

Tall, balding and wearing a big apron over jeans and a white T-shirt, he walked over and slapped Wyatt on the back. "How the hell are you, kid?"

"I'm fine. Great." He looked around. "Wow. The place hasn't changed one iota in fifteen years."

"People like consistency."

"Yep." He knew that from running his own company, but there was a difference between consistent and run-down. Still, it wasn't his place to mention that. "I'm surprised you don't have any of Missy's cakes in here."

Monty stepped back. Returning to the wood-topped island, he picked up his spatula. "Oh, she doesn't bake for me anymore."

"Too busy with her own cakes, I guess."

Monty glanced up. "Is she doing good? I mean, one businessman to another?"

Wyatt laughed. Having seen a bit of her pride that morning, he guessed she probably hadn't told her father anything about her business beyond the basics. Maybe he'd also made the mistake of offering her money?

"She's doing great. Three future brides corralled her when she tried to leave yesterday's wedding reception."

"Wow. She is doing well."

"Exceptionally well. She's a bit stubborn, though, about some things."

"Are you helping her?"

He winced. "She's not much on taking help."

Monty snorted. "Never was."

Well, okay. That pushed his mood even further up the imaginary scale. If she wouldn't take help from her dad, why should Wyatt be surprised she wouldn't take help from him?

The outing got him back to normal, but not so much that he braved going into Missy's house the next morning. He went to the sandbox and five minutes later Owen, Lainie and Claire came racing out of the house.

While playing Wiffle ball with the kids,

he ascertained that their mom was working on a new cake.

"This one will be yellow," Lainie said.

Not knowing what else to do, he smiled. "Yellow. That's nice. I like yellow."

"I like yellow, too."

"Me, too."

"Me, too."

He laughed. He didn't for one minute think yellow was that important to any one of the triplets, but he did see how much they enjoyed being included, involved. His heart swelled. He liked them a lot more than he ever thought he could like kids. But it didn't matter. He and their mother might be attracted, but they didn't see eye to eye about anything. Maybe it was time to step up the jewelry search and get back to Tampa?

CHAPTER FIVE

WYATT THREW HIMSELF into the work of looking for the Scottish heirlooms in the mountain of closet boxes.

He endured the scent of sachets, billowing dust and boxes of things like panty hose—who saved old panty hose and why?—and found nothing even remotely resembling jewelry.

To break up his days, he played with Owen every morning and all three kids every afternoon, but he didn't go anywhere near Missy.

Still, on Saturday afternoon, when she came out of the house dressed in a sunny yellow dress that showed off her shoulders and accented her curves, lugging the bottom of a cake with the babysitter, he knew he couldn't let her go alone. Particularly since her SUV had already had trouble starting once that week.

While she brought the rest of the cake

to her vehicle, he changed out of his dirty clothes into clean jeans and a T-shirt. Looking at himself in the mirror, he frowned. His hair was growing in and looked a little like Owen's, poking out in all directions. He also needed a shave. But if he took the time to shave, she'd be gone by the time he was done.

No shave. No comb. Since he usually didn't have hair, he didn't really own a comb. So today he'd be doing grunge.

Once again, he didn't say anything. Simply walked over to her SUV and got in on the passenger's side as she got in on the driver's side.

"Don't even bother to tell me one person can handle this big cake. I watched you and the babysitter cart it out here. I know better. If the caterer can't spare a waiter you'll be in a world of trouble."

She sighed. "You don't have to do this."

"I know."

"You haven't spoken to me since we fought on Sunday."

He made a disgusted noise. "I know that, too."

"So why are you going?"

He had no idea. Except that he didn't want to see her struggle. Remembering her fierce independent streak, he knew that reply wouldn't be greeted with a thank-you, so he said, "I like cake."

Apparently expecting to have to fend off an answer that in some way implied she needed help, she opened her mouth, but nothing came out. After a few seconds, she said, "I could make you a cake."

He peered over at her. In her sunny yellow dress, with her hair all done up, and wearing light pink lipstick, she was so cute his selfish inner demon returned. He'd forgotten how hard it was to want something he couldn't have.

"Oh, then that would be charity and we can't have that. If you can't take my money, I can't take your cake."

She sighed. "Look, I know I got a little over-the-top angry on Sunday when you offered me money. But there's a good reason I refused. I need to be independent."

"Fantastic."

She laughed. "It is fantastic. Wyatt, I need to be able to support myself and my kids. And I can. That's what makes it fantastic. *I can do this.* You need to trust me."

"Great. Fine. I trust you."

"Good, because I feel I owe you for playing

with the kids, and a cake would be a simple way for me to pay that back."

He gaped at her. "Did you hear what you just said? You want to pay me for playing."

She shoved her key into the ignition and started the SUV. "You're an idiot."

"True. But I'm an idiot who is going to get cake at this wedding."

But in the car on the way to the reception venue, he stared out the window. He couldn't remember the last time anybody had ordered him around like this. Worse, he couldn't remember a time a *woman* had ordered him around like this—and he *still* liked her.

He sighed internally. And there it was. The truth. He still liked her.

The question was what did he do about it?

Avoiding her didn't work. She wouldn't take his money so he could recategorize her. And even after not seeing her all week, the minute he was in the same car with her all his feelings came tumbling back.

He was nuts.

Wrong…

Really? Wrong? They were healthy, single, attracted people. Why was liking her wrong?

Because she didn't want to like him.

* * *

They arrived at the wedding reception more quickly than the week before because this venue was closer. As they unloaded the square layers with black lace trim, Missy gazed at each one lovingly. In high school, she'd hated having to bake fancy cakes for the diner, but now she was so glad she had. At age thirty-three she had twenty years of cake-baking experience behind her. And she was very, very good.

"The kids told me this one is yellow."

She peeked over at Wyatt, relieved he was finally talking. "It is. It's a yellow cake…with butter cream fondant and rolled fondant to make the black lace."

"How do you make lace?"

His question surprised her. Most people saw the finished product and didn't care how it got that way.

"There are patterns and forms you can buy, but I made my own."

He studied the intricate design. "That couldn't have been easy."

"I do things like this when you're playing with the kids."

He shot her a funny look and she turned away. The little spark of attraction she'd felt when she'd seen his scruffy day-old beard and butt-hugging jeans that morning flared again. With his sexy, fingers-run-through-it-in-frustration hair and his long, lean body, he was enough to drive her to distraction.

But she wouldn't be distracted.

Well, maybe a little. She was a normal woman and he was extremely sexy. Was it so wrong to be attracted? No. The trick would be not letting him see.

They arranged the black-and-white cake from the big square layer to the smallest layer, which had a top hat and sparkly wedding veil at the peak.

"Cute."

She stood back. "Different. I'll say that."

"You act as if you didn't know how it would turn out."

"I didn't. The bride is a Goth who wanted something black with hints of Victorian. She told me what she wanted and I made it."

"Can you eat the top hat?"

"Yep. And the veil, too."

"Amazing."

Their gazes caught. The flare of attraction became a flicker of need. She tried to squelch it, but in four years she hadn't felt anything like this. Oh, who was she kidding? She'd never felt anything like this. Wyatt was bold, sexy, commanding. And he liked her. The real her. Not the pretend version most men saw when they looked at her. He'd seen her stubborn streak, and still helped her—was still attracted to her.

What if there really was something going on between them? Something real. He could walk away. Hell, after she'd yelled at him on Sunday he should have walked away. But he hadn't. Even though they'd had a fairly nasty difference of opinion—which they'd yet to get beyond—here they were. He was still attracted to her. She was still attracted to him.

The bride arrived in her black-and-white wedding gown with her tuxedo-clad groom in tow. At least fourteen tattoos were visible above the bodice of her strapless gown.

Wyatt's eyebrows rose. "Different."

"Very her," Missy replied, standing beside him, off to the left of the cake, out of the way so they didn't detract from it.

He looked at the bride, looked at the cake. "You're really very good at this."

Missy's smile came slowly. Anybody could throw batter into a pan and get a cake. But not everybody could match baking ability with artistry. It was a gift. She never took it for granted.

"I know."

"I can see why you're so confident."

"Thanks."

"Someday you are going to be the best."

She laughed. There was an unimaginable joy in having something she was good at. But an even greater joy at having people appreciate it. "Thanks."

He growled and she frowned at him. "What?"

"I can never seem to say the right thing to you."

Music from the string quartet blended with the noise of wedding guests taking seats. The best man took the microphone, hit it to make sure it was live. The tap, tap, tap rolled into the room like thunder.

Wyatt caught Missy's hand. "Let's go outside."

Confused, she let him lead her through the French doors to a wide wooden deck, which was filled with milling wedding guests. Avoiding them, he guided her to the steps, and they clambered down until they stood in a quiet garden.

She looked around. She hadn't done a lot of exploring of the country clubs and other wedding venues where she took her cakes, but seeing how beautiful, and inspiring, this garden was, maybe she should.

"This is nice."

He sighed heavily. "Let's not change the subject until I get out what I want to say."

She peeked over at him, suddenly realizing how alone they were. All her nerve endings sprang to life. She'd never been attracted to a man like this. And he wasn't just nice, he was thoughtful. Or trying. When he made a mistake he wanted to fix it. He didn't just walk away.

Her thoughts from before popped into her brain again.

What if something really was happening between them? Something real? Something important? Something permanent?

"I understand why my offering you money doesn't fit your plan. But I still feel like we're not beyond the insult."

She pressed her lips together. She was right. He didn't walk away. He fixed what he broke. So different from her dad and her ex.

"What you said in the car today about being able to support yourself...I thought it was pride, but I finally get it. I see the bride-cake connection. You don't want money or help because you *know* this is going to work because you have that instinct. The thing that's going to push you above the rest. You are going to be one of the best in your business. You don't *need* help."

Her insides melted. She loved it when a bride gushed over a cake, or wedding guests sought her out to compliment her, but this wasn't just a compliment. This was Wyatt. A successful entrepreneur. Somebody who knew good work when he saw it. Somebody who saw that she had what it took to be successful.

Her blood warmed with pleasure that quickly turned to yearning. He was gorgeous and attracted to her. Plus, he understood her. Would it be so wrong to start something with him?

It had been so long since she'd wanted something for herself, purely for herself, that she instinctively tried to talk herself out of it. She told herself it felt wrong, because she knew she had to be self-sufficient before she started anything serious with a man.

But this was Wyatt. This was a guy who understood. A guy who didn't run. A guy who fixed things. A guy who liked her and believed in her. The little voice in her heart told her to relax and let it happen.

She smiled sheepishly, not quite sure what a woman did nowadays to let a man know she'd changed her mind and was willing to go after what they both seemed to want. "Thanks for the compliment."

He sighed again, this time as if relieved. "You're welcome."

Silence settled over them. It should have been the nice, comfortable silence of two friends. But her stomach quivered and her nerve endings lit up, as if begging to be touched. She'd never before felt this raw, wonderful need, and she wished with all her might that he'd kiss her.

As if reading her mind, he stepped close again. He laid a hand on her cheek. "Missy."

His head began to descend.

She swallowed hard. Even as the sensations rushing through her begged to be explored, new fear leaped inside her. It had been four long years since she'd kissed someone.

Four years.

And she wasn't just considering kissing. What burned between them was so hot she knew they'd end up in bed sooner rather than later. With their faces mere inches apart, her heart hit against her ribs. Was she ready for this?

His mouth met hers and liquid heat filled her. Like lava, it erupted from her middle and poured through her veins. She put her hands on his cheeks, just wanting to touch him, but when his tongue slipped inside her mouth, she used them to bring him closer.

She'd never felt anything like this. The pleasure. The passion. The pure, unadulterated sensuality that left her breathless and achy.

His hands roamed from her shoulders to her waist and back up again. Hers fell from his cheeks to his shoulder, down his long, lean back, and slowly—enjoying every smooth demarcation of muscle and sinew beneath his T-shirt—drifted up again. He was so strong. So solid. Everything inside her wept with yearning. For four years she'd been nothing but a mom. A busy mom. Right now she felt like a woman. Flesh and blood. Heat and need.

As his mouth continued to plunder hers, she pictured them tangled in the covers of her big four-poster bed. Desire whooshed through her. Everything was happening so fast that her head spun.

She thought she knew him…but did she?

He thought he knew her…but he didn't. Nobody did.

She stopped kissing him, squeezed her eyes shut. *That* was the real reason she shied away from men. Nobody knew her. Sure, Wyatt had seen her stubborn streak. He'd seen her with the kids, in full mom mode, but nobody knew about her dad. Nobody knew about the beatings, the alcoholism, the gambling that had colored her childhood and had formed who she was. And at this stage in her life, she wasn't sure she could tell anybody. Just as she was equally sure Wyatt, this Wyatt who fixed things, who probed into things, who wanted to make everything right, would never let her get away with the usual slick answers she gave when anyone asked her if she'd seen her dad lately.

Wyatt would realize there'd been trouble in her past and he'd demand she talk about it.

She stepped away. "I'm sorry. I can't do this."

He caught her hand and tugged her back. "Seems to me you were 'doing' it just fine."

She couldn't help it; she laughed. He was such a fun guy, but her past was just too much to handle. Even for him.

She slipped away from him. "I'm serious. I don't want a relationship—"

He caught her hand and yanked her back. "That's perfect, because I don't want a relationship, either."

That confused her so much she frowned. "You don't want a relationship?"

He chuckled. "No."

She pointed at him, then herself, then back at him. "Then what's this?"

"A fling?"

She blinked. A fling? While she was worried about telling him her deepest, darkest secret, he was thinking fling?

"Look, I've only been divorced for two weeks—"

She stepped back, her mind reeling. Before thoughts of her secret had ruined the moment, she'd felt things she'd never felt before. And he wanted a fling? "But—"

"But what? We're single, adults and attracted to each other. There's no reason we can't enjoy each other while I'm here."

She blinked again. The emotions careening through her didn't match up with the word *fling*. "Let me get this straight. You want to sleep with me, no strings attached, no thought of a relationship. No possibility of falling in love?"

His face scrunched. "You're making it sound tawdry."

She'd never once considered sex just for the sake of sex. Even though it solved the problem of telling him about her dad, her stomach took a little leap. He didn't want to love her. He wasn't even considering it.

He caught her shoulders and forced her to look at him. "You said that your ex leaving you with three kids and no money made you independent?"

She nodded.

"Well, think about this. Think about working for something from the time you're sixteen, and one mistake—picking the wrong person to trust—causes you to lose one-third of it. But it's about more than the money. My ex cheated on me. Lied to me. Tried to undermine me with people in the industry, saying that when she got half the company she could take over with a little bit of help, positioning herself to take everything I'd worked for. She didn't just want money. She wanted to boot me from my own company. She wanted to ruin me."

"Oh." Hearing the hurt in his voice, understanding rose in Missy, but it didn't salve the emptiness, the letdown she felt from realizing he didn't even want to *consider* loving her. It seemed in her life there'd been nobody who'd ever really loved her. At home, her dad wasn't ever sober enough to have a real emotion. Her mom stayed too busy keeping up appearances that if she kissed her or hugged her, Missy always knew it was for show, not for real. Her sister locked herself away. Like Wyatt, she'd studied. The first chance she'd gotten, she'd left.

In going along, living the lie, Missy had been alone.

Alone.

Confused.

Not wanted.

He sighed. "I just don't believe relationships last, and I don't want either one of us to get hurt."

"Sure." She understood. She really did. No one wanted to be taken for granted, and hurt as he'd been by his ex. It could be years before he would trust again.

Which was why she stepped back. "I get it."

He sighed with relief. "Good."

But when he reached for her, she moved

farther away. Put a distance between them that was as much emotional as physical.

"I can't have a fling." At his puzzled look, she added, "The things you didn't factor into your fling are my kids."

He frowned. "Your kids?"

"I can't leave them to be with you and you can't...well, sleep over."

His frown deepened. "I can't?"

"No. They're kids. Sweet. Impressionable. I don't want to confuse them."

"So you won't have a fling because of your kids?"

"I don't want them confused." Tears welled behind her eyes and she struggled to contain them. She hadn't ever quite realized how alone she was until a real relationship, a real connection, seemed to be at her fingertips, only to disappear in a puff. "I don't want them involved. And until they're old enough, I'm... well, I'm just not going to..." She reddened to the roots of her hair. "You know."

"Sleep with anybody." He shook his head. "You're not going to sleep with anybody until your kids are teenagers."

"I hadn't really thought it through, but I guess that's what I'm saying." Determined to be mature about this, she held out her hand to shake his. "No hard feelings?"

He took it. Squeezed once. "Lots of regret, but no hard feelings."

She nodded, but when he released her hand, disappointment rattled through her.

She liked him. But he didn't want to like her.

CHAPTER SIX

SUNDAY MORNING, Wyatt wanted nothing more than to stay in bed. He looked at the clock, saw it was only seven, and pulled the covers over his head. Then a car door slammed and he realized he'd woken because he'd heard a vehicle pull into the drive. He bounced out of bed, confused about who'd be coming to his Gram's house at seven o'clock on a Sunday morning. But when he walked to the kitchen window and peered out, he realized the caller had parked in Missy's driveway.

Who would visit Missy at seven o'clock on a Sunday?

With a sigh he told himself not to care about her. Ever. For Pete's sake. She'd rebuffed him twice, and the night before out-and-out told him she didn't want anything to do with him. She even made him shake on it.

Did he have no pride?

He ambled to the counter, put on a pot of coffee and opened the back door to let the stale night air out and the cool morning air in.

Leaning against the counter, he waited for his jolt of caffeine. When the coffeemaker gurgled its final release, he poured himself a cup.

Turning to walk to the table, he almost tripped over Owen.

Still wearing his cowboy pajamas, the little boy grinned. "Hey."

"Hey." He stooped down to Owen's height. "What are you doing here?"

"There's a man talking to my mom."

Even as Owen spoke, dark-haired Lainie opened Wyatt's screen door and stepped inside. Dressed in a pink nightgown, she said, "Hi," as if it were an everyday occurrence for her to walk into his house in sleepwear.

"Hi."

Before he could say anything else, Claire walked in. Also in a pink nightgown, she smiled sheepishly.

Still crouched in front of Owen, Wyatt caught the little boy's gaze. "So your mom's talking to somebody and I'm guessing she didn't see you leave."

"She told us to go to our woom."

At Wyatt's left shoulder, Lainie caught his chin and turned him to face her. "He means room."

"Your mom sent you to your room?"

Owen nodded. "While she talks to the man."

Wyatt's blood boiled. For a woman who didn't want to get involved with him, she was engrossed enough in today's male guest that she hadn't even seen her kids leave.

Maybe he'd just take her kids back and break up her little party?

Telling himself that was childish, he nonetheless set his coffee cup on the counter and herded the three munchkins to the door. Missy would go nuts with worry if she realized they were gone. Albeit for better reasons than to catch her in the act, he had to take her kids back.

"Let's go. Your mom will be worried if she finds you gone."

Owen dug in his heels. "But she's talking to the man. She doesn't want us to sturb her."

His eyebrows rose in question and he glanced at Helaina, the interpreter.

Who looked at him as if he was crazy not to understand. "Yeah. She doesn't want us to sturb her."

"Sturb?"

"Dee-sturb." Claire piped in.

"Oh, disturb."

Lainie nodded happily.

Well. Well. Little Miss I-Don't-Want-A-Fling didn't want to be disturbed. Maybe his first guess hadn't been so far off the mark, after all? She might not want a relationship with *him,* but she was with somebody.

Wyatt corralled the kids and directed them to the porch.

When they were on the sidewalk at the bottom of the steps, Helaina caught his hand. "We stay together when we walk."

Claire shyly caught his other hand.

Warmth sputtered through him. He seriously wasn't the kind of guy to hang out with kids, but not only was he playing in dirt and organizing Wiffle ball games, now he was holding hands.

Owen proudly led the way. He skipped to the hedge and pulled it aside.

Lainie stooped and dipped through. Claire stooped and dipped through. Owen grinned at him.

Wyatt took one look at the opening provided and knew that wasn't going to work. "You go first. I need to hold it up higher for myself."

Owen nodded and ducked down to slip through.

Wyatt pushed the hedge aside and stepped into Missy's backyard, where all three kids awaited him.

He pointed at the porch. "Let's go."

But only a few feet across the grass, Missy's angry shout came from the house, as if she was talking to someone on the enclosed front porch.

"I don't care who you are! I don't care what you think you deserve! You're not getting one dime from me!"

Wyatt's blood ran cold. That didn't sound like the words of a lover. It didn't even sound like the words of a friend.

Could the man in her house be her ex? Returning for money? From her? After draining their accounts?

His nerve endings popped with anger. He dropped Claire's and Helaina's hands. "Wait here."

But when he looked down at their little faces, he saw Claire's eyes had filled with tears. Owen's and Helaina's eyes had widened in fear. The shouting had scared them. He couldn't leave them out here alone when they were obviously frightened.

"Oh, come on, darlin'. You know I should have gotten this house when your grandmother died. I'm just askin' for what you owe me."

Wyatt's mouth fell open. That was Monty.

"I heard you've got a sweet deal going with this wedding cake thing you're doing. I just want what's coming to me."

"What should be coming to you is jail time!"

"Aren't you being a little melodramatic?"

"Melodramatic? You beat Mom to within an inch of her life so often I'm not surprised her heart gave out. And you beat me and Althea." She stopped. A short cry rang out.

Then Missy said, "You get the hell away from me! Now. Mom may not have wanted to call the police, but the next time you show up here I'll not only call the police, I'll quite happily tell every damned person in this town that you beat us. Regularly. They'll see that the happy-go-lucky diner owner everybody loves doesn't really exist."

"You'd never get anybody to believe you."

"Try me."

By now the kids had huddled around the knees of Wyatt's sweatpants. No sound came from the house, but the front door slammed shut. With his hands on the kids' shoulders,

Wyatt quickly shepherded them to his side of the shrubs, where Monty couldn't see them.

As her father screeched out of the driveway, Missy came barreling out the kitchen door. Standing on the porch, she screamed, "Owen! Lainie! Claire!" as if she'd gone looking for them after Monty left, found them gone and was terrified.

Wyatt quickly stepped out from behind the thin leafy branches, three kids at his knees. "We're here. They came to get me to play in the sandbox."

She ran down the porch steps and gathered her children against her. "They haven't eaten breakfast yet."

"I didn't know that or I would have given them cereal. I have plenty." Not knowing what else to do, he babbled on. "Gram had enough for an army, and most of it still hasn't hit the expiration date."

She looked up at him. Tears poured from her blue eyes, down her cheeks and off her chin.

He stooped down beside her and the kids. "Hey." His heart thudded against his breastbone. What did a man say to a woman when he'd just heard that her dad had beaten her when she was a child?

Wyatt didn't have a clue. But he did have a sore, aching heart. She'd had a crappy husband and a rotten father. While he'd had two perfect parents, talent, brains and safety, she'd lived in fear.

The knowledge rattled through him like an unwanted noise in an old car. He couldn't deny it, but he didn't know how to fix it.

And the last thing he wanted to do was say the wrong thing.

He set his hand on her shoulder. "You go inside. Take a shower. I'll feed the kids."

"I'm fine."

"You're crying." He hated like hell stating the obvious, but sometimes there was no way around that. "Give yourself a twenty-minute break. I told you I have lots of cereal. We'll be okay for twenty minutes."

Owen broke out of her hug. "We'll be okay, Mommy."

Fresh tears erupted. She gave the kids one last hug, then rose. Her voice trembled as she said, "If you're sure."

"Hey, we'll make a game out of it."

Owen tugged on the leg of his sweatpants. "Can we wook for tweasure?"

Wyatt laughed. "Yeah. We'll wook for treasure."

* * *

She'd never abandoned her kids.

Never handed them over to another person just to give herself time to pull herself together. But she also hadn't had a visit from her dad in…oh, eight years?

And he'd decided to show up today? Knowing she had money in her checking account? Demanding that she give it to him?

How the hell did he know she had money?

She put her head under the shower spray. Now that she'd had a minute to process everything, she wasn't as upset as she was surprised. Shocked that he'd shown up at her house like that. But now that she knew she was on his radar again, she wouldn't cower as her mom had. She'd stand her ground. And she *would* call the police. If he touched her or—God forbid—her kids, he'd be in jail so fast his head would spin.

She got out of the shower and dried her hair. In ten minutes she had on clean shorts and a T-shirt. Her hair was combed. Her tears were dry.

She headed outside.

She expected to find Wyatt and the kids in the yard. Instead, they were nowhere in sight.

When she knocked on his kitchen door there was no answer, so she stepped inside.

"Wyatt?"

"Back here."

She followed the sound of his voice to the large corner bedroom, the 1960s version of a master suite, just like the one in her house. Old-fashioned lamps and lacy curtains reminded her of the room she'd inherited herself.

But the bed was covered in boxes, and more boxes were piled on the floor. Taking a bite of cereal from a bowl on the bedside table, Owen saw her. He grinned. "Hi, Mommy."

Lainie popped up from behind the bed. Claire peeked around a tall stack of shoe boxes. "We're looking for treasure."

Missy walked into the room. "In the boxes?"

Owen said, "Yeah. But Lainie spilled her milk."

Wyatt came running out of the bathroom, holding a roll of toilet paper. "Okay, everybody stand back…." Then he saw Missy. "Hey."

She took the toilet paper from him and rushed to the other side of the bed, where rolling milk rapidly approached the edge of the area rug. She spun off some tissue and caught the milk just in time.

Wyatt rubbed his index finger across his nose. "Things look worse than they really are."

On her way to dump the milk-sodden tissue in the bathroom, she said, "What is all this?"

"This," Wyatt said, following her to the bathroom, "is everything I found in the closet."

"Are you kidding me? How'd your gram get all that in a closet?"

"She was quite the crafty packer."

"I suppose." Missy glanced around. "So it looks like you haven't found the jewelry from Scotland yet."

"Nope. And the kids were fine. Great, actually, until Lainie spilled her milk."

"She gets overeager."

He laughed. "She wants to do everything at once."

"I can take them home now."

"Why? We're having fun. And I'm actually getting through three boxes a minute."

"Three boxes a minute?"

"They open, dump, get bored and move on to the next one. And that leaves me to collect up everything they dumped, and get it back in the box. As I'm collecting, I'm checking for jewelry. At this rate I'll have this whole room done by noon."

She laughed.

And he sighed with relief. But the relief didn't last long. With her tears dry and her mood improved, he knew she'd never tell him about her dad. And he couldn't just say, "Hey, I saw Monty running out of your house this morning." It would be awkward for her, like dropping someone in an ice-cold swimming pool.

Still, he couldn't let this go. He'd been the one to tell Monty she was doing well. He'd thought he was doing her a favor. Turns out he had everything all wrong. And somehow he had to fix it.

"So what happened this morning?"

She strolled back into the bedroom and walked over to Helaina, who'd dumped out a box of panty hose.

"What is this?"

He grabbed the ball of panty hose and stuffed it back into the shoe box. "My grandmother never met a pair of panty hose she didn't want to save."

"My grandmother saved them, too. She used them as filler when she made stuffed animals or couch pillows."

"Thank God. I was beginning to think my grandmother was nuts." And he'd also noticed Missy had changed the subject. "So what happened this morning?"

She sucked in a breath, ruffling Lainie's dark hair as the little girl picked up another shoe box, popped the lid and dumped the contents.

Bingo. Jewelry.

He swung around to that side of the bed. Beads and bobbles rolled across the floral comforter. "Well, what do you know?"

Missy caught his gaze. "Don't get your hopes up. Most of this looks like cheap costume jewelry."

He picked up a necklace, saw a chip in the paint on a "pearl."

"Drat."

"Finding jewelry is a good sign, though. At least you know it's here somewhere."

He dropped the string of fake pearls to the bed. "Yeah, well, she has three furnished bedrooms. I found clothes in the drawers in the dressers in each room. All the closets are full of boxes like these." He sighed. "Who wants to go play in the yard?"

Missy laughed. "Is that how you look for jewelry? In the yard?"

He faced her. "In case you haven't noticed, I'm sort of, kind of, the type of guy who doesn't do anything he doesn't want to do."

Shaking her head, she laughed again. "So how do you intend to find the jewelry?"

He shrugged. "Not sure yet. But I'm an idea guy. That's how I got rich." It was true. Even his writing was a form of coming up with ideas and analyzing them to see if they'd work. "So eventually I'll figure out a way to find the jewelry without having to look through every darned drawer and box in this house."

"Well, I'd volunteer to help you, but I have some thinking of my own to do today."

"Oh, yeah." He sat on the bed, patted the spot beside him. That was as good of an opening as any to try again to get her to talk to him. "I just told you I'm a good idea man. Maybe I could help you with that thinking."

"No. You and I have already been over this. Your idea to solve my financial problem was to give me money."

He remembered—and winced.

"So this morning I need to go over my books again, think through how I can get a van and an assistant."

"Why the sudden rush?"

She shrugged. "No reason." She clapped her hands. "Come on, kids. Let's go."

A chorus of "Ah, Mom," echoed around him.

He rose from the bed, suddenly understanding that maybe she didn't want to talk about her dad because the kids were around. Which meant they wouldn't talk until the triplets took their naps. "I promised them time in the sandbox."

She sighed. "They're not even out of their pajamas yet."

"How about if you go get them dressed while I clean up some of this mess? Then I'll take them when you're done."

"I do want that thinking time this morning." She blew her breath out in another sigh. "I don't know how to pay you back for being so good to them."

"I already told you it makes me feel weird to hear you say you want to pay me for playing. So don't say it again."

She laughed. Then she faced the kids. "All right. Let's go. We'll get everybody into clean shorts, then you can go out to the sandbox with Wyatt."

Owen jumped. "Yay!"

Lainie raced to the door.

Claire took her mom's hand.

Wyatt watched them go, then fell to the bed again. She'd been beaten by her dad, left by her husband with three babies, and now struggled with growing a business. It didn't seem right that he couldn't give her money. But that ship had sailed. Worse, he had to confess that he was the one who'd told her dad how well she was doing.

Wyatt looked at his watch, counting down the hours till naptime, feeling as if he was counting down the hours to doomsday.

CHAPTER SEVEN

STILL TOO WORKED UP to sit at a table and run numbers, Missy pulled a box of flour from her pantry, along with semisweet chocolate chips, sugar and cornstarch. Wyatt taking the kids without pushing for answers as to why she was so upset was about the nicest thing anyone had ever done for her, so she would repay him with a cake. A fancy chocolate cake with raspberry sauce.

While the cake baked, she took snacks and juice boxes out to the kids, with an extra for Wyatt. Though he accepted the cookies and juice box, he more or less stayed back, but she understood why. Not only had he seen her sobbing that morning, but she'd rejected his advances the night before. She didn't blame him for not wanting to talk to her.

But the cake would bring them back to their normal footing.

As it cooled, she put raspberry juice, cornstarch and a quarter cup of sugar into a saucepan. After it had boiled, she strained it to remove the seeds, then set it aside. Using more chocolate chips, she made the glaze for the cake.

By the time the kids returned to the house for lunch, the cake was ready. As usual, Wyatt didn't come inside with them. He went to his own house for lunch. But that was okay. While the kids napped, she'd take the baby monitor receiver with her and deliver the cake to him.

The kids washed up, ate lunch, brushed their teeth and crawled into their little beds.

Missy took a breath and tucked the monitor under her arm. She grabbed the cup of sauce in one hand and the cake in the other and carried the best-looking cake she'd ever baked across her yard, under the shrub branch and to his porch.

She lightly kicked the door with her foot. "Wyatt?"

He appeared on the other side of the screen. "Yeah?"

She presented the cake. "I made this for you."

He glanced down at the cake, then back at

her. "I thought we talked about you baking me a cake?"

She laughed. "It's a thank-you for helping me out this morning. Not a thank-you for playing, because we both know that's wrong. It's thanks for helping me."

When he said nothing, she laughed again. "Open the door, idiot, so we can cut this thing and see if it tastes as good as it looks."

He opened the door and she stepped inside the modest kitchen. She set the cake on the table. "Where did your gram keep her knives?"

He walked to the cabinets, opened a drawer and retrieved a knife.

"Might as well get two forks and two plates while you're gathering things."

He silently did as he was told. She happily cut the cake. Dewy and moist, it sliced like a dream. She placed a piece on each plate, then drizzled raspberry sauce over them.

Handing one to Wyatt, she said, "There was supposed to be a whipped cream flower on each piece, but I didn't have enough hands to carry the whipped cream."

He sniffed a laugh, but didn't say anything.

That was when she felt the weirdness. Something was definitely up.

"The cake really is just a simple thank-you. No strings attached." She paused, pointing at his piece. "Try it."

He slid his fork into it and put a bite in his mouth. His eyes closed and he groaned. "Good God. That's heaven on a fork."

Pride tumbled through her. "I know! It's a simple recipe I found online. But it tastes like hours of slave labor."

She laughed again, but Wyatt set down his fork. "We have to talk."

At the stern tone of his voice, her appetite deserted her. She set her fork down, too. "You want to know what made me cry this morning."

He squeezed his eyes shut again, then popped them open. "Actually, that's the problem. I already know what made you cry this morning. When I was bringing the kids back after their surprise visit to my house, I overhead you and Monty."

"Oh." Embarrassment replaced pride. Heat slid up her cheeks. Her chest tightened.

"I heard him ask for money."

She said nothing, only stared at the pretty cake between them.

"I also heard what you said about him beating your mom, you and your sister."

She pressed her lips together.

"But that's not the worst of it."

Her head shot up and she caught his gaze. "Really? What can be worse than my dad beating me? About living a lie? About worrying every damn night that he was going to kill my mom, until she finally did die? What can be worse than that?"

"Look. I know it was a terrible thing."

"You know nothing." And she didn't want him to know anything. If she believed there was a chance for them to have a relationship, she might have told him. The timing was perfect. He already knew the overall story. She might have muddled through the humiliating details, if only because she was sick to death of living a lie. But knowing there was no chance for them, not even the possibility of love, she preferred to keep her secrets and her mortification to herself.

"I don't want to talk about it."

"Okay." His quiet acceptance tiptoed into the room. From his tone she knew he wasn't happy with her answer, but he accepted it. "But I have to tell you one more thing." He dragged in another breath. "One day last week I ate at the diner. When I was done, I went back to the kitchen to say hello to your dad, and somehow the subject of you and your business came up—"

She jumped out of her seat. "Oh, my God! *You* told him?"

"I'm sorry."

She gaped at him, horrible things going through her brain. She'd spent years staying away from her dad, not going to town picnics and gatherings or anything even remotely fun to protect her kids. And in one casual conversation, Wyatt had ruined years of her sacrifice.

She grabbed the monitor and turned to leave.

"I'm sorry!"

She spun to face him. "He's a leech. A liar. A thief. I don't want him in my life! I especially don't want him around the kids!"

"Well, you know what?" Wyatt shot out of his chair and was in front of her before she could blink. "Then you should tell people that. Because normal people don't keep secrets from their dads. Which means other normal people don't suspect you're keeping a secret from yours."

Her chin rose. "I guess that means I'm not normal, then. Thanks for that." She pivoted and smacked her hands on his screen door, opening it. "I need to get back to the kids."

When she was gone, Wyatt fell to his chair. Part of him insisted he shouldn't feel bad. He hadn't known. She hadn't told him.

But he remembered his charmed childhood. He might not have been well liked at school, but he was well loved at home. What the hell did he know about being abused? What did he know about the dark reasons for keeping secrets?

He'd been born under a lucky star and he knew it.

He scrubbed his hands down his face. Looked over at the cake. It was the best thing he had ever tasted. Missy had talent. With a little help, she would succeed. Maybe even beyond her wildest dreams.

But like an idiot, he'd blocked his chance to help her, by offering her money so he could stop being attracted to her.

Her life was about so much more than sex and marriage and who was attracted to whom. It was about more than being praised and admired. All she wanted to do was make a living. Be safe. Keep her kids safe.

And Wyatt kept hurting her.

He was an idiot.

* * *

Missy spent the rest of the kids' nap in tears. Not because Wyatt had ratted her out to her dad. He couldn't have ratted her out. As he'd said, he hadn't known she kept her success a secret from her dad. Because she didn't tell anybody about him.

And if she really dug down into the reasons she was suddenly so sad, so weary of it all, that hit the top of the list.

She didn't talk to anybody. At least not beyond surface subjects. No one knew her. It was the coldest, emptiest, loneliest feeling in the world, to exist but not be known. In high school, she could pretend that the life she led during the day, in classes, at football games, cheering and being chosen to be homecoming queen, snowball queen and prom queen, was her real life. But as she got older, her inability to have real friends, people she could talk to, wore on her. And when she really got honest with herself, she also had to admit that her company was a nice safe way of having to connect with people in only a superficial way. Once a wedding was over, she moved on to new people. No one ever stayed in her life.

Of course, she had wanted to connect with

Wyatt, but he didn't want a relationship. He wanted a fling.

She swiped away her tears. It didn't matter. She was fine. When her dad was out of the picture, her life was good. And that morning she'd scared him off. He wouldn't be back. And if he did come back, testing to see if she was serious about her threats, she'd call the police. After a night or two in jail he would stay away for good. Because he was a coward.

Then the whole town would know and she'd be forced to deal with it. But at least her life wouldn't be a lie anymore.

And maybe she could come out from under this horrible veil of secrets that ended with nothing but loneliness.

When the kids awoke, she kept them inside, working on a special project with them: refrigerator art. She got out the construction paper, glue and little round-edged plastic scissors. They made green cats and purple dogs. Cut out yellow flowers and white houses. And glued everything on the construction paper, creating "art" she could hang for Nancy to see on Saturday when she babysat.

And outside, Wyatt sat on the bench seat of his gram's old wooden picnic table, peering through the openings in the tall shrubs, waiting for them to appear.

But the kids and Missy didn't come outside. Because she was angry? Or sad? Or in protection mode?

He didn't know.

All he knew was that it was his fault.

He rose from the picnic table and walked into his house, back to the bedroom littered with shoe boxes. He sat on the bed and began the task for looking for the jewelry, trying to get his mind off Missy.

It didn't work. He was about to give up, but had nothing else to do—damn his mother for canceling the cable. So he forced himself to open one more box, and discovered a stack of letters tied with a pink ribbon. He probably would have tossed them aside except for the unique return address.

It was a letter from his grandfather, Sergeant Bill McKenzie, to his grandmother, sent from Europe during World War II.

Wyatt sat on the bed, pulled the string of the bow.

Though his grandfather had died at least twenty years before, Wyatt remembered him as a tall, willowy guy who liked to tell jokes, and never missed a family event like a birthday party or graduation. He'd liked him. A lot. Some people even said Wyatt "took after" him.

He opened the first letter.

Dear Joni...

I hope this letter finds you well. Things here are quiet, for now. That's why I have time to write. I wanted to thank you and everyone at home for your efforts with the war bonds. I also know rationing is hard. I recognize what a struggle it is to do without and to work in the factories. Tell everyone this means a great deal to those of us fighting.

The letter went on to talk about personal things, how much he missed her, how much he loved her, and Wyatt had to admit he got a bit choked up. A kid never thought of his grandparents loving each other. He'd certainly never pictured them young, fighting a war and sacrificing for a cause. But he could see his grandmother working in a factory, see his grandfather fighting for freedom.

What Wyatt hadn't expected to find, in letter after letter, was how much encouragement his grandfather had given his grandmother. Especially since, of the two, she was safer.

Still, his gram would have been a young woman. Working in a factory. Going without nylons—which might explain why she saved old panty hose. Getting up at the crack of dawn, doing backbreaking labor. He'd never thought of his grandparents this way, but now that he had, their lives and their love took on a new dimension for him.

Hours later, feeling hungry, he ambled to the kitchen and saw the cake. He took a chunk of the half-eaten slice he'd left behind. Flavor exploded on his tongue like a recrimination.

He sat at the table, staring at the cake. His grandfather was such a people-smart guy that he never would have let anyone suffer in silence the way Missy was. Sure, she baked cakes and attended weddings, looking pretty and perky, as if everything was fine. But everything wasn't fine. She worked her butt off to support her kids, and probably lived her life praying her dad would forget she existed.

And Wyatt had blown that in a one-minute conversation after eating pie.

He had to do something to make that up to her. He had to do something to make her life better. He already watched her kids while she worked every morning, but from the way she'd kept them inside after their naps, she might be changing her mind about letting him do even that.

So that left her business. If he wanted to do something to help her, if he wanted to do something to make up for the things he'd done wrong, then he had to figure out how she could afford to hire an assistant and buy a van.

Without him giving her money.

The next morning, Missy got up, put on a pot of coffee, poured three bowls of cereal and three glasses of milk, and sat at the table.

"So what are you going to do today?"

Owen said, "Pway with Wyatt."

She stirred her coffee. "That sounds like a lot of fun, but he might not come over, so you should think about what you'd like to do with your sisters."

Lainie's head shot up and she gave her mom a wide-eyed look. Claire's little mouth fell open. For the past two weeks, they'd enjoyed a small heaven, playing dolls without being forced to also entertain their brother. Neither seemed happy to have that change.

A knock at the door interrupted them, turning Missy around to see who it was.

Wyatt opened the door. "I brought your cake plate and sauce cup back."

She rose, wiped her sweating palms down her denim shorts. She took the plate and cup from him. "Thanks."

He smiled slightly. "Aren't you going to offer me a cup of coffee?"

Actually, she hoped he'd just go. Like Owen, she'd gotten accustomed to having someone to talk to, to be with. She hadn't even realized it until the night before, when she'd thought about how everybody came into her life, then left again. Even Wyatt would soon leave. But as they were jointly caring for her kids, and he helped her deliver her cakes, spending entire Saturdays with her, she'd been so preoccupied with her work that she'd been growing accustomed to having him around.

But he'd told her he didn't want to be in her life, and she had accepted that. She wished he'd just leave, so she could start her healing process.

Still, after years of working at the diner as a teenager, if someone asked for coffee, she poured it. "Sure. I have plenty of coffee."

He ambled to the table. "Hey, kids."

Lainie said, "Hi, Wyatt!"

Owen said, "Hey, Wyatt."

Claire smiled.

Owen said, "Are we going to pway?"

Wyatt pulled out a chair and sat. "As soon as I talk to your mom about some things." He pointed at the boy's bowl. "Are you done eating?"

Owen picked up his little plastic bowl and drank the contents in about ten seconds. Then he slapped the bowl on the table and grinned at Wyatt from behind a milk mustache.

Wyatt laughed. "Now you need to go wash up."

"You can all wash up, brush your teeth and head outside. Wyatt won't be far behind."

Missy knew that probably sounded rude. At the very least high-handed. But she'd made up her mind the night of the wedding. Even before he'd seen her dad at her door. If she got involved with him, she wanted something more. He didn't. Plus, in another day or week, he'd be gone. He wasn't really her friend, didn't want to be her lover, except temporarily. She had to break her attachment to him.

The kids scrambled along the short hall to their bathroom. She sat across from Wyatt.

"I'm not going to talk about my dad."

"That's not what I came to talk about."

"It isn't?"

"No. You know yesterday how I told you I was a thinker?"

"I thought you were just bragging."

He winced. "I was…sort of."

Her eyebrows rose, as if she was silently asking him what the hell that had to do with anything.

He squirmed uncomfortably. "The thing is, last night as I thought about your situation…"

"You can't help me. I have to handle my dad alone."

"I'm not talking about your dad. I'm talking about your business."

"And I thought we'd already been over this, too. I don't want your money."

"I'm not offering you money. I solve business problems all the time. And sitting there last night, I realized that if I'm such a hotshot, I should be able to solve yours, too."

She laughed. That hadn't occurred to her, but it was true. If he was such a hotshot he should be able to muddle through her measly little expansion problem. "Without offering me money."

"Right. We took that off the table the first week I was here."

"So. Now you're going to think about my problem?"

He picked up the saltshaker, turned it over in his hands as if studying it. "Actually, I solved it."

She snorted a laugh. "Right."

He finally caught her gaze. "I did. I don't know if you're going to be happy with the answer, but I took all the variables I knew into consideration, and realized that if I were in your position, I'd use the house as collateral for a line of credit."

She gasped. "Use my house?"

"I woke up my chief financial officer last night and had him run some numbers."

Wyatt pulled a paper from his back pocket. "He checked the value of your house against comps in the area, and estimates your house's value here." Wyatt pointed at the top number. "Which means you could easily get a hundred thousand dollar line of credit with the house as collateral."

She raised her gaze to his slowly. "But then I'd have a payment every month."

"You'd also have a van and an assistant, and you could take more weddings."

The truth of that hit her with a happy lift of her spirits. Though part of her struggled against it, her mind shifted into planning mode. "And maybe birthday cakes."

"And birthday cakes." He smiled sheepishly. "I ate that whole damned cake."

"Wyatt! That much sugar's not good for you."

"I know, but I'm out of food except for cereal, and I couldn't go to the diner."

Her face heated. "You can go wherever you want."

"I'll be damned if I'll give money to a guy who beat his family."

Owen came barreling into the kitchen. "Ready to pway?"

Wyatt pointed at the door. "You get everything set up outside. I'll be there in a minute." Owen raced out the door as Claire and Lainie appeared with their dolls.

"Are you going outside?"

They nodded.

Missy straightened the collar of Claire's shirt. "Okay. You know the rules. Stay in the yard."

They left and Wyatt caught her hand. "So?

What do you think? Could you be okay with a line of credit?"

The warmth of his hand holding hers rendered her speechless for a few seconds, but she reminded herself he wasn't interested in her romantically, unless it was for an affair. What he was doing now was making up for talking about her to her dad.

Of course, that was sort of nice, too. If he didn't think of her as a friend, he'd blow off what he'd done. Instead, he was making it up to her. As a friend would.

She relaxed a bit. It wasn't wrong to take advice from a friend. Especially a friend who had business expertise. "It's a big step. I don't want to lose this house."

"Hey, who yelled at me for not having faith in you?"

"I did."

"Then have some faith in yourself. And diversify. I have a couple of people on staff who could look into markets for your cakes. Or you could just go to the grocery stores and restaurants in neighboring towns and offer them a cake or two. Make the first week's free. When they see the reaction to them, they'll order."

Warmth spread through her. A feeling of normalcy returned. "You think I can do this?"

"Hell, yeah." Wyatt rose. "But it's more important that you know you can do it."

CHAPTER EIGHT

At lunchtime she fed the kids, wondering what Wyatt was eating. Then she saw him leave on his bike. She wouldn't let herself consider that he might be going to the diner. He'd said he wouldn't, but in her life people said a lot of things, then did the opposite. She just hoped he'd respect her enough not to say anything to her dad, not to warn him away or yell at him.

Twenty minutes later, when he returned with a bag from the grocery store, she relaxed. From the size of the bag, she knew he hadn't had enough time to shop as well as visit her dad. Maybe he really was a guy true to his word?

Falling into her normal daily routine, she straightened up the house while the kids napped. She picked up toys and vacuumed the living room and playroom floors. When she walked into the kitchen, she saw Wyatt at the door.

"How long have you been standing there?"

"Long enough to know you're a thorough vacuumer."

She laughed and opened the screen door. "Did you get lunch?"

"I stopped at the store for bread and deli meat. Do you know they don't have an in-house bakery anymore? They could use some homemade cakes in their baked goods section."

"You can stop spying for me. Once I get an assistant I'll investigate every store in the area."

"So you've decided to get the line of credit?"

"Yes. Using the house as collateral."

He walked to the table. "Can we sit?"

"Why? Are you going to help me call the bank?"

He pulled some papers from his back pocket. "Actually, I'd like to be the bank."

She gasped. "I told you I don't want your money."

"And I told you that I feel responsible for the mess with your dad yesterday. This is my way of making that up to you." He caught her gaze. "Besides, I'm going to give you a point and a half below the current interest rate at the bank, and my people have worked out a very flexible repayment schedule. No matter what happens with your business, you will not lose this house."

Her heart tripped over itself in her chest. *She wouldn't lose her house?* She didn't know a bank that promised that. And Wyatt hadn't gone to the diner. He'd bought deli meat. Even though she knew he was growing tired of not eating well, he'd been true to his word.

"And it's a loan?"

He handed the papers to her. "Read the agreement. Though I promise not to take the house if you default, a new payment schedule will be created. But if you sell the house, you have to pay me the balance of the loan with the proceeds. No matter what happens, you have to pay back the hundred grand." He pointed to a paragraph at the bottom of page one. "And you have to take out a life insurance policy in the amount of a hundred thousand dollars with me as beneficiary, if you die."

Hope filled her. He hadn't merely stayed away from her dad; he'd listened to everything she'd been saying the past few weeks. "So it really is a business deal?"

"Albeit with very good terms for you. I know you don't want any special favors, but even you have to admit I owe you."

She licked her lips. Lots of people had done her wrong, but no one had ever even acknowledged that, let alone tried to make up for it.

"You can take that to an attorney, if you want."

She smiled up at him. "I could take it to my former boss at the law firm."

Wyatt rose. "Smart businesswoman that you are, I would expect no less from you."

That night, Wyatt sat on the big wicker chair on his back porch, once again wishing his mom hadn't canceled the cable. He'd dug through more boxes, read a few more of his grandfather's letters and still wasn't tired enough for bed. Leaning back in the big chair, he closed his eyes.

"Hey, are you asleep?"

He bounced up with a short laugh. Missy stood at the bottom of his porch steps, holding two bottles of beer and the papers he'd given her that afternoon.

"I guess I was."

She waved the papers. "Can I come up?"

He rose. "Sure. Your lawyer's already looked at those?"

She wore a pink top and white shorts, and had the front of her hair tied back in some sort of clip contraption, but her smile was what caught him. Bright and radiant as the closest star, it raised his hopes and eased his guilt.

She handed him a beer. "To celebrate. My old boss squeezed me in, read the papers in about ten minutes and told me I'd be a fool not to sign." She clanked her beer bottle against Wyatt's. "He's read your comics, by the way. He called you a genius."

Wyatt scuffed his tennis shoe on the old gray porch planks. "I don't know about genius."

"Oh, don't go getting all modest on me now."

He laughed. "So you're signing?"

She handed the papers to him. "It's already signed and notarized. My lawyer kept a copy and made a copy for me."

Wyatt took the papers, glanced down at her signature. "Good girl." Then he clanked his bottle to hers again. "Congratulations. Someday you're going to be the superstar this town talks about."

She fell into one of the big wicker chairs. "This town doesn't care about superstars. We're all about making ends meet."

He sat, too. It was the first time since he'd been home that she'd been totally relaxed with him. He took a swig of his beer, then said, "There's no shame in that."

"I think about ninety percent of America lives that way."

The conversation died and he really wished it hadn't. There was a peace about her, a calmness that he'd never seen before.

"So you're happy?"

"I'm ecstatic. Within the next month I'll have a van, an assistant and day care for the kids." She turned to him. "Do you know how good it is for kids to socialize?"

He didn't. Not really. He knew very little about kids. What he knew was business and comics. So he shrugged. "I guess pretty important."

"Owen will have other boys to play with."

Though Wyatt got a stab of jealousy over that, he also knew he was leaving soon. With or without the jewelry, he couldn't stay away from his work more than a month, five weeks tops.

"That can't be anything but good."

Another silence fell between them. After a

few minutes she turned to face him. "I don't know how to deal with someone who knows about my dad."

"Really?"

"Yeah. I've been keeping the secret so long it feels odd that another person knows. It's almost like who I am around you is different."

He laughed. "That's funny, because I've been thinking the same thing since I came here."

"That I'm different?"

"No. More that I can't get my footing. In Florida I'm king of my company. Here, I know nothing about kids or cakes or weddings. Plus, I'm the guy you remember as a nerd."

"You're so not a nerd."

"Geek then."

She shook her head. "Have you looked at yourself in the mirror lately?"

He glanced down at his jeans, then back at her. "I wore jeans in high school."

"Yeah. But not so well."

He laughed.

She smiled. "It's like you're the first person in my life to know the whole me. Past and present."

"And you're the first person to know the whole me. Geek and sex god."

She laughed and rose from her seat. "Right." Reaching for his empty beer bottle, she said, "Before that little display of conceit, I was going to ask if you wanted to help me van shop."

"I'd *love* to help you van shop."

"See? Old Wyatt wouldn't have been able to do that."

"Old Wyatt?"

"The geeky high school kid."

"Right."

"But older, wiser Wyatt can."

He chuckled. No one ever called him old, let alone wise. But he sort of liked it. Just as she had her fortes with kids and cakes, he had his expertise, too. "So you're going to let me go with you?"

"Yes." She turned and started down the stairs. "And don't go getting any big ideas about buying some tricked out supervan. I saw the clause in the agreement where you can raise the amount of the loan to accommodate expansion. I don't want any more money. I have to grow the business in stages. We get a normal van. I hire a normal assistant. The kids go to local day care."

By the time she finished she was at the bottom of the steps. She turned to face him.

He saluted her. "Aye, aye, Captain."

She laughed. "I also like your new sense of humor. Young Wyatt didn't laugh much."

He leaned on the porch railing. Since they were being honest, it was time to admit the truth. "He was always too busy being nervous. Especially around you. You're so beautiful you probably make most men nervous."

She shook her head as if she thought he was teasing, then pointed at the hedge. "I've gotta go. See you tomorrow."

"See you tomorrow."

He pushed away from the railing, smiling to himself. She was correct. He felt odd around her because she was the first, maybe the only person in his life to know both sides of him.

But now he also knew her secret. Instead of that scaring him the way he knew it probably should, because her secret was dark and frightening and needed to be handled with care, he felt a swell of pride. She hadn't told him her secret, but she clearly trusted him with it. He felt honored.

"Hi, Mommy."

Missy opened her eyes and smiled down at the foot of the bed. Claire grinned at her.

She never awoke after the kids. She couldn't imagine why she'd slept so late. Except that being honest with Wyatt about her dad, and accepting the loan, had relaxed her. She didn't have to pretend that everything was fine around him. She could be herself.

"Hey, sweetie. Want some cereal?"

Her daughter's grin grew and she nodded.

Missy rolled out of bed. Normally she was already in shorts and a T-shirt before she went to the kitchen. Today she was so far behind she didn't have time to change. Still, she slept in pajama pants and a tank top. There was no reason to change or even to find a robe. She sleepily padded from her bedroom in the back corner of the downstairs into the kitchen. As she got cereal from the cupboard and Claire climbed onto a chair, Lainie and Owen ambled into the kitchen. They also climbed onto chairs.

She'd barely gotten cocoa chunks cereal into three bowls and a pot of coffee on before there was a knock at her door. Without waiting for her to invite him in, Wyatt entered.

"Are you here to mooch coffee?"

He laughed. "No, but I wouldn't say no if you'd offer me a cup."

She motioned for him to take a seat at the

table, grabbed a cup from the cupboard and poured some coffee into it for him.

When she set it in front of him, his gaze touched on her tank top, then rippled down to her pajama pants. "I guess I'm early for the van shopping."

She stifled the warmth and pleasure that saturated her at his obvious interest. Saturday they'd decided against any kind of relationship because they wanted two different things. Yesterday, when she'd signed the line of credit papers, they'd cemented that. Even if he wanted to get involved with her—which he didn't—she wouldn't get involved with a man who owned the "mortgage" on her house.

"You want to go today?"

"No time like the present. My bank wire transferred the hundred grand into a new account set up for you. We can stop at the bank for you to sign the paperwork, and the money will be at your disposal immediately."

Her attraction to him was quickly forgotten as her heart filled with joy. This was really happening. She was getting a van, a helper… She would expand her business!

"Let me call Nancy to babysit." Missy popped out of her chair and raced back to the bedroom to get her phone. After Nancy agreed to come over, she hopped into the shower. Halfway done shampooing her hair, she realized she'd left the kids with Wyatt. Without thinking.

She trusted him.

She ducked her hair under the spray. She did trust him.

She waited for her tummy to twist or her breathing to become painful at the thought of trusting someone so easily, so completely, that she didn't even think to ask him to mind the kids, but nothing happened.

She finished her shower, fixed her hair and slid into jeans and a blue T-shirt. In a way she was glad they'd decided on Saturday night against a relationship, because her feelings for him had nothing to do with her attraction— or his. The trust she felt for him was simple, honest. Just as she'd realized his lending her money was like something a friend would do to make up for a wrong, her leaving her kids without thought was also the act of a friend.

They were becoming *friends*.

Tucking her hair behind her ears, she walked into the kitchen to find Wyatt filling the sink with soapy water as her children brought their cereal bowls to him.

"How'd you get them to do that?"

"Bribery."

Her mouth fell open. "Wyatt—"

"Relax. I promised them another trip to my grandmother's house to look through boxes. Nothing sinister like ice cream."

She casually walked to the table. "Ice cream isn't a bad idea."

He turned from the sink. "It isn't?"

"No. There's a nice place a mile or so out of town." She peeked at him, testing this friendship they were forming. Though her stomach jumped a bit at how handsome he was, she reminded herself that was normal. "Maybe we could take the kids there when I get the van. You know? Use getting ice cream as a maiden voyage."

He appeared surprised. "Sounds great."

Nancy knocked on the door and walked into the kitchen. "I heard there's a bunch of kids here who want to play house with me."

The girls jumped for joy. "Yay!"

But Owen deflated.

Wyatt stooped down to talk to him. "Don't worry. Van shopping won't take all day. And when we get back you can do whatever you want."

"Wook for tweasure?"

"Sure."

Missy's heart swelled. If they hadn't had the talk about their relationship she'd be in serious danger of falling in love with this guy. But they had had the talk. Then he'd overheard her argument with her father. And now they were friends.

Outside, she rummaged through her purse for her SUV keys. But when she reached the driver's side door, she noticed he hadn't followed.

"Aren't you sick of that beast yet?"

She laughed. "What?"

He jangled his keys. "It's such a beautiful day. Let's take the bike."

Happiness bubbled in her veins. "I haven't been on a bike since high school."

He grabbed the thin shrub branch and pushed it aside for her. "Then it's time."

With a laugh, she dipped under and walked over to the garage door. He opened it and there sat his shiny black bike.

"I don't have a helmet."

"You can use mine."

He handed her the helmet and straddled the bike.

She licked her suddenly dry lips. For all her fancy, happy self-talk that morning about being glad they were becoming friends, the thought of straddling the bike behind him sent shivers up her spine.

She'd danced with him. She'd kissed him. She knew the potency of his nearness.

And in spite of all that happy self-talk, she was susceptible. He was good to her. He was good to her kids. And around him she felt like a woman. Not just a mom.

She liked that feeling as much as she liked the idea of being his friend.

"Come on! Don't be a chicken."

Glad that he mistook her hesitancy for fear, she sucked in a breath. She could stop this just by saying she'd changed her mind and wanted to take the SUV. But then she'd miss the chance to hold him without worry he'd get the wrong impression. The chance to slide her cheek against his back. The chance to inhale his scent.

And the chance to enjoy him for a few minutes without consequences. Because, God help her, she did like him as more than a friend. He was the one who didn't want her. And if she refused this chance to be close to him, she'd regret it.

She slid onto the bike.

He revved the engine as she plopped the helmet on her head. Within seconds they shot out of the garage and onto the quiet street. She wrapped her arms around his middle, not out of a desire to hold him, but out of sheer terror.

Then the wind caught her loose hair beneath the helmet and whooshed along her limbs. Gloriously free, she raised her arms, let them catch the breeze and yelled, "Woo hoo!"

She felt rather than heard him laugh. In under five minutes, they were at the bank. She pulled off the helmet and he wrapped the straps around the handlebars before they walked into the lobby.

The customer service representative quickly found her file. Missy signed papers. Wyatt signed papers. And within what seemed like seconds they were on the bike again.

He pulled out onto Main Street and stopped at the intersection. He turned his head and yelled, "What car dealer do you want to go to?"

"I thought you'd know."

"I haven't been around here for a while." He revved the bike and smiled at her. His dark eyes shone with devilishness that called to her. "We could just get on the highway and drive until we find something."

Part of her wanted to. The kids were cared for. She was in a wonderful, daring mood. And he was so close. So sweet. So full of mischief...

Mischief with someone she really liked was dangerous to a mother of three who was knee-deep in a fledgling business. She pulled out her phone. "Or I could look up dealers online."

"Spoilsport." He revved the bike. "I like my idea better." He shot out into the street again. They flew down Main Street and again she had to stifle the urge to put her hands in the air and yell, "Woo hoo!"

But she stifled it. Because as much fun as this was, she had to get a van and get home to her kids.

A little voice inside her head disagreed. She didn't need to get home. Nancy was at the house. The kids were fine. And Missy was out. Out of the house. On her way to buy a van. On her way to having a wonderful future because her business would succeed. She knew it would.

Then she remembered the look of mischief in Wyatt's eyes. That was why she needed to get home. She liked him. Really liked him. And he wanted an affair. That was a bad combo. She hit a few buttons on her phone and began looking for a used car dealer.

Wyatt got them on the highway. The bike's speed picked up. Wind rushed at her. The sun warmed her arms. She put her face up and inhaled.

"Find a place yet?"

When Wyatt's voice whispered in her ear, she almost flew off the bike. He chuckled. "I turned on the mic." He showed her the mouthpiece hanging from the phone piece in his ear.

She said, "Oh." She shouldn't have been surprised by the communications equipment. In his real world, Wyatt probably had every gadget known to mankind. After a few flips through the results of her internet search on her phone screen, she said, "There's a place right off the highway about a mile down the road."

"Then that's where we'll go."

They drove the mile, took the exit ramp and stopped in the parking lot of a car dealer. Shiny new cars, SUVs, trucks and vans greeted them.

She slid off the bike. "Wow. There are so many cars here."

Wyatt smoothed his hand along the fender of a brand-new red truck. "Too bad you need a van." He whistled as he walked along the back panels. "Look at this thing."

She laughed. "You should buy it for yourself."

He lovingly caressed some chrome. "I should." He turned toward the big building behind the rows and rows of vehicles. "I think I'll just go find a salesman."

He came back ten minutes later with a salesman who first told him all the finer points of the brand-new red truck, then turned to her as Wyatt climbed into the truck cab.

"I hear you need a van."

She smiled slightly. "Yes."

"Do you know what you want?"

"Yes. A white one."

He laughed. "No. I was talking about engine size, cargo bay versus seating."

Wyatt jumped out of the truck. "She wants a V-8, with seats that retract so that she has enough space to deliver goods."

"What kind of goods? How much space?"

"She bakes wedding cakes. The space doesn't need to be huge. We just need to know that the van can be easily air-conditioned."

"Are you sure she doesn't want to order a refrigerated van?"

Missy opened her mouth to speak, but

Wyatt said, "She's on a limited budget. She doesn't need to go overboard."

They looked at several vans. Test drove three. In the end, she bought a white van that was used rather than new. She didn't know anything about refrigerated vans, but it sounded like something she might need in the future. Given that the used van was twelve thousand dollars less than a new one, she wouldn't be wasting as much if she decided a year or two from now to get the refrigerated van. Exclusively for business. She might even be able to keep the used van for her kids.

She suddenly felt like a princess—buying what she needed, planning to buy something even better in the future.

They walked into the office to write up the papers for her van. She called the bank and made arrangements to do a wire transfer of the purchase price, then signed on the dotted line.

The salesman stapled her papers together and gave her a set. "Okay. Van will be delivered tomorrow morning."

He then passed a bunch of papers to Wyatt. "And for the truck."

He said, "Thanks," and signed a few things.

The salesman handed him the keys. "Pleasure doing business with you, Mr. McKenzie. You know, if you get tired of the red one, I also have it in blue and yellow."

Wyatt laughed.

It was then that it hit her how rich he was. Sure, she'd always known in an abstract way that he had money. But watching him see something he wanted and buy it without a moment's hesitation or a single second thought made it real. This guy she liked, someone who was a friend, had more money than she could even imagine.

They walked out into the bright sunshine. He slid onto the bike. She put the helmet on her head and got on behind him. As he started off, she slid her arms around his waist and squeezed her eyes shut. He was so far out of her league. So different than anybody she knew.

Sadness made her sigh. Still, she leaned in close to him. Because he couldn't see her, she let her eyes drift shut, and enjoyed the sensation of just holding him. Because he was tempting. Because she was grateful. Because for once in her life, she really, really wanted somebody, but she was smart enough to know she couldn't have him.

And if she didn't take this chance to hold him, to feel the solidness of him beneath her chest, she might not ever get another.

When they returned to his gram's, she removed the helmet. He looped the strap over the handlebars.

"So? Fun?"

She refused to let her sadness show and spoil their day. "Oh, man. So much fun. I loved the bike ride, but I loved buying the van even more. I've never been able to get what I wanted. I've always had to take what I could afford."

He grinned. "It's a high, isn't it?"

"Yeah, but I'm not going to let myself get too used to it. For me, it's all part of getting my business up and running."

He nodded. "So, go feed the kids lunch and I'll be over around two to play with Owen."

She said, "Okay," and turned to go, but then faced Wyatt again. He was great. Honest. Open. Generous. And she'd always had her guard up around him. But now he knew her secret. He knew the real her. And he still treated her wonderfully.

She walked over and stood on her tiptoes. Intending to give him a peck on his check, in the last second she changed her mind. When her toes had her tall enough to reach his face, she kissed his lips. One soft, quick brush of her mouth across his that was enough to send electricity to her toes.

"Thanks."

He laughed. "I'd say you're welcome, but you owed me that kiss."

"I did?"

"If you'd kept our date graduation night, you'd have kissed me."

"Oh, really?"

"I might have been a geek, but that night I knew what I wanted and I was getting it."

She laughed, but stopped suddenly.

"What?"

She shook her head, turned away. "It's nothing."

He caught her hand and hauled her back. "It's something."

She stared at the front of his T-shirt. "The first day you arrived, I wanted to say I was sorry I broke that date." She swallowed. "I was all dressed to go, on my way to the door..." She looked up. "But my dad hit my mom. Bloodied her lip."

Wyatt cursed. "You don't have to tell me this."

"Actually, I want to. I think it's time to let

some of this out." She held his gaze. "I trust you."

"Then why don't we go into the house and you can tell me the whole story?"

She almost told him she should get back to the kids, but her need to rid herself of the full burden of this secret told her to take a few minutes, be honest, let some of this go.

She nodded and they walked to the back door of his grandmother's house and into her kitchen. He made a pot of coffee, then leaned against the counter.

"Okay…so what happened that night?"

"We'd had a halfway decent graduation. It was one of those times when Dad had to be on his best behavior because we were in public, so everything went well. I actually felt normal. But driving home, he stopped at a bar. When he got home, he freaked out. He'd been on good behavior so long he couldn't keep up the pretense anymore and he exploded. He slammed the kitchen door, pivoted and hit my mom. Her lip was bleeding, so I took her to the sink to wash it off and get ice, and he just turned and punched Althea, slamming her into the wall." Missy squeezed her eyes shut, remembering. "It was a nightmare, but then again lots of times were like that."

"Scary?"

She caught his gaze. "More than scary. Out of control. Like playing a game where the rules constantly change. What made him happy one day could make him angry the next. But even worse was the confusion."

"Confusion worse than changing rules?"

She swallowed. "Emotional, personal confusion."

Wyatt said nothing. She sucked in a breath. "Imagine what it feels like to be a little girl who wants nothing but to protect her mom, so you step in front of a punch."

He cursed.

"From that point on, I became fair game to him."

"He began to beat you, too?"

She nodded. "It was like I'd given him permission when I stepped into the first punch." She licked her lips. "So from that point on, my choice became watch him beat my mom, or take some of the beating for her."

Wyatt's eyes squeezed shut, as if he shared her misery through imagining it. "And you frequently chose to be beaten."

"Sometimes I had to."

She walked to the stove, ran her finger along the shiny rim. "But that night he couldn't reach me. I'd taken my mother to the sink, stupidly believing that without anyone to hit, he'd get frustrated and head for the sofa. But he went after Althea."

"How old was she?"

"Twelve. Too young to take full-fist beating from a grown man."

"I'm sorry."

Missy sucked in another breath. Hearing the truth coming from her own mouth, her anger at herself, disappointment in herself, and the grief she felt over losing Althea began to crumble. She'd been young, too. Too young to take the blame for things her father had done.

She loosened her shoulders, faced Wyatt again. "I could see her arm was broken, so I didn't think. I didn't speak. I didn't ask permission or wait for instructions. I just grabbed the car keys to take her to the hospital, and my dad yanked the bottle of bleach off the washer by the back door." Missy looked into Wyatt's dark, solemn eyes. "He took off the cap and, two seconds before I would have been out of range, tossed it at me. It ran down my skirt, washing out the color, eating holes right through the thin material."

Wyatt shook his head. "He was insane."

"I'd earned that dress myself." Her voice wobbled, so she paused long enough to strengthen it. She was done being a victim, done being haunted by her dad. It appeared even her ghosts of guilt over Althea leaving were being exorcized. "I worked for every penny I'd needed to buy it. But when he was drunk, he forgot things like that. As I was scrambling out of the dress, before the bleach burned through to my skin, he called me a bunch of names. I just tossed the dress in the trash and walked to my room. I put on jeans and a T-shirt and took Althea to the hospital. His screams and cursing followed us out the door and to the car."

Wyatt said nothing.

She stayed quiet for a few seconds, too, letting it soak in that she'd finally told someone, and that in telling someone she'd seen that she wasn't to blame. That she had no sin. No part in any of it except victim. And she was strong enough now not to accept that title anymore.

"At the hospital, a social worker came into the cubicle. Althea wanted to tell, to report our dad. I wouldn't let her." Missy glanced up at him again. "I feared for Mom. I knew the social worker would take us away, but Mom would be stuck there. And because we'd embarrassed him, he'd be even worse to her than he already was."

"Why didn't your mom leave?"

"She was afraid. She had no money. No skills. And he really only beat her about twice a month."

Wyatt sniffed in derision. "He's a bastard."

"I left the next day. Got a clerical job in D.C. and an apartment with some friends. Althea spent every weekend with us. I guess that was enough for my dad to realize we didn't need him—didn't depend on him— and we could report him, because he stopped hitting Mom. When Althea graduated, she left town. Went to college in California. We haven't really heard from her since." Saying that aloud hurt. Missy loved and missed her sister. But she wasn't the reason Althea had gone. She could let go of that now. "When one of my roommates moved out, I tried to get my mom to move in with me, but she refused. A few weeks later she had a heart attack and died."

Wyatt gaped at her. "How old was she?"

"Not quite fifty. But she was worn down, anorexic. She never ate. She was always too worried to eat. It finally killed her."

With her story out, exhaustion set in. Missy's shoulders slumped.

He turned to the coffeepot, poured two cups. "Here."

She smiled shakily. "That wasn't so bad."

"Secrets are always better if you tell them."

She laughed. "How do you know?"

He shrugged. "School, I guess. In grade school I hid the fact that I was bullied from my parents. But in high school I knew I couldn't let it go on. The kids were bigger, meaner, and I was no match. So I told them. They talked to the school principal. At first the bullies kept at me, but after enough detention hours, and seeing that I wasn't going to be their personal punching bag anymore, they stopped."

Missy laughed, set her cup on the counter beside him and flattened her hands on his chest. "Poor baby."

"I'd have paid good money to have you tell me that in high school."

"I really did like you, you know. I thought of you as smart and honest."

"I was."

She peeked up at him. "You are now, too."

The room got quiet. They stood as close as lovers, but something more hummed between them. Emotionally, she'd never been as connected to anyone as she was to him right now. She knew he didn't want anything permanent, but in this minute, she didn't, either. All she wanted was the quiet confirmation that, secrets shared, she would feel in the circle of his arms. She wanted to feel. To be real. To be whole.

Then she heard the kids out in the yard. Her kids. Her life. She didn't need sex to tell her she was real, whole. She had a life. A good life. A life she'd made herself. She had a cake to bake this Saturday. Soon she'd have an assistant. She'd make cakes for grocery stores and restaurants. Her life had turned out better than she'd expected. She had good things, kids to live for, a business that made her happy.

She stepped away. A one-night stand would be fun. But building a good life was better. "I've gotta go."

He studied her. "You're okay?"

"I'm really okay." She smiled. "I'm better than okay. Thanks for letting me talk to you."

"That's what friends do."

Her smile grew. The tension in her chest eased. "Exactly. So if you have any deep, dark secrets, I'm here for you, friend."

"You know my story. Stood up to bullies in high school, made lots of money, bad marriage, worse divorce—which I'm beginning to feel better about, thank you for asking."

She laughed and headed for the door. "Well, if you ever need to talk, you know where I am."

"Like I said, I have no secrets."

She stopped, faced him again. He might not have secrets, but he did have hurts. Hurts he didn't share.

Were it not for those hurts, she probably wouldn't push open the door and walk away. She'd probably be in his arms right now. But she did push on the screen door, did leave his kitchen. They were both too smart to get involved when he couldn't let go of his past.

CHAPTER NINE

Saturday morning Wyatt didn't wait until Missy was ready to leave to get dressed to help deliver her cake. She hadn't yet hired an assistant. She'd put an ad in the papers for the nearby cities, and a few responses had trickled in. But she wasn't about to jump into anything. She wanted time for interviews and to check references.

He couldn't argue with that. Which meant he'd need to help her with that week's wedding.

So Friday he'd bought new clothes, telling himself he was tired of looking like a grunge rocker. Saturday morning, after his shower, he had black trousers, a white shirt and black-and-white print tie to put on before he ambled to her house. As had become his practice, he knocked twice and walked in.

Then stopped.

Wearing an orange-and-white-flowered strapless sundress, and with her hair done up in a fancy do that let curls fall along the back of her neck, she absolutely stopped his heart. In a bigger city, she would have been the "it" girl. In a little town like Newland, with nowhere to go but the grocery store or diner, and no reason to dress up, she sort of disappeared.

"You look amazing." He couldn't help it; the words tumbled out of their own volition.

She smiled sheepishly. "Would you believe this is an old work dress? Without the little white jacket, it's perfect for a garden wedding."

He looked her up and down once again, his heart pitter-pattering. "I should get a job at that law firm if everyone looks that good."

Because he'd flustered her, and was having a bit of trouble keeping his eyes off her, he searched for a change of subject. Glancing around her kitchen, he noticed the five layers of cake sitting in a row on her counter. Oddly shaped and with what looked to be steel beams trimming the edges, it wasn't her most attractive creation.

"Is the bride a construction worker?"

"That's the Eiffel Tower." Missy laughed. "The groom proposed there."

"Oh." Wyatt took a closer look. "Interesting."

"It is to them."

Owen skipped into the room. "Hey, Wyatt."

"Hey, kid." He faced Missy, asking, "When's Nancy get here?" But his heart sped up again just from looking at her. She had the kind of legs that were made to be shown off, and the dress handled that nicely. Nipped in at the waist, it also accented her taut middle. The dip of the bodice showed just enough cleavage to make his mouth water.

And he thought *he* looked nice. She put him and his white shirt and black trousers to shame—even with a tie.

"She should be here in about ten minutes. If you help me load up, we can get on the road as soon as she arrives."

Making several trips, Missy and Wyatt put the layers of cake into the back of her new van. Together they carried the bottom layer, which had little people and trees painted on the side, mimicking street level around Paris's most famous landmark.

"Cute."

"It is cute. To the bride and groom." She grinned. "And it's banana walnut with almond filling."

He groaned. "I'll bet that's delicious."

Sixteen-year-old Nancy walked up the drive. Her dark hair had been pulled into a ponytail. In a pair of shorts and oversize T-shirt, she was obviously ready to play.

"Hi, Missy. Wyatt."

The kids came barreling out. She scooped them into her arms. "What first? Cartoons or sandbox?"

Owen said, "Sandbox."

The girls whined. But Nancy held her ground. "Owen has to get the chance to pick every once in a while."

After a flurry of goodbyes and a minute for Missy to find her purse, she and Wyatt boarded the van. He glanced around with approval. "So much better than the SUV."

"I know."

She started the engine and pulled out of the driveway onto the street. In a few minutes they were on the highway.

She peeked over at him. "So…you look different. Very handsome."

Her compliment caused his chest to swell with pride. He'd had hundreds of women come on to him since he'd become rich, but none of their compliments affected him as Missy's did. But that was wrong. They'd decided to be friends.

Pretending to be unaffected, he flipped his tie up and let it fall. "You know, I don't even dress like this for my own job."

"That's because you're the boss. Here I'm the boss."

"You never told me you wanted me to dress better."

"I think it was implied by the way everybody around you dressed. It's called positive peer pressure."

He chuckled, then sneaked a peek at her. Man. He'd never seen anybody prettier. Or happier. And what made it even better was knowing he'd played a part in her happiness. She wanted this business to succeed and it would. Because she'd let him help.

Pride shimmied through him, but so did his darned attraction again, stronger and more potent than it had been before she complimented him. But they'd already figured out they wanted two different things. The night before, she'd even offered to listen to his troubles. Smart enough not to want to get involved with him, she'd offered them the safe haven of friendship. He shouldn't be thinking of her any way, except as a friend.

It took two hours to get to the country club where the reception was being held. The

party room of the clubhouse had been decorated in green and ivory, colors that flowed
out onto the huge deck. The banister swirled
with green and ivory tulle, down stairs that
led guests to a covered patio where tables and
chairs had been arranged around two large
buffet tables.

As they carried the cake into the clubhouse,
Missy said, "Wedding was at noon. Lunch
will be served around one-thirty. Cake right
after that, then we're home."

He snorted. "After a two-hour drive."

"Now, don't be huffy. Because we get home
early, I'm making dinner and insisting you
eat with us."

"You are?"

"Yep. And I'm not even cooking something
on the grill. I'm making real dinner."

"Oh, sweetheart. You just said the magic
words. *Real dinner.* You have no idea how
hungry I am."

She laughed. They put the cake together
on a table set up in a cool, shaded section of
the room. When the wedding guests arrived,
however, no one came into the building or
even climbed up to the deck. Instead, they
gathered on the patio, choosing their lunch
seats, getting drinks from the makeshift bar.

The bride and groom followed suit. On the sunny, beautiful May day, no one went any farther than the patio.

"One of two things has to happen here," Missy said as she looked out the window onto the guests who were a floor below them. "Either we need to get people in here or we need to get the cake out there."

He headed for the door. "I'll go talk to somebody."

She put her hand on his forearm to stop him. "*I'll* go talk to somebody."

She walked through the echoing room and onto the equally empty deck, down the stairs to the covered patio. Wyatt watched her look through the crowd and finally catch the attention of a tuxedo-clad guy.

She smiled at him and began talking. Even from a distance Wyatt saw the sparkle in her eyes, and his gaze narrowed in on the guy she was talking to. Tall, broad-shouldered, with dark curly hair, he wasn't bad looking… Oh, all right, he was good-looking, and was wearing a tux. Wyatt knew how women were about men in tuxes. He'd taken advantage of that a time or two himself. And Missy was a normal woman. A woman he'd rejected. She had every right to be attracted to this guy.

Even if it did make Wyatt want to punch something.

As she and the man in the tux walked up the stairs to the deck, he scrambled away from the window. She opened the door and motioned around the empty room.

"See? No one's even come in here."

The man in the tux glanced around, his gaze finally alighting on her creation. "Is that the cake?"

She smiled. "Yes."

Tux man strolled over. He examined the icing-covered Eiffel Tower, then looked over his shoulder at Missy, who had followed him. "You're remarkable."

Her cheeks pinkened prettily. Wyatt's eyes narrowed again.

"I wouldn't say remarkable." She grinned at him. "But I am good at what I do."

"And beautiful, too."

Unable to stop himself, Wyatt headed for the cake table.

Missy's already pink cheeks reddened. "Thanks. But as you can see, the cake—"

"I don't suppose you'd give a beleaguered best man your phone number?"

Her eyes widened. Wyatt's did, too. Beleaguered best man? Did he think he was in a Rodgers and Hammerstein play?

"I—"

He slid his hand into his pocket. "I have a pen."

Wyatt finally reached them. "She's got a pen, too, bud. If she wanted to give you her phone number, she could. But it seems she doesn't want to."

Missy shot Wyatt a stay-out-of-this look, then smiled politely at the best man. "What my assistant is trying to say is that I'm a very busy person. I keep a pen and paper for brides-to-be, who see my cakes and want to talk about me baking for them."

The best man stiffened. "So you wanting to get the cake downstairs, into the crowd, is all about PR for you?"

"Heavens, no." She laughed airily. "I want the bride to see the cake she designed."

But the best man snorted as if he didn't believe her. He shoved his hands into his pockets, casually, as if he held all the cards and knew it. "I guess you'll just have to figure out a way to get the bride up here yourself, then."

But Missy didn't bite. She smiled professionally and said, "Okay." Not missing a beat, she walked over to the French doors leading to the deck and went in search of the bride.

His threat ignored, the best man deflated and headed for the door, too.

Wyatt chuckled to himself. She certainly was focused. The best man might have temporarily knocked her off her game, but she'd quickly rebounded.

A few minutes later, Missy returned to the room in the clubhouse, the bride and groom on her heels.

"As you can see, nobody's here."

The bride stopped dead in her tracks. "That's my cake?"

Missy pressed her hand to her throat. "You said you wanted the Eiffel tower."

The bride slowly walked over. She ambled around the table, examining the cake. Wyatt stifled the urge to pull his collar away from his neck. In the quiet, empty room, the click of the bride's heels as she rounded the table was the only sound. Her face red, Missy watched helplessly.

Finally the bride said, "It's beautiful. So real. Isn't it, Tony?"

Tony said, "Yeah. It's cool. I like it."

"I think I'll have the band announce that

we're cutting the cake up here, and ask everyone to join us."

Missy sighed with relief. "Sounds good."

Tony caught the bride's hand and they went back to the patio.

As soon as they were gone, Missy turned on Wyatt. "And *you*."

"Me?" This time he did run his fingers under his shirt collar to release the strangled feeling. "What did I do?"

She stalked over to him. In her pretty orange-and-white-flowered dress and her tall white sandals, with her hair all done up, she looked like a Southern belle on the warpath.

"I fight my own battles. He was a jerk, but I handled him. Professionally. Politely."

"He was a letch."

She tossed her hands in the air. "I've handled letches before. Sheesh! Do you think he's the first best man to come on to me?"

Wyatt's blood froze, then heated to boiling and roared through his veins. "Best men come on to you?"

"And ushers and fathers of the bride—or groom." She stepped into his personal space. "But I'm a big girl. I can handle myself with bad boys."

He snorted. "Oh, really?"

"You think I can't?"

His hands slipped around the back of her neck, pulling her face to his as he lowered his head. His lips met hers in a flurry of passion and desire. He expected her to back off, to be stunned—at the very least surprised. Instead, she met him need for need. When his tongue slipped into her mouth, she responded like someone as starved for this as he was.

Heat exploded in his middle, along with a feeling so foreign he couldn't have described it to save his life. Part need, part entitlement, part something dark and wonderful, it fueled the fire in his soul and nudged him to go further, take what he wanted, salve this crazy ache that dogged him every time he was around her.

The door opened and sounds from the wedding below billowed inside. Missy jerked away, her eyes filled with fire. From passion or from anger, Wyatt couldn't tell.

She pulled a tissue from her pocket, quickly dabbed her lips, turned and faced the bride, groom and photographer with a smile.

"Come in. We're all set up."

What the hell was that?

Missy smiled at the bride and groom, leading them and the wedding party to the Eiffel Tower cake. As the crowd gushed, complimenting the detail, retelling the story of how the groom had proposed, her thoughts spun away again.

Had Wyatt kissed her out of jealousy?

Her stomach knotted. He'd absolutely been jealous. But she'd bet her bottom dollar the kiss hadn't been out of jealousy, but was meant to teach her a lesson. She'd responded to prove she was able to take care of herself. And instead...

Well, she'd knocked them both for a loop.

The question was—

How did they deal with it?

The bride and groom posed for pictures with the cake, along with their parents and the bridal party. They served each other a bite of the cake as the photographer snapped more pictures. Almost as quickly as they'd come, they left, taking the bridal party with them.

And the room went silent.

Missy sighed, calmly walking to the cake table, though inside she was scrambling for something to say. Anything to get both their minds off that kiss.

"My best cake ever and I won't be getting any referrals from it."

He didn't even glance at her. "How do you know?"

Either he wasn't happy about being jealous or he wasn't happy that this kiss had been better than their first. "Only the wedding party and the bride and groom saw it."

He sniffed a laugh. "Give people time to taste it. You'll get your referrals."

"That's just it. They didn't leave instructions to serve it." She sighed. "I'm going to find the bride's mom."

With that, she left, and Wyatt collapsed against the silent, empty bar behind him. He didn't need to wonder what had happened when they kissed. He didn't need to probe why he'd been jealous. He was falling for her. A few weeks past his divorce and like a sucker he was falling for somebody new.

He couldn't let it happen. Not just to protect himself, but to protect her. She didn't want to fall in love with a guy who wasn't ready for a commitment, any more than he wanted to fall in love so soon after he'd ended his marriage. Only beginning to get her feet wet with her business, she wanted the fun, the thrill, of stepping into her destiny. Of making money. Running the show.

Her response to his kiss had started out as

a way to tell him to back off, that she could handle herself. No matter that it ended up with both of them aroused and needy. The original intent had been clear. Now he had to return them to sanity.

Though he was starving, he begged off her homemade dinner and drove ten miles to the next town over to eat meat loaf that was a disgrace. Sunday, he played with the kids but avoided seeing Missy. On Monday morning, however, he arrived at her back door as soon as he saw the kitchen light go on. He knocked twice, then let himself inside.

Without turning around, she said, "Come in, Wyatt."

The laugh in her voice told him she wasn't as afraid to be around him as he was to be around her. That served to strengthen his resolve. Wrapped up in her new business venture, she was too busy to dwell on runaway emotions the way he was. Not just the rumble of attraction, the longing to kiss her senseless and make her his, but the urge to protect her, bring her into his home…really make her his.

He knew these urges were wrong. With the ink barely dried on his divorce papers, they could simply be rebound needs. So he had to get hold of himself. To protect himself, but also to protect her. Whether she knew it or not, she was vulnerable. He could be a real vulture when he went after something he wanted. She wouldn't stand a chance.

And after he got what he wanted, he'd get bored, and he'd leave her hurt and broken.

He would not do that to her.

Since their biggest temptation time seemed to be weddings, there was an easy answer.

"This week we're going to have to find that assistant for you."

She walked away from the coffeepot, holding two steaming mugs. She handed one to him and they sat at the table, where all three kids sleepily played with cereal that swam in milk made chocolate by the little bites bobbing in it.

"Did you get any responses to your ad?"

"Lots. I'm just not sure where to interview people."

"Since you're going to be baking here at your house, I think the interviews should take place here."

"Okay." She sipped her coffee, then smiled. "Want some cocoa bites?"

"I thought you'd never ask."

They called the four candidates Missy deemed best suited for her company, and set up interviews for Tuesday, Wednesday and Thursday.

Wyatt sat with her through the interview for the first candidate, Mona Greenlee, a short, squat woman who clearly loved food. But after a comment or two at the beginning of the meeting, he stopped talking and let Missy ask her questions, give Mona a tour of the house and introduce her to the kids.

Mona laughed about how unusual it was to bake from a house, but Missy assured her that her kitchen had passed inspection. After she left, Wyatt headed for the door.

"Where are you going?"

He turned slowly. When he finally caught her gaze, she saw a light in his eyes that caused her heart to stutter. His focus fell from her eyes to her mouth, then rose again. "You can handle these interviews on your own."

Though complimented by his faith in her, she got a funny feeling in her stomach. Was he leaving because he was thinking about kissing her?

Remembering the kiss from Saturday made her stomach flip again. That was one great kiss. A kiss she wouldn't mind repeating. But they'd been attracted to each other right from the beginning and they'd managed to work together in spite of it. Wanting to kiss shouldn't cause him to leave.

"You don't want to help?"

"You're fine without me."

But I like spending time with you. I like your goofy comments. I like you.

The words swirled around in Missy's head so much, she almost said them. But she didn't. First, the intensity of her feelings surprised her, and she needed to think them through. Second, if she'd grown so accustomed to having him around that she didn't mind having him neb his nose into her business, then maybe things had gone further than she wanted them to.

He didn't want a relationship. She didn't want a fling. It was better not to encourage these feelings. And maybe he was right. They shouldn't spend so much time together.

She did the next interview alone and didn't have a problem until Jane Nelson left. Then she scurried outside to find Wyatt. Not to ask for help, but to talk. To tell him about Jane. To show him that she could handle all this alone, and how excited she was.

But when she walked into the backyard where he was playing Wiffle ball with the kids, he barely spoke to her. He complimented the job she had done interviewing Jane, but he didn't ask questions or go into detailed answers. He was distancing himself from her.

Disappointment followed her back into the house. She didn't *need* him, but suddenly everything she did felt empty without him.

At the end of the next two interviews, she didn't bother looking for Wyatt, but that didn't stop the emptiness. After so many weeks of having him underfoot, it seemed wrong that he was pulling away from her.

Except he'd be leaving in a few days. Maybe he was preparing them both?

That would be okay, except she didn't want to be prepared. She wanted to enjoy the last few days she had with him. What was the point of starting the empty feeling early? It would find a home in her soon enough, when he really did leave.

Thursday evening she offered Elaine Anderson the job. She'd blended in best with the chaos and the kids, and was able to start immediately.

To celebrate, Missy made fried chicken, and sent Owen over to get Wyatt. She knew that was a tad underhanded, but after several days of not seeing him, she was tired of wasting the precious little time they had left together. Plus, spending a few days without him had forced her to see that she liked him a lot more than she thought she did. So tonight she intended to figure out what was really going on with him.

If he was upset about their kiss and didn't want to repeat it, she would back off.

But if he was struggling with jealousy and the lines they'd drawn about their relationship, maybe it was time to change things. He didn't want a relationship. She didn't want a fling, but surely they could find a compromise position? Maybe agree to date long distance for a few months to see if this thing between them was something they should pursue.

He strolled over to the picnic table behind bouncing Owen, who was thrilled to be getting his favorite fried chicken, and in general thrilled with life these days. She no longer worried about his transition after Wyatt left. With money to put the kids in day care for four hours every morning, she knew Owen would find friends. Her life was perfect.

Except for the empty feeling she got every time she thought about Wyatt leaving.

But tonight she intended to set this relationship onto one course or another. Either ask him to work something out with her or let him go. And then stick by that decision.

"I hope you like fried chicken."

He reached for two paper plates, obviously about to help her dish up food for the kids. "I don't think there's a person in the world who doesn't like fried chicken."

Watching him help Owen get his dinner, she pressed her lips together. There was so much about Wyatt that was likable, perfect. And she wasn't just talking about his good looks, charm and sex appeal. He liked her kids. Genuinely liked them. Plus, with the exception of the last wedding, they always had fun together. They understood each other.

Hell, he was the first person—the only person—to know her whole story. It didn't seem right that this had to end.

She put three stars on the plus column for a relationship. He liked her kids. He was fun to be around. He knew her past and didn't think any less of her for it.

They settled on the worn bench seats, said grace and dug into dinner.

He groaned with ecstasy.

She smiled. Whoever said the way to a

man's heart was his through stomach must have known tall, perpetually hungry Wyatt.

"This is fantastic."

"Just a little something I can whip up at a moment's notice." Not that she was bragging, but it never hurt to remind him that she wasn't just a businesswoman and mother. There were as many facets to her as there were to any of the women he dated in Florida. She smoothed her palms down the front of her shorts. After cooking the chicken, she'd changed into her best pink shirt, the one her former coworkers told her brought out the best in her skin tones. And thinking of the bikini-clad beach bunnies he probably met in Florida, she was glad she looked her best. But sitting across from him, acknowledging the realities of his life, she fought the doubts that beat at her brain.

How did a thirty-three-year-old mother of triplets compete with beach bunnies?

Should she even try?

Wasn't she setting herself up for failure?

They ate dinner with Owen and the girls giggling happily. Owen grinned with his mouth full and made Lainie say, "Oh, gross! Tell him to stop that."

But Missy only smiled, glad to have her mind off Wyatt for a few seconds. It was good to see Owen behave like a little boy. Gross or not.

When they were done eating, Wyatt helped her clear the picnic table and bring everything into the kitchen. She persuaded him to help her tidy up, delaying his visit, but she could see he was eager to go.

Fears and doubts pummeled her. He'd talked so little she was beginning to believe he'd already made up his mind. And if he'd set his course on forgetting her, wouldn't it be embarrassing to talk about thinking of a compromise for them? That kiss on Saturday, the one that had gotten away from them and knocked both of them to their knees, proved there was something powerful between them. Something she wanted. Something he seemed to be afraid of.

And even now he was straining toward the door.

Owen popped into the kitchen, already bathed. His sisters were now in the tub. With his pajama top on backward, he raced to Wyatt with a huge storybook. Big and shiny, with a colorful cover, it hid half his body.

"You wead this to me?"

"I don't know, buddy. I should get going."

Missy waited in silence. She could nudge

Wyatt into reading the book, but this was a big part of what she'd want in any man she let into her life. A real love for her kids. Wyatt had shown he loved to play. He'd also shown a certain kinship with Owen. But when the chips were down, when he wanted to leave, would he stay?

He stooped down. "I'm kinda tired."

Owen rolled his eyes. "It takes five minutes."

Then the most wonderful thing happened. Wyatt laughed. He laughed long and hard. When he was done, he scooped Owen up, book and all, and carried him down the hall. "Which one's your room?"

Missy scrambled behind them. "They all still sleep in the same room. I'm waiting until Owen's a little older before I make him sleep by himself."

When they reached the bedroom, Wyatt tossed Owen on his bed. He giggled with delight.

The girls ran into the bedroom. Dressed in their pink nighties, they raced to their beds and slid under the covers.

Wyatt sat on the edge of Owen's bed. He opened the book.

"'The adventures of Billy Bunny,'" he read,

and Missy leaned against the door frame, "'began behind the barn.'"

He glanced back at Missy. "A lot of alliteration in this thing."

"Kids like that…and things that rhyme."

He nodded. "Point taken."

He turned his attention back to the book. "'A curious bunny, he spent his days exploring.'"

Missy watched silently, noting how the girls lay on their backs and closed their eyes, letting the words lead them to dreamland. But Owen sat up, looked at the pages, looked at Wyatt with real love in his eyes.

And that's when Missy fell in love. Or maybe admitted the love she'd had for Wyatt ever since they'd been on his bike and she'd laid her head on his back. This guy wasn't just sexy and smart. He had a real heart. For her kids. For her—if that kiss was anything to go by.

And she suddenly knew that was why he'd been so closed off. He was falling for her and he didn't want to be. What he felt for her was about more than sex. And it scared him.

When the story ended, he shut the book. Owen had snuggled into his side, but his eyes drooped.

"Wead it again."

Wyatt rose, shifting Owen to his pillow as he did so. "You're sleepy."

"But I wike it."

He pulled the covers to Owen's chin. "And you can hear it again tomorrow."

Owen's eyes drifted shut. Missy pushed away from the door frame, smiling at Wyatt as he flicked off the bedside lamp and walked out of the room.

"Thanks."

He stepped into the hall.

She closed the door behind him. If what he felt for her was about more than sex, more than a fling, then she definitely wanted it. "Want a beer?"

He cleared his throat. "I need to get home."

"Please? Just five minutes."

He rubbed his hand along the back of his neck. "Let's talk on the porch."

On the way to her kitchen door, she grabbed two bottles of beer. She understood why he was afraid. If falling for him had scared and confused her, she could only imagine what it felt like to be a newly divorced guy falling for a woman with three needy kids. But she wasn't asking him to marry her. At least not now. All she wanted was a little time. A visit or two after he returned to his real life, and maybe the option for her and the triplets to visit him this winter.

As the screen door slapped closed behind her, she handed him a beer.

He looked at the bottle, looked at her. "We shouldn't do this."

"What? Drink? We're both over twenty-one. Besides, we limited ourselves to a bottle. We're strong, mature and responsible that way."

He let out a sigh. "That's just it. You are strong and mature and responsible. I am not."

"You think you're not, but I see it every day."

"Trust me. You're seeing a side of me that few people ever do."

She smiled. "I suspected that."

As if wanting to prove himself to be irresponsible and immature, he guzzled his beer and handed the empty to her.

"In Florida I'm moody, bossy and pushy."

"You've been pretty moody, bossy and pushy here, too, but you're also good to the kids, good to me, fun to be around, considerate."

He groaned and turned away. When he

faced her again frustration poured from him. "Don't make me into something I'm not!"

At his shout, she backed up a step. "I'm not."

"You are! What you see as good things, I see as easy steps. Who wouldn't enjoy a few weeks of playing with kids, no stress, no pressure? Even helping you with cakes and money and finding a van—those things were fun. But in a few days I go home, and when I do, I'll be back to working ten- and twelve-hour days, pushing my employees, making my parents crazy when I bow out of invitations I'd agreed to because they suddenly don't suit me." His voice softened on the last words. He reached out and gently stroked Missy's cheek. "I wish I was the guy you think I am. But I'm not." He snorted. "Just ask my ex-wife."

He took one final long look at her, then bounded off the porch, down the steps and across her yard. She stood watching him, her heart sighing in her chest.

His anger had surprised her, but the way his voice had softened and his eyes filled with longing meant more than his words. He talked about a person she didn't know. Someone impossible to get along with. He'd been a little pushy and bossy around her, but not so much that he was offensive or even hard to handle. Yet it was clear he saw himself as impossible to get along with.

So how could the guy who was so good to her kids, so good to her, think himself impossible to get along with?

Running his company couldn't make him feel that way. He'd never been anything but calm, cool and collected when discussing her business. He knew he was smart. He knew what he was doing.

Unless dealing with a scheming wife, a woman who'd insinuated herself into his company, had made him suspicious, bossy, difficult—out of necessity?

And being away from his ex and the business had brought back the nice guy he was?

That had to be it. It was the only theory that made sense.

Around his ex-wife, he'd always had to be on guard and careful, so he didn't see how good he was. But Missy did. And somehow between now and the day he left, she was going to have to get him to see it, too.

CHAPTER TEN

WHEN WYATT GLANCED OUT the window Saturday afternoon, Missy wasn't carrying a cake with Nancy, the babysitter. She and her assistant, Elaine, lugged the huge violet creation to the back of her new van.

Pride enveloped him. This week's cake was huge and fancy. Flowers made ropes of color that looped from layer to layer. It reminded him of the Garden of Eden.

But as he admired her in her pretty pink dress, a dress that complemented the cake, he realized he wouldn't be scrambling to put on clean clothes, or driving with her to a wedding reception, helping to set up, telling her how much he liked her latest cake, dancing, almost kissing—actually kissing. His breath stalled. That last kiss had been amazing.

Still, forcing her to hire her assistant quickly had been the right thing to do. He didn't want any more time with her. He didn't want to lead her on and he didn't want her getting any more wild ideas that he was a nice guy. This—her leaving without him—was for the best.

She got behind the steering wheel and her assistant jumped into the passenger's side. As Missy put the van into Reverse and started out of the driveway, she called, "See you later, kids!"

He watched her leave, his heart just heavy enough to make him sad, but not so heavy that he believed he'd done the wrong thing in standing her on her own two feet and then stepping back.

He turned to face another bed full of boxes, this one in the first of two extra bedrooms. His grandmother might have been a neat, organized hoarder, but she'd been a hoarder all the same. He worked for hours, until his back began to ache. Then he glanced out the window longingly. On this sunny May afternoon, he had no intention of spending any more time inside, looking for jewelry that he was beginning to believe did not exist.

He slid into flip-flops and jogged down his back porch steps. Ducking under the shrub, he noticed the kids were in the sandbox. Nancy sat on the bench seat of the old wooden picnic table.

He ambled over. "Hey."

Owen's head shot up. "Hey, Wyatt."

"Hey, Owen." He faced the babysitter. "Can I play?"

Nancy rose from the picnic table. "Actually, I was hoping you'd come over."

He peeked at her. Sixteen, pretty and probably very popular, she reminded Wyatt of the sitters his mom used to hire when he was a kid. Young. Impressionable.

He wasn't sure he should be glad she was hoping he'd come over. "You were?"

She winced. "Tomorrow's Mother's Day and I forgot to get my mom a gift."

"Oh, shoot!" He winced with her, happy her gladness at seeing him was innocent, but also every bit as guilty as she was about the Mother's Day gift. "I forgot, too."

"I'll tell you what. You give me fifteen minutes to run to the florist and I'll order both of our moms flowers."

He waved his hand in dismissal. "That's okay. I can do mine online. You go, though. There's nothing worse than forgetting Mother's Day."

"My mother would freak."

He laughed. "My mother would double freak."

"So you're okay with the kids? The florist is on Main Street and I can be there and back in fifteen minutes."

"If they're not crowded."

She grimaced. "Yeah. If they're not crowed."

He slid out of his flip-flops. "Take your time. We'll be fine."

When she was gone, the triplets shifted and moved until there was enough space for Wyatt in the sandbox. They decided to build a shopping center, which made Owen happy and also pleased the girls, who—though he hadn't thought them old enough to understand shopping—seemed to have the concept down pat.

After five minutes of moving sand, Owen suddenly said, "What's Mother's Day?"

"That's the day you buy your mom…" Wyatt stopped, suddenly understanding the three big-eyed kids who hung on his every word. He didn't have to do the math to know that they'd never bought their mother a gift for Mother's Day. Their dad had been gone on their first Mother's Day. Missy's mom was dead, so they'd never seen Missy buy a Mother's Day gift. Missy's dad was worthless, so there had been no one to tell them about Mother's Day, let alone help them choose gifts.

"It's the day kids buy their mom a present—usually flowers—so she knows that they love her."

Owen studied him solemnly. "We love our mom."

Wyatt's heart squeezed. The temptation to help them order flowers was strong, but this was exactly the kind of thing he shouldn't be doing. It was easy, goofy things like this that made Missy think he was nice.

He wasn't. He was a cutthroat businessman.

He cleared his throat. "Yeah. I know you love your mom."

Lainie tapped on his knee. "So we should get her flowers."

The desire to do that rumbled through him. He didn't just want to help these kids; he also knew Missy deserved a Mother's Day gift.

Ah, hell. Who was he kidding? Wild horses couldn't stop him from helping them. Somehow he'd downplay his role in things.

He pulled out his phone. "And that's why we're going to order some."

All three kids stared at him, hope shining

from their big eyes. He looked down at the small screen before him. It seemed too impersonal to buy their first ever Mother's Day gift from a tiny screen on a phone. Particularly since the babysitter had said the florist was a five-minute walk away.

He rose, dusted off his butt. "You know what? I think we should do a field trip."

Lainie gaped at him as if he'd grown a second head. "We're going to a field?"

He laughed. "We're going to the florist." He looked down. All three kids had on tennis shoes. They were reasonably clean. He had credit cards in his wallet in his back pocket. They were set.

He caught Lainie's hand, then Claire's. "Owen, can you be a big boy and walk ahead of us?"

His chest puffed out with pride. "Yeth."

Lainie dropped his hand. "I can walk ahead, too."

Wyatt laughed. The little brunette had definitely inherited her mother's spunk—and maybe a little of her competitiveness. "Go for it."

They strode out of the drive, Claire holding his hand, Owen sort of marching and Lainie pirouetting ahead of him. Wyatt directed them to turn right, then herded them across the quiet street and turned right again.

The walk took more like ten minutes, not the five Nancy had said, and Wyatt ended up carrying Claire, but they made it.

Owen opened the door to the florist shop and a bell sounded as they entered.

Because it was late afternoon, probably close to closing time, the place was almost empty. Nancy was at the counter, paying for her flowers.

She grinned when she saw the kids. "Hi, guys." Then she glanced at Wyatt. "What's up?"

"We've decided to get flowers, too. For Missy."

Her eyes widened with understanding. "What a great idea! Do you want me to stay and help?"

"No. We'll meet you back at the house."

She kissed each kid's cheek, then headed for the door, a huge purple flowery thing in her hands.

Wyatt faced the clerk. "What was that?"

The fifty-something woman smiled. "Hydrangeas." She peered into Claire's face. "I recognize the little Brooks kids, but I'm not familiar with you."

"I'm Wyatt…" His eyes narrowed as he read her name tag. "Mrs. Zedik?"

"Yes?"

"You taught me in fourth grade."

She looked closer. "I can't place you."

"That's because I wear contacts instead of big thick glasses. I'm Wyatt McKenzie."

She gasped. "Well, good gravy! Wyatt McKenzie. What brings you home?"

"Looking through things in Gram's house. Making sure she doesn't have a Rembrandt that gets sold for three dollars and fifty cents at the garage sale the real estate agent is going to have once we put the house on the market."

The woman laughed. "And what are you doing with the Brooks triplets?"

Lainie and Owen blinked up at her.

From her position on Wyatt's arm, Claire said, "We're shopping for Mother's Day flowers."

Mrs. Zedik came out from behind the counter. "And what kind of flowers do you want?"

Lainie said, "Pink."

Claire said, "Yellow."

Owen pointed at a huge bushlike thing. "Those."

Mrs. Zedik laughed. "Well, I might be able

to find the azaleas the boy wants in pink. That way two kids would get what they want."

Claire caught Wyatt's face and turned it to her. "I want yellow."

He said to Mrs. Zedik, "She wants yellow."

"So we'll pick two flowers."

"How about if we let each kid get the flower they want?" He set Claire on the floor and reached for his credit card. "Sky's the limit on this thing."

With a chuckle she took the card. "I heard you made some money."

"Yeah. And it's no fun having money if you can't use it to make people happy." He stooped to the kids' level. "Pick what you want. Everybody gets a flower to give to your mom." Then he rose. "Any chance I can get these delivered?"

She winced. "Depends on how soon you want them. Van's out making deliveries now. Won't be back for at least two hours."

"It would be nice if she'd get them tomorrow morning."

Mrs. Zedik made a face. "We don't actually deliver on Mother's Day. It's Sunday."

"How about this? You deliver these flowers to my house this evening and I'll take care of the kids getting them to their mom in the morning."

"That sounds good."

Even as he spoke, Lainie called out, "I want this one."

Claire said, "I want this one."

Lainie looked at Claire's flower, then her own. "I want that one, too."

Mrs. Z walked up behind him. "I do have two of those."

"Okay, we'll get two of those and Owen's bush."

Owen said, "I want one of these, too." He pointed at an arrangement.

Lainie said, "I want one of those, too."

Mrs. Z's eyebrows rose.

Wyatt sucked in a quick breath. "Might be easier to let them each pick two."

"Can I have one of those?" This time Owen pointed at a vase in a cooler with a long-stemmed red rose.

"Owen, that would be three flowers."

He nodded.

Wyatt laughed.

Mrs. Z smiled. "You said money was no fun unless you spent it."

"I'm just hoping you have a van big enough to get them everything they want."

"I think it's sweet."

He didn't like thinking about how sweet it was. He'd told Missy the last time they'd talked that he was grouchy and bossy, and usually he was. But how could he resist helping her kids show her that they love her? "Actually, it's more of a necessity, since I haven't yet figured out how to tell these kids no."

Mrs. Z rounded the counter. "Just let me get a tablet and start writing some of this down."

In the end, they bought nine flower arrangements, three long-stemmed roses in white vases, three Mother's Day floral arrangements and three plants.

He walked the kids back to the house, Owen in the lead with Lainie pirouetting behind him. But when Wyatt slid Claire to the ground again, another thought hit him. He directed them to sit on the bench seat of the picnic table, and crouched in front of them.

"Mother's Day is a special day when moms don't just get flowers, they also aren't supposed to work."

The kids gave him a blank stare.

"At the very least somebody should take them out to breakfast or lunch. So I was thinking we could—"

Owen interrupted him. "We can make breakfast."

"Yeah, we can make breakfast."

Claire tugged on his hand. "I can make toast."

"Well, that would be really cute, but it might be even cuter if—"

The sound of a vehicle pulling into the driveway stopped him. He turned and saw Missy's new van.

He rose as she got out. "What are you doing home so early?"

"Garden wedding. Fifteen-minute service. Then an hour for pictures. Then cake and punch and we were done."

"Where's Elaine?"

"I dropped her off at home."

Missy stooped down and opened her arms. The kids raced into them. "So did you have fun today?"

"We went to—"

"We played in the sandbox," Wyatt interrupted, giving Owen a significant look. "Why don't you go wash up? At least get out of that dress?"

She glanced down at herself. "I guess I should."

"Great. The kids and I will be out here when you're done."

When she was gone, he whirled to face the kids. "The flowers are a secret."

Lainie frowned. "A secret?"

"So that tomorrow morning, we can have a big surprise. We'll hide the flowers at my house tonight, then tomorrow morning I'll sneak them over and we can have them on the kitchen table and your mom will be so surprised."

Owen frowned at him.

"Trust me. Secrets are fun." He paused to let that sink in. "Okay?"

They just looked at him.

Nancy came out of the back door and ambled over. "If you're trying to get them to keep a secret, it's not going to work. Your best bet is to entertain them so well they forget what you did today. And above all else don't say the one word that will trigger the memory."

This time he frowned. "What word is that?"

"F-l-o-w-e-r-s."

He got it. "Okay. Keep them busy, don't remind them of what we did."

Nancy ambled away, tucking her babysitting money in the back pocket of her jeans.

Heeding her advice, Wyatt said, "So, aren't we building a shopping mall?"

All three kids raced to the sandbox. When Missy came out, he kept them superinvolved in digging sand. She told Wyatt a bit about the wedding and the cake and the bride and groom, but then got bored and went into the house to make supper.

Wyatt all but breathed a sigh of relief, but fifteen minutes later she brought out hamburger patties and asked him to light the grill.

He didn't want to stay for dinner, and give him and Missy so much time together that his feelings overwhelmed him again, but he had no choice.

The girls picked up their dolls and began to follow Missy into the house. Panicking, he said, "Hey, wanna learn how to grill?"

The girls stopped, grinned and raced back to him.

Missy stopped, too, and faced him. "I was okay with you showing Owen how to light the grill, because he doesn't get to do a lot of boy things, but honestly, they're a little young to learn how to light charcoal briquettes."

"Maybe. But I don't want them to help with

the grill so much as I…want to finish our shopping center."

She laughed. "Really? It's that important to you to be done?"

"We're about to lose the light."

"It's early. You have plenty of light."

"We also have lots of work to do."

She shook her head. "Suit yourself. But everybody has to wash up before they eat."

When she was gone, he directed the kids to the sandbox. "That was close."

Lainie said, "What was close?"

"Nothing." He pointed at some blocks in the sand. "Aren't you building a Macy's?"

She grinned and picked up the blocks.

All three kids got back to work as easily as if building block shopping malls was their real job. Wyatt waited fifteen minutes before he checked on the grill, found the briquettes a nice hot white and set the hamburgers on to cook.

Just as the hamburgers were getting done, Missy came out with buns and potato salad. His mouth watered.

"Are those buns homemade?"

She said, "Mmm-hmm."

His mouth really watered and he made a mental note to find himself a half-decent restaurant, because everything inside him was really liking this. And he knew he could have it, all of it, the kids, Missy, good food, if he could just pretend that he was the nice guy she thought he was.

But he wasn't.

They sat down to eat and Wyatt forced himself not to gush with praise over how delicious the food was. Then Owen unexpectedly said, "Hey, you know where we went today?"

It was everything Wyatt could do not to slap his hand over Owen's mouth to keep him quiet. Instead he said, "We went for a walk," as he gave Owen a look he hoped would remind him they weren't supposed to talk about the florist.

Owen's eyes widened, then he sheepishly looked away. But Lainie said, "I danced in the street."

Missy's head jerked up. "What?"

"When we went for our walk, I let her walk ahead of me and she sort of did those circle things ballet dancers do," Wyatt said.

"In the street?"

"There were no cars coming."

"No. But you're teaching them bad habits

if you let them get too casual about crossing the street."

"Good point," he said, hoping that his easy acquiescence would smooth things over. "So your bride really liked your cake?"

Missy took a breath. Wyatt couldn't tell if it was an annoyed breath or a relieved breath.

Then she said, "Yes. The bride loved the cake." She set her fork down and smiled. "I told you I got four referrals."

"So how's your calendar looking these days?"

"Really good. I'll have to work with Elaine a lot to see if she can handle setting up a cake alone, but that's all part of being a start-up business. Everything's an experiment."

"Do you like yellow flowers?"

Wyatt's gaze jumped to Claire, who was sliding her fork around her plate as if she was bored, then over to Missy.

Missy's gaze had gone to the rows of yellow flowers around her house. She laughed. "Yes. I obviously love yellow flowers."

Claire grinned and glanced at Owen. "Told you."

Lainie said, "I like pink."

Wyatt jumped from his seat. "You know

what? I think we should help your mom with these dishes."

Missy laughed. "Sit. We have plenty of time. Besides, they're paper plates. We'll toss them."

"I know, but shouldn't we get this potato salad into the refrigerator?"

She frowned. "Because of the mayonnaise?"

He didn't have a clue in hell, but he said, "Yes."

"Hmm." She rose. "Maybe."

He waved her down. "Sit! The kids and I will do it."

"Why are you spoiling me?"

"We're not spoiling you. We're—" Shoot. He almost said something about starting Mother's Day early. He wasn't any better at this than the kids.

"We know you worked hard."

Owen tugged on his jeans. "I worked hard."

"We all worked hard," Wyatt agreed. "But your mom's the only one who got paid for her work, so the rest of us are freeloaders."

Owen's face scrunched in confusion.

"Which is why we need to earn our supper by cleaning up."

Not entirely on board with the idea, Owen

nonetheless got up from the table and helped Wyatt and his sisters clear away the paper plates and gather the silverware. In the kitchen, he gave each triplet a dish towel and stood over them as they dried silverware.

Missy came in carrying the potato salad. "I thought the whole purpose of getting up from the table was to bring this in."

He winced. "Sorry."

She laughed. "Your memory's about as good as mine."

They finished the silverware and cleared the kitchen table, and then there was nothing to do.

No reason to keep himself in their company.

No way he could make sure none of the kids talked about their surprise.

Owen tugged on his jeans. "You weed me a stowwy?"

Right! Story! "Only if you take your bath first."

Owen's head swiveled to Missy. "Can we?"

She frowned. "It's early."

"I never heard of a mother thinking her kids were settling in for the night too early."

Her frown deepened. "I suppose not. It's just not like them."

"Well, we did have a busy day."

She sighed. "Okay."

"Yippee!" Owen raced to the bathroom. Missy tried to fill the tub, but Wyatt shooed her away. "I'll bathe Owen. You do the girls."

When Owen was bathed and in his pj's, Wyatt stood at the closed bathroom door, listening to the girls' chatter, hoping they didn't mention the flowers.

Apparently the promise of a story was enough to take their minds in another direction. Both Claire and Lainie raced through their baths. He smiled, listening to them talk to their mom, who told them about the bride's dress and how handsome the groom looked in his tux, making her work that day seem like part of a big fairy tale. A sweet, wonderful fairy tale where moms loved their kids and grooms didn't get divorced.

Wouldn't that be nice?

"What are you doing?"

Wyatt glanced down at Owen, who had the big Billy Bunny book again. "Waiting for the girls."

"Oh." He grinned. "I'll wait, too."

Wyatt almost argued, but with the little boy quiet beside him, he decided to take his victories where he could. When the doorknob rattled, he turned Owen toward the bedroom and they scooted down the hall. When the girls arrived in their pink nighties, he and Owen were on Owen's bed, looking as if they'd been there the whole time.

Owen handed him the book.

He frowned. "Billy Bunny again?"

"We wike it."

"Yeah," Claire said as she climbed into her bed. "We like it."

He opened the book. "Okay."

He read it twice, dragging out the story as much as he could, hoping to tire the kids. By the end of the second read through, the girls were asleep and Owen was nodding off.

When Wyatt finished, he slid out of bed, put Owen's head on the pillow and leaned down to brush a kiss across his forehead. For three kids who loved to talk, keeping their secret had probably been something akin to torture, but they'd come through like three little troupers.

He straightened away and saw Missy in the doorway, watching him with a smile. He remembered her portrayal for the girls of that day's wedding, with the handsome groom and the love-struck bride. He could almost see him and Missy standing in a flower-covered gazebo, him in a tux, her in a gown. Lainie pirouetting everywhere.

He shook his head to clear the picture. That was so wrong.

As he reached the door, he shooed her into the hall and closed the door behind him. Faking a yawn, he said, "I guess I better get going, too."

"Seriously? If I didn't know better I'd think the four of you really had been working on a shopping mall."

"Actually, I think keeping track of three kids for eight hours is harder than building a shopping mall."

She laughed, her pretty blue eyes filled with delight. "It's how I keep my girlish figure."

He glanced down, took in every curve of her nearly perfect form and swallowed hard. "You should write a book. It could be the newest diet craze. You could call it 'how to look eighteen even though you're thirty-three.'"

"You think I look eighteen?"

I think you look fantastic. The words tickled his tongue, pirouetted like Lainie across his teeth. He held them back only because he knew it was for her own good that she didn't know how beautiful he thought she was.

"Listen, I really have to go."

"Oh."

The disappointment in her voice nearly did him in. He hesitated, but gritted his teeth. He wasn't right for her. She deserved somebody better.

He headed for the door. "I'll see you tomorrow."

"Oh?"

Damn it! He really wasn't any better at this than the kids. Worse, he knew the flowers the next day would make her like him again.

He really wasn't very good at this.

That night he set his alarm for five o'clock, wanting to get up before Missy did. Still tired, he groaned when it rang, but he forced himself out of bed. Missy deserved a Mother's Day.

One by one, he carried the flower arrangements to her porch. When he realized he didn't have a key, he felt along the top of the door, looked under the mat and finally found one under an odd-looking rock in the small flower garden beside the bottom step to her porch.

He let himself in and began carrying flowers into the kitchen. With all nine pots and vases on the table, he found eggs in her refrigerator and bread for the toaster and started their simple breakfast.

Before even the first two slices of bread popped, Owen sleepily ambled into the kitchen. Claire followed a few seconds behind him and Lainie a few seconds after that.

"Everybody has to be quiet," he whispered as the kids raced to the table filled with their flowers.

Missy awakened to the oddest noise. She could have sworn it was a pop. Or was it a bang?

Oh, Lord. A woman with three kids did not like to hear a bang. She whipped off her covers and ran to the kitchen, only to find a table full of flowers, Wyatt with his arms up to the elbows in sudsy water and Claire standing on the step stool making toast.

Missy walked into the kitchen. "What's this?"

Everybody froze at the sound of her voice.

Wyatt said, "What did we practice?"

All three kids shouted, "Happy Mother's Day."

Owen raced over and caught her around the knees, hugging for all he was worth. Claire bounced off the step stool and ran over, too. Lainie danced to the flowers. "These are yours."

Her heart stuttered. Tears pricked her eyelids. She pressed her fingers to her lips. Three azalea bushes towered over the lower "fancy" arrangements, which had plastic decorations stuck among the flowers that proclaimed Happy Mother's Day! Three long-stemmed red roses sat in tall milk-glass vases.

She swallowed. Four Mother's Days had come and gone with no recognition, and truth be told, she'd been too busy to notice. If anything, she mourned her mom on Mother's Day.

She walked to the table, ran her fingers along the velvety petal of one of the roses. How could a man who thought to help her kids get her flowers for Mother's Day—a man who was making her breakfast, which she could smell was now burning—think he wasn't nice?

Her eyes filled with tears, half from the surprise and half from sorrow for him. His ex had really done a number on him.

She peeked over at Wyatt. "Thanks."

Flipping scrambled eggs, which smoked

when he shifted them, he said, "It was nothing."

It was everything. But she couldn't tell him that.

This guy, who was probably the kindest, most considerate person she'd ever known, didn't have any idea how good he was.

She looked at him—organizing the kids, tossing Claire's burned toast into the trash, starting over with the scrambled eggs—and something happened inside her chest.

She'd already realized that she loved him. She'd tried a few halfhearted attempts to let him know, and even an attempt to ask him if she could visit him or if he could visit her again. But somehow she'd never been able to get out the right words. And she'd never actually led him into the will-you-visit-us or can-we-visit-you conversation.

Still, the sense she had this time, the strong sense that burst inside her and caused her spine to straighten and her brain to shift into gear, told her the days of halfhearted attempts were gone. She wanted this man in her life forever.

And by God, she would figure out a way to keep him.

CHAPTER ELEVEN

AFTER BREAKFAST, Owen and his sisters directed Missy to the living room recliner. Wyatt handed her the Sunday paper. Lainie found the side controller and flipped up the footrest.

Missy laughed. "You're spoiling me."

"Oh, I have a feeling one day of spoiling won't hurt you." Wyatt turned to the door. "We'll clean the kitchen, then get the kids out of pj's into shorts so that we can play outside."

Laughing again, she opened the paper and read until Wyatt had all three kids dressed and on their way out the door.

As soon as they were gone, she leaped out of the chair and found her cell phone.

"Nancy? It's me, Missy Brooks. Are you busy tonight?"

If she was going to seduce Wyatt McKenzie, she couldn't do it with a baby monitor in her right hand. She needed a sitter.

A little after nine that night, a knock on the door surprised Wyatt. He was in bedroom number three now. After caring for the kids that afternoon, giving Missy a break, his heart had hurt so much he'd come home and begun digging. He needed to find his grandmother's jewelry and get home before he said or did something he'd regret. Something that would ultimately hurt Missy.

The knock sounded again. "I'm coming! I'm coming!"

He raced to the door and whipped it open. There stood Missy, her hair wet from the unexpected spring rain, her eyes shining with laughter.

She displayed a bottle of wine. "It's a thank-you."

He looked at the bottle. What he'd done for her, the flowers, the breakfast, those were simple things someone should have thought to do four years ago. Yet she didn't let a kindness go unnoticed. She took the time to do something nice in return.

That was part of why he liked her so much.

Part of why she was so tempting. Part of why she was too good for him.

He opened the door and took it. "Thanks. But I'm—"

But as he tried to close the door again, she wedged her way inside. "I brought the wine for *us* to drink."

"Oh." That couldn't happen. Wine made him romantic. And after an afternoon with three kids he was coming to adore, and an emotional morning of being proud of himself for helping her kids give her a real Mother's Day, the two of them alone with a bottle of wine was not such a good idea.

Thinking fast, he said, "Well, then we'll have to drink it while we look for jewelry. That's the agenda for tonight."

She rolled up her sleeves. "I don't mind."

Of course she didn't. She might like him, but she didn't seem to be experiencing the heart-stopping, fiery attraction he had for her. Drinking wine like two friends, digging through boxes for Scottish jewelry that may or may not exist, was a fun evening for her.

Watching her, hearing her laugh, wanting her so much he ached all over, would be an evening of torture for him.

Still, he got two glasses, pulled the cork from the wine and led her to the bedroom.

He poured two glasses of wine and handed one to her.

She peeked up and smiled. "Thanks."

His heart zigzagged through his chest. Her eyes sparkled. Her face glowed with happiness. He knew he was responsible for her happiness and part of him just wanted to take the credit for what he'd done, to accept her gratitude by kissing her senseless and—

Oh, boy. That "and" was exactly where they shouldn't go.

He turned away. "You're welcome." He put his glass to his lips, but instead of taking a sip, he gulped, then had to refill his glass.

She laughed. "I know you hate looking for this jewelry, but be careful with the wine."

"I'm not going anywhere." He couldn't keep his voice from sounding just a tad childish and bitter. And why shouldn't he be? The woman he'd always loved was at his fingertips, but he was too much of a gentleman to take her.

Damn his stupid manners! He was going to have a long talk with his mother when he got home.

"Let's just get to work."

She looked around with a smile, sipped her wine, then turned her smile on him. "Where do we start?"

"Those boxes there." He pointed at a tall stack. "Are all things I've gone through." He pointed at another stack. "So start there."

She walked over to the pile, sat on the floor and went to work on the shoe boxes, popping lids, pouring out junk, sifting through it for jewelry, and then moving on to the next box, as he'd explained to her the day her kids had helped him.

They worked in silence for at least twenty minutes. Done with her stack, she moved to the one beside it.

"I had to go through a lot of junk when my gram died, too."

Her voice eased into the silent room. Okay with the neutral comment, he said, "Really?"

"Yep. She wasn't quite the packrat your gram seemed to be, but she kept a lot of mason jars in the basement."

He laughed. "So she was a jelly maker."

"And she loved to can her own spaghetti sauce." Missy sighed. "She was such a bright spot in my life."

"My gram was, too. That's why I moved her down to Florida with us."

"So what do you have down there to fit all these people? A mansion?"

He laughed again. "No one lives with me. I got my gram a town house and my parents have a house near mine on the Gulf."

"Sounds nice."

He glanced over. Usually when he told someone he had a house on the Gulf, they oohed and ahhed. She seemed happy for him, but not really impressed. "It's a six-thousand-square-foot mansion with walls of windows to take advantage of the view."

She winced. "You're lucky you can afford to hire someone to clean that."

His gaze winged over to her. Was she always so practical? "I don't get it very dirty."

"Was that the house you shared with your wife?"

"She got the big house."

Missy gaped at him. "She didn't think six thousand square feet was good enough?"

"She didn't think anything was good enough." He stopped himself. Since when did he talk about Betsy? About his marriage?

Missy shrugged. "Makes sense."

Cautious, but curious, because to him nothing about Betsy made sense, he said, "What makes sense?"

"That you divorced. It sounds like you had two different ideas of what you wanted."

He'd never thought of it that way. "I guess we did."

"So what was she like?"

"Tall, pretty." The words were out before he even thought to stop them. "She'd been a pageant girl."

"Oh, very pretty then."

He laughed. "Why are you asking questions about my ex?"

Missy caught his gaze. "Scoping out the competition."

He choked on his wine. "The competition?"

"Yeah. I like you." She said it naturally, easily, as if it didn't make any difference in the world. "I really like you. And I don't want to find out what to do or not do to get you to like me. I'm just trying to figure out what makes you you."

He set his wineglass down on the table. "Don't."

"Why not?"

"Because we've already been over this. My ex did a number on me. Even if I wasn't only a month out of a divorce, I wouldn't want to get involved again."

"It might be a month since you divorced,

but if you fought over the settlement for four years, you haven't been married for four years."

"What?"

"You heard me. You keep saying you've only been divorced a month, but you've been out of your relationship a lot longer." She took a sip of wine. "Have you dated?"

His eyebrows rose. "I was separated. I was allowed to date."

"I'm not criticizing. I'm just helping you to understand something." She paused with a gasp. "Hey, look at this!"

The enthusiasm in her voice drew his gaze. She held up a small round thing with a woman's face on it.

She beamed. "It's a cameo."

He cautiously said, "That's good?"

"Not only does it look really old, but it's clear it was expensive." She examined it. "Wow."

He scrambled over. "What else is in that box?"

She rose, taking the box with her, and sat on the bed.

He sat beside her.

She pulled out matching combs. "These

are hair combs." She studied them. "They're so pretty."

He reached in and retrieved a delicate necklace. Reddish stones and silver dominated the piece. "No wonder my mom wanted them."

"Yeah."

Missy's voice trembled on the one simple word, and even though she hadn't said it, he knew what troubled her. He set the necklace back in the box, as sadness overwhelmed him, too. "So. I found what I came for."

"Yeah. You did."

And now he could go home.

Silence settled over them. Then he peeked at her and she peeked at him. He'd never see her again. Oh, tomorrow morning after he packed, he'd walk over and say goodbye to her and the kids. But this was the very last time they'd be alone together. Once he returned to Florida, he wasn't coming back. He had a life that didn't include her, and in that life he wasn't this normal, selfless guy she was falling in love with. He was a bossy, moody, selfish businessman who now had to deal with an ex-wife who owned one-third of his company. She might not have controlling interest, but she had enough of a say to make his life miserable.

And he wouldn't waste the ten or so minutes he had with the genuinely kind, selfless woman sitting beside him, by thinking about his bad marriage.

Though Missy had paid him back for the kiss they should have had graduation night, he bent and brushed his lips across hers. He went to pull back, but she caught him around the neck and kept him where he was, answering his kiss with one that was so soft and sweet, his chest tightened.

When her tongue peeked out and swiped across his lips, his control slipped. This was the one person he'd felt connected to since he was a geek and she was a prom queen. For once, just once, he wanted to feel what it would be like to be hers. He took over the kiss, and suddenly they were both as greedy as he'd always wanted to be.

As his mouth plundered hers, his hands ran down her arms, then scrambled back up again. Her velvety skin teased him with the promise of other softer skin hidden beneath her clothes. She wrapped her arms around his back and the feelings he'd had when she'd clung to him that day on the motorcycle returned. All that trust, all that love, in one simple gesture.

She loved him.

The thought stopped him cold. No matter what he did now, she would be hurt when he left. So would it be so bad to make love, to give them both a memory?

Yes. It would be bad. It would give her false hope. It would tear him up inside to leave her.

When he pulled away, he didn't merely feel the physical loss, he felt the emotional loss. But he knew he'd done the right thing.

Missy rose from the bed. She paced around the little room as if deliberating, then swung to face him. "You know, I never felt alone. Not once in the four years after my husband left, until I began missing you."

The sadness in her voice pricked his heart. He'd deliberately held himself back the past few days. He knew that's why she'd missed him. Still, he said, "I'm not even gone yet."

"No, but you always pull away."

"I have to. One of us has to be smart about this."

"How do you know I want to be smart? Couldn't I once, just once, get something I want without worrying about tomorrow?"

Yearning shuddered through him. He wanted this night, too. And if she didn't stop pushing, he would take it. "Right from the beginning you've told me your kids come first, and the best way to protect them is to keep yourself from doing stupid things."

She faced him with sad blue eyes. "Would making love with the first guy I've been attracted to in four years really be stupid?"

His blasted need roared inside him. For fifteen years he'd wished she was attracted to him. Now that she was, he had to turn her away. Everything inside him rebelled at the idea. Everything except the gentleman his mother had raised. He knew this was the right thing. "That's not a reason to do this."

"Okay, then." She smiled. "How about this? I love you."

The very thought stole his breath. Missy Johnson, prettiest girl he'd ever met, girl he'd been in love with forever, woman who'd made the past four weeks fun, loved him.

He'd guessed that already, but hearing her say it was like music. Still, practicality ruled him. He snorted a laugh. "Right. In four weeks, you've fallen in love?"

"What's so hard to believe about that?"

"It's not hard to believe. It's just not love. Since I've been here, you haven't merely had company, you've also had an ally for your business. Somebody who saw your potential and wouldn't let you back down or settle for less than what you deserve."

"You know, in some circles that might be taken to mean you love me, too."

Oh, he did. Part of him genuinely believed he did. And the words shivered on his tongue, begging to be released. But his practical side, the rational, logical, hard-nosed businessman, argued that this wasn't love. That everything he believed he felt was either residual feelings from his teen years or rebound feelings. Feelings that would disappear when he went home. Feelings that would get her hopes up and then hurt her.

"I care about you. But I didn't have a good marriage. And for the past four years I've been trapped in hearings and negotiations to keep my wife—ex-wife—from taking everything I'd worked for. In the end we compromised, but I'd be lying if I said I wasn't bitter. And what you think I feel—" He snorted a laugh. "Hell, what I think I feel isn't love. It's rebound. You're everything she wasn't. And I need to go home. Get back to my real life."

Hurt to her very core, Missy walked around the bedroom. There was no way she could let the conversation end like this. She picked up one of the broaches that meant so much to his family. He had roots. He'd always had stability. He didn't know what it was like to be alone and wanting. So he didn't know how desperate she was to hang on to the first person in her life she really loved. And the first person, she believed, to really love her.

"You've never once seemed bitter around me."

"That's because I've been happy around you." When her gaze darted to his, he held up his hand to stop what she wanted to say. "Or maybe it was more that around you I was occupied." He ran his fingers through his hair. "Look, I'm not going to lie to you by telling you leaving will be easy. It won't. You and the kids mean more to me than anybody ever has. But the timing is wrong. And if I stay or ask you to come with me, one of us is going to get hurt." He sucked in a breath. "And it won't be me. I'm selfish. I'm stubborn. I usually take what I want, so be glad I'm giving you a way out."

Her lips trembled. She'd presented all her best arguments and he wasn't budging. She had a choice. Stay and embarrass herself by crying in front of him, maybe even begging him to stay, or go—lose any chance of keeping him here, but salvage her pride.

She glanced up at him, saw the look of sadness on his face and knew the next step was pity. Pity for the woman who was left by her ex. Pity for the woman who was only now getting her life together after her father's abuse.

Pride rescued her. She would never settle for anybody's pity.

She softly sucked in a breath to hold off the tears, and smiled. Though it killed her, she forced her lips to bow upward, her tears to stay right where they were, shimmying on her eyelids.

"You know what? You're right. You probably are a totally different guy in Florida. I *am* just starting out. It is better not to pursue this."

"Two years from now you'll be so busy and so successful you'll forget who I am."

Oh, he was wrong about that. She'd never forget him. But he was also right. She would be busy. Her kids would be well dressed, well loved, happy. She would have all the shiny wonderful toys every baker wanted. Hell, she'd probably have her own building by then.

Still, she wouldn't let him off the hook. In

some ways she believed he needed to be loved even more than she did. She loved him and he needed to know that. "I will be busy, but I won't forget you."

Her heart caught in her throat and she couldn't say any more. She turned to the door and walked out.

He didn't try to follow her.

CHAPTER TWELVE

MISSY AWAKENED before the kids, rolled out of bed and began baking. Wyatt rejecting her again the night before had stung, but the more she examined their conversation, the tortured expression on his face, the need she felt rolling from him, the more she knew he loved her.

That was the thing that bothered her about his rejecting her. Not her own loss. His. He kept saying he was protecting her from hurt, but in her own sadness she hadn't seen his loss. It took her until three o'clock in the morning to realize that to keep her from hurt he was hurting himself.

If she really believed he didn't want her, she'd let him go without a second thought. But she wasn't going to let him walk away just to protect her. Risk was part of love. Unfortunately, both of them had been in relationships that hadn't panned out, so they were afraid to risk.

Well, she wasn't. Not with Wyatt. He was good, kind, loving. He would never leave her. And she would never leave him. She loved him.

In her pantry, she found the ingredients for lemon cake and meringue frosting. When the kids woke at eight, she fed them, then shooed them out the door to play.

As they sifted through the sand, she took a few peeks outside to see when Wyatt came out to be with them. He didn't. But that didn't bother her. He'd found his jewels the night before. He could be on the phone with his mom or even his staff, making plans to go home.

Which was why she had to get her lemon cake to him as soon as possible so she would have one more chance to talk him out of leaving, or one more chance to talk him into staying in touch, visiting her every few weeks or letting her and the kids visit him.

Elaine arrived at nine. Missy brushed her hands on her apron, then removed it. "Would you mind watching the kids while I quickly deliver this cake next door to Wyatt?"

With a laugh, Elaine said, "No. Go."

Pretty yellow-and-white cake in hand, she

walked through the backyard and dipped through the hole in the shrub. Sucking in a breath for courage, she pounded up the back porch steps and knocked on the kitchen door.

"He's not here."

She spun around to find Owen on her heels. "What?"

"He just weft."

"He just weft?"

Owen nodded. "He said to tell you good-bye."

"Oh."

Wow. Her chest collapsed, as if someone had punched it. Wyatt wasn't even going to tell her goodbye? Shock rendered her speechless, but also prevented her from overtly reacting.

"Well, then let's go home. We'll eat this cake for dessert at suppertime."

Owen eagerly nodded.

But as they clomped down the stairs, the shock began to wear off. Her throat closed. Tears filled her eyes.

It really was over. He didn't want her. All the stuff she'd convinced herself of, that he loved her, that he was protecting her, it was crap.

How many times had he told her he was

a spoiled man, accustomed to getting what he wanted? How many times had he warned her off?

God, she was stupid! What he'd been saying was that if he wanted her, he would have her. And all that pain over leaving her that she'd been so sure she'd seen the night before? She hadn't.

She set the cake on the counter, gave Elaine a list of chores for the day and went to her bedroom. About to throw herself across the bed and weep, she faltered. A shower would cover the noise of her crying. Then she wouldn't have to worry about yet another person, Elaine, feeling sorry for her. She stripped, got into the shower and let the tears fall.

He might not have loved her, but like a fool, she'd fallen for him.

Wyatt had decided to take the bike home. He loved the truck, but he needed the bike. He needed the feeling of the wind on his face to remind him of who he was and what he did and why he hadn't taken what Missy had offered.

Damn it! She'd have slept with him, even after all his warnings.

He stifled the urge to squeeze his eyes shut. She was such a good person. Such a wonderful person. And such a good mom.

A vision of his last five minutes with Owen popped into his head. He'd thought he could slide out the front door, zoom down the steps and get on the bike without being noticed. But the little boy had been at the opening in the shrubs. Just as he had been the day Wyatt arrived.

"Where you goin'?"

He'd stopped, turned to face him. "Home."

"You didn't give me a wide."

No longer having trouble understanding Owen's lisp, he'd laughed, dropped his duffel bag in the little pouch that made the back of the bike's seat, and headed to the opening. When he reached Owen he'd crouched down.

"Actually, I think you're too small to ride a bike."

Owen looked at his tennis shoes. "Oh."

"But don't worry, someday you'll be tall. Not just big enough to ride a bike, but tall."

The little boy grinned at him.

Wyatt ruffled his hair. He started to rise to go, but his heart tightened and he stopped. He opened his arms and Owen stepped into them. He wrapped them around the boy, his eyes filling with tears. This time next week, when the kids went to day care, Owen would forget all about him. But Wyatt had a feeling he'd never forget Owen.

He let him go and rose. "See ya, kid."

"See ya."

Then he'd gotten on his bike and rode off.

Damn it. Now his head was all cloudy again and his chest hurt from wanting. Wanting to stay with Missy. Wanting to be around her kids. Wanting to stay where he was instead of return to the home that was supposed to be paradise, but he knew would be empty and lifeless.

Seeing a sign for a rest stop, he swung off the highway and drove up to the small brick building.

He took off his helmet and headed for the restroom. Parked beside the sidewalk was a gray-blue van. As he approached, the side door slid open and six kids rolled out. Three girls. Three boys. They barreled past him and giggled their way to the building.

"Might as well mosey instead of running." The man exiting the van smiled at him. "They'll be taking up most of the bathroom stalls and all the space in front of the vending machines for the next twenty minutes."

Last month that would have made Wyatt grouchy. This month it made him smile. He could see Missy's kids doing the same thing a few years from now. "Yours?"

"Three grandkids. Three kids with my new wife." He pointed at the tall, willowy redhead who followed the kids, issuing orders and in general looking out for them.

"Oh." Wyatt was all for polite chitchat, but he wasn't exactly sure what to say to that. The closer the stranger got to Wyatt the more obvious it was that he wasn't in his twenties, as the redhead was. Early fifties probably. Plus, he'd admitted three of those kids were his *grandkids*.

The man batted a hand in dismissal. "Everybody says raising kids is a younger man's game, and that might be true, but I love them all."

"Bet your older kids aren't thrilled."

He laughed. "Are you kidding? Our house is the in place to be. We have movie night every Friday, so every Friday both of my daughters get a date night with their husbands."

"Well, that's handy."

"And I feel twenty-eight again."

Wyatt laughed. He guessed that was probably the redhead's age.

"Didn't think I'd pull through after my first wife left me." He tossed Wyatt a look. "Dumped me for my business partner, tried to take the whole company from him." He chuckled. "My lawyers were better than theirs."

Wyatt couldn't stop the guffaw that escaped. It was nice to see somebody win in divorce wars.

"But now I have a wife I know really loves me. Three new kids to cement the deal. And very good relationships with my older kids, since I am a convenient babysitter for weekends."

"That's nice."

The older man sucked in a breath. "It is nice." He slapped Wyatt on the back. "I'm telling you, second chances are the best. Just when you think you're going to be alone forever, love finds you in the most unexpected ways." He stopped, his mouth fell open and he began racing up the sidewalk. "Come on, Tommy! You know better than that."

By the time Wyatt got out of the restroom, the van, the older man and the kids were gone. He shook his head with a laugh, thinking the guy really was lucky. Then he walked up to a vending machine and inserted the coins to get a two-pack of chocolate cupcakes. He pushed the selection button. They flopped down to the takeaway tray.

He opened them and shoved an entire cupcake into his mouth, then nearly spit it out.

Compared to the cake he'd been eating the past few weeks, it was dry, tasteless. And made him long for Missy with every fiber of his being. Not because he wanted cake, but because she made him laugh, made him think, made him yearn for things he didn't even realize he wanted.

He wanted kids.

Someday he wanted to be the dad in the van taking everyone on an adventure. He wanted his house to be the one that hosted Friday night movie night—with the triplets' friends.

He wanted to have a bigger family than his parents and Missy's parents had given them. So his grandkids could have cousins and aunts and uncles. Things he didn't have.

But most of all he wanted her. He wanted to laugh with her, to tease with her, to wake up beside her every morning and fall asleep with her at night. He didn't want the noise in Tampa. He didn't want to fight any more battles in courtrooms or in his boardroom. He wanted a real life.

He glanced around the crowded rest stop. What the hell was he doing here? He never ran away from something he wanted. He went after it.

And the first step was easy. He climbed on his bike, but before he started the engine, he pulled out his cell phone. He hit Betsy's speed dial number.

When she answered, he said, "Here's the deal. You come up with ten percent over the market value for my shares, or you sell me yours for their real value."

She sputtered. "What?"

"You heard me. If you want to play hardball, I'm countering your offer. I'll buy your shares for market value. If that doesn't suit you, then you buy me out. But I'm not working with you. And I'm not running the company for you. One of us takes all. The other gets lost. I don't care which way it goes."

"We're not supposed to negotiate without our lawyers."

"Yeah, well, I found something I want more than my company. I'd be happy to keep it and run it, as long as I don't have to deal with you.

We never were a good match. We're opposites who argue all the time. If we try to run the company together, all we'll do is fight. And I'm done fighting. If you don't want to buy my shares, I'll find somebody who will."

She sighed. "Wyatt—"

"You have ten seconds to answer. Either let me buy your shares for what they're really worth or you buy mine and I disappear. Or I sell them to a third party."

"I don't want your company."

"Clock's ticking."

"Fine. I'll take market value."

"I'll call my accountant and lawyer."

He clicked off the call with a grin. He was free. Finally free to walk into the destiny he'd known was his since ninth grade. He was gonna marry Missy Johnson.

He started the bike and zipped onto the highway, this time going in the opposite direction, back home.

He was going to get his woman.

Missy cried herself out in the shower, put on clean clothes and set about making gum paste. While it cooled, she could have made a batch of cupcakes. Her plan was to deliver the cupcakes to every restaurant in a three-county area this week, but her heart wasn't in it. After Wyatt's rejection, she needed to feel loved, wanted. So as Elaine gathered the ingredients for a batch of chocolate cupcakes, she went outside to plant the azalea bushes the kids had bought her for Mother's Day.

The problem was she could see splashes of red through the shabby hedge. Her heart stuttered a bit. Wyatt's truck. He'd have to come home for that.

She stopped the happy thoughts that wanted to form. Even if he did come home, he wouldn't come over to see her. He'd made his choices. Now she had to live with them. With her pride intact. She didn't beg. She'd never begged. She sucked it up and went on.

She would go on now, too.

But one of these days she'd dig up those shrubs and replace them with bushes thick enough that she couldn't see the house on the other side. True, it would take years for them to grow tall enough to be a fence, but when they grew in they would be healthy and strong…and full. So she wouldn't be able to see into the McKenzie yard, and any McKenzie who happened to wander home wouldn't be able to see into hers.

She snorted a laugh. No McKenzie would

be coming home. He'd probably send somebody to pick up the truck, and hire a Realtor to sell the house. She had no reason to protcct herself from an accidental meeting. There would be no accidental meeting.

The roar of a motorcycle in her driveway brought her back to the present. Her first thought was that someone had chosen to turn around in her drive. Still, curious, she spun around to see who was.

Wyatt.

Her heart cartwheeled. *Wyatt.*

She removed her gardening gloves and tossed them on the picnic table, her heart in her throat.

As he removed his helmet and headed into her yard, all three kids bounced up with glee. He got only midway to the picnic table before he was surrounded. He reached down and scooped up Claire. Helaina and Owen danced around him as he continued toward the picnic table.

"Are we going to play?" Owen's excited little voice pierced her heart. This was just like Wyatt. Come back for two seconds, probably to give her keys to the truck for whoever he sent up to retrieve it, and undo all the progress she'd made in getting the kids to understand that he'd left and wasn't coming back.

"In a minute." He slid Claire to the ground again. "I need to talk to your mom."

All three kids just looked at him.

He laughed. "If you go play now, I'll take you for ice cream later."

Owen's eyes widened. "In the twuck?"

Missy sighed. Now he was just plain making trouble for her. "The truck doesn't have car seats."

Wyatt sat on the bench across from hers and casually said, "We'll buy some."

That was good enough for the triplets. With a whoop of delight from Owen and a "Yay!" from Claire and Lainie, the three danced over to the sandbox.

"Why are you here?" There was no point delaying the inevitable. "Did you forget something?"

He laughed. "Yes. I forgot you guys."

"Right." She glared at him across the table. "What the hell is that supposed to mean?"

"It means I don't want to go back without you."

Her heart tripped. She caught herself. She hadn't precisely misinterpreted everything he'd said and done to this point, but she had done a lot of wishful thinking. She liked him. But they were at two different places in their lives. And even if they weren't, they lived in two different parts of the country.

"I shouldn't have gone."

She sniffed a laugh. "You seemed pretty certain about it last night."

"Last night I was an idiot. This morning I left without talking to you because I didn't want to hurt you. Turns out I hurt myself the most by leaving."

She shook her head. "So this is all about you?"

"This is all about us. About how we fit. About how we would be a family."

For the first time since he'd walked over from her driveway, hope built in her heart. But hope wasn't safe. She'd spent her childhood hoping her dad would change. Her marriage hoping her husband would stay with her. Every time she hoped, someone hurt her or left her.

"Hey." His soft voice drifted over to her as his strong hand reached across the table and caught hers. "I'm sorry. I shouldn't have gone. I didn't even want to leave. But something inside me kept saying I couldn't do this. That I'd hurt you and hurt the kids."

She didn't look at him. She couldn't. If she glanced over and saw those big brown eyes sad, she'd melt. And she didn't want to melt. She needed to be strong to resist whatever nonsense he was about to say.

"Then I saw this guy and his family at a rest stop on I-95. His first wife had dumped him for his business partner and he married this really hot chick who had to be at least thirty years younger than he was."

Missy couldn't help it. She looked over at him with a laugh. "Are you kidding me?"

"No. Listen." He rose from his side of the picnic table and walked over to hers. Sitting almost on top of her, he forced her to scoot over to accommodate him. "He had six kids in a van that sort of looked like yours."

"Six kids?"

"Half of them were his with his new wife."

"Half?"

"The other half were grandkids."

That made her laugh out loud. "Grandkids?"

"Grandkids and kids all mingled together, and they were having a blast."

She suddenly realized they were talking like normal people again. Just two old friends, sitting on her picnic table, talking about the daily nonsense that happens sometimes.

It hurt her heart because this was what she wanted out of life. A companion. A lover, sure. But more than that, every woman wanted a guy who talked, shared his day, shared his hopes, his dreams. And the easy, casual way Wyatt sat with her, talked with her, got her hopes up more than any apology.

If she didn't leave now, she'd let those hopes take flight and she'd end up even more hurt than she already was.

She rose. "Well, that's great."

He grabbed her hand and tugged her back down again. "You're not listening to what I'm telling you."

Annoyed, she turned on him. "So what are you telling me?"

"Well, I was going to say I love you, but you seem a little too grouchy to hear it."

She huffed a laugh. "You don't love me. You said so last night. You said you *cared* about me but didn't love me."

"Geez, did you memorize everything I said verbatim?"

"A woman doesn't forget the words that hurt her."

He caught her chin and made her look at

him. "I do love you. I love you more than any-body or anything I've ever thought I loved. I got confused because I thought I wasn't ready or supposed to love. That guy in the van, the guy with all the kids and enough family to be an organizational chart for a Fortune 500 company? He showed me that you don't have to be ready. Sometimes you can't be ready. When life and love find you, you have to grab them. Inconvenience, messiness, problems and all."

The hope in her heart swelled so much it nearly exploded. "Are you saying we're in-convenient?"

"Good God, woman, you have triplets. Of course this is inconvenient. You're starting a business here, which means you can't leave. My business is a thousand miles away. You haven't met my parents. Not that they won't love you, but it's going to be a surprise to suddenly bring three kids into their world. Especially since if we're going to make this work, I'm going to be spending a big chunk of my time up here." He shook his head. "They moved to Florida to be with me and now I'm going to be living at least half the year up here."

She laughed a bit. That was sort of ironic.

His serious brown eyes met her gaze. "But I love you. I want what you bring to my world."

"Messiness, inconvenience and problems?"

"Happiness, joy and a sense of belonging."

With every word he said his face got closer. Until when he said, "Belonging," their lips met.

This time there was no hesitation. There was no sense that as soon as he got the chance he would pull away. This time there was only real love. The love she'd been searching for her whole life was finally here.

Finally hers.

EPILOGUE

Two years later they got married on a private island about an hour down the coast from Tampa. The triplets, now six, were more than happy to be the wedding party. Owen looked regal in his little black tux that matched Wyatt's, and the girls really were the princesses they wanted to be, dressed in pale pink gowns with tulle skirts.

Nancy, their longtime babysitter, now a college sophomore, had been invited to the wedding as a guest, but ended up herding the triplets into submission as they stood at the end of the long white runner that would take Missy to the gazebo on the beach, where she would marry the love of her life.

She and Wyatt had decided to date for a year, then had been engaged for a year. Not just to give her a chance to get her company running smoothly, with a baking supervisor and actual delivery staff, but also to give the two of them time to enjoy being in love. Though Wyatt spent most of his time in her house when he visited, he'd kept his gram's house. He was very sentimental when it came to Missy, to their past, and especially to the picnic tables where he'd taught her how to solve equations.

"Okay, Owen, you're first."

Nancy gave him a small push to start him on his journey down the white runner to the gazebo, where Wyatt and the minister waited. Owen hesitated at first, but when he saw all the people urging him on, especially Wyatt's parents, his first grandparents, it was as if someone had flashed a light indicating it was showtime. He grinned and waved, taking his time as he went from the back of the beach to the gazebo.

Wyatt caught him by the shoulders and got him to stand still, but he couldn't stop Owen's grin. This was the day they officially became a family. A mom and dad, three kids and actual grandparents more than happy to spoil them rotten. Yeah. Owen was psyched for this.

Then the girls ambled up the aisle, more se-rious than their brother. They had rose petals to drop. Nancy had skirted the rows of folding chairs to get to the end of the runner and help the girls up the two steps into the gazebo.

Owen gave the thumbs-up signal. The crowd laughed.

Missy smiled. Then she pressed her hand to her tummy as she circled behind the last row of chairs to the runner. When she stood at the threshold of her journey up the aisle, she saw Wyatt, and all her fears, all her doubts disappeared.

His black tux accented his dark good looks, but with Owen standing just a bit above knee height beside him, and the girls a few feet away, waiting for their mom, he also looked like the wonderful father that he was.

She watched his eyes travel from her shoulders to the bodice of her strapless gown and down the tangle of tulle and chiffon that created the short skirt. His gaze paused at her knees, where the dress stopped, and he smiled before he raised his eyes and their gazes locked.

She walked down the aisle alone, because that's what she was without Wyatt. Then she carefully navigated the two steps to the gazebo and handed the two bouquets she carried to the girls.

Wyatt took her hands.

They said their vows and exchanged rings with the sound of the surf behind them. Then they posed for pictures in the gazebo, on the shore, with the kids, without the kids, with his parents and even with Nancy.

In the country club ballroom, they greeted a long line of guests, mostly Wyatt's friends and employees, as well as a swell of friends she'd made once she felt comfortable in Tampa.

As they walked to the main table for dinner, she guided Wyatt along a path that took them past their cake.

"Banana walnut?" he whispered hopefully.

"With a layer of chocolate fudge, a layer of almond, a layer of spice and an extra banana walnut layer at the top for us to take home for our first anniversary." She paused, her critical gaze passing over every flower of the five-layer cake.

He nudged her to get moving. "Everybody knows what you're doing."

She stopped, faced him with a smile. "Really?"

"You're judging that cake! Elaine was paralyzed with fear that she'd somehow ruin it."

"That's not what I'm doing."

He frowned, then his eyes narrowed. "So what are you doing?"

"I'm deciding if she's good enough to take responsibility for the wedding-cake division."

He gaped at her. "You'd give that up?"

"Not give up per se. I'd like to go back to baking. Let her supervise."

"Wow."

"It means I'd be home all winter."

His stupefied expression became a grin. "Here? In Florida?"

Her hands traveled up his lapels and to his neck. "It is our home."

"Our home. I like the sound of that."

"I want cake!"

Missy didn't even have to glance down to know the triplets had gathered at their knees.

She ruffled Owen's hair. "You always want cake. Just like your dad."

Wyatt smiled. "I like the sound of that."

"What? That you have a son?"

"Nope. I like that he already takes after me."

He stooped to Owen's height. "Don't worry. I'm guessing the guests won't eat even half that thing. You and I will be eating cake for a week."

Owen high-fived him. "All right."

They walked to the main table, raised enough for all the guests to see them. They settled Lainie and Claire in chairs to the right of Missy, and Owen between Wyatt and his parents.

When Owen grinned, Missy knew, of all the people at the wedding, herself and Wyatt included, her son was the happiest. He hadn't just gotten a dad and a grandpa; finally he wasn't the only man in the family.

* * * * *

Her Pregnancy Surprise

CHAPTER ONE

"You aren't planning on driving back to Pittsburgh tonight, are you?"

Danny Carson walked into the third floor office of his Virginia Beach beach house talking to Grace McCartney, his newest employee, who stood behind his desk, hunched over her laptop. A tall brunette with bright violet eyes and a smile that lit the room, Grace was smart, but more than that she was likable and she genuinely liked people. Both of those qualities had helped enormously with the work they'd had to do that weekend.

Grace looked up. "Would you like me to stay?"

"Call it a debriefing."

She tilted her head to one side, considering the suggestion, then smiled. "Okay."

This was her real charm. She'd been working every waking minute for three days, forced to spend her entire weekend assisting Danny as he persuaded Orlando Riggs—a poor kid who parlayed a basketball scholarship into a thirty-million-dollar NBA deal—to use Carson Services as his financial management firm. Not only was she away from her home in Pittsburgh and her friends, but she hadn't gotten to relax on her days off. She could be annoyed that he'd asked her to stay another night. Instead she smiled. Nothing ruffled her feathers.

"Why don't you go to your room to freshen up? I'll tell Mrs. Higgins we'll have dinner in about an hour."

"Sounds great."

After Grace left the office, Danny called his housekeeper on the intercom. He checked his email, checked on dinner, walked on the beach and ended up on the deck with a glass of Scotch. Grace took so long that by the time Danny heard the sound of the sliding glass door opening behind him, Mrs. Higgins had already left their salads on the umbrella table and their entrées on the serving cart, and gone for the day. Exhausted from the long weekend of work, and belatedly realizing Grace probably was, too, Danny nearly suggested they forget about dinner and talk in the morning, until he turned and saw Grace.

Wearing a pretty pink sundress that showed off the tan she'd acquired walking on the beach with Orlando, she looked young, fresh-faced and wholesome. He'd already noticed she was pretty, of course. A man would have to be blind not to notice how attractive she was. But this evening, with the rays of the setting sun glistening on her shoulder-length sable-colored hair and the breeze off the ocean lightly ruffling her full skirt, she looked amazing.

Unable to stop himself he said, "Wow."

She smiled sheepishly. "Thanks. I felt a little like celebrating Orlando signing with Carson Services, and though this isn't exactly Prada, it's the best of what I brought."

Danny walked to her place at the table and pulled out her chair. "It's perfect." He thought about his khaki trousers, simple short-sleeved shirt and windblown black hair as he seated her, then wondered why he had. This wasn't a date. She was an employee. He'd asked her to stay so he could give her a bonus for the good job she'd done that week, and to talk to her long enough to ascertain the position into which he should promote her—also to thank her for doing a good job. What he wore should be of no consequence. The fact that it even entered his head nearly made him laugh.

He seated himself. "Mrs. Higgins has already served dinner."

"I see." She frowned, looking at the silver covers on the plates on the serving cart beside the table, then the salads that sat in front of them. "I'm sorry. I didn't realize I had stayed in the tub so long." She smiled sheepishly again. "I was a little more tired than I thought."

"Then I'm glad you took the extra time." Even as the words tumbled out of his mouth, Danny couldn't believe he was saying them. Yes, he was grateful to her for being so generous and kind with Orlando, making the athlete feel comfortable, but the way Danny had excused her lateness sounded personal, when he hardly knew this woman.

She laughed lightly. "I really liked Orlando. I think he's a wonderful person. But we were still here to do a job. Both of us had to be on our toes 24/7."

When she smiled and Danny's nerve endings crackled to life, he realized he was behaving out of character for a boss because he was attracted to her. He almost shook his head. He was so slow on the uptake that he'd needed an entire weekend to recognize that.

But he didn't shake his head. He didn't react at all. He was her boss and he'd already slipped twice. His "wow" when he'd seen her in the dress was inappropriate. His comment about the extra time that she'd taken had been too personal. He excused himself for those because he was tired. But now that he saw what was happening, he could stop it. He didn't date employees, but also this particular employee had proven herself too valuable to risk losing.

Grace picked up her salad fork. "I'm starved and this looks great."

"Mrs. Higgins is a gem. I'm lucky to have her."

"She told me that she enjoys working for you because you're not here every day. She likes working part-time, even if it is usually weekends."

"That's my good fortune," Danny agreed, then the conversation died as they ate their salads. Oddly something inside of Danny missed the more personal chitchat. It was unusual for him to want to get friendly with an employee, but more than that, this dinner had to stay professional because he had things to discuss with her. Yet he couldn't stop the surge of disappointment, as if he were missing an unexpected opportunity.

When they finished their salads, he rose to serve the main course. "I hope you like fettuccini alfredo."

"I love it."

"Great." He removed the silver covers. Pushing past the exhaustion that had caused him to wish he could give in and speak openly with her, he served their dinners and immediately got down to business. "Grace, you did an exceptional job this weekend."

"Thanks. I appreciate the compliment."

"I intend to do more than compliment you. Your work secured an enormous account for Carson Services. Not only are you getting a bonus, but I would like to promote you."

She gaped at him. "Are you kidding?"

Pleased with her happy surprise, Danny laughed. "No. Right now you and I need to talk a bit about what you can do and where in the organization you would like to serve. Once we're clear, I'll write up the necessary paperwork."

She continued to stare at him slightly open-mouthed, then she said, "You're going to promote me anywhere I want to go?"

"There is a condition. If a situation like Orlando's ever comes up again, where we have to do more than our general push to get a client to sign, I want you in on the persuading."

She frowned. "I'm happy to spend time helping a reluctant investor see the benefits of using your firm, but you don't need to promote me for that."

"The promotion is part of my thank-you for your assistance with Orlando."

She shook her head. "I don't want it."

Positive he'd heard wrong, Danny chuckled. "What?"

"I've been with your company two weeks. Yet I was the one chosen for a weekend at your beach house with Orlando Riggs—a superstar client most of the men and half of the women on staff were dying to meet. You've already given me a perk beyond what employees who have been with you for years have gotten. If there's an empty position somewhere in the firm, promote Bobby Zapf. He has a wife and three kids and they're saving for a house. He could use the money, and the boost in confidence from you."

Danny studied her for a second, then he laughed. "I get it. You're joking."

"I'm serious." She took a deep breath.

"Look, everybody understood that you chose me to come with you this weekend because I'm new. I hadn't worked with you long enough to adopt your opinions, so Orlando knew that when I agreed with just about everything you said I wasn't spouting the company party line. I hadn't yet heard the party line. So I was a good choice for this. But I don't want to be promoted over everybody's head."

"You're worried about jealousy?"

She shook her head. "No! I don't want to take a job that should go to someone else. Someone who's worked for you for years."

"Like Bobby Zapf."

"In the two weeks I spent at the office, I watched Bobby work harder than anybody else you employ. If you want to promote somebody he's the one."

Danny leaned back in his chair. "Okay. Bobby it is." He paused, toyed with his silverware, then glanced up at her, holding back a smile. He'd never had an employee turn down a promotion—especially not to make sure another person got it. Grace was certainly unique.

"Can I at least give you a bonus?"

She laughed. "Yes! I worked hard for an entire weekend. A bonus is absolutely in order."

Continuing to hold back a chuckle, Danny cleared his throat. "Okay. Bonus, but no promotion."

"You could promise to watch my performance over the next year and then promote me because I'd had enough time to prove myself."

"I could." He took a bite of his dinner, more pleased with her than anybody he'd ever met. She was right. In his gratitude for a weekend's work, he had jumped the gun on the promotion. She reeled him in and reminded him of the person who really deserved it. If he hadn't already been convinced she was a special person, her actions just now would have shown him.

Grace smiled. "Okay. It's settled. I get a bonus and you'll watch how well I work." Then as quickly as she'd recapped their agreement, she changed the subject. "It's beautiful here."

Danny glanced around. Darkness had descended. A million stars twinkled overhead. The moon shone like a silver dollar. Water hit the shore in white-foamed waves.

"I like it. I get a lot of work done here because it's so quiet. But at the end of the day I can also relax."

"You don't relax much, do you?"

Lulled by the sounds of the waves and her calming personality, Danny said, "No. I have the fate of a company that's been around for decades on my shoulders. If I fail the company fails and the legacy my great-grandfather sweated to create crumbles into nothing. So I'm focused on work. Unless relaxation happens naturally, it doesn't happen."

"I don't relax much, either." She picked up her fork again. "You already heard me tell Orlando I grew up the same way he did. Dirt poor. And in the same away he used his talent to make a place for himself, I intend to make a place for myself, too."

"Here's a tip. Maybe you shouldn't talk your bosses out of promotions?"

"I can't take what I don't deserve." She wiggled her eyebrows comically. "I'll just have to make my millions the old-fashioned way. I'll have to earn them."

Danny laughed and said, "I hate to tell you this, but people who work for someone else rarely get rich. So if you want to make millions, what are you doing working for me?"

"Learning about investing. When I was

young I heard the theory that your money should work as hard for you as you work for it. Growing up, I didn't get any experience seeing how to make money work, so I figured the best place to get the scoop on investing was at an investment firm." She smiled, then asked, "What about you?"

"What about me?"

She shrugged. "I don't know. Anything. Did you want your family's business? Were you a happy child? Are you happy now?" She shrugged again. "Anything."

She asked the questions then took a bite of her dinner, making her inquiry into his life seem casual, offhand. But she'd nonetheless taken the conversation away from herself and to him. Still, she didn't seem as if she were prying. She seemed genuinely curious, but not like a bloodhound, like someone trying to become a friend.

He licked his suddenly dry lips and his heart rate accelerated as he actually considered answering her. A part of him really wanted to talk. A part of him *needed* to talk. Two years had passed. So much had happened.

He took a breath, amazed that he contemplated confiding in her, yet knowing he wouldn't. Though he couldn't ignore her, he wouldn't confide. He'd never confide. Not to her. Not to anyone.

He had to take the conversation back where it belonged. To business.

"What you see is who I am. Chairman of the Board and CEO of Carson Services. There isn't anything to talk about."

She blinked. "Really?"

"From the time I was six or eight I knew I would take over the company my great-grandfather started. I didn't have to travel or experiment to figure out what I wanted. My life was pretty much mapped out for me and I simply followed the steps. That's why there's not a lot to talk about."

"You started training as a kid?"

"Not really training, more or less being included in on conversations my dad and grandfather thought were relevant."

"What if you didn't like investing?"

"But I did."

"It just sounds weird." She flushed. "Sorry. Really. It's none of my business."

"Don't be sorry." Her honesty made him laugh. More comfortable than he could remember being in years, he picked up his fork and said, "I see what you're saying. I was lucky that I loved investing. I walked into the job as if it were made for me, but when my son—"

He stopped. His chest tightened. His heart rate kicked into overdrive. He couldn't believe that had slipped out.

"But your son what?"

"But when my son began to show artistic talent," he said, thinking quickly because once again the conversation had inadvertently turned too personal. And this time it was *his* fault. "I suddenly saw that another person might not want to be CEO of our company, might not have the ability to handle the responsibility, or might have gifts and talents that steer him or her in a different direction. Then the company would have to hire someone, and hiring someone of the caliber we would require would involve paying out a huge salary and profit sharing. The family fortune would ultimately deplete."

She studied him for a second, her gaze so intense Danny knew the mention of his son had her curious. But he wouldn't say any more about Cory. That part of his life was so far off-limits that he didn't even let himself think about it. It would be such a cold, frosty day in hell that he'd discuss Cory with another person that he knew that day would never come.

Finally Grace sighed. "I guess you were lucky then—" she turned her attention back to her food "—that you wanted the job."

Danny relaxed. Once again she'd read him perfectly. She'd seen that though he'd mentioned his son, he hadn't gone into detail about Cory, and instead had brought the discussion back to Carson Services, so she knew to let the topic go.

They finished their dinner in companionable conversation because Grace began talking about remodeling the small house she'd bought when she got her first job two years before. As they spoke about choosing hardwood and deciding on countertops, Danny acknowledged to himself that she was probably the most sensitive person he'd met. She could read a mood or a situation so well that he didn't have to worry about what he said in front of her. A person who so easily knew not to pry would never break a confidence.

For that reason alone an intense urge to confide in her bubbled up in him, shocking him. Why the hell would he want to talk about the past? And why would he think that any woman would want to hear her boss's marital horror stories? No woman would. No *person* would. Except maybe a gossip. And Grace wasn't a gossip.

After dinner, they went inside for a drink, but Danny paused beside the stairway that led to his third-floor office suite.

"Bonuses don't pass through our normal accounting. I write those checks myself. It's a way to keep them completely between me and the employees who get them. The checkbook's upstairs. Why don't we just go up now and give you your bonus?"

Grace grinned. "Sounds good to me."

Danny motioned for Grace to precede him up the steps. Too late, he realized that was a mistake. Her perfect bottom was directly in his line of vision. He paused, letting her get a few steps ahead of him, only to discover that from this angle he had a view of her shapely calves.

He finished the walk up the stairs with his head down, gaze firmly fixed on the Oriental carpet runner on the steps. When he reached the third floor, she was waiting for him. Moonlight came in through the three tall windows in the back wall of the semidark loft that led to his office, surrounding her with pale light, causing her to look like an angel.

Mesmerized, Danny stared at her. He knew she was a nice person. A *good* person. He also knew that was why he had the quick mental picture of her as an angel and such a strong sense of companionship for her. But she was an employee. He was her boss. He needed to keep his distance.

He motioned toward his office suite and again she preceded him. Inside, he sat behind the desk and she gingerly sat on the chair in front of it.

"I think Orlando Riggs is the salt of the earth," Danny said as he pulled out the checkbook he held for the business. "You made him feel very comfortable."

"I felt very comfortable with him." She grimaced. "A lot of guys who had just signed a thirty-million-dollar deal with an NBA team would be a little cocky."

"A little cocky?" Danny said with a laugh. "I've met people with a lot less talent than Orlando has and a lot less cash who were total jerks."

"Orlando seems unaffected."

"Except that he wants to make sure his family has everything they need." Danny began writing out the check. "I didn't even realize he was married."

"And has two kids."

Kids.

Danny blinked at the unexpected avalanche of memory just the word kids brought. He remembered how eager he'd been to marry Lydia and have a family. He remembered his naive idea of marital bliss, and his chest swelled from the horrible empty feeling he got every time he realized how close he'd been to fulfilling that dream and how easily it had all been snatched away.

But tonight, with beautiful, sweet-tempered, sincere Grace sitting across the desk, Danny had a surprising moment of clarity. He'd always blamed himself for the breakdown of his marriage, but what if it had been Lydia's fault? He'd wanted to go to counseling. Lydia had simply wanted to *go*. Away from him. If he looked at the breakdown of his marriage from that very thin perspective, then the divorce wasn't his fault.

That almost made him laugh. If he genuinely believed the divorce wasn't his fault then—

Then he'd wasted years?

No. He'd wasted his life. He didn't merely feel empty the way he'd been told most people felt when they lost a mate; he felt wholly empty. Almost nonexistent. As if he didn't have a life. As if every day since his marriage had imploded two years ago, he hadn't really lived. He hadn't even really existed. He'd simply expended time.

Finished writing the check, Danny rose from his seat. It seemed odd to think about feeling empty when across the desk, eager, happy Grace radiated life and energy.

"Thank you for your help this weekend."

As he walked toward her, Grace also rose. He handed her the check. She glanced down at the amount he'd written, then looked up at him. Her beautiful violet eyes filled with shock. Her tongue came out to moisten her lips before she said, "This is too much."

Caught in the gaze of her hypnotic eyes, seeing the genuine appreciation, Danny could have sworn he felt some of her energy arch to him. If nothing else, he experienced a strong sense of connection. A rightness. Or maybe a purpose. As if there was a reason she was here.

The feeling of connection and intimacy could be nothing more than the result of spending every waking minute from Friday afternoon to Sunday night together, but that didn't lessen its intensity. It was so strong that his voice softened when he said, "No. It isn't too much. You deserve it."

She took a breath that caused her chest to rise and fall, calling his attention to the cleavage peeking out of the pink lace of her dress. She looked soft and feminine, yet she was also smart and sensitive. Which was why she attracted him, tempted him, when in the past two years no other woman had penetrated the pain that had held him hostage. Grace treated him like a person. Not like her rich boss. Not like a good catch. Not even like a guy so far out of her social standing that she should be nervous to spend so much one-on-one time. But just like a man.

"Thanks." She raised her gaze to his again. This time when Danny experienced the sense of intimacy, he almost couldn't argue himself out of it because he finally understood it. *She* felt it, too. He could see it in her eyes. And he didn't want to walk away from it. He *needed* her.

But then he saw the check in her hands and he remembered she was an employee. An affair between them had consequences. Especially when it ended. Office gossip would make him look foolish, but it could ruin her. Undoubtedly it would cost her her job. He might be willing to take a risk because his future wasn't at stake, but he couldn't make the decision for her.

CHAPTER TWO

DANNY CLEARED HIS throat. "You're welcome. I very much appreciated your help this weekend." He stepped away and walked toward the office door. "I'm going downstairs to have a drink before I turn in. I'll see you in the morning."

Grace watched Danny go, completely confused by what was happening between them. For a few seconds, she could have sworn he was going to kiss her and the whole heck of it was she would have let him.

Let him? She was so attracted to him she darned near kissed him first, and that puzzled her. She should have reminded herself that he was her boss and so wealthy they were barely on the same planet. Forget about being in the same social circle. But thoughts of their different worlds hadn't even entered her head, and, thinking about them now, Grace couldn't muster a reason they mattered.

Laughing softly, she combed her fingers through her hair. Whatever the reason, she couldn't deny the spark between her and Danny. When Orlando left that afternoon, Grace had been disappointed that their weekend together had come to an end. But Danny had asked her to stay one more night, and she couldn't resist the urge to dress up and hope that he would notice her the way she'd been noticing him. He'd nearly ruined everything by offering her a promotion she didn't deserve, but he showed her that he trusted her opinion by taking her advice about Bobby Zapf.

The real turning point came when he mentioned his son. He hadn't wanted to talk about him, but once Danny slipped him into the conversation he hadn't pretended he hadn't. She had seen the sadness in his eyes and knew there was a story there. But she also recognized that this wasn't the time to ask questions. She'd heard the rumor that Danny had gone through an ugly divorce but no report had mentioned a child from his failed marriage. Nasty divorces frequently resulted in child custody battles and his ex-wife could very well make him fight to see his son, which was undoubtedly why he didn't want to talk about him.

But tonight wasn't the night for probing into a past that probably only reminded him of unhappy times. Tonight, she had to figure out if he felt for her what she was beginning to feel for him. The last thing she wanted was to be one of those employees who got a crush on her boss and then pined for him for the rest of her career.

And she wouldn't get any answers standing in his third floor office when he was downstairs!

She ran down the steps and found him in the great room, behind the bar, pouring Scotch into a glass.

He glanced up when she walked over. Though he seemed surprised she hadn't gone to her room as he'd more or less ordered her to, he said, "Drink?"

Wanting to be sharp and alert so she didn't misinterpret anything he said or did, Grace smiled and said, "No. Thanks."

She slid onto one of the three red leather bar stools that matched the red leather sofas that sat parallel to each other in front of the wall of windows that provided a magnificent view of the Atlantic Ocean. A black, red and tan Oriental rug between the sofas protected the sand-colored hardwood floors. White-bowled lights connected to thin chrome poles suspended from the vaulted ceiling, illuminating the huge room.

Danny took a swallow of his Scotch, then set the glass on the bar. "Can't sleep?"

She shrugged. "Still too keyed up from the weekend I guess."

"What would you normally do on a Sunday night?"

She thought for a second, then laughed. "Probably play rummy with my mother. She's a cardaholic. Loves any game. But she's especially wicked with rummy."

"Can't beat her?"

"Every once in a while I get lucky. But when it comes to pure skill the woman is evilly blessed."

Danny laughed. "My mother likes cards, too."

Grace's eyes lit. "Really? How good is she?"

"Exceptional."

"We should get them together."

Danny took a long breath, then said, "We should."

And Grace suddenly saw it. The thing that had tickled her brain all weekend but had never really surfaced. In spite of her impoverished roots and his obviously privileged upbringing, she and Danny had a lot in common. Not childhood memories, but adult things like goals and commitments. He ran his family's business. She was determined to help her parents out of poverty because she loved them. Even the way they viewed Orlando proved they had approximately the same beliefs about life and people.

If Danny hadn't asked for her help this weekend, eventually they would have been alone together long enough to see that they clicked. They matched. She knew he realized it, too, if only because he'd nearly slipped into personal conversation with her four times at dinner, but he had stopped himself. Probably because she was an employee.

It was both of their loss if they weren't mature enough to handle an office relationship. But she thought they were. Her difficult childhood and his difficult divorce had strengthened each of them. They weren't flip. They were cautious. Smart. If any two people could have an office relationship without it affecting their work, she and Danny were the two. And she wasn't going to miss out on something good because, as her boss, Danny wouldn't be the first to make a move.

She raised her eyes until she caught his gaze. "You know what? Though you're trying to fight it, I think you like me. Would it help if I told you I really like you, too?"

For several seconds, Danny didn't answer. He couldn't. He'd never met a woman so honest, so he wasn't surprised that she spoke her mind. Even better, she hadn't played coy and tried to pretend she didn't see what was going on. She saw it, and she wanted to like him as much as he wanted to like her.

And that was the key. The final answer. She wanted to like him as much as he wanted to like her and he suddenly couldn't understand why he was fighting it.

"It helps enormously." He bent across the bar and kissed her, partly to make sure they were on the same page with their intentions, and partly to see if their chemistry was as strong as the emotions that seemed to ricochet between them.

It was. Just the slight brush of their lips knocked him for a loop. He felt the explosion the whole way to his toes.

She didn't protest the kiss, so he took the

few steps that brought him from behind the bar and in front of the stool on which she sat. He put his hands on her shoulders and kissed her deeply this time, his mouth opening over hers.

White-hot desire slammed through him and his control began slipping. He wanted to touch her, to taste her, to feel all the things he'd denied himself for the past two years.

But it was one thing to kiss her. It was quite another to make love. But when he shifted away, Grace slid her hand around his neck and brought his lips back to hers.

Relief swamped him. He'd never had this kind of an all-consuming desire to make love. Yet, the yearning he felt wasn't for sexual gratification. It was to be with Grace herself. She was sweet and fun and wonderful...and beautiful. Having her slide her arms around him and return his kisses with a passion equal to his own filled him with an emotion so strong and complete he dared not even try to name it.

Instead he broke the kiss, lifted her into his arms and took her to his bed.

The next morning when Grace awoke, she inhaled a long breath as she stretched. When her hand connected with warm, naked skin, her eyes popped open and she remembered she'd spent the night making love with her boss.

Reliving every detail, she blinked twice, waiting for a sense of embarrassment or maybe guilt. When none came she smiled. She couldn't believe it, but it was true. She'd fallen in love with Danny Carson in about forty-eight hours.

She should feel foolish for tumbling in over her head so fast. She could even worry that he'd seen her feelings for him and taken advantage of her purely for sexual gratification. But she wasn't anything but happy. Nobody had ever made love to her the way he had. And she was sure their feelings were equal.

She yawned and stretched, then went downstairs to the room she'd used on Friday and Saturday nights. After brushing her teeth and combing her hair, she ran back to Danny's room and found he was still sleeping, so she slid into bed again.

Her movements caused Danny to stir. As Grace thanked her lucky stars that she had a chance to fix up a bit before he awoke, he turned on his pillow. Ready, she smiled and caught his gaze but the eyes that met hers were not the warm brown eyes of the man who had made love to her the night before. They were the dark, almost black eyes of her boss.

She remembered again the way he'd made love to her and told herself to stop being a worrying loser. Yes, the guy who ran Carson Services could sometimes be a real grouch, but the guy who lived in this beach house was much nicer. And she was absolutely positive that was the real Danny.

Holding his gaze, she whispered, "Good morning."

He stared at her. After a few seconds, he closed his eyes. "Tell me we didn't make a mistake."

"We did not make a mistake."

He opened his eyes. "Always an optimist."

She scooted closer so she could rest her head on his outstretched arm. "We like each other. A lot. Something pretty special happened between us."

He was silent for a few seconds then he said, "Okay."

She twisted so she could look at him. "Okay? I thought we were fantastic!"

His face transformed. The caution slipped

from his dark eyes and was replaced by amusement. "You make me laugh."

"It's a dirty job but somebody's got to do it."

Chuckling, he caught her around the waist and reversed their positions. But gazing into her eyes, he softened his expression again and said, "Thanks," before he lowered his head and kissed her.

They made love and then Danny rolled out of bed, suggesting they take a shower. Gloriously naked, he walked to the adjoining bathroom and began to run the water. Not quite as comfortable as he, Grace needed a minute to skew her courage to join him, and in the end wrapped a bedsheet around herself to walk to the bathroom.

But though she faltered before dropping the sheet, when she stepped into the shower, she suddenly felt bold. Knowing his trust was shaky because of his awful divorce, she stretched to her tiptoes and kissed him. He let her take the lead and she began a slow exploration of his body until he seemed unable to handle her simple ministrations anymore and he turned the tables.

They made love quickly, covered with soap and sometimes even pausing to laugh, and

Grace knew from that moment on, she was his. She would never feel about any man the way she felt about Danny.

CHAPTER THREE

WHEN GRACE AND Danny stood in the circular driveway of his beach house, both about to get into their cars to drive back to Pittsburgh, she could read the displeasure in his face as he told her about the "client hopping" he had scheduled for the next week. He wanted to be with her but these meetings had been on the books for months and he couldn't get out of them. So she kissed him and told him she would be waiting when he returned.

They got into their vehicles and headed home. He was a faster driver, so she lost him on I-64, but she didn't care. Her heart was light and she had the kind of butterflies in her tummy that made a woman want to sing for joy. Though time would tell, she genuinely believed she'd found Mr. Right. She'd only known Danny for two weeks, and hadn't actually spent a lot of that time with him since he was so far above her on the company organizational chart. But the weekend had told her everything she needed to know about the real Danny Carson.

To the world, he was an ambitious, demanding, highly successful man. In private, he was a loving, caring, normal man, who liked her. A lot.

Yes, they would probably experience some problems because he owned the company she worked for. He'd hesitated at the bar before kissing her. He'd asked her that morning if they'd made a mistake. But she forced herself not to worry about it. She had no doubt that once they spent enough time together, and he saw the way she lived her beliefs, his worries about dating an employee would vanish.

What they had was worth a few months of getting to know each other. Or maybe the answer would be to quit her job?

The first two days of his trip sped by. He called Wednesday morning, and the mere sound of his voice made her breathless. Though he talked about clients, meetings, business dinners and never-ending hand-shaking, his deep voice reminded her of his whispered endearments during their night together and that conjured the memory of how he tasted, the firmness of his skin, the pleasure of being held in his arms. Before he disconnected the call, he whispered that he missed her and couldn't wait to see her and she'd all but fainted with happiness.

The next day he didn't call, but Grace knew he was busy. He also didn't call on Friday or Saturday.

Flying back to Pittsburgh Sunday, Danny nervously paced his Gulfstream, fighting a case of doubt and second thoughts about what had happened between him and Grace. In the week that had passed, he hadn't had a spare minute to think about her, and hadn't spoken with her except for one quick phone call a few days into the trip. The call had ended too soon and left him longing to see her, but after three days of having no contact, the negatives of the situation came crowding in on him, and there were plenty of them.

First, he didn't really know her. Second, even if she were the perfect woman, they'd gone too far too fast. Third, they worked together. If they dated it would be all over the office. When they broke up, he would be the object of the same gossip that had nearly ruined his reputation when his marriage ended.

He took a breath and blew it out on a puff. He couldn't tell if distance was giving him perspective or calling up all his demons. But he did know that he should have thought this through before making love to her.

Worse, he couldn't properly analyze their situation because he couldn't recall specifics. All he remembered from their Sunday night and Monday morning together were emotions so intense that he'd found the courage to simply be himself. But with the emotions gone, he couldn't summon a solid memory of the substance of what had happened between them. He couldn't remember anything specific she'd said to make him like her—like? Did he say like? He didn't just like Grace. That Sunday night his feelings had run more along the lines of a breathless longing, uncontrollable desire, and total bewitching. A man in that condition could easily be seduced into seeing traits in a woman that weren't there and that meant he had made a horrible mistake.

He told himself not to think that way. But the logical side of his brain called him a sap. He'd met Grace two weeks before when she'd come to work for his company, but he didn't really know her because he didn't work with new employees. He worked with their bosses. He said hello to new employees in the hall. But otherwise, he ignored them. So he hadn't "known" her for two weeks. He'd glimpsed her.

Plus, she'd been on her best behavior for Orlando. She had been at the beach house to demonstrate to Orlando that Carson Services employed people in the know. Yes, she'd gone above and beyond the call of duty in her time with Orlando, making him feel comfortable, sharing personal insights—but, really, wasn't that her job?

Danny took a long breath. Had he fallen in love with a well polished persona she'd pulled out to impress Orlando and simply never disengaged when the basketball star left?

Oh, Lord!

He sat, rubbed his hands down his face and held back a groan. Bits and pieces of their Sunday night dinner conversation flitted through his brain. She'd grown up poor. Could only afford a house that needed remodeling. She wanted to be rich. She'd gone into investing to understand money.

He *had* money.

Technically he was a shortcut to all her goals.

He swallowed hard. It wasn't fair to judge her when she wasn't there to defend herself.

He had to see her. Then he would know. After five minutes of conversation she would either relieve all his fears or prove that he'd gone too fast, told her too much and set himself up for a huge disappointment.

The second his plane taxied to a stop, he pulled out his cell phone and called her, but she didn't answer. He left a message but she didn't return his call and Danny's apprehensions hitched a notch. Not that he thought she should be home, waiting for him, but she knew when he got in. He'd told her he would call. He'd said it at the end of a very emotional phone conversation in which he'd told her that crazy as it sounded, he missed her. She'd breathlessly told him she missed him, too.

Now she wasn't home?

If he hadn't given her the time he would be landing, if he hadn't told her he would be calling, if he hadn't been so sappy about saying how much he missed her, it wouldn't seem so strange that she wasn't home. But, having told her all those things, he had the uncontrollable suspicion that something was wrong.

Unless she'd come to the same conclusions

he had. Starting a relationship had been a mistake.

That had to be it.

Relief swamped him. He didn't want another relationship. Ever. And Grace was too nice a girl to have the kind of fling that ended when their sexual feelings for each other fizzled and they both eagerly walked away.

It was better for it to end now.

Content that not only had Grace nicely disengaged their relationship, but also that he probably wouldn't run into her in the halls because their positions in the company and the building were so far apart, he went to work happy. But his secretary buzzed him around ten-thirty, telling him Grace was in the outer office, asking if he had time for her.

Sure. Why not? Now that he'd settled everything in his head, he could handle a debriefing. They'd probably both laugh about the mistake.

He tossed his pencil to the stack of papers in front of him. "Send her in."

He steeled himself, knowing that even though his brain had easily resolved their situation, his body might not so easily agree. Seeing her would undoubtedly evoke lots of physical response, if only because she was beautiful. He remembered that part very, very well.

His office door opened and she stepped inside. Danny almost groaned at his loss. She was every bit as stunning as he remembered. Her dark hair framed her face and complemented her skin tone. Her little pink suit showed off her great legs. But he wasn't meant for relationships and she wasn't meant for affairs. Getting out now while they could get out without too much difficulty was the right thing to do.

"Good morning, Grace."

She smiled. "Good morning."

He pointed at the chair in front of his desk, indicating she should sit. "Look, I know what you're going to say. Being away for a week gave me some perspective, too, and I agree we made a mistake the night we slept together."

"What?"

Confused, he cocked his head. "I thought you were here to tell me we'd made a mistake."

Holding the arms of the captain's chair in front of his desk, she finally sat. "I came in to invite you to dinner."

He sat back on his chair, knowing this could

potentially be one of the worst conversations of his life. "I'm sorry. When you weren't home last night when I called, I just assumed you'd changed your mind."

"I was at my mother's."

"I called your cell phone."

She took a breath. "And by the time I realized I'd hadn't turned it on after I took it off the charger, it was too late for me to call you back." She took another breath and smiled hopefully. "That's why I came to your office."

He picked up his pencil again. Nervously tapped it on the desk. "I'm sorry. Really. But—" This time he took the breath, giving himself a chance to organize his thoughts. "I genuinely believe we shouldn't have slept together, and I really don't want to see you anymore. I don't have relationships with employees."

He caught her gaze. "I'm sorry."

That seemed to catch her off guard. She blinked several times, but her face didn't crumble as he expected it would if she were about to cry. To his great relief, her chin lifted. "That's fine."

Pleased that she seemed to be taking this well—probably because his point was a valid one—bosses and employees shouldn't date—

he rose. "Do you want the day off or something?"

She swallowed and wouldn't meet his gaze. She said, "I'm fine," then turned and walked out of his office.

Danny fell to his seat, feeling like a class-A heel. He had hurt her and she was going to cry.

Grace managed to get through the day with only one crying spurt in the bathroom right after coming out of Danny's office. She didn't see him the next day or the next or at all for the next two weeks. Just when she had accepted that her world hadn't been destroyed because he didn't want her or because she'd slept with him, she realized something awful. Her female cycle was as regular as clockwork, so when things didn't happen on the day they were supposed to happen, she knew something was wrong.

Though she and Danny had used condoms, they weren't perfect. She bought an early pregnancy test and discovered her intuition had been correct. She had gotten pregnant.

She sat on the bed in the master suite of her little house. The room was awash with warm colors: cognac, paprika, butter-yellow in satin pillows, lush drapes and a smooth silk bedspread. But she didn't feel any warmth as she stared at the results of the EPT. She had just gotten pregnant by a man who had told her he wanted nothing to do with her.

She swallowed hard and began to pace the honey-yellow hardwood floors of the bedroom she'd scrimped, saved and labored to refinish. Technically she had a great job and a good enough income that she could raise a child alone. Money wasn't her problem. And neither was becoming a mother. She was twenty-four, ready to be a mom. Excited actually.

Except Danny didn't want her. She might survive telling him, but she still worked for him. Soon everybody at his company would know she was pregnant. Anybody with a memory could do the math and realize when she'd gotten pregnant and speculate the baby might be Danny's since they'd spent a weekend together.

He couldn't run away from this and neither could she.

She took a deep breath, then another, and another, to calm herself.

Everything would be fine if she didn't panic and handled this properly. She didn't have to tell Danny right away that she was pregnant. She could wait until enough time had passed that he would see she wasn't trying to force anything from him. Plus, until her pregnancy was showing, she didn't have to tell anybody but Danny. In six or seven months the people she worked with wouldn't necessarily connect her pregnancy with the weekend she and Danny together. They could get out of this with a minimum of fuss.

That made so much sense that Grace easily fell asleep that night, but the next morning she woke up dizzy, still exhausted and with an unholy urge to vomit. On Saturday morning, she did vomit. Sunday morning, she couldn't get out of bed. Tired, nauseated and dizzy beyond belief, she couldn't hide her symptoms from anybody. Which meant that by Monday afternoon, everybody would guess something was up, and she had no choice but to tell Danny first thing in the morning that she was pregnant. If she didn't, he would find out by way of a rumor, and she couldn't let that happen.

Grace arrived at work an hour early on Monday. Danny was already in his office but his secretary had not yet arrived. As soon as he was settled, she knocked on the frame of his open door.

He looked up. "Grace?"

"Do you have a minute?"

"Not really, I have a meeting—"

"This won't take long." She drank a huge gulp of air and pushed forward because there was no point in dilly-dallying. "I'm pregnant."

For thirty seconds, Danny sat motionless. Grace felt every breath she drew as the tension in the room increased with each second that passed.

Finally he very quietly said, "Get out."

"We need to talk about this."

"Talk about this? Oh, no! I won't give credence to your scheme by even gracing you with ten minutes to try to convince me you're pregnant!"

"Scheme?"

"Don't play innocent with me. Telling the man who broke up with you that you're pregnant is the oldest trick in the book. If you think I'm falling for it, you're insane."

Grace hadn't expected this would be an easy conversation, but for some reason or another she had expected it to be fair. The Danny she remembered from the beach house might have been shocked, but he would have at least given her a chance to talk.

"I'm not insane. I am pregnant."

"I told you to get out."

"This isn't going to go away because you don't believe me."

"Grace, I said leave."

His voice was hard and cold and his office fell deadly silent. Knowing there was no talking to him in that state and hoping that after she gave him a few hours for her announcement to sink in he might be more amenable to discussing it, Grace did as he asked. She left his office with her head high, controlling the tears that welled behind her eyelids.

The insult of his reaction tightened her chest and she marched straight to her desk. She yanked open the side drawer, withdrew her purse and walked out of the building as if it were the most natural thing in the world for her to do. When she got into her car, she dropped her head to her steering wheel and let the tears fall.

Eventually it would be obvious she hadn't lied. But having Danny call her a schemer was the absolute worst experience she'd ever had.

Partially because he believed it. He believed she would trick him.

Grace's cheeks heated from a sudden rush of indignation.

It was as if he didn't know her at all—or she didn't know him at all.

Or maybe they didn't know each other.

She started her car and headed home. She needed the day to recover from that scene, but also as sick as she was she couldn't go back to work until she and Danny had talked this out. Pretty soon everybody would guess what had happened. If nothing else, they had to do damage control. There were lots of decisions that had to be made. So when she got home she would call her supervisor, explain she'd gotten sick and that she might be out a few days. Then she and Danny would resolve this *away* from the office.

Because she had written down his home number and cell number when he left the message on her answering machine the Sunday night he'd returned from his business trip, Grace called both his house and his cell that night.

He didn't answer.

She gave him forty-eight hours and called Thursday morning before he would leave for work. Again, no answer.

A little more nervous now, she gave him

another forty-eight hours and called Saturday morning. No answer.

She called Monday night. No answer.

And she got the message. He wasn't going to pick up her calls.

But by that time she had something a little more serious to handle. She couldn't get well. Amazed that she'd even been able to go to work the Monday of her encounter with Danny, she spent her days in bed, until, desperate for help and advice, she told her mother that she was pregnant and sicker than she believed was normal. They made a quick gynecologist appointment and her doctor told her that she was simply enduring extreme morning sickness.

Too worried about her baby to risk the stress of dealing with Danny, Grace put off calling him. Her life settled into a simple routine of forcing herself out of bed, at least to the couch in her living room, but that was as far as she got, and watching TV all day, as her mother fussed over her.

Knowing the bonus she'd received for her weekend with Orlando would support her through her pregnancy if she were frugal, she quit her job. Swearing her immediate supervisor to secrecy in their final phone conversation, she confided that she was pregnant and having troubles, though she didn't name the baby's father. And she slid out of Carson Services as if she'd never been there.

She nearly called Danny in March, right before the baby was born, but, again, didn't have the strength to handle the complexities of their situation. Even though he would be forced to believe she hadn't lied, he might still see her as a cheat. Someone who had tricked him. She didn't know how to explain that she hadn't, and after nine months of "morning sickness" she didn't give a damn. A man who behaved the way he had wasn't her perfect partner. His money didn't make him the special prize he seemed to believe he was. It was smarter to focus on the joy of becoming a mother, the joy of having a child, than to think about a guy so hurt by his divorce that he couldn't believe anything anyone told him.

When Sarah was born everything suddenly changed. No longer sick and now responsible for a child, Grace focused on finding a job. Happily she found one that paid nearly double what she'd been making at Carson Services. Because her parents had moved into her house to help while she was pregnant, she surprised them by buying the little bungalow down the street. Her mother wanted to baby-sit while Grace worked. Her dad could keep up both lawns. And the mortgage on the new house for her parents was small.

Busy and happy, Grace didn't really think about Danny and before she knew it, it was September and Sarah was six months old. Everything from baby-sitting to pediatrician appointments was taken care of. Everyone in her little family was very happy.

And Grace wondered why she would want to tell Danny at all.

But holding Sarah that night she realized that this situation wasn't about her and Danny anymore. It was about Sarah. Every little girl had a right to know her daddy.

The following Saturday evening, Grace found herself craning her neck, straining to read the small sophisticated street signs in the development that contained Danny's house. It hadn't been hard to find his address. Convincing herself to get in the car and drive over had been harder. Ultimately she'd come to terms with it not for Danny's sake, but for Sarah's. If Grace didn't at least give Danny the chance to be a dad, then she was no better than he was.

She located his street, turned onto it and immediately saw his house. Simple stone, accented by huge multipaned windows, his house boasted a three-car garage and space. Not only was the structure itself huge, but beyond the fence that Grace assumed protected a swimming pool, beautiful green grass seemed to stretch forever before it met a wall of trees. Compared to her tiny bungalow, his home was a palace.

She parked her little red car in his driveway, got out and reached into the back seat to unbuckle Sarah. Opting not to put her in a baby carrier, Grace pulled her from the car and settled her on her arm.

Holding her squirming baby and bulky diaper bag, she strode up the stone front walk to Danny's door, once again noting the differences in their lifestyles personified by decorative black lantern light fixtures and perfect landscaping.

Grace shook her head, trying to stop the obvious conclusion from forming, but she couldn't. She and Danny were different. Too difference to be together. Why hadn't she recognized that? He probably had. That's why he'd told her he didn't want to see her. They *weren't* made for each other. Not even close.

And he'd now had fifteen months to forget her. She could have to explain the entire situation again, and then face another horrible scene.

Still, as much as she dreaded this meeting, and as much as she would prefer to raise Sarah on her own, she knew it wasn't fair for Sarah to never know her father. She also knew Danny should have the option to be part of his daughter's life. If he again chose not to believe Grace when she told him Sarah was his child, then so be it. She wouldn't beg him to be a father to their baby. She wouldn't demand DNA testing to force him in. If he wanted a DNA test, she would comply, but as far as she was concerned, she was the one doing him the favor. If he didn't wish to acknowledge his child or be a part of Sarah's life that was his decision. She wasn't going to get upset or let him hurt her again. If he said he wanted no part of her or her baby, this time Grace and Sarah would leave him alone for good.

Again without giving herself a chance to think, she rang the doorbell. Waiting for someone to answer, she glanced around at his massive home, then wished she hadn't. How could she have ever thought she belonged with someone who lived in this part of the city?

The door opened and suddenly she was face-to-face with the father of her child. Though it was Saturday he wore dress slacks and a white shirt, but his collar was unbuttoned and his tie loosened. He looked relaxed and comfortable and was even smiling.

Then his eyes darkened, his smile disappeared and his gaze dropped to Sarah, and Grace realized he remembered who she was.

She took a breath. "Can we come in?"

The expression in his eyes changed, darkening even more, reminding Grace of a building storm cloud. For the twenty seconds that he remained stonily silent, she was positive he would turn her away. For those same twenty seconds, with his dark eyes condemning her, she fervently wished he would.

But without saying a word, he pulled open his door and stepped aside so she could enter.

"Thank you." She walked into the echoing foyer of his big house, fully expecting this to be the worst evening of her life.

CHAPTER FOUR

As GRACE BRUSHED by Danny, a band of pain tightened his chest. At first he thought the contraction was a result of his anger with Grace, fury that she'd continued with her pregnancy scheme. He wondered how she intended to get around DNA since he would most certainly require the test, then he actually looked at the baby in her arms, a little girl if the pink one-piece pajamas were any indication. She appeared to be about six months old—the age their baby would be if he had gotten Grace pregnant that Sunday night at his beach house. More than that, though, the baby looked exactly as Cory had when he was six months old.

Danny stood frozen, unable to do anything but stare at the chubby child in Grace's arms. Suddenly the baby smiled at him. Her plump lips lifted. Her round blue eyes filled with laughter. She made a happy gurgling sound that caused playful spit bubbles to gather at the corners of her mouth. She looked so much like Cory it was as if Danny had been unceremoniously flung back in time.

Feeling faint, he pointed down the corridor. "There's a den at the end of the hall. Would you please wait for me there?"

Grace caught his gaze with her pretty violet eyes and everything inside of Danny stilled. In a hodgepodge of pictures and words, he remembered bits and pieces of both the weekend they'd spent together with Orlando and the morning he'd kicked her out of his office—wrongly if his assumptions about the baby were correct. In his mind's eye, he saw Grace laughing with Orlando, working with him, making him comfortable. He remembered her soft and giving in his arms. He remembered her trembling when she told him she was pregnant, and then he remembered nothing but anger. He hadn't given her a chance to explain or even a sliver of benefit of the doubt. He'd instantly assumed her "pregnancy" was a ruse and wouldn't hear another word.

"I don't think we want to be interrupted," he said, grasping for any excuse that would give him two minutes to come to terms with some of this before he had to talk to her. "So I need to instruct my housekeeper that we're to be left alone."

She pressed her lips together, nodded and headed down the hall. Once Danny saw her turn into the den, he collapsed on the bottom step of the spiral staircase in his foyer and dropped his head to his hands.

They were shaking. His knees felt like rubber. Pain ricocheted through him and he squeezed his eyes shut. In vivid detail, he saw Cory's birth, his first birthday party, and every Christmas they'd had together. He remembered his giggle. He remembered his endless questions as he grew from a toddler into a little boy. He remembered how he loved garbage trucks and mailmen.

Pain overwhelmed him as he relived every second of the best and worst six years of his life and then realized he could very well go through it all again. The first birthday. Laughing, happy Christmases. Questions and curiosities. And pain. One day he was a doting dad and the next he was living alone, without even the possibility of seeing his son again.

He fought the anger that automatically surged up in him when the thought about his marriage, about Lydia. In the past year, his sense of fair play had compelled him to examine his marriage honestly and he had to admit that Lydia hadn't been a horrible shrew. *He* hadn't been a terrible husband. Their marriage hadn't ended because he and his ex-wife were bad people, but because they'd hit a crossroad that neither had anticipated. A crossroad where there had been no choice but to separate. They had once been the love of each other's life, yet when their marriage had begun to crumble, they'd both forgotten the eight good years, only remembered their horrible final year, and fought bitterly. They'd hurt each other. Used Cory as a weapon. And both of them had walked away damaged.

Remembering that only made his upcoming showdown with Grace more formidable. He and Grace didn't have two years of courtship and six years of marriage to look back on to potentially keep them from hurting each other. So how did he expect their confrontation to turn out any better than his fight with Lydia had?

He didn't.

He wouldn't shirk his responsibility to Grace's baby. But he had learned enough from the past that the key to survival was not being so in love with his daughter that she could turn into Grace's secret weapon.

Finally feeling that he knew what he had to do, Danny rose from the step, went to the kitchen and told his housekeeper he and Grace weren't to be disturbed, then he walked to the den.

Unfortunately he couldn't keep the displeasure out of his voice when he said, "Let me see her."

Grace faced him. "Save your anger, Danny. I was the one left to have this baby alone. I was so sick I had to quit my job and depend on my parents to basically nurse me for nine months. The bonus you gave me went to support me until I had Sarah and could go back to work. I was sick, exhausted and worried that if anything went wrong when she was born I wouldn't be able to pay for proper care. You could have helped me through all of that, but you never even followed up on me. So the way I see this, you don't have anything to complain about."

She was right, of course. It didn't matter that he was still hurting from the end of his marriage when she told him she was pregnant. He hadn't for two seconds considered Grace or her feelings. Still, he had no proof that she was the innocent victim she wanted him to believe she was. The weekend they'd spent together, he'd made himself an easy mark for a woman he really didn't know. He'd never wanted another relationship, let alone a child. And now he had one with a stranger. A woman he genuinely believed had tricked him.

"What made it all worse was wondering about your reaction when I did bring Sarah to you." She sat on the leather sofa in the conversation area, laid the gurgling baby on the cushion and pulled the bonnet ribbon beneath the little girl's chin, untying the bow.

Danny's breathing stuttered as he stared at the baby. *His daughter.* A perfect little pink bundle of joy. She punched and pedaled her legs as Grace removed her bonnet.

Grace's voice softly intruded into his thoughts. "I understood when you told me you didn't want to see me anymore. I had every intention of respecting that, if only because of pride. But this baby was both of our doing."

Sarah spit out her pacifier and began to cry.

Grace lifted the little girl from the sofa cushion and smoothed her lips across her forehead. "I know. I know," she singsonged. "You're hungry."

She rose and handed the baby to Danny. "Can you take her while I get her bottle?"

Panic skittered through him and he backed away. He hadn't held a baby since Cory.

To his surprise Grace laughed. "Come on. She won't bite. She doesn't have teeth yet."

"I've…I'm…I just—"

Realizing he was behaving like an idiot, Danny stopped stuttering. He wasn't an idiot. And he would always think of Cory every time he looked at Sarah, but there was no way he'd admit that to Grace. She already knew enough about him and he didn't know half as much about her. Seeing Cory every time he looked at Sarah would be his cross to bear in private.

He reached out to take the baby, but this time Grace pulled her back.

"Sit," she said as if she'd thought his hesitancy was uncertainty about how to hold the baby. "I'll hand her to you."

Deciding not to argue her assumption, Danny lowered himself to the sofa and Grace placed the baby in his arms. "Just set her bottom on your lap, and support her back with your left hand."

He did that and the baby blinked up at him,

her crying becoming sniffles as she lost herself to confusion about the stranger holding her.

Staring at her mutely, Danny identified. The first time he'd seen Cory was immediately after he'd slid into the doctor's hands. He'd been purple and wrinkled and when the doctor slapped his tiny behind he'd shrieked like a banshee. The little girl on Danny's lap was clean and now quiet. The total opposite of her half brother.

Grace pulled a bottle from her diaper bag. Dripping formula onto her wrist, she checked the bottle's temperature and said, "Can I take this to your kitchen and warm it?"

"Go back to the foyer, then turn right. The door at the end of the hall leads to the kitchen. My housekeeper is there. She'll help you."

Grace nodded and left.

Danny glanced down at the blue-eyed, rather bald baby. He took a breath. She blinked at him again, as if still confused.

"I'm your father."

She cocked her head to the right. The same way Cory used to. Especially when Danny would tell him anything about Carson Services, about responsibility, about carrying on the family name, as if the idea of doing anything other than paint was absurd.

Remembering Cory's reaction tightened Danny's chest again, but this time it wasn't from the memory of how, even as a small child, Cory had seemed to reject the idea of taking over the family business. Danny suddenly realized this little girl was now the one in line to run Carson Services. Grace might not know it, but Danny did.

Grace ran to the kitchen and didn't find a housekeeper, but she did locate a microwave into which she quickly shoved the bottle. She'd never seen a person more uncomfortable with a baby than Danny appeared to be, which was surprising considering he had a son, but she wasn't so insensitive that she didn't realize that meeting Sarah hadn't been easy for him.

She'd been preoccupied with Sarah's needs and hadn't factored Danny's shock into the equation. But having watched his facial expression shift and change, she realized that though he might not have believed Grace when she told him she was pregnant he seemed to be accepting that Sarah was his.

When the timer bell rang, she grabbed the bottle and headed back to his den. Walking down the hall she heard Danny's soft voice.

"And that's why mutual funds are better for some people."

Grace stopped just outside the door.

"Of course, there are times when it's more logical to put the money of a conservative investor in bonds. Especially a nervous investor. Somebody who can't afford to take much risk. So you always have to question your investor enough that you can determine the level of risk his portfolio and personality can handle."

Standing by the wall beside the door, Grace twisted so she could remain hidden as she peered inside. Sarah gripped Danny's finger and stared up at him. Her blue eyes sharp and alert. Danny appeared comfortable, too, holding the baby loosely on his lap, and Grace realized that talking about something familiar was how Danny had overcome his apprehensions. Still, stocks? Poor Sarah!

"It's all about the individual. Some people are afraid of the stock market. Which is another reason mutual funds are so great. They spread the risk over a bunch of stocks. If one fails, another stock in the fund could skyrocket and balance everything out."

If it had been under any other circumstances, Grace would have burst out laughing. Danny looked up and saw her standing there. He grimaced. "Sorry. I didn't know what else to talk about."

She shrugged. "I guess it doesn't really matter. All a baby really cares about is hearing your voice." She walked into the room and lifted Sarah from Danny's lap. Nestling the baby into the crook of her arm, she added, "When in doubt, make up something. Maybe a story about a bunny or a bear. Just a short little anything."

Danny didn't reply, but rose and walked to the window. "You should be the one to sit."

Not about to remind him that there was plenty of space for both of them on the leather sofa, Grace took the place he had vacated. With two silent parents, the sound of Sarah greedily sucking filled the room.

"I almost wish you hadn't brought her to me."

Grace hadn't forgotten that he'd broken up with her before she told him she was pregnant. Still, that was his tough luck. He'd created a child and she wasn't letting him pretend he hadn't.

"She's your child."

"Yes. And I know you think there are all

kinds of reasons that's great, but you're not going to like the way this has to play out."

"The way this has to play out?"

"I have to raise my daughter."

Not expecting that, Grace stared at his stiff back. But rather than be offended by his defiant stance, she remembered the feeling of his corded muscles beneath her fingertips. The firmness of his skin. Her own shivers of delight from having his hands on her.

Reaction flared inside her but she quickly shook it off. She wouldn't let herself fall victim to his charm again. Too much was at stake. She didn't know the official definition of "raise his daughter," but it sounded as if he intended to get more than a Saturday afternoon with Sarah every other weekend. There was no way Grace would let him take Sarah and ignore her. He hadn't ever wanted her. If he took her now, it would probably be out of a sense of duty to his family.

Still, if Grace argued, if she didn't handle this situation with kid gloves, her reply could sound like an accusation and accusations only caused arguments. She did not want to argue. She wanted all this settled as quickly and amicably as possible.

"It's good that you want to be involved—"

Danny suddenly turned from the window and caught her gaze, but Grace couldn't read the expression in his eyes and fell silent. She didn't know what he was thinking because she didn't know him. Not at all. She hadn't worked with him long enough to even know him as a boss. With Orlando he had been fun and funny. But when she'd told him about being pregnant he'd been hard, cold, unyielding. As far as she knew he had two personalities. A good guy and a bad guy and she had a sneaking suspicion few people saw the good guy.

"I want my daughter to live with me."

"Live with you?" *Grace* would be the one getting a visit every other Saturday afternoon? He had to be joking. Or insane.

"I've got money enough and clout enough that if I take you to court I'll end up with custody."

Grace gaped at him. It had been difficult to bring her child to meet him. As far as she was concerned, he could have stayed out of their lives forever. She was only here for Sarah's sake. Trying to grasp that he wanted to take Sarah away from her was staggering. Could his money really put Grace in a position where she'd be forced to hand over her innocent, defenseless baby daughter to a complete stranger? A man who didn't even want her?

She pulled in a breath and said, "That's ridiculous."

"Not really. When I retire, the option to take over Carson Services will be Sarah's. She'll need to be prepared. Only I can prepare her."

"But your son—"

"Never wanted the job. It falls to Sarah."

Overwhelmed, Grace shook her head. "This is too much in one day. I never even considered the possibility that you wanted to know I'd had a baby. Yet the day you find out, you're suddenly demanding custody."

"I don't have any other choice."

Grace sat in stunned silence. The whole hell of it was he didn't want Sarah. He wasn't asking for any reason except to fulfill a duty. Which was just wonderful. Grace would lose the baby she adored to a man who didn't want her, a man who intended to *train* her for a job. Not to love and nurture her, but to assure there was someone to take over the family business.

The injustice of it suffocated Grace at the same time that she understood it. Danny might not want Sarah, but he had a responsibility to her and to his family.

She wondered if he really needed to live with Sarah to teach her, then unexpectedly understood his side again. Preparing to take over a family fortune required more than a formal education. It required knowledge of family history and traditions. It required social graces. It required building social relationships.

All of which Grace didn't have. Sarah had to live with him at least part of the time.

Part of the time.

Suddenly inspired, Grace said, "You know what? I think I have a compromise."

"I don't compromise."

No kidding.

"Okay, then maybe what I have is a deal to propose."

His eyes narrowed ominously. "I don't need a deal, either."

"Well, listen anyway. The problem I see is that you don't know Sarah—"

"Living together will take care of that."

"Just listen. You don't know Sarah. I don't think you really want her. You're asking for custody out of a sense of duty and responsibility not to her but to your family, and, as bad as it is for my cause, I understand it. But as Sarah's mother I can't let you take my baby when you don't want her. So what I'm going to propose is that you come to live with Sarah and me for the next two weeks."

His face scrunched in confusion. "How exactly would that help?"

"If nothing else, in two weeks, I'll get to know you and you'll get to know her. Especially since I don't have a housekeeper or nanny. You and I will be the ones to care for her."

His shrewd brown eyes studied her, as if he were trying to think of the catch. Since there was no catch, Grace continued.

"The deal is if you can spend two weeks with us, learning to care for her, and if at the end of that two weeks I feel comfortable with you having her, I won't contest *shared* custody. Week about. I get her one week. You have her the next. That way, as she gets older, you can schedule the functions you think she needs to be involved in, and I won't have to give her over to you permanently."

Danny shook his head. "Grace—"

"I won't give her over to you permanently. Not for any reason. Not any way. The best you'll get from me is week about and only if I believe you can handle her."

"You're not in a position to name terms," Danny said, shaking his head. "I can beat you in court."

"And then what?" Grace asked barely holding onto her temper. This time yesterday he didn't know he had a daughter. This time last year he didn't want to even hear Grace was pregnant. He couldn't expect her to hand over their child. She'd spend every cent of money she had before she'd recklessly hand over her baby to a man who didn't want Sarah, a man who probably would keep his distance and never love her.

"Say you do beat me in court. What are you going to do? Pass off your daughter's care to nannies, and let her be raised by a stranger when she could be spending that time with her mother? Is that your idea of grooming her? Showing her how to walk all over people?"

He ran his hand along the back of his neck.

She had him. They might not have spent much time together, but she'd noticed that when he rubbed the back of his neck, he was thinking.

"It sure as hell isn't my idea of how to teach

her," Grace said quietly, calming down so he would, too. "If nothing else, admit you need some time to adjust to being her dad."

He sighed. "You want *two* weeks?"

"If you can't handle her for two weeks, how do you expect to have her permanently?"

Danny said nothing and Grace retraced her argument, trying to figure out why two weeks made him hesitate. A person who wanted full custody couldn't object to a mere two-week stay with the same baby he was trying to get custody of—

Unless he wasn't worried about two weeks with Sarah as much as he was worried about two weeks with Grace. The last time they'd spent three *days* together they'd ended up in bed.

The air suddenly filled with electricity, so much that Grace could almost see the crackles and sparks. Memories—not of his accusations when she told him she was pregnant, but his soft caresses that Sunday night and Monday morning—flooded her mind and the attraction she'd felt the weekend they'd spent together returned full force.

But she didn't want it. She did not want to be attracted to this man. He'd come right out and said he didn't want a relationship with her. Plus, he had clout that she didn't have. Grace needed all her facilities to fight for Sarah's interests. She couldn't risk that he'd push her around in court the way he'd steamrolled her when she told him she was pregnant.

The reminder of how he'd kicked her out of his office without hearing her out was all she needed. Her chin came up. Her spine stiffened. She would never, ever trust him again. She would never give in to the attraction again.

"You're perfectly safe with me. Our time together was a mistake. I wouldn't even speak to you were it not for Sarah."

He remained silent so long that Grace sighed with disgust. He hadn't had a clue how painful his words had been to her. He hadn't cared that she could have misinterpreted everything he'd said and drawn the conclusion that he'd had his fun with her but she wasn't good enough to really love. He'd been so wrapped up in his own wants and needs that he never considered hers.

Or anyone's as far as Grace knew.

Another reason to stay the hell away from him.

"I mean it, Danny. I want nothing to do with you and will fight tooth and nail before

I let you take Sarah even for weekends if only because you're a virtual stranger."

Obviously controlling his anger, he looked at the ceiling then back at her. "If I spend two weeks with you and the baby you won't contest shared custody," he said, repeating what he believed to be their arrangement.

"*If* by the end of those two weeks I believe you'll be good to Sarah."

Sarah had stopped sucking. Grace glanced down to see the baby had fallen asleep in her arms. "If you wish, we can have our lawyers draw up papers."

"Oh, I *will* have my lawyer write an agreement."

"Great. Once we get it signed we can start."

"You'll have it tonight. Do you have an email address?"

"Yes."

"Watch your computer. You'll have the agreement before you go to bed. You can email me directions to your house and I'll be there tomorrow."

CHAPTER FIVE

WHEN GRACE RECEIVED Danny's email with their agreement as an attachment, she realized that no matter how simple and straightforward, she couldn't sign any legal document without the advice of counsel. She replied saying she wanted her own lawyer to review the agreement before she signed it, expecting him to be angry at the delay. Instead he was surprisingly accommodating of her request.

She spoke with a lawyer Monday morning, who gave her the go-ahead to sign, and emailed Danny that she had executed the agreement and he could sign it that evening when he arrived at her house.

Busy at work, she didn't give Danny or the agreement another thought until she walked into the foyer of her little bungalow and saw something she hadn't considered.

The downstairs of her house had an open

floor plan. Pale orange ceramic tile ran from the foyer to the back door. An oatmeal-colored Berber area rug sat beneath the burnt-orange tweed sofa and the matching love seat, delineating that space. Similarly the tan, brown and black print rug beneath the oak table and chairs marked off the dining area. A black-and-tan granite-topped breakfast bar separated the living room from the kitchen, but because there were no cabinets above it, people in the kitchen were clearly visible from any point downstairs.

Grace wasn't afraid that Danny wouldn't like her home. She didn't give a damn if he liked it or not. What troubled her was that with the exception of the two bedrooms, both upstairs, there was nowhere to hide. Anytime they were downstairs they would technically be together.

"Well, Sarah," she said, sliding the baby out of her carrier seat and giving her a quick kiss on the cheek. In her yellow one-piece outfit, Sarah looked like a ray of sunshine. "I guess it's too late to worry about that now."

As the words came out of her mouth, the doorbell rang, and Grace winced. If that was Danny, it really was too late to worry about the close quarters of her house now.

Angling the baby on her hip, Grace walked to the door and opened it. Danny stood on her small porch, holding a garment bag, with a duffel bag sitting beside his feet. Dressed in jeans and a loose-fitting sport shirt, he looked comfortable and relaxed, reminding her of their time together at his beach house.

A sudden avalanche of emotion overtook her. She had really fallen hard for him that weekend. Not just because he was sexy, though he was. He had an air of power and strength that—combined with his shiny black hair, piercing black eyes and fabulous body— made him one of the sexiest men Grace had ever met. Staring into his eyes, she remembered the way he made love to her. She remembered their pillow talk and their one phone conversation. He had definitely felt something for her that weekend, too, but in the one short week he was out of town he'd lost it. He hadn't believed her when she told him she was pregnant. He'd kicked her out of his office. And now they were here. Fighting over custody of a baby he hadn't wanted.

"This house doesn't look big enough for two people, let alone three."

"It's got more space than you think," Grace said, opening the door a little wider so he could enter, as she reminded herself she had to do this because she couldn't beat him in court. "It looks like a ranch, but it isn't. There are two bedrooms upstairs."

"Yeah, they're probably no bigger than closets."

Grace told herself she could do this. She'd dealt with grouchy Danny every time she'd spoken to him—except for that one weekend. The person she'd met that weekend was more likely the exception and grouchy Danny was the rule. She wasn't about to let their two weeks begin with her apologizing.

Ignoring his closet comment, she said, "Let's take your bags upstairs and get them out of the way."

Grace turned and began walking up the steps, and, following after her, Danny got a flashback of following her up the steps of his beach house. It intensified when he glanced down at the steps to avoid looking at her shapely legs. The memory was so clear it made him dizzy, as if he were stepping back in time.

But he wasn't. They were here and now, fifteen months later. She'd had his child. She might have done it without him, but ultimately she'd brought the baby to him. And why not? As far as Grace knew little Sarah could inherit a fortune—even before Danny was dead if she became the CEO of Carson Services when Danny retired.

He didn't want even a portion of the family fortune to go to an opportunist, but his threat of taking Grace to court to get full custody had been empty. An attempt to pressure her into giving him their daughter. Then Grace had come up with a compromise and to Danny's surprise it really did suit him. He could train Sarah without paying off her mother.

Plus, he no longer had the worry that a custody battle gave her reason to dig into his past.

All he had to do was spend two weeks with Grace, a woman who he believed tricked him.

At the top of the steps, Grace turned to the right, opened a door, and stepped back so he could enter the room. To his surprise, Grace was correct, the bedroom was more spacious than he'd thought from the outward appearance of the house. Even with a double bed in the center of the room, a knotty pine armoire and dresser, and a small desk in the corner, there was plenty of space to walk.

He hesitantly said, "This is nice."

"We have to share the bathroom."

He faced her. She'd taken a few steps into the room, as if wanting to be available to answer questions, but not exactly thrilled to be in the same room with him. Especially not a bedroom.

Her soft voice triggered another batch of beach house memories. Grace telling him to promote someone else. Grace looking like an angel in front of the upstairs widows. Grace ready to accept his kiss...

He shoved the memories out of his brain, reminding himself that woman probably didn't exist. "I'll keep my things in a shaving kit. I won't take up any room."

She turned away from him with a shrug. Walking to the door, she said, "It doesn't matter one way or the other to me."

He couldn't tell if she intended to insult him or prove to him that his being there had no meaning to her beyond their reaching an accord about custody, but the indifference he heard in her voice was just fine with him. He didn't want to be involved with her any more than she wanted to be involved with him.

Which should make for a fabulous two weeks.

He tossed his duffel bag on the bed and walked the garment bag to the closet before going downstairs. At the bottom of the steps, he realized that the entire first floor of the house was open. He could see Grace puttering in the compact kitchen and Sarah swinging contentedly in the baby swing sitting in the space between the dining area and living room.

Walking to the kitchen, he said, "Anything I can help you with?"

"You're here for Sarah. So why don't you amuse her, while I make dinner?"

"Okay." Her cool tone of voice didn't affect him because she was correct. He was here for Sarah. Not for Grace. Not to make small talk or plans or, God forbid, even to become friendly.

He glanced at the cooing baby. A trip to the department store that morning to arrange for baby furniture to be delivered to his house had shown him just how behind the times he had become in the nine years that had passed since Cory was a baby. Playpens were now play yards. Car seats had become downright challenging. He didn't have to be a genius to know that if the equipment had changed, so had the rules. He wouldn't do anything with Sarah without asking.

"Should I take her out of the seat?"

Pulling a salad bowl from a cabinet, Grace said, "Not when she's happy. Just sit on the floor in front of her and chat."

Chat. With a baby. He'd tried that the day Grace brought Sarah to his house and hadn't known what to say. Obviously he had to think of something to talk about other than investing. But he wasn't sitting on the floor. After a quick look around, he grabbed one of the oak ladder-back chairs from the table in the dining room section and set it in front of the swing.

"Hey, Sarah."

She pulled the blue plastic teething ring from her mouth and cooed at him. He smiled and settled more comfortably on the chair as he studied her, trying to think of something to say. Nothing came. She gurgled contently as she waved her arms, sending the scent of baby powder through the air to his nose. That brought a burst of memories of Cory.

He'd been so proud of that kid. So smitten. So enamored with the fun of having a baby that he'd thought his life was perfect. Then Cory had shown artistic ability and Lydia wanted to send him to special school. Danny had thought she was jumping the gun, making a decision that didn't need to be made until Cory was older.

Taking a breath, Danny forced himself back to the present. He had to stop thinking of Cory. He had to focus on Sarah. He had to create an amicable relationship so their time together would be happy and not a horrible strain.

Then he noticed that the one-piece yellow thing she wore made her hair appear reddish brown. "I think somebody's going to be a redhead."

The baby gooed. Danny smiled. Curious, he turned toward the kitchen. "My parents are French and English. So I don't think the red hair comes from my side of the family. How about yours?"

Grace grudgingly said, "Both of my parents are Scottish."

"Well, that explains it."

Danny's comment fell on total silence. Though he was here for Sarah, he and Grace had two long weeks to spend together. He might not want to be her friend, but he didn't want to be miserable, either. Studying Grace as she ripped lettuce and tossed it into a bowl, he swore he could see waves of anger emanate from her. It might have been her idea to share custody, but she clearly didn't want to spend two weeks with him any more than he wanted to spend two weeks with her. He'd forced her hand with the threat of taking her baby away.

Taking her baby away.

He hadn't really looked at what he was doing from her perspective and suddenly realized how selfish he must seem to her.

"Had I gone for full custody, I wouldn't have shut you out of her life completely."

"No, but you would have demanded that she live with you and I'd be the one with visitation."

She walked over to him and displayed a plate with two steaks. "I'm going to the back deck to the grill." She waited a heartbeat, then said, "You're not afraid to be alone with her, are you?"

As if any man would ever admit to being afraid of anything. "No. But I'm guessing you're a better choice to stay inside with her, which means I should grill the steaks."

"Great." She handed him the plate. "I'll finish the salad."

She pivoted and returned to the kitchen without waiting for his reply. Danny rose from his seat and walked out to the deck.

He agreed with her nonconversation policy. There was no point in talking. She didn't like him. And, well, frankly, he didn't like her.

He dropped the plate of steaks on a small table and set the temperature on the grill. Still, whether he agreed with her or not, not talking guaranteed that the next two weeks would be two of the longest of his life. Torture really. Maybe payback for his not believing her? He slapped the steaks on the grill rack.

That was probably it. Payback. But what Grace didn't realize was that the way she treated him was also proof that she wasn't the sweet innocent she'd pretended to be.

He almost laughed. What a mess. All because he couldn't keep his hands off a woman. He'd never make *that* mistake again.

He closed the lid and looked out over the expanse of backyard. Grace didn't have a huge space but what she had was well tended. Her bungalow was neat and clean, newly remodeled. Her yard was well kept. He hoped that was an indicator that Grace would take good care of Sarah during the weeks she had her.

He heard a giggle from inside the house. Turning, he saw he hadn't shut the French doors. He ambled over and was just about to push them closed when he heard Grace talking. "So, somebody needs to go upstairs and get a fresh diaper."

She lifted the baby from the swing and rubbed noses with her. "I swear, Sarah, there's got to be a better system."

The baby laughed. Danny sort of chuckled himself. A person would think that after all the generations of babies, somebody, somewhere would have thought of a better system than diapers.

"Let's take care of that. Then we'll feed you something yummy for dinner."

The baby giggled and cooed and Danny felt a quick sting of conscience for worrying about Sarah when she was in Grace's care. Grace obviously loved the baby.

He took a quick breath. She might love the baby but there was a lot more to consider in child rearing than just love. Grace was on trial these next two weeks every bit as much as he was. He wouldn't be convinced she was a good mom, just because she was sweet. She wasn't sweet. As far as he knew she was a conniver. She could have seen the French doors were open and put on a show with the baby for him to see.

He closed the doors and checked the steaks. They were progressing nicely. He sat on one of the deck chairs. The thick red, yellow and tan striped padding felt good to his tired back and he let his eyelids droop. He didn't raise them again until he heard the French doors open.

"How's it going?" Grace asked quietly. Sarah sat on her forearm, once again chewing the blue teething ring.

Danny sat up. "Fine. I was just about to peek at the steaks." He poked and prodded the steaks, closed the lid and chucked Sarah under the chin. "You're just about the cutest kid in the world, aren't you?"

Sarah giggled and cooed and Grace regretted her decision to bring the baby with her when she checked on him. When she least expected it, he would say or do something that would remind her that she'd genuinely believed he was a nice, normal guy the weekend they'd spent at the beach house. Volunteering to help her in the kitchen when he first came downstairs hadn't been expected. His wanting to know Sarah's heritage had struck her as adorable. And now he looked perfectly natural, perfectly comfortable on her back deck.

But he was also here to convince Grace

that he would be able to care for Sarah. Technically he was on good behavior. She refused to get sucked in again as she had at the beach house.

She turned to go back into the house, but he said, "Grace?" And every nerve ending she had went on red alert. He had a sexy quality to his voice that was magnified when he spoke softly. Of course, that took her back to their pillow talk the night they had slept together and that made her all quivery inside.

Scowling because she didn't want to like him and did want to let him know that if he thought he could charm her he was wrong, she faced him. "Yes?"

"You never told me how you wanted your steak."

Feeling embarrassment heat her cheeks, she quickly turned to the door again. "Medium is fine."

With that she walked into the house. She put Sarah in her high chair and rummaged through the cupboards for a jar of baby food, which she heated. By the time she was done feeding Sarah, had her face cleaned and the rubber teething ring back in her chubby hands, Danny brought in the steaks.

"Salad is on the counter," she said, as she

laid plates and silverware on the table. "Could you bring that in, too?" Her new strategy was to put him to work before he could volunteer. This way, he wouldn't seem nice, he would only be following orders.

He did as she asked and they sat down at the table, across from each other, just as they had been sitting that Sunday night at his beach house. She'd dressed up, hoping he would notice her. But tonight, on the trip upstairs to change Sarah's diaper, she'd put on her worst jeans, her ugliest T-shirt. What a difference fifteen months made.

"Your house is nice."

"Thank you."

Silence reigned for another minute, before Danny said, "So, did you buy it remodeled like this?"

She bit back a sigh, loath to tell him anything about herself. More than that, though, they'd discussed this that night at the beach house. He'd forgotten. So much for thinking she'd made any kind of impression on him

"It was a wreck when I bought it."

"Oh, so you did the remodeling—I mean with a contractor, right?"

"No. My cousin and I remodeled it." And she'd told him that, too.

He smiled. "Really?"

Grace rose from her seat. "You know what? I'm really not all that hungry and it's time for me to get Sarah bathed and ready for bed." She smiled stiffly. "If you'll excuse me."

Alone at the table Danny quietly finished his steak. If Grace was going to continually take Sarah and leave the room, maybe he shouldn't cancel tomorrow's dinner engagement? He drew in a breath, then expelled it quickly. He couldn't dodge or fudge this commitment. He wanted at least shared custody of his daughter, and Grace had handed him the way to get it without a custody battle that would result in her investigating his past and probably result in him losing all but scant visitation rights. So he couldn't leave. He had to be here every minute he could for the next two weeks.

The problem was he and Grace also had to be together. He'd thought they could be at least cordial, but this was what he got for his positive attitude. The silent treatment. Well, she could save herself the trouble if she intended to insult him. His ex-wife had been the ultimate professional when it came to the silent treatment. Grace would have to go a long way to match that.

But when he'd not only finished eating his dinner and stacking the dishes in the dishwasher and Grace still hadn't come downstairs, he wondered if maybe she couldn't give Lydia a tip or two in the silent treatment department. Angry, because the whole point of his being here was to spend time with his daughter, Danny stormed up the steps. He stopped outside Grace's bedroom door because it was ajar and what he saw compelled him to rethink everything.

Though Grace's bedroom was pretty, decorated in warm colors like reds, yellows and taupe, a big white crib, white changing table and two white dressers took up most of the space. Still, there was enough adult furniture pushed into the room's corners that Danny could almost envision how she probably had her room before the baby was born. When she met him, she had had a pretty house, a sanctuary bedroom and a budding career. When she got pregnant, she'd lost her job. When she actually had Sarah, most of her pretty house had become a nursery.

"Oh, now, you can't be sleepy yet."

Grace's soft voice drifted out into the hallway.

"You still need to spend some time with your daddy."

Danny swallowed when he heard himself referred to again as a daddy. He was only getting used to that.

"I know you're tired, but just stay awake long enough to say good-night."

She lifted Sarah from the changing table and brushed her cheek across the baby's little cheek. Mesmerized, Danny watched. He'd forgotten how stirring it was to watch a mother with her baby.

"Come on," Grace said, turning to the door. Danny jumped back, out of her line of vision.

Thinking fast, he leaped into his room and quickly closed the door. He counted to fifty, hoping that gave her enough time to get downstairs, then opened the door a crack and peered out into the hall. When he found it empty, he walked downstairs, too. Grace sat on the sofa, Sarah on her lap.

"Can I hold her before she goes to bed?"

"Sure."

She made a move to rise, but Danny stopped her. "I'll take her from your lap."

Grace nodded and Danny reached down to get Sarah. Lifting her, he let his eyes wander over to Grace and their gazes caught. Except now he knew why he was no longer dealing with the sweet, innocent woman he'd slept with at the beach house. Her life had changed so much that even if she hadn't tricked him, she couldn't be the same woman. She'd gotten pregnant to a stranger. He'd rejected her. She'd lost her job and was too sick to get another. She'd had her baby alone. Any of those would have toughened her. Made her cynical. Maybe even made her angry.

No. She was no longer the woman he knew from the beach house.

CHAPTER SIX

DANNY AWAKENED TO the sounds of the shower.
Grace was up before him and already started
on her day. He waited until the shower
stopped, then listened for the sounds of the
bathroom door opening before he got out of
bed, slipped on a robe and grabbed his shaving kit.

In the hall he heard the melodious sounds
of Grace's voice as she spoke to Sarah and
laughed with her. He stopped. Her soft laughter took him back to their weekend at the
beach house. He shook his head and walked
into the bathroom. He had to stop remembering. As he'd realized last night, that Grace no
longer existed. Plus, they had a child. Sarah's
future was in their hands. He didn't take that
responsibility lightly anymore.

After a quick shower, Danny dressed in a
navy suit, ready for a long day of business

meetings. He jogged down the stairs and was immediately enfolded in the scent of breakfast.

Walking to the small dining area, he said, "Good morning."

Grace breezed away from the table and strode into the kitchen. "Good morning."

Sarah grinned up at him toothlessly. He smiled down at her. "And how are you today?"

Sarah giggled. Danny took a seat at the table. Grace set a dish containing an omelet, two slices of toast and some applesauce in front of him. Suddenly her coolness made sense. He'd forced her to have their baby alone, yet she'd nonetheless suggested shared custody, allowing him into her home to give him the opportunity to prove himself. Even if the Grace who'd seduced him that night no longer existed, the woman who'd taken her place had her sense of generosity. Even to her detriment. She wouldn't cheat him out of time with her daughter. Or use Sarah as a weapon. She was fair and it cost her.

Grace set her dish at the place opposite Danny and sat down. She immediately grabbed her napkin, opened it on her lap and picked up her fork.

Sarah shrieked.

Grace shook her head. "You already ate."

Sarah pounded her teething ring on the high chair tray.

"A tantrum will do you no good," Grace said to Sarah, but Danny was painfully aware that she didn't speak to him. She didn't even look at him.

His chest tightened. She'd been such a fun, bubbly, lively person. Now she was cautious and withdrawn. And he had done this to her.

Grace all but gobbled her breakfast. She noticed that Danny had become quiet as she drank a cup of coffee, but she didn't have time to care. She wasn't entirely sure she would care even if she had time. He'd basically accused her of lying. He clearly believed she'd tricked him. And if both of those weren't enough, he intended to take her child every other week. She didn't want to be his friend. He was only in her house because she couldn't risk that he'd get full custody, and she also wouldn't risk her child's happiness with a grouch. So he was here to prove himself. She didn't have to entertain him.

He was lucky she'd made him breakfast. That was why she was late, and rushing, so if he expected a little morning chitchat, that was his problem.

Having eaten enough food to sustain herself until lunch, Grace rose from her seat and took her dish to the kitchen. To her surprise Danny was right behind her when she turned from the dishwasher. Her heart thudded in her chest, half from surprise, half from being so close to him. He radiated warmth or energy, or something, that made being near him intoxicating. And trouble. His being irresistible was what had caused her to let her guard down in the first place.

He handed her his plate, though most of his food hadn't been eaten.

She took a quick gulp of air to try to rid herself of the breathless feeling and looked up at him. His eyes mirrored an emotion she couldn't quite read, except that he was unsure of what he was supposed to be doing.

"I'm rushing because I'm late. You can stay and finish. Just rinse your plate when you're through and put it in the dishwasher."

"I've had enough," Danny said and as Grace turned away from the dishwasher she saw him glance around her small kitchen. "Since I'm the boss I don't have to worry about being late, so if you'd like I could clean up in here."

In his neat navy blue suit, white shirt and blue print tie, he might look like the guy who ran Carson Services, but he behaved like the Danny Grace had met at the beach house, and that wasn't right. Being attracted to him wasn't right. Even being friendly wasn't right, if only because they were on opposite ends of a custody battle.

"No, thank you," she coolly replied. "It will take me only a minute or two to wipe the skillet and stove. You go on ahead. I'm fine."

"Grace," he said with a chuckle. "It's not a big deal."

"Really?" Try as she might, she couldn't keep the sarcasm out of her voice. "I'm surprised a rich guy like you even knows how to clean a skillet."

He laughed. The sound danced along her nerve endings, reminding her again of how he'd been the night they'd made love. She fought the happy memories by recalling the scene in his office. The one where he'd called her pregnancy a scheme.

"I couldn't exactly take a maid to university. My parents might have gotten me an apartment, but unless I wanted to live in squalor I had to do at least a little straightening up."

Grace felt herself softening to him and squeezed her eyes shut. It was much easier dealing with mean Danny. No expectations were better than unmet expectations.

Opening her eyes, she faced him. "Look, I don't want you to be nice to me. I don't need you to be nice."

"Helping clean up isn't nice. It's common courtesy."

"Well, save it. You're here to prove yourself with Sarah. And you did fine this morning just by saying good morning. You noticed her. You didn't ignore her. You're on the right track."

"I'm not going to let you wait on me while I'm here."

Grace removed her apron and set it on the counter. She didn't have time or the inclination to argue. She also couldn't give a damn what he did. That only tripped memories of a man she was absolutely positive didn't exist. She couldn't get into arguments that tempted her to believe otherwise.

"Fine. Dishcloths are in the bottom drawer." She walked out of the kitchen and over to the high chair, where she lifted Sarah into her arms before she headed for the stairway.

But from the corner of her eye she could see Danny standing in the kitchen, plate in hand, watching her. He looked totally out of place and equally confused and Grace again fought against emotions she couldn't afford to have.

How could he make her feel like the one in the wrong when he had done such terrible things to her?

After a horrifically long day, Danny finally had ten minutes alone in his office. Though he tried to make a few phone calls before leaving he couldn't. Being with Grace at her house and yet not really being with Grace was driving him crazy. He could not live with someone for two whole weeks who barely spoke to him. Not that he wanted lively conversation, but he couldn't handle being ignored, either. Plus, if they didn't at least discuss Sarah and her care, especially her likes and dislikes, how were these two weeks supposed to prove to Grace that she could relax when Sarah was with him?

Knowing it wouldn't help matters if he were late for dinner that night, Danny stuffed a few files into a briefcase and left early. At her front door, he hesitated. He felt so ill at ease just walking inside that he should ring the bell. But he was living here. The next two weeks this was his home. And maybe walking in would jar Grace into realizing she had to deal with him.

He opened the door and saw Grace on the floor with Sarah, playing peekaboo.

"Hey."

Sarah squealed her delight at seeing him. Grace glanced over. "Hey."

He didn't smell anything cooking and finally, finally saw a golden opportunity. "I was thinking this afternoon that things might go easier if we just went out to dinner." He paused, but she didn't say anything. "On me, of course."

She sighed, lifted Sarah into her arms and rose from the floor. "It's not practical to go out to a restaurant with a baby every night." She walked into the kitchen, Sarah on her hip.

With Grace's reply ringing in his head, Danny looked around again. Two bears sat on the sofa. A baby swing was angled in such a way that the baby inside could be seen from the kitchen, dining room or living room. A high chair sat by the dining table. Blocks were stacked on the buffet. The room smelled of baby powder.

He remembered this now. For the first few years of a baby's life everything revolved around the baby. That had been a difficult enough adjustment for a married couple. But it had to be all-consuming for a single mom. Not just because she didn't have assistance with Sarah, but because it affected everything.

He walked into the kitchen. "Can I help with dinner?"

She pulled a package of hamburger from the refrigerator. "Do you want to grill the hamburgers?"

Eager to do his share, Danny said, "Sure."

He reached for the hamburger, but Grace pointed at his jacket and tie. "You can't cook in that."

He grimaced. "Right."

After changing into jeans and a T-shirt, he took the hamburger from the refrigerator and headed for the back deck and the grill. Grace was nowhere around, but he assumed she and the baby were in her room. Maybe because the baby needed a diaper change.

Gazing out over the short backyard Danny studied the houses near Grace's. Realizing none was as well kept as hers, he remembered her telling him about remodeling her home the night they spent at his beach house. That was why her comments about wanting to be rich hadn't struck him oddly that night. He knew she was a hard worker. But three weeks later when she told him she was pregnant, he'd forgotten how eager she was to earn her way in life. He only remembered that she'd wanted to be rich and he'd assumed the worst.

He'd seduced her, left her for a week, said he didn't want to see her again when he returned, refused to believe her when she told him she was pregnant and then threatened to file for full custody of their baby. While he'd acted on inaccurate "interpretations" of things she'd done, he'd given her five very real reasons to hate him.

It was no wonder she was cool to him. He'd not only misjudged her. He'd behaved like a horrible person.

The sound of a car pulling into her driveway brought him out of his thoughts. He strode to the far end of the deck and glanced around the side of the house just in time to see Grace pulling Sarah from the car seat. With a grocery bag hooked over her arm and

Sarah perched on the other, she walked, head down, into the house.

Danny's heart squeezed in his chest. Would he ever stop hurting people?

Grace stepped into her house at the same time that Danny walked in from the deck. "Where did you go?"

"I needed milk and hamburger buns." Carrying Sarah, she went to the kitchen to deposit her purchases.

Danny grabbed the gallon jug that dangled from her hand and put it in the refrigerator. "I could have gone to the store."

"Well, I did."

He sighed. "Grace, I want to help but I can't do things that I don't know need done."

"I didn't ask you to do anything."

But even as the words were coming out of her mouth, Grace regretted them. She slid Sarah into the high chair and turned to face Danny. He might be a difficult person, but she wasn't. And she refused to let him turn her into one.

"Here's the deal. I'm accustomed to being on my own. There's no point in breaking that habit because you'll only be here for another twelve days. So don't worry about it. Okay?"

He nodded, but he kept looking at her oddly as if she'd just discovered the secret to life. He continued to steal peeks at her all through dinner, making her nervous enough that she chattered to Sarah as they ate their hamburgers and salads, if only to bring some sound into the room.

When she could legitimately slip away to feed Sarah a bottle and put her to bed, she felt as if she were escaping a prison. She extended her alone time with a long, soothing shower, but rather than slip into her usual nightgown and robe she put on sweatpants and a T-shirt and shuffled downstairs to watch a little TV to unwind before trying to sleep.

She had just turned off all the lights and settled on the sofa with a cup of cocoa, when Danny came down the steps.

Seeing her curled up on the couch, he paused. "Sorry."

He pivoted to go back upstairs and Grace said, "Wait." She didn't want to be his friend. She didn't want to like him. She most certainly didn't want to get romantically involved with him. But she couldn't take the silence anymore and she suspected he couldn't, either.

"You don't have to leave. For the next two

weeks this is your home. We might as well get accustomed to each other."

At first he hesitated, but then he slowly made his way down the steps and into the sitting area.

"Would you like some cocoa?"

As he lowered himself to the love seat, he chuckled softly. "I haven't had cocoa in—"

He stopped. Grace suspected that the last time he'd had cocoa it had been with his son, but she was also tired of tiptoeing around his life. He'd told her very little about himself the night they had dinner at the beach house and she'd not pushed him. But if she had to accept him into her house and Sarah's life, then he had to accept her into his. They couldn't pretend his other life didn't exist.

"In?" Grace prompted, forcing him to talk about his son.

"In years." He took a breath and caught her gaze. "Since I had cocoa with my son."

The words hung in the room. Danny kept his gaze locked with Grace's, as if daring her to go further. But she had no intention of delving into every corner of his world. She only wanted them to begin having normal conversations, so the tension between them would ease.

"See. We can talk about both of your children." She rose from the sofa. "Let me make you a cup of cocoa."

Without waiting for his reply, she walked into the kitchen, pulled a small pot from the cupboard by the stove and set it on a burner. Danny lowered himself to one of the stools by the counter, reminding Grace of how she had sat at the beach house bar while he poured himself a glass of Scotch.

Danny suddenly bounced from the seat, as if he'd had the memory, too, and didn't want it. He strode into the kitchen and reached for the refrigerator door handle. "I'll help you."

Removing the cocoa from a cupboard, Grace turned so quickly that she and Danny nearly ran into each other in the compact kitchen.

He caught her elbows to steady her, and tingles of awareness skipped along her skin. This close she could feel the heat of his body. Memories of making love, of how different he had been that night and how happy she had been, flipped through her brain. The sizzle between them was so intense she suddenly wondered what might have happened if they hadn't made love that night. Would the nice guy she'd met at the beach house have pursued her? Would he have remained nice? Would they have discovered differences and gone their separate ways or lived happily ever after?

Pulling her arms away, she turned toward the stove. What might have been wasn't an issue. If she thought about what might have been for too long she might get starry-eyed again and that would be insane. The guy had hurt her and now he wanted her child. She wouldn't be reckless with him again.

"Hand me the milk."

He did.

"Thanks." Exaggerating the task of pouring it into the pan so she didn't have to look at him, she said, "How are things at Carson Services?"

He walked back to the counter, but didn't sit. Instead he leaned against it. "Fine."

"How's Orlando?"

Danny laughed. "Great. He's a dream client. Because he does his homework, we're always on the same page when I suggest he move his money."

"That's so good to hear. I liked him."

"He's asked about you."

Dumping three scoops of cocoa on top of

the milk, she grimaced. "What did you tell him?"

Danny shifted uncomfortably. "That you'd moved on."

She heard the stirring of guilt in his voice. Though part of her found it fitting, she couldn't pretend she was innocent. She'd recognized from the beginning that losing her job was one of the potential consequences of a failed relationship between them. So she wouldn't pretend. She would discuss this like an adult.

She faced him. "So you told him the truth."

"Excuse me?"

"What you told him was the truth. I *had* moved on."

He barked a laugh. "Yeah."

Grace walked over to him and stood in front of him, holding his gaze. "We won't survive twelve more days of living together if we don't admit here and now that we both made mistakes that weekend. We don't need to dissect our sleeping together and place blame. But we do need to admit that we *both* made mistakes."

"Okay."

"It is okay because we both moved on."

"Bet you wish you had stayed moved on."

She might be willing to agree to be polite and even friendly, but she didn't intend to discuss nebulous things like regrets. So she fell back on humor to get her out of the conversation. Batting her hand in dismissal, she said, "Nah. What fun is having a nice, quiet life with no one pestering you for custody of your child?"

He laughed again. She turned to leave, but he caught her fingers and stopped her. Her gaze swung back to his.

"You're one of only a few people who make me laugh."

Memory thrummed through her. Her being able to make him laugh had been their first connection. But the touch of his fingers reminded her that they'd taken that connection so much further that night. She remembered the way his hands had skimmed her body, remembered how he'd held her, remembered the intensity of the fire of passion between them.

But in the end, passion had failed them. The only thing they had between them now was Sarah. And everything they did had to be for Sarah.

Grace cleared her throat and stepped back. "We'll work on getting you to laugh more often for Sarah." She pulled her hand away from his, walked to the stove and poured Danny's cocoa into a mug. "So what do you like to watch?"

"Watch?"

"On TV."

He took the mug she handed to him. "Actually I don't watch TV."

"Then you're in for a treat because you get to watch everything I like."

That made him laugh again, and Grace's heart lightened before she could stop it, just as it had their weekend together. But she reminded herself that things at the beach house had not turned out well. And she didn't intend to make the same mistake twice. He needed to be comfortable and relaxed for Sarah. She and Danny also needed to be reasonably decent to each other to share custody. But that was all the further she could let things between them go.

They spent two hours watching crime dramas on television. Danny was oddly amused by them. The conversation remained neutral, quiet, until at the end of the second show the eleven o'clock news was announced and Grace said she was going to bed.

"Ripped from the headline is right," he

said, when Grace hit the off button on the remote and rose from the sofa. "That program couldn't have been more specific unless they'd named names."

"That's the show's gimmick. The writers take actual situations and fictionalize them. It's a way to give curious, gossip-hungry viewers a chance to see what might have happened, and how it would play out in court."

Danny said, "Right," then followed her up the stairs. In the little hallway between their closed bedroom doors, Danny put his hand on his doorknob, but he couldn't quite open the door. It didn't seem right to leave her just yet. And that spurred another beach house memory. He hadn't wanted to leave her after he'd given her her bonus. He'd tried to ignore the feeling, but Grace had followed him down to the bar in his great room.

That made him smile. The hall in which they stood was far from great. It was a little square. Only a bit wider than the bar that had separated them at the beach house. He'd closed that gap by leaning forward and kissing her, and he'd experienced one of the most wonderful nights of his life.

And he'd ruined even the pleasant memo-

ries he could hold on to and enjoy by not believing her. Not appreciating her.

"Thanks for the cocoa."

She faced him with a smile. "You're welcome."

He took a step away from his door and toward hers. He might not have appreciated her
the weekend at the beach house, but tonight
he was beginning to understand that she probably had been the woman he'd believed her to
be when he seduced her. Everything that had
happened between them was his fault. Especially their misunderstandings.

He caught her gaze. "I'm glad you moved
on."

He took another step toward her, catching
her hand and lifting it, studying the smooth
skin, her delicate fingers. He recalled her fingers skimming his back, tunneling through
his hair, driving him crazy with desire, and
felt it all again, as if it were yesterday.

"I'm a lot stronger than I look."

Her words came out as a breathy whisper. The same force of attraction that swam
through his veins seemed to be affecting her.
In the quiet house, the only sound Danny
heard was the pounding of his heart. The

only thought in his mind was that he should kiss her.

Slowly, holding her gaze, watching for reaction, he lowered his head. Closing his eyes, he touched his lips to hers. They were smooth and sweet, just as he remembered. Warmth and familiarity collided with sexual hunger that would have happily overruled common sense. Their chemistry caused him to forget everything except how much he wanted her. How happy she made him. How natural it was to hold her.

But just when he would have deepened the kiss, she stepped away.

"This is what got us into trouble the last time." She caught his gaze. "Good night, Danny."

And before he could form the words to stop her, she was behind her closed bedroom door.

CHAPTER SEVEN

Danny awoke feeling oddly refreshed. He opened his eyes, saw the sunny yellow bedroom around him and was disoriented until he remembered he was living with Grace.

Grace.

He'd kissed her, but she'd reminded him that was what had gotten them into trouble the last time. And he didn't think she was talking about creating Sarah. Sarah wasn't trouble. Sarah was a joy. Their "trouble" was that they had slept together when they didn't know each other, which was why he hadn't trusted her enough to continue the relationship, and why he hadn't believed Grace when she told him she was pregnant. He'd thought she was lying to him. Tricking him. Because he didn't know her well enough to realize Grace would never do something like that.

He now knew his accusations were the

product of an overly suspicious mind, but he also had to admit to himself that he hadn't changed much from the man who had dismissed her as a liar. Yes, he'd gotten past the tragedies of his life and to the outside world he appeared normal. And he really could be normal at work, normal with friends, normal with a woman only looking for an evening of entertainment. But his divorce had soured him on commitment. He wasn't marriage material. He wasn't even a good date for anyone who wanted anything other than a fun night out or no-strings-attached sex. Forget about being the right guy for someone as wonderful as Grace. She deserved better. Even he knew it.

She needed a husband. A mate. Someone to share her life. He was not that guy.

He rolled out of bed and tugged on his robe. But once the slash belt was secured, he stopped again. He'd nearly forgotten he was sharing a bathroom.

Sharing a bathroom.

Watching TV.

And happy.

How long had it been since he could say he was happy? Years. He'd accustomed himself to settling for surface emotions, convinced that if he loved anything, life would yank it away. But though he might not believe he could make a commitment to a woman, living with Grace made him consider that he could love Sarah and he could be a real dad. Especially since Grace was kind enough, honest enough, fair enough that she was willing to share custody. Not as adversaries, but as two friends. Both having the best interests of their little girl at heart. And without a hearing that would air his less-than-perfect past.

He grabbed his shaving kit, opened his bedroom door and glanced down the short hall. The bathroom door was open and Grace wasn't anywhere to be seen. Good. He didn't want to bump into Grace dressed only in a robe. As she'd reminded him last night, kissing—or more appropriately runaway emotions and hormones—had gotten them into trouble the last time. He wasn't going to make the same mistake twice. Getting romantically involved had cost them. He'd lost a good employee and someone who probably would have turned into a friend.

And he'd hurt her.

He wouldn't let himself forget that. He also wouldn't let himself hurt her again. He could say that with absolute certainty because he wouldn't get involved with her again. That was a promise he was making to himself.

He showered and shaved and was back in his bedroom before he heard the sound of Grace's alarm. Removing a suit from the garment bag he'd hung in the closet, he heard Sarah's wailing and Grace's words of comfort. He put the suit back in the closet, and yanked on jeans and a T-shirt, listening to Grace soothing Sarah as she carried her downstairs. He heard Grace quietly return upstairs and knew that the lack of crying meant Sarah was sucking her bottle.

He listened for the sound of Grace's door closing and then sneaked downstairs. It had been years since he'd made his "world famous" blueberry pancakes, but if anybody ever deserved a little treat, it was Grace.

After taking a last peek to be sure her black skirt and print blouse were in the proper position, Grace shifted away from her full-length mirror to lift already-dressed Sarah from her crib. But as she turned, the scent of something sweet stopped her.

Whatever it was it smelled like pure heaven. Her mouth watered.

She grabbed Sarah and rushed down the

steps. In the kitchen, dressed in jeans and a T-shirt and wearing a bib apron, stood Danny.

"What is that smell?"

He turned with a smile. "Pancakes. My one and only specialty."

"If they taste as good as they smell, they are absolutely your specialty."

"Oh, they do."

The ringing endorsement—combined with the growling of Grace's tummy—had her scampering into the dining area. She slid Sarah into her high chair and went to the kitchen to retrieve plates from the cupboard. "More stuff you learned while at school?"

He winced. "Not really. These are the only thing I can cook. Unless you count canned soup and fried eggs."

Avoiding her eyes, he set two fluffy blueberry pancakes on each of the two plates she held. Grace took them to the table. She set her dish at the seat beside the high chair and the second across the table from her.

The night before he'd kissed her and just the memory of that brought a warm fuzzy somersault feeling to her empty tummy. She hadn't let the kiss go too far. But there was something between them. Something special. Something sharp and sexual. It wasn't something that would go away with the press of a button, or just because it complicated things. And today he'd made her breakfast. Though she appreciated it, she also knew she had to tread lightly. She didn't want to get involved with him again and he was tempting her.

Danny brought the syrup to the table and sat across from her. "I think there are some things you and I need to discuss."

Her stomach flip-flopped again. The last thing she wanted was to talk about their one-night stand. Or whatever it was that had happened between them. But disliking him hadn't worked to keep them apart. So maybe it was best to talk?

"Okay."

He took a breath. "All right. Here's the deal. That kiss last night was wrong and I don't want you to have to worry about it happening again."

She looked across the table at him, her heart in her throat, and praying her eyes weren't revealing the pain that brought. She also didn't think getting involved was a good idea, but he hadn't needed to say the words.

"The truth is I know you deserve better than me."

Grace blinked. That wasn't at all what she

was expecting and she had absolutely no idea how to reply.

"The night we slept together, I was going through a bad time," he said, glancing down at his pancake before catching her gaze again. "Not that that makes what happened right, but I think it might help you to understand that now that I'm past those personal problems, I can see I misjudged you and I'm sorrier than I can ever say."

Grace took a breath. Once again he was talking about himself, but not really about anything. Still his apology was a big step for them. "Okay."

"Okay you understand or okay you accept my apology?"

She took another breath. Her gut reaction was to accept his apology, but she simply didn't trust him. He had a powerful personality. He might say that she needn't worry about him kissing her again, but she didn't believe either of them could say that with absolute certainty. There was something between them. Chemistry, probably. Hormones that didn't listen to reason. She was afraid that if she accepted his apology and told him she understood it would open the door to things she couldn't control. Things neither one of them could control.

Before she could answer, Danny said, "I hate excuses for bad behavior, but sometimes there are valid reasons people do all the wrong things." He took a breath. "Because that weekend was the two-year anniversary of my son's death, I wasn't myself."

Grace blinked. "What?"

"Cory had died two years before. Six months after his accident my wife and I divorced. I spent the next year and a half just going through the motions of living."

Shocked into silence, Grace only stared at him.

"That weekend you reminded me of happiness." He combed his fingers through his hair. "I don't know. Watching you with Orlando and hearing the two of you make jokes and have a good time, I remembered how it felt to be happy and I began to feel as if I were coming around." He caught her gaze. "You know...as if I were ready to live again."

Stuck in the dark place of trying to imagine the crushing blow of the death of a child and feeling overwhelmed at even the thought, Grace only nodded.

"But I'd always believed you and I had

gone too far too fast by making love the very first weekend we really even spoke, and when I went away for that week of client hopping my doubts haunted me. I started imagining all kinds of reasons you'd sleep with me without really knowing me, and some of them weren't very flattering." He took a breath. "When you told me you were pregnant it just seemed as if every bad thing I had conjured had come true." He held her gaze steadily. "I was wrong and I am sorry."

Grace swallowed hard. She'd left the beach house happy, thinking she'd found Mr. Right and believing all things good would happen for them. But Danny had left the beach house worried about the potential bad. It was no wonder neither of them had seen the other's perspective. They were at two ends of a very broad spectrum.

"I'm sorry, too. I was so happy I didn't think things through. Had I known—"

Sarah pounded on her tray with a squeal. Grace grimaced. "I forgot to feed her."

Danny calmly rose. "I can get that."

Grace's first instinct was to tell him to sit back down. Their discussion wasn't really over. But wasn't it? What else was there to say? He was sorry. She was sorry. But they couldn't change the past. She didn't want a relationship. He'd hurt her and she rightfully didn't trust him. And he didn't want a relationship. Otherwise he wouldn't have promised not to kiss her again. There was nothing more to say. The discussion really was over.

"Do you remember how to make cereal?" Grace asked.

"The stuff in the box with a little milk, right?"

She nodded.

"I can handle it."

He strode into the kitchen and Grace took several long, steadying breaths.

His child had died.

She had always believed that nothing he could say would excuse the way he treated her when she told him she was pregnant.

But this did.

It didn't mean she would trust her heart to him, but it did mean she could forgive him.

That night Grace had dinner nearly prepared when Danny arrived. She directed him upstairs to change while she fed Sarah some baby food and by the time Sarah had eaten, Danny returned wearing jeans and a T-shirt. He looked as relaxed as he had their night at the beach house. Confession, apparently, had done him a world of good.

Incredibly nervous, Grace fussed over the salads. Now that she knew about Danny's son everything was different. She almost didn't know how to treat him. His admissions had opened the door to their being friends, and being friendly would work the best for Sarah's sake. But could two people with their chemistry really be friends?

While Grace brought their salads to the table, Danny took his seat.

"You know, we never have gotten around to discussing a lot of things about Sarah."

Glad for the neutral topic, Grace said, "Like what?"

"For one, child support."

"Since we'll each have Sarah two weeks a month, I don't think either one of us should be entitled to child support. So don't even think of filing for any."

He laughed. "Very funny."

A tingle of accomplishment raced through her at his laughter, but she didn't show any outward sign of her pleasure. Instead she shrugged casually. "Hey, I make a decent salary. How do I know it wasn't your intention to file?"

"You never did tell me where you got a job."

"I work for a small accounting firm. Johnson and O'Hara."

"So you do okay financially?"

"Yeah." Grace smiled. "Actually they pay me double what your firm did."

He chuckled. "You got lucky."

"Yes, I did."

He glanced into the kitchen, then behind himself at the living room. "And you seem to know how to use your money wisely."

"I bought this house the day I got my first job."

"The night I was grilling, I remembered you told me about remodeling your house while we ate that Sunday night at the beach house." He smiled across the table at her, and Grace's stomach flip-flopped. Lord, he was handsome. And nice. And considerate. And smart. And now she knew he wasn't mean-spirited or selfish, but wounded. Life had hurt him and he needed somebody like her to make him laugh.

Oh, God, she was in trouble!

"You did a good job on the remodel."

"My cousin did most of it." Shifting lettuce on her dish, Grace avoided looking at him.

"I was the grunt. He would put something in place, tack it with a nail or two then give me the nail gun to finish."

"It looks great." He took another bite of salad.

But Grace was too nervous to eat. She couldn't hate him anymore. But she couldn't really like him, either.

Or could she?

By telling her about his son, he'd both explained his behavior and proved he trusted her.

But he'd also said she didn't need to worry about him kissing her anymore.

Of course, he might have said that because she'd pushed him away the night before, reminding him that kissing only got them in trouble.

They finished their salads and Grace brought the roast beef, mashed potatoes and peas to the table. Unhappy with being ignored, Sarah pounded her teething ring on her high chair tray and screeched noisily.

"What's the matter, Sarah Bear," Grace crooned, as she poured gravy onto her mashed potatoes. Sarah screeched again and Grace laughed. "Oh, you want to sit on somebody's lap? Well, you can't."

She glanced at Danny. "Unless your daddy wants to hold you?"

Danny said, "Sure, I'll—"

But Grace stopped him. "No. You can't hold a baby in front of a plate with gravy on it. You would be wearing the gravy in about twenty seconds."

"If you want to eat your dinner in peace, I could take her into the living room, then eat when you're done."

He was so darned eager to please that Grace stared at him, drawing conclusions that made her heart tremble with hope. There was only one reason a man wanted to please a woman. He liked her. Which meant maybe Danny had only promised not to kiss her again because she'd stopped him, not because he didn't want to kiss her anymore.

Or she could be drawing conclusions that had absolutely no basis in fact.

"I'm fine. I like having Sarah at the table. When I said you might want to hold her I was just teasing her."

"Oh, okay."

Determined to keep her perspective and keep things light and friendly, Grace turned to the high chair. "So, Miss Sarah, you stay where you are."

"What's that thing your mother's got you wearing?" Danny asked, pointing at the fuzzy swatch of material in the shape of a stuffed bear that had been sewn onto Sarah's shirt.

"It's a bear shirt."

Danny's fork stopped halfway to his mouth and he gave Grace a confused look. "What?"

"A bear shirt." Grace laughed. "From the day she was born, my dad called her Sarah Boo Beara…then Sarah Bear. Because the name sort of took, my parents buy her all kinds of bear things." She angled her fork at the bear on Sarah's shirt. "Push it."

"Push it?"

"The bear. Push it and see what happens."

Danny reached over and pushed the bear on Sarah's shirt. It squeaked. Sarah grinned toothlessly.

Danny jumped as if somebody had bitten him. "Very funny."

"It makes Sarah laugh and some days that's not merely a good thing. It's a necessity."

"I remember."

Of course, he remembered. He'd had a son. Undoubtedly lots of things he did for Sarah or things Sarah did would bring back memories for him. If he needed anything from Grace it might not be a relationship as much as a friend to listen to him. Just listen.

"Would you like to talk about it?"

Danny shook his head. "Not really."

Okay. She'd read that wrong. She took a quiet breath, realizing she'd been off base about him a lot, and maybe the smart thing here would be to stop trying to guess what he thought and only believe what he said. Including that he wouldn't be kissing her anymore. So she should stop romanticizing.

"If you ever do want to talk, I'm here."

"I know." He toyed with his fork then he glanced over at her with a wistful smile. "I sort of wonder what might have happened between us if I'd told you everything the morning after we'd slept together, as I had intended to."

Her heart thudded to a stop. "You were going to tell me?"

He nodded. "Instead the only thing I managed to get out was that I had to go away for a week." He paused, glancing down at the half-eaten food on his plate. "I really shouldn't have slept with you that night. I was still raw, but fighting it, telling myself it was time to move on. And I made a mistake."

"You don't get sole blame for that. I was the one who went down to the bar."

"Yeah, but I was the one who knew I wasn't entirely healed from my son's death and my divorce. The whole disaster was my fault."

"It takes two—"

"Grace, stop. Please."

His tone brooked no argument—as if she'd been pushing him to talk, when she hadn't—and Grace bristled. Though he'd said he didn't want to talk about this, he'd been the one to dip their toes into the conversation. Still, because it was his trouble, his life, they were discussing, he also had to be the one with the right to end it. "Okay."

He blew his breath out on a long sigh. "I'm not trying to hide things or run from things, but I just plain don't want to remember anymore. I'm tired of the past and don't like to remember it, let alone talk about it. I like living in the present."

"I can understand that."

"Good." He set his fork on his dish. "So do you want help with the dishes?"

She almost automatically said no, but stopped herself. Giving him something to do made life easier for both of them. "Sure."

He rose, gathering the plates. She lifted the

meat platter and walked it to the refrigerator. The oppressive tension of the silence between them pressed on her chest. If the quiet was difficult for her, she couldn't even imagine how hard it was on Danny. Knowing he didn't want to think, to remember, she plunged them into the solace of chitchat.

"So what did you do at work today?"

Danny turned on the faucet to rinse their dishes. "The same old stuff. What did you do?"

"I'm in the process of reviewing the books for a company that wants to incorporate."

That caught his interest. "Oh, an IPO."

Grace winced at the excitement in his voice. "No, a small family business. The corporation will be privately held. The principals are basically doling out shares of stock to the family members who made the company successful, as a way to ensure ownership as well as appropriate distribution of profits."

"Ah."

"Not nearly as exciting as investing the fortunes of famous athletes, but it's good work. Interesting."

"Have you begun to do any investing for yourself?"

His question triggered an unexpected memory of telling him she'd gone to work for his investment firm because she wanted to learn about investing to be rich. The heat of embarrassment began to crawl up her neck. She'd meant what she said, but given everything that had happened between them, her enthusiastic pronouncement had probably fed the fire of his suspicions about her.

They'd really made a mess of things that night.

She walked back to the dining room table and retrieved the mashed potato bowl. "I'm working on getting the house paid off. So I haven't had a lot of spare cash."

"Since we'll be splitting expenses for Sarah, you should have some extra money then, right?"

She shrugged. "Maybe."

"Grace, I want to pay my fair share. And I can be pretty stubborn. So no maybes or probablys or whatevers. Let's really be honest about the money."

"Okay."

He stacked the dishes in the dishwasher. "Okay. So once we get everything straightened out I would like to open an account for you at Carson Services."

Grace laughed. "Right. Danny, even if I

have spare cash from our sharing expenses for Sarah, I'm not sure I'll have more than a hundred dollars a month or so."

"A hundred dollars a month is good."

"Oh, really? You're going to open an investment account with a hundred dollars?"

He winced. "I thought I'd open it with a few thousand dollars of my own money. You know, to make up for what you've spent to date and you could add to it."

Grace sighed. "You told me to stop talking about the past and I did. So now I'm going to tell you to stop fretting about the money."

"But I—"

"Just stop. I don't want your money. I never did. When I said I wanted to be rich that night at the beach house, I was actually saying that I wanted my parents and me to be comfortable." She motioned around her downstairs. "Like this. This is enough. I am happy. I do not want your money. Can you accept that?"

He held her gaze for several seconds. Grace didn't even flinch, so that he would see from her expression that this was as important to her as no longer discussing the past was for him.

"Yes, I accept that."

"Okay."

* * *

Sliding under the covers that night, Grace was still annoyed by their money discussion. Not because he wanted to pay his fair share, and not even because she had brought his suspicions about her on herself, but because that one memory opened the door to a hundred more.

She remembered what it felt like to be with him. He'd made her feel so special. Wonderful. Perfect.

Warmth immediately filled her. So did the sense that she'd had during their weekend together. That they fit. That they were right for each other. She had been so happy that weekend, but she also remembered that *he'd* been happy too.

Was she so wrong to think *she* brought out the nice guy in him? And was it so wrong to believe that there was a chance that the nice guy could come out and stay out forever? And was it so wrong to think that maybe—just maybe—if the nice guy stayed out forever they could fall in love for real? Not fall into bed because they were sexually attracted. But fall in love. For real. To genuinely care about each other.

She didn't know, and she couldn't even

clearly analyze the situation, because they'd slept together and that one wonderful memory clouded her judgment.

Plus she'd already decided she wouldn't be second-guessing him anymore. He'd said she didn't have to worry about him kissing her again.

He didn't want her. She had to remember that.

CHAPTER EIGHT

GRACE AWAKENED TO the scent of pancakes and the sound of Sarah slapping her chubby hands against the bars of her crib.

"I'm coming."

She groggily pulled herself out of bed and lifted Sarah into her arms. Rain softly pitter-pattered on the roof. The scent of blueberry pancakes wafted through the air. It would have been a perfect morning except Grace had tossed and turned so much the night before that she'd slept in.

Though she had said she didn't want to get accustomed to having Danny around, after dressing Sarah for the day, she padded downstairs and into the kitchen area.

"Hey."

Danny looked up from the newspaper he was reading at the kitchen counter. "Good morning."

"I'm sorry, but I slept in. Could you take her?"

"And feed her?"

Grace nodded.

"Sure. Come on, Sarah Bear."

Sarah easily went to Danny and Grace turned and walked back though the living room, but at the stairs she paused, watching Danny as he held Sarah with one arm and prepared her cereal with the other. Rain continued to tap against the roof, making the house cozy and warm. Breakfast was made. She would have privacy to dress. It all seemed so perfect that Grace had a moment of pure, unadulterated sadness, realizing that *this* was what sleeping together too soon had cost them.

She drew in a breath and ran upstairs. There was no point crying over spilled milk. No point wishing for what might have been. And no way she could jeopardize the comfort level they had by yearning for a romance. Particularly with a man who so desperately needed to do things at his own pace, in his own way.

She showered, dressed and returned downstairs. Sarah sat in her high chair and cooed when Grace approached. Danny rose from the dining room table and walked into the kitchen.

"I'll microwave your pancakes. Just to warm them up."

"Thanks."

"Want some coffee?"

"Yes, but I'll get it." She laughed. "I told you, I don't want to get too accustomed to having help."

He leaned against the counter and crossed his arms on his chest. "We could share the nanny I hire."

She held up her hands to stop him. "Don't tempt me."

"Why not? What else is she going to do during the weeks you have Sarah?"

"Take yoga."

He burst out laughing. "Come on, Grace, at least think about it."

She poured herself a cup of coffee, then grabbed the cream from the refrigerator. "The part of me that wants help is being overruled by the part of me that loves the one-on-one time with Sarah."

He nodded. "Okay. Makes sense."

She turned and smiled at him. "Thanks."

He returned her smile. "You're welcome."

For a few seconds, they stood smiling at each other, then Grace's smile faded and she quickly turned away. She really liked him, and that triggered more pheromones than a thousand bulging biceps. They were better off when she had disliked him, before his explanation and apology. Now instead of disagreeing and keeping their distance they were becoming friends, getting close, and she was wishing for things she couldn't have.

"By the way, my lawyer called this morning."

Brought back to the present by a very timely reminder, Grace faced him. "Oh, yeah?"

Danny winced. "Yeah. The guy's a nut. He called me while he was shaving. He actually woke me." The microwave buzzer rang. Unfolding his arms, Danny pushed away from the counter. "He asked about the progress on our agreement. I told him that you had told me you contacted a lawyer, and that lawyer had told you it was okay to sign, so you signed it, right?"

The casual, cozy atmosphere of Grace's little house shifted. Tension seeped into the space between them with words left unsaid. He hadn't signed their agreement. She had. But he hadn't. And it worried his lawyer. Or maybe it worried *him* and he used the call from his lawyer as a cover?

She swallowed, calling herself crazy for

being suspicious. Shared custody was *her* idea. "I signed it."

"Great. Give it to me and I'll sign it, then we'll be set. According to my lawyer, once we have that in place we won't even need a hearing." Plate of warm pancakes in his hand, he faced her. "We simply begin sharing custody."

His pancakes suddenly looked like a bribe, and Grace froze, unable to take them from his hand. Until she reminded herself that Danny had nothing to gain by being nice to her. If anything *she* benefited from any agreement that kept them out of court.

She forced a smile and took the plate from his hands. "Sounds good. It's upstairs. I'll get it."

He glanced at his watch, then grimaced. "I have an early meeting today so unless you want your pancakes to get cold again, how about if you get it for me tonight. Tomorrow's Saturday, but I can take it to work on Monday and sign it in front of my secretary who can witness it. Then we'll make copies."

Calling herself every sort of fool for being suspicious, Grace walked to the table. "That sounds good." Eager to make up for her few seconds of doubt, she added, "But it's on top of my dresser. You could get it."

He waved a hand in dismissal. "We'll handle it tomorrow."

Grace drove to work, feeling like an idiot for mistrusting him. But walking from the parking garage, she reminded herself that it wasn't out of line for her to be suspicious of him. She might be prone to a little too much second-guessing about him, but he hadn't really told her a lot about his life. And he stopped the discussion any time they began to edge beyond surface facts.

Plus, *they* had a past. An unusual, unhappy past. He mistrusted her. When she told him she was pregnant, he kicked her out of his office. After that, she never tried to contact him again because she hadn't trusted him. She only took the baby to him for Sarah's sake. She hadn't expected him to want visitation, let alone have a hand in raising their daughter. But he did. He wanted full custody and had agreed to shared custody. To get Grace to give him that, he had to prove himself. Everything they'd done had been a negotiation of a sort.

She shouldn't magically feel that things between them had been patched up.

Except that he'd trusted her enough to tell him about his son.

Didn't that count as at least a step toward mending fences?

Yes, it did. Yet even knowing that he had good reason to be off his game something bothered her. Something in her gut said that Danny was too eager about their agreement and accepting shared custody, and she had no idea why.

Grace couldn't come up with a solid answer, even though the question popped into her head a million times that day. She returned home that evening edgy and annoyed, tired of running this scenario through her brain. Shared custody and the agreement had been *her* idea. She'd already signed the agreement. Week about with Sarah was the fair thing to do in their circumstance. The man had offered her the use of his nanny. He'd told her about his son. Yet something still nagged at her.

It didn't help that Sarah was grouchy. After a quiet and somewhat strained dinner, Danny excused himself to go to his room to work on a project that needed to be completed on Monday morning. Grace tried to stack the dishes in the dishwasher with Sarah crying in her high chair, but her patience quickly ran out. She lifted the baby and carried her up to Danny's room.

"Can you watch her while I finish clearing the kitchen?"

Looking too big for the little corner desk Grace had in her spare room more for decorative purposes than actual use, Danny faced her. "Grace, I—"

"Please." Grace marched into the room. "I know you have to get this project done for Monday morning, but I had a miserable day and I just need a few minutes to clean up." She dropped Sarah onto his lap. "When the dishes are done, I'll take her again."

With that she walked out, closing Danny's bedroom door behind her, leaving nothing but silence in her wake.

Danny glanced down at the little girl on his lap. "One of us made her angry and since I've been up here and you were the one with her in the kitchen, I'm blaming you."

Sarah screeched at him.

"Right. You can argue all you want but the fact remains that I was up here and you were down there with her."

He rose from the little desk chair and walked to the door, intending to take the baby to the living room where he and Sarah could watch TV or maybe play on the floor. But even before his hand closed around the knob, he had second thoughts. Grace said she wanted to clean the kitchen, but maybe what she needed was some peace and quiet. He glanced around, unsure of what to do. The room wasn't tiny, but it wasn't a center of entertainment, either.

"Any suggestions for how we can amuse ourselves for the next hour or so?" he asked Sarah as he shifted her into his arms so that he could look down at her. She smiled up at him and his heart did a crazy flip-flop. From this angle he didn't see as much of Cory in her features as he saw Grace. Were he to guess, he would say Sarah's eyes would some day be the same shade of violet that Grace's were.

She rubbed her little fist across her nose, then her right eye, the sign babies used when they were sleepy. Danny instinctively kissed the top of her head.

She peeked up and grinned at him and this time Danny's heart expanded with love. Not only had Sarah grown accustomed to him, but also he was falling in love with her. He was falling in love with the baby, happy living in

Grace's home and having feelings for Grace he didn't dare identify. He knew she deserved a better man than he was. He'd made a promise to himself not to hurt her and he intended to keep it.

He looked down at Sarah, who yawned. "On, no, Sarah! You can't fall asleep this early. You'll wake up before dawn, probably ready to play and tomorrow's Saturday, the only day your mom gets to sleep in—"

He stopped talking because inspiration struck him. The thing to do would be to get Sarah ready for bed. That way she wouldn't fall asleep for at least another half hour and who knew? Maybe a bath would revive her? Plus he might make a few brownie points with Grace by keeping them so busy she could relax.

Pleased with that idea, he held Sarah against his shoulder, quietly opened his bedroom door and looked down the hall. Grace was nowhere in sight, and he could still hear the sounds of pots and pans in her kitchen.

He sneaked across the little hall and into her room. Inside he was immediately enfolded in a warm, sheltered feeling, the sense a man got when he felt at home. He squeezed his eyes shut, telling himself not to get so attached to Grace and her things that he again did something they'd both regret. He took a breath, then another and then another, reminding himself of all the reasons being too cozy with her was wrong.

Sarah wiped her nose in his shirt and snuggled into his shoulder, bringing him back to reality.

"No. No," he said, manipulating her into a different position before she could get too comfortable. "You'll be able to go to sleep soon enough if you let your daddy get you ready for bed."

He searched around the room for her baby tub, but realized it was probably in the bathroom. Remembering that preparation was a parent's best trick when caring for a baby, he decided to get everything ready before he brought his sopping wet baby from the bathroom. He laid a clean blanket on the changing table, then pulled open the top draw of a white chest of drawers that had bears painted on the knobs. Inside were undershirts and socks so tiny they looked about thumb-size. Knowing those were too small, he closed the drawer, and opened the next one, seeking pajamas. He found them, then located the stash of disposable diapers, and arranged them on the changing table.

With everything ready he took Sarah to the bathroom. Holding her with one arm, he filled the baby tub he'd placed inside the regular bathtub, found her soap and shampoo and the baby towel that hung on the rack.

That was when he realized she was fully dressed and he was still wearing his suit trousers. In an executive decision, he pronounced it too late to do anything about his trousers and laid her on the fluffy carpet in front of the tub to remove her clothes.

She giggled and cooed and he shook his head. "Let's just hope you're this happy after I put you in the water."

She grinned at him.

Returning her smile, he lifted her to eye level. "Ready?"

She laughed and patted his cheeks.

"Okay, then." He dipped her into the tub and when she didn't howl or stiffen up, he figured she was one of the babies who loved to sit in water. Grateful, he kept one hand at her back as he wet a washcloth and squeezed a few drops of liquid soap on it, amazed by how quickly baby care was coming back to him.

"So you like the water?" Danny said, entertaining Sarah with chitchat as he washed her, just in case any part of bathtime had the potential to freak her out. She merely gooed and cooed at him, even when he washed her hair. Pleased by his success, he rinsed off all the soapsuds, rolled her in the soft terry-cloth baby towel and carried her back to Grace's room.

Not in the slightest uncomfortable, Sarah chewed a blue rubber teething ring while Danny put on her diaper and slid her into pajamas.

When she was completely dressed, he took her out into the hallway. He heard the sounds of the television—indicating Grace was done filling the dishwasher and probably waiting for the cycle to be complete so she could put everything away—and turned to the stairs, but his conscience tweaked. He'd been here five days and he hadn't done anything more than make pancakes, help with dishes and grill a few things. This was the first time he'd really helped with the baby. It seemed totally wrong to take Sarah downstairs and disturb the only private moments he'd allowed Grace.

He turned and walked back into Grace's bedroom. "So what do we do?"

Sarah rubbed her eyes again.

Danny frowned. He didn't have a bottle for her, but she didn't seem hungry. Or fussy. All she appeared to be was sleepy. Now that they'd wasted almost an hour getting her ready for bed, it didn't seem too early to let her fall asleep. The only question was, could she fall asleep without a bottle?

He remembered a comment Grace had made about making up stories for Sarah, and walked to the bed. If he laid Sarah in her crib, he ran the risk that she'd cry and Grace's private time would be disturbed. It seemed smarter to sit on the bed and tell Sarah a story and see if she'd fall asleep naturally.

He sat. Sarah snuggled against his chest. But sitting on the edge of Grace's bed was incredibly uncomfortable, so he scooted back until he was leaning against the headboard.

"This is better."

Sarah blinked up at him sleepily.

"Okay. Let's see. You clearly like bears since your grandfather blended a bear into your name, so let's make up a story about a bear."

She blinked again. Heavier this time. He scooted down a little farther, then decided he might as well lie down, too.

* * *

Two hours later, Grace awoke on the sofa. She'd fallen asleep! Danny was going to kill her.

She ran up the steps and to Danny's room, but it was empty. Panicked, she raced across the hall and without turning on the light saw his shadowy form on her bed. She tiptoed into the room and peered down to discover he was not only sleeping on her bed with Sarah, he'd also put the baby in her pajamas for the night.

Both the baby and her daddy slept deeply, comfortably. Little Sarah lay in the space between his chest and his arm, snuggled against him in a pose of trust. Danny looked naturally capable. Grace wished she had a camera.

Careful not to disturb Danny, she reached down and lifted Sarah from his arms. The baby sniffled and stretched, but Grace "Shhed," her back to sleep and laid her in her crib.

Then she turned to her bed, her heart in her throat. Danny looked so comfortable and so relaxed that she didn't want to disturb him. The peaceful repose of his face reminded her of the morning she'd awakened in his bed in the beach house, and she involuntarily sat down beside him.

Unable to help herself, she lovingly brushed a lock of hair from his forehead. She wasn't going to fall into her black pit of recriminations again about sleeping together. She already knew that had been a mistake. No need to continue berating herself. Life had handled their punishment for prematurely sleeping together by using it to keep them apart. What she wanted right now was just a couple of seconds, maybe a minute, to look at him, to be happy he was here, to enjoy the fact that he loved their daughter so she wouldn't have to worry when Sarah was in his care.

She scooted a little closer on the bed, remembered waking up that morning at the beach house, laughed softly at how glad she had been that she'd had the chance to sneak away and brush her teeth before he woke up, and then sighed as she recalled making love in the shower.

She remembered thinking that she'd never love another man the way she loved Danny and realized it was still true. He had her heart and she wasn't even sure how he'd done it. Except that he was cute, and sweet, and nice, and she desperately wanted to fill the aching need that she could now see he had.

But he wouldn't let her.

And that was what was bothering her. That was why she grabbed onto her suspicions like a lifeline. As long as she mistrusted him, she could hold herself back. But now that he'd told her about his son, explaining his irrational behavior, she had forgiven him. And once she'd forgive him, she'd begun falling in love again.

But he didn't love her. He didn't want to love her. If she didn't stop her runaway feelings, she was going to get hurt again.

After another breath, she lightly shook his shoulder and whispered, "Danny?"

He grumbled something unintelligible and she smiled. Damn he was cute. It really didn't seem fair that she had to resist him.

"Danny, if you don't want to get up, I can sleep in your room, but you'll have to wake up with Sarah when she cries for her two o'clock feeding."

The threat of being responsible for Sarah must have penetrated, because he took a long breath, then groggily sat up.

"Want help getting across the hall?"

He stared at her, as if needing to focus, and reached for her hand, which was still on his shoulder. His fingers were warm and his touch gentle, sending reaction from Grace's fingertips to her toes. She remembered how sweet his kisses had been. She remembered how giving, yet bold he was as a lover. She remembered how safe she'd felt with him, how loved.

In the silence of the dark night, their gazes stayed locked for what felt like forever, then he put his hands on her shoulders and ran them down her back, along the curve of her waist and up again.

Grace swallowed and closed her eyes, savoring the feeling that she remembered from that summer night. Not sexual attraction, but emotional connection, expressed through physical attraction. Whatever was between them was powerful, but it was also sweet. By caring for Sarah tonight he'd shown her what she'd instinctively understood about him. That deep down he was a good guy. He'd kept Sarah beyond the time he'd needed to for Grace to get her work done, dressed her in pajamas and fallen asleep with the baby in his arms.

He might dismiss it or downplay it, but he couldn't deny it and that meant they were at a crossroad. He liked her enough to do something kind for her. It might be too soon for him to fall in love again. Or he might not want to fall in love again. But he was falling. And she didn't have to tell him she was falling, too. He could surely see it in her eyes.

Gazing into his dark eyes, Grace held her breath, hoping, almost praying he was thinking the same thing she was and that he had the courage to act on it.

CHAPTER NINE

IN THE DARK, quiet bedroom that radiated warmth and the comfort of home, Danny stared at Grace. All he wanted to do was crawl under the covers of her bed with her. Not to make love but to sleep. He was tired, but also he simply needed the succor of this night. The peaceful feeling a man got when his baby was tucked away in her crib, sleeping like an angel, and the mother of his baby was tucked under his arm. The desire was instinctive, nearly primal, and so natural he hadn't thought it. It had overtaken him. Almost as if it wasn't something he could stop or change.

But every time he'd given in to his instincts, he'd failed somebody. He'd failed Lydia, he'd failed Cory, and he'd even failed Grace by not believing her when she told him she was pregnant. Did he really want to fail her again?

No.

He backed away from the temptation of Grace, his hands sliding off her in a slow, sad way, savoring every second of her softness for as long as he could before it was gone.

He hadn't said anything foolish, like how beautiful she was or how much he had missed her or how the instant closeness they had shared was coming back to him. He hadn't done anything he couldn't take back like kiss her. He could get out of this simply by saying good-night and leaving the room.

"Good night."

She swallowed. "Good night."

And Danny walked out of the room.

Grace sat on the bed. It was still warm from where he lay. She could smell the subtle hint of his aftershave.

She dropped her head to her hands. If she'd needed any more reason to stay away from Danny, he'd given it to her tonight. She'd watched the play of emotions on his face display the battle going on in his brain as he'd stared at her, wanting her, yet denying himself. She could have been insulted or hurt; instead she saw just how strong he was. How determined he could be to deny himself what he wanted, even when it was probably clear to him that she wanted it, too.

And it was her loss. She knew it the whole way to her soul.

For the second time since he'd moved in with Grace, Danny awakened happy. The night before he'd spent time with Sarah and had very successfully cared for her, proving to himself that he didn't need to be afraid about the weeks he would spend with his daughter. He'd also successfully stepped away from temptation with Grace. He wanted her, but he didn't want to hurt her. Some day she would thank him.

As he dressed, he heard the sounds of Sarah awakening and Grace walking down the stairs to get her a bottle. When he was sure she had returned to her room to dress and get the baby ready for the day, he rushed downstairs, strode into the kitchen and retrieved the ingredients for pancakes.

Twenty minutes later she came down the stairs and he turned from the stove. "Good morning."

Wearing jeans and a pale blue top that made her eyes seem iridescent, Grace carried the baby to her high chair.

"Good morning."

She was beautiful in an unassuming, yet naturally feminine way that always caused everything male in Danny to sit up and take notice. But he didn't mind that. In fact, now that he knew he could control the emotional side of their relationship, he actually liked noticing Grace. What man didn't want to appreciate a beautiful woman?

As she puttered, getting the baby settled in the high chair with a teething ring, Danny looked his fill at the way her T-shirt hugged her full breasts and her blue jeans caressed her bottom. But what really drew him was her face. Her violet eyes sparkled with laughter and her full lips lifted in a smile. If his walking away the night before had affected her, she didn't show it. She was one of the most accepting, accommodating people he'd ever met.

He took a stack of pancakes to the table and she sniffed the air. "Blueberry again."

He winced. "They're my only specialty."

She surprised him by laughing. "You say that as if you'd like to learn to cook."

His reaction to that was so unexpected that he stopped halfway to the kitchen and he faced her again. "I think I do."

She took her seat at the table. "I don't know why that seems so novel to you. Lots of men cook."

But Danny didn't want to cook. He wanted to please Grace. Not in a ridiculous, out-of-control way, but in a way that fulfilled his part of the responsibility. Still, with only a week left in their deal to live together it was too late now to find a class.

Grace plopped a pancake on her plate as Sarah pounded her high chair tray. "You could get a cookbook."

Now that idea had merit.

"Or I could teach you."

And that idea had even more merit. He would get the knowledge he needed to do his part, and he'd have a perfect opportunity to spend time with Grace. Normal time. Not fighting a middle-of-the-night attraction. Not wishing for things he couldn't have. But time to get even more adjusted to having her in his world without giving in to every whim, sexual craving or desire for her softness.

"I'd like that."

She smiled at him. "Great. This morning we'll go shopping for groceries."

Reaching into the cupboard for syrup, he said, "Shopping?"

"Shopping is the first step in cooking. You can't make what you don't have. If you'd tried to prepare these pancakes tomorrow," she said, pointing at her dish, "you would have been sadly disappointed because the blueberries would have been gone. That's why we're going shopping today."

He didn't really want to go to a store, but she had a point. Unfortunately her suggestion also had a fatal flaw. "How am I going to know what to buy if I don't yet know how to cook anything?"

"I'm going to help you."

"Right."

Sarah screeched her displeasure at being left out of the conversation. Danny took his seat at the table and before Grace could turn to settle the baby, he broke off a small bite of pancake and set it in her open mouth.

She grinned at him.

And Danny felt his world slide into place. What he felt was beyond happiness. It was something more like purpose or place. That was it. He had a place. He had a child, and a friend in his child's mother. In a sense, Grace getting pregnant had given him back his life. As long as he didn't try to make this relationship any more than it was, he had a family of sorts.

In the grocery store, Grace had serious second thoughts about her idea of teaching Danny to cook. He wanted to learn to steam shrimp and prepare crème brûlée. Her expertise ran more along the lines of pizza rolls and brownies. And the brownies weren't even scratch brownies. They were from a boxed mix.

"How about prime rib?"

"I'm not exactly sure how that's made, either."

"We need a cookbook."

"Or we could start with less complex things like grilled steak and baked potatoes."

Standing by the spice counter, he slowly turned to face her, a smile spreading across his mouth. "You don't know how to cook, either."

"That's a matter of opinion. I know the main staples. I can bake a roast that melts in your mouth, fix just about any kind of potato you want and steam vegetables. My lasagna wins raves at reunions—"

"Reunions?"

"You know. Family reunions. Picnics. Where all the aunts and uncles and cousins get together and everybody brings his or her specialty dish, plays volleyball or softball, coos over each other's kids and the next morning wakes up with sore muscles because most of us only play sports that one day every year."

He laughed.

"You've never been to a family reunion?"

"I don't have much of a family. My dad was an only child, and though my mother had two siblings, her brother became a priest and her sister chose not to have kids."

She gaped at him. "You're kidding."

"Why are you so surprised. *Your* parents had only one child."

"My parents had one child because my dad was disabled in an automobile accident. He appears fine and he can do most things, but he never could go back to work. It's why my parents have so little money. We had to live on what my mother could make."

"Oh."

Seeing that he was processing that, Grace stepped over to the spices and pulled out a container of basil. She had to wonder if the reason Danny couldn't seem to love wasn't just the mistake of his marriage, but a result of his entire past. Could a person who'd only seen one marriage, then failed at his own, really believe in love?

"I can also make soup."

"What kind?"

"Vegetable and chicken and dumpling."

"Ah. A gourmet."

"Now, don't get snooty. I think you're really going to like the chicken and dumpling. I have to use a spaetzle maker."

"What the hell is a spaetzle maker?"

His confusion about a cooking utensil only served to confirm Grace's theory that Danny couldn't love because he knew so little about the simple, ordinary things other people took for granted. "It's a fancy word for a kitchen gadget that makes very small dumplings."

"Why don't you just call it that?"

"Because I'm not the one who decided what it's called. It's German or something. Besides, spaetzle maker sounds more official."

"Right."

Grace laughed. She was having fun. Lots of fun. The kind of fun they probably would have had if she and Danny had let their relationship develop slowly. They were so different that they'd desperately needed time to get to know each other, to become familiar with each other's worlds, and to integrate what worked and get rid of what didn't. From Danny's eagerness to learn and his curiosity, it was clear something was missing in his world. And from the way he reacted to the simplicity of her life it was obvious she wouldn't have been able to stay the same if they'd actually had a relationship. That was also why Sarah needed both of them. Neither one of them was *wrong* in the way they lived. It was all a matter of choices.

They spent over double what Grace normally allotted for food, but Danny paid the bill. When she tried to give him her share, he refused it, reminding her that she'd paid for the first week's groceries. Another proof that Danny was innately fair. A good man. Not the horrible man who tossed her out of his office when she told him she was pregnant. But a man trying to get his bearings after the loss of a child.

At two o'clock that afternoon, with Sarah napping and Danny standing about three inches behind her, Grace got out her soup pot.

"Could you watch from a few feet back?"

"I'm curious."

"Well, be curious over by the counter." He stepped away from her and to keep the conversation flowing so he didn't pout, Grace said, "Soup is good on a chilly fall day like this."

Danny leaned against the counter and crossed his arms on his chest. "I think you're showing off."

"Showing off?"

"I doubted your abilities, so you're about to dazzle me with your spaetzle maker."

She laughed. "The spaetzle maker doesn't come into play for a while yet. Plus, there's very little expertise to soup," she said, dropping the big pot on the burner. "First you get a pot."

He rolled his eyes.

"Then you fill it halfway with water." She filled a large bowl with water and dumped the water into the big pot on the stove. "You add an onion, one potato, a stalk of celery and a chicken."

He gaped at her. "You're putting that entire chicken into the pot?"

"Yes."

Now he looked horrified.

She laughed. "Come on. This is how my grandmother did it." While he stood gaping at her, looking afraid to comment, she reached for the chicken bouillion cubes.

His eyes widened. "You're cheating!"

"Not really. The only thing bouillion cubes accomplishes is to cut down on cooking time."

"It's still cheating."

"I'm starting to notice a trend here. You're against anything that saves time."

"I want to learn to cook correctly."

She shrugged. "I need to be able to save time." With everything in the pot, she washed her hands then dried them with a paper towel.

"Now what?"

"Now, I'm going to take advantage of the fact that Sarah's still napping and read."

"Really?"

"Even with the bouillion cubes, the soup needs to cook at least an hour. It's best if we give it two hours." She glanced at the clock on the stove. "So until Sarah wakes I'm going to read."

"What should I do?"

"Weren't you working on something last night?"

He pouted. "Yeah, but I can't go any further because I left an important file at my office."

She sighed. "So I have to entertain you?"

He actually thought about that. For a few seconds Grace was sure the strong man in him would say no. Instead he laughed and said, "Yes. Somebody's got to entertain me."

Grace only stared at him. The night before she would have sworn he was firmly against getting involved with her, but today he was happy to be in her company. It didn't make sense—

Actually it did. The night before they were both considering sleeping together. Today they were making soup. Laughing. Happy. Not facing a life choice. Just having fun in each other's company. No stress. No worries. And wasn't that her real goal? To make him comfortable enough that Sarah's stays with him would be pleasant?

That was exactly her goal. So she couldn't waste such a wonderful opportunity.

"Do you know anything about gardening?"

"No."

"Ever played UNO?"

He gave her a puzzled look. "What's an Uno?"

"Wow, either you've led dull life or I've been overly entertained." Deciding she'd been overly entertained by a dad who couldn't do much in the way of physical things, Grace had a sudden inspiration. "If your mother's an expert at rummy, I know you've played that."

He glanced down at his fingernails as if studying them. "A bit."

"Oh, you think you're pretty good, don't you?"

"I'm a slouch."

"Don't sucker me!"

"Would I sucker you?"

"To get me to let my guard down so you could beat me, yes." She paused, then headed to the dining room buffet and the cards. "If you think you have to sucker me, you must not be very good."

"I'm exceptional."

She grinned. "I knew it."

Just then, a whimper floated from the baby monitor on the counter.

Grace set the cards back in the drawer. "So much for rummy. I'll try to get her back to sleep but I'm betting she wants to come downstairs."

"Why did she wake up so soon?"

"She probably heard us talking. That's why she didn't roll over and go back to sleep. She wants to be in on the action."

"Great. We'll play rummy with her in the high chair."

She paused on her way to the steps. "We could, but wouldn't it be more fun to spend a few minutes with Sarah first?"

He nodded. "Yeah. You're right."

As Grace went up the steps Danny took a long breath. He, Grace and the baby had had a good time shopping. He and Grace had had fun putting away the groceries and getting the soup into the pot. Now they would spend even more time together, and no doubt it would be fun.

He rubbed his hand across the back of his neck. The whole morning had been so easy—so right—that he knew he was correct in thinking that a friendship between him and Grace gave him the family, the connection, he so desperately wanted. But he also knew he was getting too close to a line he shouldn't cross—unless he wanted to fall in love with her and make their family a real family. He didn't want to hurt her, but right now, in his gut, he had an optimistic sense that he wouldn't. And the night before he'd seen in her eyes that she wanted what he wanted. For them to fall in love. She didn't have to say the words for Danny to know that she trusted him. She believed in him. He'd hurt her once, yet she trusted that he wouldn't hurt her again.

She believed in him and maybe the trick to their situation wouldn't be to take this one step at a time, but to trust what Grace saw in him, rather than what he knew about himself.

He walked into the kitchen and lifted the lid from the pot. He sniffed the steam that floated out and his mouth watered. Even if soup was simple fare and even though he absolutely believed Grace had cheated with the bouillion cube, it smelled heavenly. He'd trusted her about spending two weeks here with her and Sarah, and had acclimated to being in a family again, albeit a nontraditional one. He'd trusted Grace about the soup, and it appeared he would be getting a tasty dinner. He'd trusted her about relaxing with Sarah and he now had a relationship with his daughter.

Could he trust her instinct that he wouldn't hurt her? Or let her down the way he'd let Lydia down?

Grace came down the steps carrying smiling Sarah.

When the baby immediately zeroed in on him, he said, "Hey, kid."

She yelped and clapped her hands.

"She does a lot of screeching and yelping. We've got to teach her a few words."

"Eventually. Right now, I think playing with the blocks or maybe the cone and rings are a better use of our time."

Danny was about to ask what the cone and rings were, but he suddenly had a very vivid memory of them. He saw Cory on the floor, brightly colored rings in a semicircle in front of him. He remembered teaching Cory to pick up the rings in order of size and slide them onto the cone.

And the memory didn't hurt. In fact, it made him smile. Cory had always had an eye for color. Maybe Sarah did, too? Or maybe Danny didn't care how smart Sarah was or where her gifts were? Maybe his being so concerned about Cory's gifts was part of what had pushed Lydia away from him?

Forcing himself into the present, Danny glanced around. "Where's the toy box?"

"I don't have one. Sarah's toys are in the bottom drawer of the buffet in the dining area."

He walked over to it. "Curse of a small house?"

"Yes. This is the other reason I hesitated

to talk with you about opening an investment account for me. I definitely need something with more space and I'm considering buying another house, and if I have extra money that's probably where it will go."

He opened the bottom drawer, found the colorful cone and rings and pulled it out. Returning to the area that served as a living room, he handed Grace the cone and sat on the sofa.

As Grace dumped the multicolored rings on the floor in front of Sarah, Danny cautiously said, "You know, we've never made a firm decision about child support."

She glanced up at him with a smile. "Yes, we did. I told you I wouldn't pay you any."

Her comment made him laugh and suddenly Danny felt too far away. He slid off the sofa and positioned himself on the floor across from Grace with Sarah between them, using the baby as a buffer between him and the woman who—whether she knew it or not—was tempting him to try something he swore he'd never try again. Even the idea of *trying* was new. He was shaky at best about trusting himself, and Sarah's happiness also tied into their situation. He couldn't act hastily, or let his hormones have control.

"Actually I think if we went to court a judge would order me to pay you something. So, come on. Let's really talk about this."

Grace busied herself making sure all the rings were within Sarah's reach. "Okay, if you want to pay something every month, why don't you put a couple hundred dollars a month into a college fund for Sarah?"

"Because she doesn't need a college fund. I can afford to pay for schooling." He took a breath, remembering that the last time they'd broached this subject she'd made him stop— the same way he made her stop when they got too far into his past. But resolving child support for their daughter was different than rehashing a past he desperately needed to forget. They had to come to an agreement on support.

"Look, I know you don't want to talk about this. But we have to. I don't feel right not contributing to her day-to-day expenses."

"I already told you that we're going to be sharing custody," Grace said as she gently guided Sarah's hand to take the ring she was shoving into her mouth and loop it onto the cone. "I will have her one week, but you will have her the next. Technically that's the way we'll share her expenses."

"I'd still like to—"

"Danny, I have a job. My house is nearly paid off. When I sell it, the money I get will be my down payment for the new one. I have a plan. It works. We're fine."

"I know. I just—"

Though Danny had thought she was getting angry, she playfully slapped his knee. "Just for one afternoon will you please relax?"

He peered at her hand, then caught her gaze. "You slapped me."

She grinned. "A friendly tap to wake you up, so you'll finally catch on that I'm right."

This was what he liked about her. She didn't have to win every argument. She also knew when to pull back. *Before* either one of them said something they'd regret, rather than after. It was a skill or sixth sense he and Lydia had never acquired. Plus, she had wonderfully creative ways of stepping away and getting him to step away. Rather than slammed doors and cold shoulders, she teased him. And she let him tease her.

"Oh, yeah? So what you're saying is that friendly tapping between us is allowed?"

"Sure. Sometimes something physical is the only way to get someone's attention."

"You mean like this?" He leaped behind

Sarah, caught Grace around the shoulders, and nudged her to the floor in one fluid movement, so he could tickle her.

"Hey!" she yelped, trying to get away from him when he tickled her ribs. "You *had* my attention."

"I had your attention, but you weren't getting my point, so I'm making sure you see how serious I am when I say you should take my money."

She wiggled away from him. "I don't need your money."

"I can see that," he said, catching her waist and dragging her back. "But I want to give it."

He tickled her again and she cried, "Uncle! I give up! Give me a thousand dollars and we'll call it even."

"I gave you more than that for helping with Orlando," he said, catching her gaze. When their eyes met, his breathing stopped. Reminded of the bonus and Orlando, vivid images of their weekend came to Danny. He stopped tickling. She stopped laughing. His throat worked.

In the year that had passed he'd all but forgotten she existed, convinced that she had lied about her pregnancy and left his employ because she was embarrassed that her scheme had been exposed. Now he knew she'd been sick, dependent upon the bonus that he'd given her for expenses and dependent upon her parents for emotional support that *he* should have given her.

"I'm so sorry about everything."

She whispered, "I know."

"I would give anything to make it up for the hurt I caused you."

"There's no need."

He remembered again how she had been that weekend. Happy, but also gracious. She wouldn't take a promotion she hadn't deserved. She wouldn't pry, was kind to Orlando, never overstepped her boundaries. And he'd hurt her. Chances were, he'd hurt her again.

Still, he wanted so much to kiss her that his chest ached and he couldn't seem to overrule the instinct that was as much emotional as it was physical. He liked her. He just plain liked her. He liked being with her, being part of her life, having her in his life.

He lowered his head and touched his lips to hers, telling himself that if he slid them into a simple, uncomplicated romance with no expectation of grandeur, she wouldn't be hurt. He wouldn't be hurt. Both would get what they wanted.

His mouth slid across hers slowly at first, savoring every second of the physical connection that was a manifestation of the depth of his feelings for her. She answered, equally slowly, as if as hesitant as he was, but also as unable to resist the temptation. When the slight meeting of mouths wasn't enough her lips blossomed to life under his, meeting him, matching him, then oh so slowly opening.

It was all the invitation Danny needed. He deepened the kiss, awash with the pleasure of being close to someone as wonderful as Grace. Happiness virtually sang through his veins. Need thrummed through him. For the first time since she'd brought Sarah to him, his thoughts didn't automatically tumble back to their beach house weekend. They stayed in the present, on the moment, on the woman in his arms and the desire to make love. To touch her, to taste her, to cherish every wonderful second. To build a future.

But the second the future came into play, Danny knew he was only deluding himself. He'd tried this once and failed. He'd lost a child, broken his wife. Spent a year mourning his loss alone in the big house so hollow and empty it echoed around him. He knew the reality of loss. How it destroyed a person. Emptied a life. He couldn't go through it again, but more than that, he wouldn't force Grace to.

CHAPTER TEN

DANNY BROKE THE kiss, quickly rose from the floor and extended his hand to Grace. When she was on her feet, he spun away and Grace's stomach knotted.

"Danny?"

He rubbed both hands down his face. "Grace, this is wrong."

"No, it isn't." Glad for the opportunity to finally discuss their feelings instead of guessing, she walked over and grabbed him by the upper arm, turning him to face her. "This is us. We like each other. Naturally. We're like toast and butter or salt and pepper. We fit."

He laughed harshly. "Fit? Are you sure you want to say you fit with me?"

She didn't hesitate. "Yes."

He shook his head. "Grace, please. Please, don't. Don't fit with me. Don't even *want* to fit with me. If you were smart you wouldn't even want to be my friend."

At that her chin came up. If he was going to turn her away again, to deny her his love, or even the chance to be part of his life, this time she would make him explain. "Why?"

"Because I'm not good for you. I'm not good for anybody."

"Why?"

He raked his fingers through his short black hair. "Stop!"

"No. You say you're not good for me. I say you are. And I will not stop pursuing you."

"Then I'll leave."

"Great. Run. If that's your answer to everything, then you run."

He groaned and walked away as if annoyed that she wouldn't let him alone. "I'm not running. I'm saving you."

"I don't think you are. I also don't think you're a coward who runs. So just tell me what's wrong!"

He pivoted to face her so quickly that Grace flinched. "Tell you? Tell you what? That I failed at my marriage and hurt the woman I adored? Tell you that I don't want to do it again?"

His obsidian eyes were bright with pain.

His voice seemed to echo from a dark, sacred place. A place of scars and black memories and wounds. A place he rarely visited and never took another person. Still, broken marriages were common. And though she understood his had hurt him, she also suspected even *he* knew it was time to get beyond his.

Her heart breaking for him, Grace whispered, "How do you know that you'll fail?"

Stiff with resistance, he angrily countered, "How do you know that I won't?"

"Because you're good. You may not know it but I see it every day in how you treat me and how you treat Sarah."

"Grace, you are wrong. I use people. Just ask my ex-wife. She'll tell you I'm a workaholic. If you called her right now, she'd probably even accurately guess that I'm only here because I need to raise my daughter because I need an heir. Carson Services needs an heir."

"Well, she'd be wrong. If you only wanted to raise Sarah because Carson Services needs an heir you could take me to court."

"Unless I didn't want you digging into my past."

That stopped her.

"What if this is all about me not wanting you to take me to court?" he asked, stepping close. "What if there is something so bad in my past that I know even you couldn't forgive it?"

She swallowed. Possibilities overwhelmed her. Not only did having a hidden sin in his past explain why he agreed to live with her and their daughter when letting his lawyers handle their situation would have been much easier, but it also explained why he always stepped back, always denied himself and her.

Still, she couldn't imagine what he could have done. He wasn't gentle and retiring by any means. But he also wasn't cruel or vindictive. He wasn't the kind to take risks or live on the edge. She might have told herself to stop guessing, to quit ascribing characteristics to him he didn't deserve, but she'd also lived with him for a week. Almost fifteen hours a day. She'd seen him *choose* to make breakfast, *choose* to bathe Sarah, *choose* to give Grace breaks. She didn't believe he could be cruel or do something so horrible it couldn't be forgiven.

She took a breath, then another. "I don't think there is something in your past that can't be forgiven."

"What if I told you that I killed my son?"

Her heart in her throat, more aware of the

pain that would cause him than any sort of ramification it would have on their relationship, she said, "You couldn't have killed your son."

"It was an accident, but the accident was my fault."

Grace squeezed her eyes shut. An accident that was his fault. Of course. That accounted for so many things in his life and how he had treated her that before this hadn't added up.

But accidents were circumstances that somehow got out of someone's control. He hadn't deliberately killed his child. He couldn't deliberately kill his child. That was why he was so tortured now.

"Danny, it wasn't your fault."

His eyes blazed. "Don't you forgive me! And don't brush it off as if my son's life was of no consequence. I was in charge of him that morning. *I* knew he was in the mood to push me. He wanted to remove the training wheels from his bike and I refused, but he kept arguing, begging, pleading. When my cell phone rang, I should have ignored it. But my natural reaction kicked in, I grabbed it, answered it and gave him the chance to prove to me how good he was on his bike by darting out into the street right into the path of an SUV."

He paused, raked his fingers through his hair again and his voice dropped to a feather-light whisper. "A neighbor hit him. She doesn't come out of her house now. I ruined a lot of lives that morning."

The tick of the clock was the only sound in the room. Grace stood frozen, steeped in his pain, hurting for him.

"Not quite as sure of me now, are you?"

She swallowed. "It wasn't your fault."

He ran his hands down his face. "It was my fault. And I live with it every day. And I miss my son and I remember the look on my wife's face." Seeming to be getting his bearings, he blew his breath out on a long gust and faced her. "And I won't do that to you."

He headed for the stairway. Panicked, knowing they were only at the tip of this discussion, Grace said, "What if I—"

He stopped at the bottom of the steps. His face bore the hard, cold expression she remembered from the day she told him she was pregnant.

"You don't get a choice. You don't get a say. This pain is mine."

He ran up the steps and Grace collapsed on

her sofa. Bending forward, she lifted Sarah from the floor and squeezed her to her chest, suddenly understanding why he didn't want her digging into his past. It could give her plenty of grounds to keep him from getting custody—even shared. But it also gave her a foot in the door to keep the baby away from him completely.

And she hated to admit she was considering it. Not because of what had happened with his son, but because he couldn't seem to get beyond it. What did it mean for Sarah that her father wouldn't let himself love again?

She took a breath, knowing her fears were premature because they had another week to live together, another week for him to recognize that though he didn't want to forget his son, he also had a daughter who needed him. She shouldn't jump to conclusions.

But twenty minutes later he came downstairs, suitcase in hand.

"We have another week to live together."

"Grace, I'm done." He shrugged into his jacket. "Besides, I never signed the agreement. This was a mistake anyway."

With that he opened the door, and stepped out, but he turned one final time and looked at Sarah, then his gaze slowly rose to catch

Grace's. She saw the regret, the pain, the need. Then she watched him quickly erase it as determination filled his dark eyes. He stepped out into the September afternoon, closing the door behind him with a soft click.

Danny walked into the empty foyer of his huge house and listened to the echo his suitcase made as he set it on the floor, knowing this was the rest of his life, and for the first time totally, honestly, unemotionally committed to accepting it. He wouldn't risk hurting Grace. Telling his story that afternoon, he remembered in vivid detail how unworthy he was to drag another person into his life. Now that Grace knew his mistake, he didn't expect to even get visitation with Sarah. He expected to live his life alone, the perfect candidate to serve Carson Services and pass on the family legacy.

To Sarah. A little girl who wouldn't know him, probably wouldn't know about Carson Services, but who shared his bloodline. When she came of age, Danny would offer her the chance to train to take over the family business, but would Grace let him? No mother would sentence her daughter to even a few hours a week with a cold, distant father.

Walking up the ornate curved stairway of the huge home that went to the next Carson, Danny had to wonder if that wasn't a good thing.

CHAPTER ELEVEN

A MONTH LATER, seated at the slim wooden table in the hearing room in the courthouse, Danny wasn't entirely sure why he had come to this proceeding. Grace's reasons for being here were a no-brainer. She'd had her lawyer set the hearing to make her case for Danny not getting custody. She could probably get enough reasons on the record to preclude him from even seeing their baby again.

But he knew she wouldn't do that. After his confession to her, and a week of wallowing in misery in his lonely house, he'd pulled himself up by his bootstraps and gone back to work like the sharp CEO he was, and his life had fallen into a strong, comfortable routine. Once he'd gotten his bearings and stopped feeling sorry for himself, he'd recognized that *all* was not lost. Grace wouldn't keep Sarah from him. She would be kind enough—or maybe fair enough to Sarah—to let him have visitation, even though she probably hated him.

Some days he hated himself. Blamed himself for the pain he'd caused both him and Grace by letting her believe in him—even if it was for one short week. Had he told Grace right from the beginning that his son was not only dead, but Danny himself was responsible for Cory's accident, Grace would have happily kept her distance. She wouldn't have mourned the loss of his love, as he'd pictured her doing. He wouldn't have again felt the sting of living alone in his big, hollow house, torturously reminded of how it felt to be whole, to be wanted, to have people in his life and a purpose beyond perpetuating the family business.

But if nothing else had come from the week he'd spent with Grace and Sarah, Danny knew Grace would be fair. He thoroughly loved his daughter. He wanted to be part of her life, not just to assure she'd be ready to make a choice about Carson Services, but because he loved having her around. He loved being with her. And she was Danny's last chance at a family. He might never have the good fortune to share his life with Sarah's mother, but he could at least have a daughter.

So he supposed he'd come to this hearing as a show of good faith, proof that if Grace intended to let him have visitation, he wanted it. He suspected that any visitation she granted him would be supervised. He'd been the one in charge when Cory was killed. Grace's lawyer would undoubtedly drop that fact into the proceeding as a way to demonstrate that Danny wasn't a good dad. But he'd take even supervised visitation. At this point, he'd take anything he could get.

Grace entered the hearing room. Wearing an electric-blue suit, with her dark shoulder-length hair swaying around her and her sexy violet eyes shining, she was pretty enough to stop his heart. Yet in spite of how gorgeous she was, Danny's real reaction to her was emotional rather than physical. He'd missed her. They'd spent a total of nine days together. Three at his beach house and six at her house and he missed her. Ached for her. Longed for everything he knew darned well they could have had together, if he hadn't looked away for one split second and changed his destiny.

Grace approached the table with her lawyer, young, handsome, Robby Malloy. The guy Danny's lawyer called pretty boy Malloy. Danny could see why. He had the face of a movie star and carried himself like a billionaire. Danny experienced a surge of jealousy so intense he had to fight to keep himself from jumping from behind the table and yanking Grace away from the sleazy ambulance chaser.

But he didn't jump and he didn't yank. Because as a father his first concern had to be assuring that he was part of his daughter's life. He'd never had the right to care about Grace, about who she dated, or even if she dated.

So why was his blood pressure rising and his chest tightening from just looking at her with another man? Her lawyer no less? A man who may not even be romantically interested, only earning his hourly fee for representing her?

The judge entered the room, his dark robe billowing around him with his every step. Danny followed the lead of his attorney, Art Brown, and rose.

Having not yet taken his seat, Malloy extended his hand to the judge. "Judge Antanazzo."

"Good morning, Mr. Malloy," Charlie Antanazzo boomed. "How's my favorite attorney today?"

Malloy laughed. "Well, I doubt that I'm your favorite attorney," he said, obviously charming the judge. "But I'm great, your honor. This is my client, Grace McCartney."

As Grace shook Judge Antanazzo's hand, he smiled. "It's a pleasure to meet you."

Danny would just bet it was. Not only did the judge smile like any man happy to meet a pretty girl, but also Danny hadn't missed the way the judge took a quick inventory that started with Grace's shiny sable hair and managed to skim her perfect figure and nice legs in under a second.

This time it was a bit harder to refrain from leaping over the desk and yanking her to him.

But that ship had sailed and Danny had to grow accustomed to watching men fawn over Grace. He'd had his chance and he'd blown it. Or maybe it wasn't so much that Danny had had his chance, as much as it was that Danny had destroyed his own life long before he met Grace.

Danny's lawyer finally spoke. "Good morning, your honor," Art said, then shook the judge's hand. "This is my client, Danny Carson."

The judge quickly shook the hand Danny extended and frowned as he looked down at the brown case file he'd brought into the hearing room with him.

"Yes, I know. Danny Carson. CEO of Carson Services. Let's see," he said, skimming the words in front of him. "Ms. McCartney was in your employ at one time." He continued reading. "She told you she was pregnant. You didn't believe her. Circumstances, including her being sick during the pregnancy, kept her from pursuing the matter. Then she took the baby to you." He read some more. "There's no record of child support." He looked at Danny. "Do you pay child support?"

Danny's lawyer said, "No, your honor, but—"

The judge ignored him. "All right then. This case boils down to a few concise facts. Ms. McCartney told you she was pregnant, brought the child to you and you don't pay child support." He glanced from Danny to Grace and held Grace's gaze. "Am I up to speed?

"There's a little more, your honor," Grace's lawyer said. "Once the court reporter is ready, I'd like to go on the record."

Danny's heart sank. Great. Just great. From the scant information the judge had read, it was pretty clear whose side he was on. Once Danny's past came out, the judge might not even let him have supervised visitation. The urge to defend himself rose up in Danny and this time rather than fight it, he let it take root. All the facts that the judge had read had made him look bad. But he wasn't. Everything he'd done wrong wasn't really a deliberate misdeed. Every one of his "bad" things were explainable—defendable.

He'd *misinterpreted* Grace's not answering the phone the night he'd flown home after his week of client hopping. As a result of that he broke off with her. So, when she came in to tell him she was pregnant, he'd thought it was a ruse to get him back, and he hadn't believed her. And when she left his employ, Danny had thought it was because her scheme had been exposed. He wasn't bad. He wasn't a schmuck. He had made some mistakes. Very defendable mistakes. Technically he could even defend himself about Cory's death.

He took a breath. That wasn't at issue right now. Sarah's custody was.

The lawyers and judge made preliminary statements for the record. Danny studiously avoided looking at Grace by tapping the eraser of his pencil on the desk. Eventually the judge said, "Mr. Malloy, ball's in your court."

"Thank you, your honor. My client would like to testify first."

Danny's lawyer had warned him that preliminary hearings could sometimes seem unofficial, but Danny shouldn't take it lightly because a court reporter would be recording the proceedings. He sat up a little straighter.

Though Grace stayed in her seat at the table, she was sworn in.

Her lawyer said, "Okay, Ms. McCartney, there is no argument between you and Mr. Carson about paternity?"

"No. And if there were we'd get a DNA test. We've agreed to that."

"But there's no need because you know Mr. Carson is the father?"

"Yes. I didn't—hadn't—" She paused, stumbling over her explanation and Danny frowned, not sure what she was getting at.

"You hadn't had relations," Robbie prompted and Grace nodded.

"—I hadn't had relations with anybody for several months before Danny—Mr. Carson—and I spent a weekend at his beach house."

Danny damned near groaned. Not because it sounded as if he'd taken her to his private hideaway to seduce her, but because for the first time since that weekend he realized how important sleeping with him must have been in her life. She didn't sleep around. Hell, she apparently barely slept with anybody. But she'd been with him that night. She'd smiled at him, made him laugh, made him feel really alive—

Robbie Malloy said, "So why are you here today, Ms. McCartney?" bringing Danny back to the present.

"I'm here today because Mr. Carson and I had a shared custody agreement."

"Briefly, what does the agreement say?"

"That if he could stay at my house for two weeks, basically to learn how to care for Sarah, I would agree to shared custody."

"Did Mr. Carson want shared custody?"

"No. At first he wanted full custody. The agreement we made about shared custody was drafted to prevent us from fighting over Sarah. Shared custody seemed like the fair way to handle things."

"But—"

Grace took a breath. Danny raised his gaze to hers and she looked directly at him. Which was exactly what he'd intended to make her do. If she wanted to testify against him, then let her do it looking into his eyes.

"But he didn't stay the two weeks."

Danny's eyes hardened.

"Ms. McCartney, is it also correct that he didn't sign the agreement?"

"No, he did not."

"And is that why we're here?"

"Well, I can't speak for Mr. Carson, but the reason I am here is to get it on the record that even though he didn't sign the agreement, or stay the two weeks, I believe Mr. Carson fulfilled its spirit and intent and I feel we should honor it."

"Which means you believe you and Mr. Carson should have shared custody?"

She held Danny's gaze. "Yes."

"You want me to have Sarah every other week?" Danny said, forgetting they were on the record.

"Yes. Danny, you proved yourself."

"I left."

"I know." She smiled slightly. "It doesn't matter. You showed me you can care for Sarah."

Robbie said, "Your honor, that's what we wanted to get on the record. No further questions."

The judge turned to Art. "Do you want to question Ms. McCartney?"

Art raised his hands. "Actually I think we'll let Ms. McCartney's testimony stand as is."

"Does Mr. Carson want to testify?"

Without consulting Danny, Art said, "No."

The judge quickly glanced down at his notes. "Technically you have a custody agreement in place. It's simply not executed. But Ms. McCartney still wants to honor it." He looked at Danny. "Mr. Carson? Do you want to honor the agreement?"

Danny nodded as Art said, "Yes."

The judge made a sound of strained patience, then said, "You're a very lucky man, Mr. Carson. Very lucky indeed."

Staring at Grace, who had begun casually gathering her purse as if what she had just said hadn't been of monumental significance, Danny didn't know what to say. Art spoke for him. "Your honor, when parents share custody it's frequently considered that each is taking his or her share of the financial burden when the child is with him—or her."

The judge closed the file. "Right. As if these two people have equal financial means." He faced Danny. "Don't screw this up." He left the room in a flurry or robes and promises about writing up an order.

Art began gathering his files. "Well, that went much better than expected," he said with a laugh, but overwhelmed with too many emotions to name, Danny watched Grace and her lawyer heading for the door.

Just as Grace would have stepped over the threshold, emotion overruled common sense and he called, "Wait!"

Grace turned and smiled at him.

Danny's throat worked. She was incredibly beautiful and incredibly generous. And he was numb with gratitude. "Why didn't you—"

She tilted her head in question. "Why didn't I what?"

Go for the jugular? Fight? Tell the court about Cory?

"Why are you letting me have Sarah?"

"You're her dad."

"I —" He took a breath. "What if I can't handle her?"

To his amazement, Grace laughed. "You can handle her. I've seen you handle her. You'll be fine."

"I'll be fine," he repeated, annoyed with Grace for being so flip, when the safety of their daughter was at stake. "What kind of answer is that!"

"It's an honest one."

"How can you trust her with me!"

"Are you telling me you're going to put her in danger?"

He glared at her. "You know I won't."

"Then there's no reason you shouldn't have your daughter."

"You trust me?"

She smiled. "I trust you. But if you're nervous, hire a nanny. You've told me at least twice that you were going to do that. So hire somebody."

Danny's heart swelled with joy. He was getting a second chance. He would have something of a family. He swallowed hard. "Okay."

She took two steps closer to him and placed her hand on his forearm. "Or, if you don't want to hire a nanny, you could come home."

Home. Her house *was* home. Warm. Welcoming. He could remember nearly every detail of their six short days. Especially how tempted he was to take what they both wanted. Just as he was tempted now to take what she was offering. A complete second chance. Not just an opportunity to be Sarah's daddy, but a second chance at life. A real life.

But he also knew he was damaged. So damaged it wasn't fair to use Grace as a step up out of his particular hell. He smiled regretfully. "You know you deserve better."

"So you say, but I don't think so. I see the part of you that you're trying to hide, or forget, or punish. I don't see the past."

"You're lucky."

"No, Danny, I'm not lucky. It's time. Time for you to move on." She held out her hand. "Come home with me. Start again."

He stared at the hand she offered. Delicate fingers. Pretty pink fingernails. Feminine things. Soft things. Things that had been missing from his life for so long. A million possibilities entered his head. A million things he would do, *could* do, if he took that hand, took the steps that would put him in Grace's world again. He could teach Sarah to walk. Hear her first word. Hear the first time she called him daddy. Sleep with Grace. Use the spaezle maker. Steal kisses. Share dreams. Spend Christmas as part of a family.

None of which he deserved.

"I can't."

CHAPTER TWELVE

Danny turned away and though Grace's gut reaction was to demand that he talk to her, she didn't. Tears filled her eyes. Tears for him as much as for the wonderful future he was denying both of them, and she turned around and walked out of the hearing room.

Robbie was waiting. "You okay?"

She managed a smile. "Yeah. I'm fine."

"You're awfully generous with him."

"That's because he's so hard on himself."

"Be careful, Grace," Robbie said, directing her to the stairway that led to the courthouse lobby. "Men like Danny Carson who have a reputation for taking what they want don't like to lose. You may think that by "granting" him shared custody you were doing him and your daughter a kindness, but you had him over a barrel and he knew it. He may have just played you like a Stradivarius. Made you feel sorry for him so that you'd give him what he wanted, since he knew he probably couldn't beat you in court."

"I don't think so. I know Danny better than you do. He wouldn't do something like that."

"You think you know Danny?"

"I *know* Danny."

"Well, you better hope so because what we got on the record today—you saying you believed he was capable of caring for Sarah—negated any possibility we had of using his son's death in future hearings."

Grace gasped. "I would never use his son's death!"

Robbie held up his hand in defense. "Hey, I'm okay with that. Actually I agree that it would be cruel to use his son's death against him. I'm just saying be careful. This whole thing could backfire and you could end up fighting for your own daughter."

"I won't."

Robbie shook his head. "God save me from clients in love."

"It's that obvious?"

"Yes." Holding open one of the two huge double doors of the courthouse entrance, Robbie added, "And if Danny's as smart as everyone claims he is, he'll use it. Better put my number on speed dial."

Reading to Sarah in the rocking chair that night, Grace thought about the look on Danny's face when she stated for the record that she wanted their shared custody agreement upheld.

She shouldn't have been surprised that he expected her to testify against him. He was angry with himself and nothing she said or did could change that. No matter how sad he appeared or how much she'd simply wanted to hug him, she couldn't. A man who couldn't forgive himself, especially for something so traumatic, wasn't ready for a relationship and he might never be. It had broken her heart when he refused her offer to return home. As much for him as for herself.

But at least she had her answer now.

With Sarah asleep in her arms, Grace set the storybook on a shelf of the changing table and rose from the rocker. She laid Sarah in her crib, covered her, kissed her forehead and walked down the steps.

It wasn't going to be easy sharing custody with a man she loved but who could never love her. But she intended to do it. Actually she intended to do the one thing she'd promised herself she wouldn't do the night she rushed down to his beach house bar to see if he felt about her the way she felt about him. She was going to pine for him. She intended to love him forever, quietly, without expectation of anything in return because the real bottom line to Danny's trouble was that nobody had ever really loved him. At least not without expectation of anything in return. His parents expected him to take over the family business. His ex-wife held him responsible for their child's death. The people who worked for him wanted a job. His investors, even investors he considered friends, like Orlando, needed his expertise. Nobody loved him without expectation of anything in return.

So she would be that person. She might never be his wife, but she would be there for him in all the right ways, so that he could see that he was okay and that life didn't always have to be about what he could give somebody.

Two Mondays later when Robbie called and told her that the judge's order had come down, Grace sat quietly and listened as her lawyer explained how she was to have Sarah ready at six o'clock that Friday night. With every word he said, her chest tightened. Her eyes filled with tears. It was easy to say she intended to love Danny without expectation of anything in return when the situation was abstract. But now that shared custody was a reality she suddenly realized loving Danny meant denying herself. At the very least, she would spend every other week without her daughter.

She hung up the phone, glad for four days to prepare herself to see him, and managed to greet him with a smile Friday evening. With Sarah's diaper bag packed and sitting by the door, she put Sarah into his arms.

"Hey, Sarah Bear," he said softly and the baby hit him on the cheek with her rattle. He laughed nervously. "I guess she's forgotten who I am."

"Maybe," Grace said, trying to sound strong and confident, but with Danny standing at her door, refusing to go beyond the foyer, wearing a topcoat and scarf because western Pennsylvania had had its first snowfall of the season, it seemed as if the Danny she loved no longer existed. The guy in jeans and a T-shirt who made pancakes seemed to have been replaced by the man who ran Carson Services.

"We won't need that," Danny said, nodding at the diaper bag, as he struggled to contain Sarah who had begun to wail in earnest and stretched away from Danny, reaching for Grace. "I have a nursery full of things." For the first time since he'd arrived, he met her gaze. "I also hired a nanny."

"Good." Tears clogged Grace's throat when Sarah squealed and reached for her. "Stay with Daddy, Sarah," she whispered, pushing the baby back in Danny's arms, then fussing with Sarah's jacket as she slowly pulled her hands way.

But with her mom this close, Sarah all but crawled out of Danny's arms again, with a squeal that renewed her crying.

Pain ricocheted through Grace. "Maybe we should have broken this up? Had her do an overnight visit or two before we forced her to spend an entire week."

"It's going to be hard no matter how we do it. Let's just get this over with."

He opened the door, not even sparing Grace a glance, taking her daughter.

"If she gives you any trouble, just call," Grace said, trying to keep her voice light and bright as he walked away, but it wobbled.

Already on the sidewalk, striding to his car, Danny said, "We're fine."

And he left.

Watching his car lights as they disappeared into the night, Grace stood on her stoop, with her lawyer's words ringing in her ears, suddenly wondering if Danny really hadn't tricked her.

Could he have put on jeans a few times, made a couple of pancakes and cruelly lured her into loving him, all to take her child?

Danny entered his home, sobbing Sarah on his arm. "Elise!" he called, summoning his nanny.

She strode into the foyer. Tall and sturdily build, Elise wore a brightly colored knit cardigan over a white blouse and gray skirt. She looked like she could have stepped out of a storybook, as the quintessential nanny.

"Oh, my. This little one's got a pair of lungs!" Elise said with a laugh, and reached out to take Sarah from his arms. But as Danny handed the baby to her nanny, he felt odd about giving over Sarah's care so easily. He remembered that Grace had told him that she didn't want to share his nanny because caring for Sarah was part of her quality time.

After shrugging out of his topcoat, he reached for Sarah again. "Tonight, I'll take care of her."

"But—"

"At least until she adjusts to being here."

Elise took a breath, gave him a confused smile and said, "As you wish."

Danny didn't care what she thought. All he cared about was Sarah. He'd thought hiring a nanny would be the perfect way to help ease Sarah into her new life, but seeing Elise with Sarah felt wrong. Sarah was his responsibility. His little girl. His daughter.

Carrying Sarah into the nursery, Danny thought of Grace. How tears had filled her eyes when Sarah had begun to cry. He'd left quickly, not to cause her pain, but to get all three of them accustomed to this every other Friday night ritual. But he'd hurt her.

Again.

It seemed he was always hurting Grace.

Still, with crying Sarah on his arm, it wasn't the time to think about that. He wrestled her out of her jacket, little black shoes, tiny jeans and T-shirt, then rolled her into a pair of pajamas.

She never stopped crying.

He put her on his shoulder and patted her

back, as he walked downstairs and to the refrigerator where he extracted one of the bottles Elise had prepared. Sitting on the rocker in the nursery, he fed her the bottle and though she drank greedily, sniffled remnants of her crying jag accompanied her sucking. The second the bottle came out of her mouth, she began to cry again.

"I'm sorry. I know this is hard. I know you miss your mom, but this is the right thing. Trust me."

He paced the floor with her, trying to comfort her, but as he pivoted to make his third swipe across the room, he saw the books beside the rocker. The designer he'd hired to create the yellow and pink, bear-theme room had strategically stationed books on a low table within reach of the rocker. After sitting again, he took one of the books, opened it and began to read.

"Once upon a time, in a kingdom far away, there lived a princess. Her name was—" He paused, then smiled. "Sarah. Sarah bear."

Sarah's crying slowed.

"She was a beautiful child with blond— reddish-brown curls," he amended, matching the description of the little girl in the book to the little girl in his arms. "And blue eyes."

Her crying reduced to sniffles and she blinked, her confused expression taking him back to the first night he'd cared for her alone—the night Grace had been edgy. The memory caused him to smile. He hadn't wanted to be alone with Sarah. Wasn't sure he could handle her. He'd only kept the baby to please Grace.

He took a breath. This time he was caring for Sarah to *protect* Grace. From him. Adding a failed marriage to ignoring her pregnancy and taking her child wouldn't help anything. He had to remember that.

"The princess lived alone with her father, the king. Her mother had died when the princess was a baby and a governess had been hired. Mrs. Pickleberry had a face puckered in a perpetual frown and Sarah would pretend to be ill, rather than spend time with her when the king was out of the palace performing his royal duties. Each time, when Mrs. Pickleberry would leave her room, sufficiently convinced that Sarah should stay in bed for the day, Sarah would crawl into her window seat, her legs tucked beneath her, her thumb in her mouth, watching, alone, for her father to return."

Danny stopped reading. The king didn't have a choice about leaving his daughter in the care of her governess, but Danny had choices. Lots of them. In the argument they'd had the day Grace brought Sarah to him, Grace had asked if it was better for Sarah to be raised by strangers rather than her mother. Still, that wasn't what was happening here. Yes, Sarah would be stuck with a governess—uh, nanny—while Danny was at work, but he wasn't taking Sarah away from her mother. Not really. Just every other week.

He glanced down. Sarah was asleep.

Thank God. He didn't think he could take any more of the story's inadvertent accusations. He laid the baby in her crib and stood for several minutes, just watching Sarah, basking in the joy of being a dad, considering all the things he could do for Sarah, and convincing himself that while he had Sarah, Grace could also do so many things, things she otherwise didn't have time to do.

But the soft smile that had lit his face suddenly died. Grace might have time to do tons of different things, but she wouldn't. She would spend every hour he had custody worrying about Sarah. Not because Danny wasn't trustworthy, but because she would miss her. And only because she would miss her. In fact, right now, Grace was probably crying, or lonely. And he absolutely couldn't stand the thought of it.

He wasn't the kind of man to hurt people. But his reasoning this time went beyond his own image of himself. He couldn't stand the thought of Grace missing Sarah because he loved her. The last thing any man wanted to do was hurt the woman he loved most in this world. And yet that was what he always did with Grace. He hurt her. When he'd met her, he was a broken, empty man. She'd reminded him of life. That Sunday night at the beach house, she'd given him a glimpse of what they'd have together if he could open up. When he couldn't, she'd gracefully accepted that he didn't want to see her anymore. But when she'd gotten pregnant, she'd tried one more time. When he rejected her again, she didn't return until she had Sarah. Offering him something he truly didn't deserve: a place in their daughter's life. A place she hadn't snatched away. Even knowing his dark secret, she had faith in him when he had none in himself.

Danny gritted his teeth. He knew the solution to this problem. He knew it as well as he knew his own last name.

In order to save Grace, he had to let go of his guilt. He had to try again. In earnest.

Or he had to take Sarah back to Grace. For good. No more shared custody.

Halfway to the kitchen to make cocoa, Grace heard a knock on her door and peered at her watch. Who would be visiting after nine at night?

Expecting it to be her parents, who were undoubtedly worried about her because this was her first night without Sarah, she turned and headed for the door. When she looked through the peephole and saw Danny holding sleeping Sarah, she jumped back and yanked open the door.

Reaching for Sarah, she said, "What happened? What's wrong?"

He motioned inside her house. "Can we talk?"

Cradling Sarah on her arm, she looked down and examined every exposed inch of her sleeping baby. Her gaze shooting to Danny, she said, "She's fine?"

He nodded. "Yeah. It's you and I who have the problem. We need to talk."

Grace's heart stopped. She'd nearly had herself convinced that Robbie was right. Danny had tricked her and he had gotten everything he wanted at Grace's expense. All because she'd fallen in love with him.

But he was back, saying they needed to talk, sounding like a man ready to give, rather than take. Still, this time she had to be strong, careful. She couldn't fall victim to the look in his beautiful dark eyes…or the hope in her heart.

She had to be strong.

"Danny, it's late and our lawyers said everything we needed to say—"

"Not mine. He hardly said anything. And there are a few things I need to say. Put Sarah to bed. In *her* bed."

The gentleness of his voice got to her. If nothing else, Grace knew with absolute certainty that Danny loved Sarah. Knowing her lawyer would probably be angry that she talked to Danny without counsel, Grace stepped aside so Danny could enter.

As she turned to walk up the steps with the baby, she saw Danny hesitate in her small entryway.

Remembering he was always more at ease in her home when she gave him something to do, she said, "I was just about to make cocoa. You could go in the kitchen and get mugs."

"Okay."

When she returned downstairs, Grace saw he had only gotten as far as the stools in front of the breakfast counter. Again noting his hesitation, Grace said, "Don't you want cocoa?"

"I'd love some."

He sounded so quiet and so unsteady that Grace didn't know what to say. She set the pan on the stove and poured in milk and cocoa, waiting for him to talk. When he didn't, she lowered the flame on the gas burner and walked to the breakfast bar.

"Did something happen with Sarah?"

"No. She was fine." He caught her gaze. "Why did you do this? Why are you letting me have her every other week?"

She shrugged. "You're Sarah's dad. She loves you. You love her."

He caught her gaze. "And that's it?"

"What else is there?"

"You didn't give Sarah to me to try to force my hand?"

"Force your hand?" She laughed. "Oh, my

God, Danny, when have I ever gotten you to do anything? You didn't believe I slept with you because I liked you. You were sure I had an agenda. You didn't believe I was pregnant when I told you. You kicked me out of your office. You were so suspicious of me when I suggested shared custody that *you* insisted on the agreement. If there's one thing I know not to do it's try to force you to do anything."

"You didn't give me Sarah so that I'd be so grateful I'd fall in love with you?"

After a second to recover from the shock of that accusation, she shook her head sadly. He really did believe that people only did nice things when they wanted something from him. "Oh, Danny, I didn't give you time with Sarah to drag you into a relationship with me."

"Really?"

"Yes. I gave you time with Sarah because you're her dad."

"And you want nothing from me."

Grace debated lying to him. She *wanted* them to be a normal family. She wanted him to be the happy, laughing guy who'd made love to her at the beach house. She wanted him to want her. To welcome her into his life with open arms. She wanted a lot, but she didn't expect anything from him. The way she saw their lives unfolding, she would spend most of the time they had together just happy to see him unwind.

But if there was one thing she'd learned about Danny over the past weeks, it was that he valued honesty. So she took a breath and said, "I want a lot. But I'm also a realist. You won't fall in love again until you're ready. Nobody's going to push you."

He slid onto the stool. "I know." Pointing at the stove, he said, "I think your pot's boiling over."

"Eeek!" She spun away from the breakfast bar and ran to the stove, where hot milk bubbled over the sides of her aluminum pot. "Looks like I'll be starting over."

"I think we should both start over."

Not at all sure what he meant by that, Grace poured out the burned milk and filled the dirty pot with water, her heart pounding at the possibilities. "And how do you propose we start over?"

"The first step is that I have to tell you everything."

She found a second pot, filled it with milk and poured in cocoa, again refusing to hurry him along or push him. This was his show. She would let him do whatever he wanted. She'd *never* misinterpret him again. "So tell me everything."

While she adjusted the gas burner, he said, "Tonight I really thought through the things that had had happened to me in the past several years, and I realized something I'd refused to see before this."

He paused again. Recognizing he might think she wasn't paying attention, Grace said, "And what was that?"

"My marriage to Lydia was over before Cory's accident."

At that Grace turned to face him. "What?"

"Tonight when I was caring for Sarah in my brand-new nursery and thinking about how sad you probably were here alone, I realized that you are very different from Lydia. She and I spent most of our married life fighting. First she didn't want children, then when we had Cory she wanted him enrolled in a school for gifted children in California. We didn't fight over my pushing him into taking over Carson Services. We fought because she kept pushing him away. She didn't want him around."

"Oh."

"I won't say I didn't love her when I married her, but I can now see that we were so different, especially in what we wanted out of life, that we were heading for divorce long before Cory's accident. Tonight, I finally saw that I needed to separate the two. Cory's accident didn't ruin my marriage. Lydia and I had handled that all by ourselves."

"I'm sorry."

He laughed lightly. "You know what? I knew you would be. And I think that's part of why I like you. Why I was drawn to you at the beach house. You really have a sixth sense about people. I saw how you were with Orlando and listened in sometimes on your conversations, and I knew you were somebody special. More than that, though, you respected the same things I did. Especially family and commitments. You and I had the thing Lydia and I lacked. Common beliefs. Sunday night when we were alone, I realized we also had more than our fair share of chemistry." He paused, then said, "But I panicked."

Since Grace couldn't dispute what he said— or add to it—she stayed silent, letting him talk.

"Tonight, rocking Sarah, thinking about

you, hating that you had to give up your child, I was angry that life had forced us into this position, but I suddenly realized it wasn't life that forced us here. It was me because I didn't think I could love you without hurting you."

Too afraid to make a hopeful guess about the end of his conclusions, Grace held her breath.

"I guess thinking about my own marriage and Lydia and Cory while holding Sarah, I finally saw something that made everything fall into place for me."

Grace whispered, "What's that?"

"That if you and I had been married, we would have weathered Cory's death. You might have honestly acknowledged my mistake in grabbing my cell phone, and even acknowledged that I would feel guilty, but you never would have let me take the blame. You and I would have survived. A marriage between us would have survived."

Grace pressed her hand to her chest. "That's quite a compliment."

"You're a very special person. Or maybe the strength of your love is special." He shook his head. "Or maybe you and I together are special. I don't know. I just know that through all this you'd been very patient. But I'm done running."

She smiled. "Thought you didn't run."

"Well, maybe I wasn't running. Maybe I was holding everybody back. Away. But I can't do that anymore."

She took a breath, her hope building, her heart pounding.

"Because I love you. I love you." He repeated, as if saying it seemed so amazing he needed to say it again. "I couldn't stand the thought of you here alone, and though I don't want to hurt you I finally saw that unless I took this step, I would always be hurting you."

Her voice a mere whisper, Grace said, "What step?"

"I want to love you. I want you to marry me."

She would have been content to hear him say he wanted to try dating. His proposal was so far beyond what she'd been expecting that her breath stuttered in her chest. "What?"

"I love you and I want you to marry me."

Dumbstruck, Grace only stared at him.

"You could say you love me, too."

"I love you, too."

At that Danny laughed. The sound filled the small kitchen.

"And you want to marry me." He took a breath. "Grace, alone with Sarah I realized I had everything I needed and I could have talked myself into accepting only that. But I want you, too. Will you marry me?"

"And I want to marry you!" She made a move to launch herself into his arms, but remembered her cocoa and turned to flip off the burner. By the time she turned back, he was at her side, arms opened, ready for her to walk into them.

He wrapped his arms around her as his mouth met hers. Without a second of hesitation, Grace returned his kiss, opening her mouth when he nudged her to do so. Her heart pounded in her ears as her pulse began to scramble. He loved her. *He loved her and wanted to marry her.* It almost seemed too good to be true.

He pulled away. "Pot's probably boiling over."

"I thought I turned that off." She whirled away from him and saw the cooling pot. "I did turn that off."

"I have a better idea than cocoa anyway." He pulled her to him and whispered something in her ear that should have made a new mother blush. But she laughed and countered something equally sexy in his ear and he kissed her deeply, reminding her of her thoughts driving up I-64 the Monday they left Virginia Beach. *She'd found Mr. Right.*

She *had* found Mr. Right, and they were about to live happily ever after.

EPILOGUE

RESTING UNDER THE shade of a huge oak, on the bench seat of a weathered wooden picnic table, Grace watched Sarah as she played in the sandbox with the children of Grace's cousins. She could also see Danny standing in left field, participating in the married against the singles softball game at the annual McCartney reunion.

The CEO and chairman of the board of Carson Services didn't look out of place in his khaki shorts and T-shirt, as Grace expected he might. It wasn't even odd to see him punching his fist into the worn leather baseball mitt he found in his attic. Everything about this day seemed perfectly normal.

The batter hunkered down, preparing for a pitch thrown so hard Grace barely saw the ball as it sliced through the air toward the batter's box, but her cousin Mark had seen it. His bat connected at just the right time to send the ball sailing through the air, directly at Danny.

With a groan, she slapped her hands over her eyes, but unable to resist, spread her fingers and peeked through. The ball sped toward Danny like a comet.

He yelled, "No worries. I've got it." Punching his fist into his mitt twice before he held it up and the ball smacked into place with a crack.

Whoops of joy erupted from the married team because Danny had made the final out of the game. For the first time in almost twenty years, the married men had beaten the younger, more energetic singles.

Danny received a round of congratulations and praise. He was new blood. Exactly what the family needed. Grace sat a bit taller on the bench seat, glancing at eighteen-month-old Sarah, who happily shoveled sand into the empty bed of a plastic dump truck.

The married team disbursed to brag to their wives about the softball victory. The singles grumbled that Danny was a ringer. Danny jogged over to Grace looking like a man about to receive Olympic gold.

"Did you see that?"

"Yes. You were great."

"I was, wasn't I?"

Grace laughed. "Men." She took a quiet breath and he sat down on the bench seat beside her.

"Are you okay?"

"I'm fine."

"You're sure?"

"I'm sure."

"It's just that the last time you were pregnant you were sick—"

She put her hand over his mouth to shut him up. "For the one-hundred-and-twenty-seven-thousand-two-hundred-and-eighty-fourth time, all pregnancies are different. Yes, I was sick with Sarah. But I'm only a little bit queasy this time."

She pulled her hand away and he said, "Maybe you were sick because—"

She put her hand over his mouth again. "I was not sick because I went through that pregnancy alone. We've been over this, Danny." Because he was so funny, she laughed. "A million times."

"Or at least one-hundred-and-twenty-seven-thousand-two-hundred-and-eighty-four."

She laughed again and he glanced around the property. "This is a beautiful place."

"That's why we have the picnic here every year. There are no distractions. Just open space, trees for shade and a brick grill to make burgers and keep our side dishes warm. So everybody has time to talk, to catch up with what the family's been doing all year."

"It's great."

"It is great."

"And your family's very nice."

She smiled. "They like you, too."

He took a satisfied breath. "Do you want me to watch Sarah for a while?"

"No. It's okay. You keep mingling. We're fine."

"But this is your family."

"And I'm mingling. Women mingle more around the food and the sandbox. At one point or another I'll see everybody." She grinned. "Besides, this may be your last day out with people for a while. You should take advantage of it."

"What are you talking about? I have to go to work tomorrow."

"Right." She rolled her eyes with a chuckle. "Tomorrow you're going to be suffering. Every muscle in your body will be screaming. You'll need a hot shower just to be able to put on your suit jacket."

He straightened on the bench seat. "Hey, I will not be sore."

"Yes, you will."

"I am an athlete."

"You push papers for a living and work out at the gym a few nights a week." She caught his gaze, then pressed a quick kiss to his lips. "You are going to be in bed for days."

The idea seemed to please him because he grinned. "Will you stay in bed with me?"

"And let Sarah alone to fend for herself with Pickleberry?" They'd found Elise to be such a stickler for rules that Danny and Grace had nicknamed her after the governess in the storybook.

"Hey, you're the one who said to keep her."

"Only so we wouldn't be tempted to over-use her."

At that Danny laughed. He laughed long and hard and Grace smiled as she studied him. All traces of his guilt were gone. He remembered his son fondly now. He'd even visited the next-door neighbor who had been driving the SUV and they'd come to terms with the tragedy enough that Mrs. Oliver was a regular visitor at their home.

He'd also hired a new vice president and delegated at least half of his responsibility to him, so they could spend the majority of their summer at the beach house in Virginia Beach. He loved Sarah. He wanted a big family and Grace was happy to oblige. Not to give him heirs, but because he loved her.

Completely. Honestly. And with a passion that hadn't died. Their intense love for each other seemed to grow every day. He had a home and she had a man who would walk to the ends of the earth for her.

Watching her other family members as they mingled and laughed, weaving around the big oak trees, sharing cobbler recipes and tales about their children, Grace suddenly saw that was the way it was meant to be.

That was the lesson she'd learned growing up among people who didn't hesitate to love.

Somewhere out there, there was somebody for everybody.

* * * * *

Have you ever dreamed of discovering that you're really a princess? That's exactly what happens to Amanda Carn in THE MAKING OF A PRINCESS by Teresa Carpenter!

"I MUST SAY good night." With obvious reluctance, Xavier saw her safely seated. And then he stepped back and raised his hand in farewell.

Amanda pressed her hand to the window and made herself drive away. Oh, boy. She was so lost. Absolutely gone. He made her feel alive, feminine, desirable.

She knew she was setting herself up for heartbreak. He'd be leaving in a few weeks and her life was here. There was no future to this relationship.

But better heartache than regret. She was tired of being afraid to trust. Tired of letting fear rule her. She felt safe with Xavier. And she longed to explore the chemistry that sizzled between them.

Xavier strolled back to the museum, his gaze locked on the vehicle carrying Amanda Carn into the night. When the car turned from his sight, he fixed his gaze forward and tried to calculate exactly how big a mistake he'd just made.

For the first time, man and soldier were at odds as desire warred with duty. He liked this woman, he wanted her physically, but if she was of the royal family, his duty was to protect her against all threats, including himself. With the addictive taste of her still on his lips, he recognized the challenge that represented.

Inside, he did a final walk-through of the entire museum, as was his habit, ending with the exhibit rooms.

He knew his duty, lived and breathed it day in and day out. Duty was what kept the soldier from kissing her when she so obviously wanted a kiss as much as he wanted to get his mouth on her. The shadow of hurt as she moved away drew the man in him forward as he sought to erase her pain.

And his.

Now may be the only time he had with her, this time of uncertainty while the DNA test was pending. Once her identity was confirmed, she'd be forever out of his reach….

If she's proved to be royalty, then Xavier will have to keep his distance, but he's been bound by royal command to protect Amanda until the truth is discovered. Keeping Amanda safe is his new mission—and where could be safer than in his own arms?

Available in June 2013 from Harlequin® Romance wherever books are sold.

LARGER-PRINT BOOKS!

GET 2 FREE LARGER-PRINT NOVELS PLUS
2 FREE GIFTS!

⊞ HARLEQUIN®

Romance

From the Heart, For the Heart

YES! Please send me 2 FREE LARGER-PRINT Harlequin® Romance novels and my 2 FREE gifts (gifts are worth about $10). After receiving them, if I don't wish to receive any more books, I can return the shipping statement marked "cancel." If I don't cancel, I will receive 4 brand-new novels every month and be billed just $4.84 per book in the U.S. or $5.24 per book in Canada. That's a savings of at least 19% off the cover price! It's quite a bargain! Shipping and handling is just 50¢ per book in the U.S. and 75¢ per book in Canada.* I understand that accepting the 2 free books and gifts places me under no obligation to buy anything. I can always return a shipment and cancel at any time. Even if I never buy another book, the two free books and gifts are mine to keep forever.

119/319 HDN F43Y

Name _____ (PLEASE PRINT) _____

Address _____ Apt. # _____

City _____ State/Prov. _____ Zip/Postal Code _____

Signature (if under 18, a parent or guardian must sign) _____

Mail to the **Harlequin® Reader Service:**
IN U.S.A.: P.O. Box 1867, Buffalo, NY 14240-1867
IN CANADA: P.O. Box 609, Fort Erie, Ontario L2A 5X3

Want to try two free books from another line?
Call 1-800-873-8635 or visit www.ReaderService.com.

* Terms and prices subject to change without notice. Prices do not include applicable taxes. Sales tax applicable in N.Y. Canadian residents will be charged applicable taxes. Offer not valid in Quebec. This offer is limited to one order per household. Not valid for current subscribers to Harlequin Romance Larger-Print books. All orders subject to credit approval. Credit or debit balances in a customer's account(s) may be offset by any other outstanding balance owed by or to the customer. Please allow 4 to 6 weeks for delivery. Offer available while quantities last.

Your Privacy—The Harlequin® Reader Service is committed to protecting your privacy. Our Privacy Policy is available online at www.ReaderService.com or upon request from the Harlequin Reader Service.

We make a portion of our mailing list available to reputable third parties that offer products we believe may interest you. If you prefer that we not exchange your name with third parties, or if you wish to clarify or modify your communication preferences, please visit us at www.ReaderService.com/consumerschoice or write to us at Harlequin Reader Service Preference Service, P.O. Box 9062, Buffalo, NY 14269. Include your complete name and address.